Also by Carl Tiktin

THE HOURGLASS MAN

Carl Tiktin

RON

ARBOR HOUSE
NEW YORK

RON

BOOK **1**

HOME, COLLEGE, HALF AND HALF

CHAPTER 1

Ron Starr's mother interrupted her own forceful murmurings from the mouth of his father's cave-like study to shout, "One-and-two-and-three-and-a-four-uneven!" while clapping her hands to emphasize the beat.

Ron took his fingers off the piano keyboard and clamped his knees around them. "Can I take a break, mom?" he yelled to the upstairs.

But Blanche Starr had returned to going at his father, and didn't answer.

Ron wanted to know exactly what was going on. He knew it had something to do with his brother Lenny working out in the little gym in the basement with Michael Pollard, the sheriff's son.

Lenny had set up a gym in the basement for weight-lifting, boxing, and wrestling. He even practiced Oriental things like jujitsu and karate down there with some of his friends, who, of course, weren't Ron's friends, as Lenny was seventeen and Ron was only fifteen.

Michael was special. Something changed whenever he arrived. Ron could feel himself getting a bit wary, like an animal sensing a distant storm, whenever on Saturday morning or Thursday evening, the two times for Michael's workouts, he would appear at the door and ask Blanche politely if Lenny were home.

Blanche would look furtively past his shoulders as if she were a lookout in a speakeasy, to see if anyone was lurking behind a parked car or a tree. She'd then greet and let him in as if legally obliged to do so.

Michael wouldn't even nod hello to Ron. He'd just smile at him with a sardonic half curl of the lips that made Ron a bit uncomfortable.

Blanche would let Michael just stand there while she became very busy in other rooms, agitatedly dusting or rearranging until Lenny would come and fetch Michael and take him to the basement.

Ron liked the way Michael had changed during the few months of working out with Lenny. Michael had been a skinny kid with a slightly effeminate walk—a floppy kind of foppishness that Ron and some of his friends would laugh at. But now there was more power to his walk and he was wearing stylish shirts with short sleeves made shorter because Michael rolled them up a notch, exposing developing arm muscles that rolled nicely.

This particular Saturday morning there had been a stampede in the kitchen when Michael showed up. Louis Starr had been there sipping tea, his soggy tea bag a wet little brown bundle on the table beside his saucer. He'd been studying the newspaper carefully making notes in the margins, looking up from time to time to address anyone whose back wasn't absolutely toward him and saying things like . . . "Not tough enough on the Russians . . . See there . . . Roosevelt sold us out to the Russians and that little storekeeper Truman rang up the cash register. And now Ike is puttering it all away."

Ron had been the most attentive to his father's dodderings even while reading his own homework so that whenever father looked up from the paper he'd have someone to mumble to.

Blanche had been very testy. She knew that *that* boy, that funny boy, was coming soon—that's why she made Louis drink his tea in the kitchen instead of his study this morning . . . Something, she didn't quite know what, had to be done about this . . . this situation. But all her husband could seem to do was make soggy lumps, like drek, she wanted to say to him, on the kitchen table. And Ron, what was he doing there? . . . She didn't like him to see this Michael boy and his brother Lenny together. Ron idolized Lenny and if something was wrong . . . she wasn't saying for sure that there was . . . but if so, then she'd have to protect Ron. She'd looked into the basement window once when they were working out and hadn't seen anything definite but the way they'd touched and looked at each other had given her a feeling that she couldn't identify. She just knew there was something wrong and that if Louis were a real man he'd prevent Michael from coming to the house—that's all!

Just before Michael had come this morning Lenny walked through the kitchen wearing a bathing suit that he hadn't worn since he was fourteen. It was a size or two too small on him. God, his thing is bulging out!—Ron had observed. Blanche and Lenny had almost hissed at each other as Lenny walked downstairs into the gym. Blanche had moved to Ron as if to shield him from a deadly ray and even Louis had looked up from the paper and frowned in Ron's general direction—hoping that Blanche had duly noted the stern look.

Ron didn't want protection, he wanted transformation. How could he be like his brother? Command the atmosphere as Lenny could. Ron was popular, kids—older people too—liked him because of a warmth that ran through him like a purring motor. He was interested, sunny, helpful and involved but he wasn't surrounded by admirers whom he didn't seem to care a damn about. He couldn't drop people with a mischievous, malicious capriciousness that was hypnotic even to those who were getting dropped. He did all right on the soccer team and next year he knew he'd make shortstop on the baseball team, but he wasn't the best gymnast in the county like Lenny and kids didn't sit around for hours just watching him on the parallel bars. Ron could do all right with a pair of boxing gloves—Lenny had taught him—but he wasn't offered a chance to go into the Golden Gloves and he didn't have the opportunity to disdainfully turn it down as Lenny had.

Ron made his mark in other ways.

Where Lenny was rebellious Ron was counterrebellious. If Lenny hit other children when they were younger, Ron didn't. When Lenny cursed, Ron spoke sweetly. When Lenny failed spelling, Ron got an "A." If Lenny demanded more spending money Ron would more than make do with what he had. Ron tried to be the balancing weight on the scale of his parents' happiness so that whenever Lenny tipped the scales one way he'd balance them the other. He did it without resentment because he vicariously enjoyed Lenny's scathing performances against the world and basked in being the "good" boy as well.

But of course in order to have the counterrevolution he had to know the revolution. And lately he had not been able to figure a damn thing out.

So Ron quietly got off the piano bench and moved slowly up the stairs toward his father's den where his mother, intruding her head into that enclave, was forcefully talking *at* his father. Blanche rarely went even this far into Louis' den and Ron could almost picture Louis sinking more deeply into his oversized leather chair.

Ron stopped on the corner of the stairs and listened.

"Stop him!" Blanche was saying. "Stop him!"

"Fuzz . . . fuzz . . . fuzz . . ."

"I don't like that boy. Make him leave."

"Why?"

Silence. Did the leather chair swallow Louis?

"Can you let this happen right in your own house?" Blanche said more loudly.

"Fuzz . . . fuzz . . . fuzz . . ."

"Schmuck!" Blanche snapped, like a rifle.

Ron scampered down the stairs, frightened, the way he always was when he heard that language.

There was a small window in the basement that could be seen through if he lay on the grass at the side of the house.

He'd thought about looking through it many times recently whenever Michael had come.

Had his mother looked through it?

If she had then why couldn't he?

He went outside, making sure the screen door made no slam as he closed it. He calculated whether his mother would listen for him to continue his practicing or not and decided that she'd be angry for at least another half hour before she'd come to the conclusion that life must go on and yell for him to complete his full hour.

He picked up a flesh-colored Spalding ball from the porch and tossed it to himself as he skipped down the steps, bouncing it a few times on the concrete walk and checking the street out. All clear.

He walked to the side of the house and tossed the ball casually near the window.

It was bouncing too close, would it rebound off the window and given Lenny warning?

Lenny could get ferocious if he thought he was being spied on. Lenny hated anything that wasn't out in the open and anytime he caught his younger brother being sneaky he would hurt him in a slow and excruciatingly painful way. Thumb-twists, earlobe pinches, and lately, because of Lenny's study of the Oriental martial arts, the promise of extreme eastern tortures gave Ron bad scares. He'd go to his room and write scenes in his secret writing book of himself being tortured by water dripping on the head, or bamboo sticks under his nails and any other torture he'd read about in the comic books. Lenny had never even threatened these things but Ron felt that they were certainly in his brother's repertory and would be invoked at something as extreme as direct spying.

Nevertheless he quickly went on his hands and knees and crawled toward the basement window. He reached the Spalding ball before the window and tossed it gently in front of him so that he'd have something to pick up if he were seen. He reached the basement window and lay flat on the grass, wishing that he didn't have to raise his head to look in. Well, he'd better do it quickly before mother wanted him to practice or father wanted to talk to him. Louis always wanted to talk to Ron after an open argument with mother.

What he saw was the most ordinary of things. Lenny was just seated on the floor drinking water from a paper cup while Michael was testing the chinning bar. They were talking and Michael seemed to be concerned about his arm muscles.

Well, he reasoned, if this is so ordinary it's not very terrible that I'm watching so if I'm caught there won't be any big deals. He made himself more comfortable and began to enjoy his position as an onlooker. He propped himself up on his elbows just a bit and spread his legs on the grass.

Lenny was measuring Michael's arm muscles with a little tape measure. They were both sweating and Ron became fascinated with the perspiration running down the sides of Michael's body. Michael wore boxy, baggy shorts as opposed to Lenny's tight bathing trunks. The contrast was funny. Fat and skinny. Loose and tight. Mutt and Jeff. Abbott and Costello.

Lenny, in that offhanded but commanding way of his, signaled that it was time for Michael to chin and Michael picked his arms up and scooped the bars, getting himself up for one chin quickly.

Ron laughed to himself about the baggy shorts—they looked so ridiculous. Michael hadn't worn them when he arrived so he must have had them in the little brown paper bag he was carrying. His pants were thrown loosely in a corner so he had to put them on right there in the basement . . . an image that made Ron strangely uncomfortable . . . Michael changing into his shorts in the basement in front of his brother . . . he shifted his body slightly so as not to press on the warm grass.

Michael was having difficulty doing the number of chins that Lenny was urging him to make. His arms quivered more and more with each one. His chin stretched to get over the bar. Sweat dribbled down more and more and Ron watched a driblet sliding under the baggy shorts.

Michael hung limply on the chinning bar. Now Lenny moved in behind him and took Michael's thighs in his arms as if they were two shopping bags and prankishly lifted Michael up for another chin. Michael laughed as his chin went easily over the bars. Michael's backside was going up and down on Lenny's upper chest as Lenny lifted him again and again, both of them laughing and having great fun. Lenny's hands were moving around Michael's thighs as well, almost going under the shorts as they made little semicircles. Lenny's right thumb disappeared under Michael's shorts and Ron became instantly very scared as Lenny's thumb flicked something under there . . . Their laughter was slightly different now. He felt that Lenny would turn toward the window in order to draw the curtains and thereby see him and he had a terrible brief vision of ten thousand furious Lennys converging on him with tons of Oriental rage. He bolted up, snatched the Spalding ball and dashed for the back of the house.

Once behind the large tree in the back yard, reassured that Lenny was not in pursuit, he laughed quietly in his relief, looking around to make sure that no one in the neighboring houses saw him acting this peculiarly. He relaxed in the warm shade, pressing his back against the hump of the tree, deciding that mother was probably too upset over what was going on (what was going on?)

9

to bother about the missing half hour of piano practice. Getting more comfortable, he lay on his stomach, folding his arms and making a pillow of them, feeling his little bulge pressing against the ground, shifting a bit so that it would be warmer against his leg, pressing himself gently, imperceptibly against the grass again and again . . .

Ron's pubescent awakenings had been slow, tentative, unformed and unfocused . . . nice feelings occasionally located in *that* area that seemed to have no direct relation to anyone or anything. He'd never masturbated but knew that one day he'd have to, at least to keep up with his friends who talked about it constantly, totaling the numbers of times they did it daily, like baseball scores.

What he'd seen vaguely reminded him of the times in the past when he and Lenny would wrestle. Lenny would bounce him around as if he were the flesh-colored Spalding ball that now lay beside him on the grass. It had happened all through their growing up and as they went into early teenage years they found that being held, bounced and gripped by each other was to be looked forward to almost every day. Sometimes Ron's thing, the thing that was only supposed to bulge for girls, would be awakened and sometimes he'd feel Lenny too. But, as it went on more and more Lenny, the older brother, wiser in the ways of what was happening, held his younger brother at an arm's length and Ron gradually accepted the stand offishness as part of their growing up.

There was a picture upstairs in Ron's room of Kim Novak from the movie *The Man with the Golden Gun* that his best friend, Joe Zapperelli, the town barber's son, had given him as a goofy gift for his fifteenth birthday. On the sides of the glossy movie-magazine full-page photo Joe had pasted comic-book hands to be manipulated at one's pleasure. He'd said when he'd given it to Ron, "Boy, I'd like to fuck her . . . What would you give to fuck her, Ron?" Then he'd moved the hands over Kim's best parts and leered. Ron, who really wouldn't have given a nickel, said with as much heat in his voice as he could conjure, "Oh yeah . . ." Then

Joe went on to confide, "You know I jerk off on her alone, not counting Marilyn Monroe or Jayne Mansfield, maybe two, three times a day."

And now he knew that he ought to go upstairs and get that picture attached to the nice feelings that were coming over him there under the tree. He quickly picked himself up and walked back around the house without even looking in the direction of the basement window, past the piano and up the stairs past the study and the bedroom where Blanche could be heard moving small pieces of furniture—something she usually did when frustrated. She'd be good for about another half hour of that before she would want him to practice some more.

He took the shiny piece of paper from his knickknack drawer where he'd carelessly thrown it and tossed it on the bed. There she was in all her sultry busty young sweetness driving poor Frank Sinatra wild. Ron gently and quietly moved his dresser an inch to block the door. If his mother tried to get in he could swear that the dresser had accidentally moved on the slightly tilted floor.

He made himself feel good again by pressing down on the bed. He concentrated on her from all angles and imagined how she'd look without that tight blouse—nothing happened, but then he saw Joe as Joe would see her with her blouse off, his pop-eyes and wild black hair crackling all over the place. Ron started to get excited. Now instead of Joe it was Michael getting excited over her and then it was Kim lifting Michael up to chin, her hands disappearing under Michael's shorts and then instead of Kim it became him and then it started to happen, without any fear or shame, as his body danced with the mattress.

Afterwards he felt proud. His first time. No guilt. He felt great. He wanted to brag but he couldn't because he'd been lying to his friends about doing it for two years. He put the picture of Kim Novak carefully in his writing book, started a new page, put the date down and wrote, "Nice. Very nice." Then he laughed at that and further wrote, "Nice is all the future great writer Ron Starr could think to write about a great milestone in his manhood on this auspicious day. If he keeps this up he certainly will be a great writer—a real *stylist.*"

A few days later, when his father came into his room awkwardly to talk to him about what was going on with his brother as Ron had anticipated, Ron instinctively moved toward the dresser as if getting ready to whip out the picture of Kim Novak in order to thwart some unknown accusation.

It had taken Louis Starr a few days to cogitate before meeting with his younger son. Louis Starr was a cogitator. That was his trouble, according to Blanche—too much cogitation and not enough agitation. She hated it whenever he said, "I have to cogitate on it."

"Cogitate" was a Protestant kind of word, and slightly old-fashioned at that, but that was Louis Stransky or Louis Starr, a man who could keep a firm grip on an identity that wasn't even his, and, in fact, wasn't quite anyone's. When he fell in love with the spire of a Protestant church is unknown. It might have been growing up in the Williamsburg section of Brooklyn as the oldest and most scholarly son of a Jewish foreman in a sweater factory and trolling up to the farm-like Flatbush area to study with his political-science teacher, or perhaps as a young law student in a midwestern university. Life around the spire seemed so pleasant —the people unpushy and kindly compared to the fast, competitive immigrants who seemed to be shoving endlessly, speaking accented English to the world and a language that made him queasy, Yiddish.

So it was ideal for Louis to take a job in a small upstate law firm in a town that embodied the very essence of supposed small-town tranquility which excited him. The firm thought themselves lucky to get one of those smart, aggressive Jewish lawyers who'd go out and chase in some business. Their first disillusionment came when Louis Stransky changed his name to Louis Starr for "professional reasons." And it accelerated as they found that they'd gotten themselves a legal Talmudic scholar-type who apologetically charged fees so small that they hardly covered secretarial costs.

Nevertheless they liked him and he was useful for having the patience to chat with poor local farmers on trivial matters, thereby freeing the other attorneys for more lucrative work; also by researching points of law that others were only willing to deal with by bombast rather than scholarship; and by having access to more of the Jewish merchants in the area who had hitherto taken their business to nearby Binghamton and were now comforted to find one of their own kind, albeit slightly in disguise, in a local law firm.

Louis made a decent enough living for up there, but when he'd come to New York to visit his family he found his brothers and uncles doing much better—in business mostly. It pained him so much—along with the sound of the Yiddish—that his trips became more infrequent as time went by.

New York City was always Louis' source of painful things, including, ultimately, his wife Blanche Rosenzweig.

He met and immediately liked her on a visit to a law firm on Park Row that handled his firm's New York City work. She was one of the legal secretaries whom he'd talked to many times on the phone. Blanche was a small, chirpy woman with a perpetual little smile and quick snappy movements—not too bad-looking. There wasn't much doing for him in that line up his way, he reasoned, so maybe he'd see a bit of her while down here in the big city.

They soon "got serious." For Louis it seemed that Blanche would be a perfect companion to share his Protestant paradise upstate. She didn't look or act Jewish. She was cultured, liked to read as he did although they read different things. He, his Emerson and Thoreau, and she, the pulsating dramatic novels that he could never quite get into. She played the piano—not much into his favorites, ragtime or jazz, but she did classical rather well and he knew that he ought to get more aware of that. He'd liked to listen to Johann Strauss when he was a boy. They both loved poetry although his was the kind with a message in it, Whittier and Longfellow, while she became dreamy-eyed over Emily

Dickinson, the brother and sister Rosetti . . . and Keats and Shelley—flowers and nature and all that. Yes, well, he ought to get into that too.

And of course she had a nice little shape on her. He was getting tired of visiting Virginia, a waitress in the Babbling Brook Diner in town who, while certainly not a prostitute was not against a few dollars carelessly dropped on the floor after each visit. One really couldn't go to the movies or a band concert with her because most of the businessmen in town had been visitors at one time or another. All and all, he was in his early thirties and ought to be getting married and raising a family of his own now that he was getting established. .

Blanche, like Carol Kennicott, the heroine of Sinclair Lewis' novel *Main Street*, dreamed of being a missionary somewhere out there in America where she could bring the light of culture to people imprisoned in the Dark Ages. Oh, sure her world of the immigrant Lower East Side was full of believers in music and poetry and literature but only as long as it didn't interfere with making a "buck." All around her she witnessed potentially sensitive, intelligent people. So many of them originally socialists too, being destroyed by the push to make it in America—to make the "bucks." Education was only to get ahead—and anything that didn't push you up the ladder was only worth a condescending pat on the head, as if you were a pet dog. An old aunt finally told her what the whole family had wanted to tell her for years, "Dickinson, Dickens, they're all very nice—I like a good story myself, but when are you going to get married to a nice Jewish boy who's making a good living and start your family."

She was in her mid-twenties and cute, but aging early—little lines already, and her nose and her lips getting tighter . . . body slouching in on itself a bit. How much longer would she be attractive? Men still liked her but she hated the way they liked her. They were all infected with a pushing sexuality like their push for the bucks. It's no coincidence, she told herself, that "buck" and that other word sound alike. She'd never come too close to

14

losing her virginity, but she felt that the reason for her premature aging was because of it. She was starting to let go of her vision of a modern poetic man with a face like Shelley and a passion like Lord Byron but with the stable kind of love for her that Browning was reputed to have had for Elizabeth Barrett . . . But if only someone could come along who would be so gentle and sweet . . . but they didn't seem to exist. Well, if she was going to shrivel, then she'd just have to shrivel rather than let some greedy character push himself into her.

She had daydreamed about Louis Starr before she ever met him. On the phone he had a quiet gentle sense of humor and a soft voice. And he never seemed to have things quite ready when he called. When they finally met and he was obviously interested in her she forced herself not to dwell on the fact that for a man in his early thirties he looked fortyish and was sort of droopy and going bald . . . He is gentle, and such a winning smile and a good mind and no greed, yes not one touch of greed . . . How did he ever get to be a lawyer? But he is a lawyer and he's Jewish too . . . He's going to be a judge. Men like that were made to be judges. And she'd be away from New York bringing culture to the community. She'd raise a family breathing spirit into her children and there'd be no more premature aging because, at last, she'd be a full woman. Lovemaking would be like waves lapping against her and washing lines away and straightening up the crouching. God, she was so happy when he finally proposed.

It went all wrong for Blanche Rosenzweig. Louis Starr was a mouse when he should have been a lion and a lion when he should have been a mouse. In the bedroom he roared, clutched and hissed and in the courtroom he squeaked. It was all the worse for Blanche in the bedroom because it came out from behind a mild-mannered disguise. He was like a demented mouse. And he wasn't going to be a judge—she saw that quickly enough. As a matter of fact she wondered why the law firm kept him at all. And there was plenty of culture up there, the bank president's wife had even had a novel published (a detective novel) and there was a flourishing Book Club and a Poetry Society. No Dark Ages waiting for her lamp. All she could do was join.

Then Leonard came.

Louis Starr hated the way his first son looked. Olive skin, thick black hair, and was that going to be a little Jewish hooked nose, as if the God of Jews—the same God who punished Moses for once denying his origin, although it certainly was reasonable at the time for Moses to have done so—had visited Leonard on him in capricious punishment for changing his name and for *underplaying*—do you hear that, God?—*underplaying* not denying his Jewishness?

Blanche worshipped the way Lenny looked because through him the mouse who had trapped her could be made to squirm. She nurtured any tendency that could be thought of as "Jewish." Lenny's pushy need for physical contact, his sharp tongue she adored secretly, yet when Lenny would get into the inevitable trouble that this sort of thing brought she would rant at Louis to *do* something about it.

And Louis couldn't stand it, couldn't understand it, so that he found himself drawing farther and farther away from the boy—sometimes repelled by the very sight of him. Except Blanche wouldn't let him get too far away. She nursed Lenny as a pet viper, letting him know through looks, moods and attitudes rather than words—never words—that the more rebellious he was, the more "pushy Jew," the better she liked it.

Later on, when Lenny would talk about it with the others and even with the "shrinks" he'd go to from time to time he'd say that he never remembered playing with dolls or having mother put pretty dresses on him and ask him to sing like a girl. He'd laugh. She encouraged him in all "masculine pursuits" except the pursuit that he turned out to pursue the most.

Even when Blanche noticed hints of Lenny's tendencies she, sensing that they would torture the mouse the most, never tried to stifle or stop them—especially when Louis was around to see his voracious teenage boy riding near-innocently on another boy or putting his hand where it just wasn't right for a hand to linger that way.

Yet there was a danger. Her darling Ron could get infected. On that there could be no equivocation. He was no sexual battleground. He was their redemption. To Louis, his small nose and good-natured fair round face were the epitome of gentile good looks. His warmth and intelligence made him a natural to be a good lawyer and a politician. To Blanche, Ron would be her artist, her beauteous man—a writer or musician certainly.

On what kind of future for Ron they couldn't agree but on keeping him utterly pure there could be no disagreement. None of this was ever in words because there were hardly any for the unspeakable suspicion about Lenny that haunted that home. Lenny was a loss from whom one must cut oneself off if necessary. Ron was everything to attach to and place one's hopes in . . .

Louis Starr looked around the room for a place to sit, letting his eyes run the walls, grateful that there were no pictures of Rock Hudson or Tab Hunter on them the way they were the last time he'd peeked into Lenny's room . . . Of course there weren't any of Marilyn Monroe either, but that was all right because Ron was a bit too young for those kind of pinups anyway.

Ron sensed by the way his father ponderously sat down, cleared his throat and put both hands on his knees that he had been cogitating on this task for days, making notes and rehearsing opening lines, so he gave his undivided attention, wanting to make whatever it was as successful and as easy as possible.

Louis delivered his well-rehearsed opening lines with a studied, man-to-man casualness designed to let Ron know that there was no more man-boy stuff in their relationship anymore.

"How're you doing with girls, son?" he asked.

"Fine, dad," Ron replied quickly and firmly.

Louis nodded his head. "Fine?"

"Well, I guess."

"Like anybody?"

"Sure. There are lots of nice girls in school, dad."

"I know these kids today are . . . pretty cute, huh?" Louis laughed. "They're cuter today then they were in my day . . . A little more forward, you know? . . ."

Louis had a repertory of dirty jokes that Ron had heard under cracks of doors for years. Whenever he told them there'd appear a special smile on his face that was there at no other time. A hint of it appeared now, and Ron inwardly cringed.

"They sure wear tight sweaters, don't they?"

"Yeah," Ron said with a short burst of laughter.

"Some of these kids today . . . They didn't seem to be built that way in my day."

"Oh yeah, some of them are wow," Ron said, putting a lot in the "wow."

Louis took full note of the animation, wishing Blanche were there. Louis leaned back, more relaxed now. "I suppose you know all about the birds and the bees at your age, huh?"

"We've gone past that, dad."

"Have you?" Louis said, the smile appearing again.

"Sure."

"You date?"

"Well, not the way the older kids do. There are girls around the ice-cream parlor and in class and on the school paper. When I'm seventeen, then I'll date . . . You know, take a girl to the movies or something."

"They start at seventeen now, huh?"

"Well, something like that."

"We didn't start till we were about nineteen, at least out of high school. You kids today have it easier."

Louis stood up and walked to the window, looking out into the street as if there were something of great importance to be gleaned out there. Ron sensed that the first step that his father was supposed to have taken had been stepped and now he would be going into Step Two. In order to make it easier he picked up the book he was reading—a collected Shakespeare—and turned at random to *Macbeth*, letting himself get lost in it so that his father wouldn't feel too uneasy about the long pause.

When Louis spoke again his voice was sharper than either of them was prepared for. "There are certain aberrations that have to be watched out for. Certain deviations, certain illnesses, no not even illness . . . That's a glorification of it that some might use but I don't believe in it. Wickedness is wickedness. There are things that are bad and evil, not sick."

Louis' sudden and hardly-ever-before-seen passion frightened Ron, yet drew him closer to his father. Had his father been like this in law school addressing mock juries and then never again in the outside world? Ron leaned forward, his apparent interest stirring Louis on. "These things must be watched out for . . . These things can sneak up on you . . . especially if you're young and open and trusting and especially if you have someone close to you who can . . . influence you."

Ron knew exactly what the subject matter was now. In some ways he'd been through it before. Once kids had made cracks about his brother being a "queer" because they'd never seen him with girls. Once some kids even called *him* one because they'd seen him with his arm around his friend Joe Zaperelli, comforting him after a big fight Joe'd had with his father. The idea that anyone, like Lenny, who could kill a guy with one blow if he wanted to, could be a homo was so ridiculous that Ron didn't even laugh at it . . . It was as if someone had accused Lenny and even him of coming from the planet Venus . . . Surely what Ron had seen in the basement had nothing to do with that word that connoted lisps, limp wrists and rolling funny eyes . . . Whatever his father was worried about had nothing to do with him, so on to Ron's main task, which was to make whatever his father had come in here for as successful as possible for his father.

"No one can influence someone who doesn't want to be influenced," Ron said strongly. His father's chest expanded visibly at this.

"Do you mean that?"

"Yes."

"Do you know this kind of thing can ruin your entire life, wreck any career that you may have, doom you to frustration, anger and disease? Do you know you can be arrested for this and that you can never be admitted to the bar or anything else you might want to do? Jobs, the army, nothing. Nothing! Do you know that?"

Now Ron became frightened. He wanted to do things in the world, perhaps be a lawyer or a doctor or a politician and if his brother was "that" and if he could be influenced . . .

"I know, dad."

Louis came close to his son and peered intently at him, a moral physician seeking some sign to tell him if his patient was infected in any way.

"Do you really know what I'm talking about?"

Ron looked squarely back at Louis. "Don't worry, dad," he said in the firmest, most manly voice that his fifteen-year-old self could command. "I know just what's going on and I want you to know that I'm all right. I've got my head screwed on right."

Louis beamed.

Ron, suddenly not frightened anymore, beamed right back at him.

Louis turned to leave, nodding his head and smiling, then paused before walking out of the door. He wanted to take his son in his arms and kiss him the way he'd always done until a few years ago. Ron took a short step toward his father, waiting for Louis to open his arms so that he could go into them. But Louis, considering the circumstances, thought better of it, awkwardly waved his hand and left the room to report to Blanche.

As soon as Louis left, he went to his writing book. There was something there that he wanted to strike out—although he'd never done that before he wanted to do it now. Someone could find the book and discover it . . . He had seen a nature movie recently that showed how a copperhead ate a rabbit by hypnotizing it and then striking. He'd written: "The copperhead is my brother Lenny and I am the rabbit. The orange and black speckled head with the two beady eyes holds me against my will, I know that I'm going to die but I wait for the pleasure of the strike. With a speed that is deliberate, he snaps me into his body. I go through the dark slime of his insides and I shiver as I slide through the long thin tube. I'd rather be a copperhead than a rabbit and now I am a copperhead." . . . It seemed sick, weird and should no longer be a part of him. He struck it out, making sure that not one word showed through the black of the pencil marks. Then, remembering a Sherlock Holmes movie that he'd seen where a chemical process could still pick up what had been written, he pulled out the page, ripping it into little pieces.

Then he found a fresh page and he wrote:

Girls. Girls who I'm going to concentrate on this week. It is time I really started. It's dumb to wait till you're seventeen.

He put down a list of names.

CHAPTER 2

Ron had no trouble being with girls. He found them fun, easy to be with—better talkers, listeners, more sympathetic, mature, better sense of humor, almost better everything than boys.

Not that he was a sissy. He had plenty of guys who were his friends too. He was popular, worked on the school paper and the French paper, *Le Courier*. He was in the Radio Club and on the soccer and baseball teams. Next term he was going into the Debating Society. His father liked that—all future lawyers went into the Debating Society in high school. Blanche was hoping that in time he'd join the Shakespeare Club, but she was content to be silent for now. At least he was writing for the paper.

Joe Zaperelli had talked about girls since he was ten years old, but now the rest of the kids . . . Stanley . . . Bill . . . all of them were catching up to Joe. They all began walking with girls, and talking about dark, sly mysterious things that went on. They bragged. He pretended extreme interest.

Everyone was pairing off. They were becoming important to each other, whereas in the past the two sexes had seemed to exist side by side, like two nations bordering one another but each with its own fish to fry.

His father would also leer more openly at girls from the porch when Ron was around, even daring it with Blanche there, poking Ron man to man. He started telling Ron dirty jokes. Little ones, not the big bad ones that he had stored up in his repertory. Ron would have the appropriate laughter or snicker for each joke even when he didn't quite catch on, taking satisfaction in the satisfaction he gave his father.

His mother, too, talked more about girls. She was full of curious questions to Ron and hints, tips on courting, what girls like and what they don't, all with a rather unmotherly naughtiness. "Young ladies are giving more away today than they did in my day, and, you know what, I don't think it's a terrible thing. Not at all," she once said.

Ron was mildly shocked to conclude that his own mother wanted him to find someone who was giving it away and wanted him to take it. Often he'd lie on his stomach in bed and gently rock himself against the mattress to feel the deliciousness—reassured that it was there, though unable to focus on any females. The Hollywood starlets, the girls in school with the tight sweaters . . . they all floated in and out like harmless ghosts . . .

It was just before he was seventeen that he started to walk with Ann. She'd been in school with him from second grade. They'd existed hardly aware of each other. If hard-pressed they knew each other's names and if further pressed, about where they lived.

Ron was president of the Radio Club when Ann joined and they were working on a radio adaptation of Edgar Allan Poe's

"The Purloined Letter." Ron was playing Arsene Dupin and Ann was helping with the sound effects. They were preparing for a state-wide competition and Ron and Ann now walked together frequently.

This particular day they were telling each other how inadequate their grade advisor Mr. Schmeil was.

"Mr. Schlemeel," Ron said.

Ann laughed and touched his arm, "Schlemeel? What's that?"

"That's a Yiddish word for jerk."

"Yiddish?"

"Jewish . . ."

"Are you Jewish?"

"Sure."

"I never would have known it."

Approaching were Joe and Bill McBride who always had this little cigarette protruding from the side of his mouth. Bill suspected that Ron was getting laid a great deal and not telling the details. Bill's cigarette was doing a lateral dance in his mouth, and Joe's eyes were snapping.

Ron realized that they must have seen Ann touch his arm. Ann, seeing them approach, quickly said goodbye and moved off.

The boys fell in step with Ron—one on each side of him. "How you *doin'?*" Joe asked.

Bill snickered.

"What's with you?" Ron asked Bill, who continued to snicker and make his cigarette move around.

"Hey, Ron," Joe said, "is that all her?" He cupped his hands, indicating Ann's well-developed bust.

"She wears falsies, doesn't she?" Bill said.

"How do I know?"

"You've been there."

"You're crazy."

"You fuck," Bill McBride said angrily, "how're we going to know who puts out and who don't if we don't swap information, huh? We tell you." Bill pushed Ron on the shoulder. "You gotta tell us."

"Get out of here," Ron said, laughing at Bill and saying to Joe as he walked away from them, "Who's your friend?"

Privately Ron was pleased that they thought that there was something between Ann and him.

Ann was attracted to boys who repelled her, greasy types—the kind that swaggered a lot and didn't talk very well. She couldn't imagine herself being kissed by Ron with his sunny, blond, round face but she was comfortable with him because there was a restful absence of threat. They formed a silent partnership. They went to parties, picnics and games together. When time for necking came they'd sit in dark places and whisper about the other people —how stupid they were.

But since each of their friends increasingly assumed they were a couple, they tended to examine each other freshly. Ann had "dirty blond" hair, as Blanche might say, and indeed, Ron suspected that she didn't shampoo it as often as other girls seemed to talk about doing. Her features were regular but on the large side and her acne tended toward the intrusive rather than the kind that could be fairly well camouflaged by makeup. Her bust was *there*, although the floppy sweaters she wore made gentle molehills out of what the more flaunty types would have made mountains. Her figure was squarish, yet with surprisingly shapely legs.

To Ann, he was a good friend, a bitching partner, an equally cynical observer of her adolescent world—yet he was a boy. Maybe he'd want to kiss her and put his hand underneath. She knew that kind of business had to start sometime. She'd never seriously been kissed, and if one of the greasers she yearned for came within a few feet of her she always ran like hell.

During this time Ron had flashes of real feelings that troubled him . . . At a party once, a boy from another school that Ron couldn't help looking at a lot because of . . . Well, he didn't know . . . watching that boy necking with his date . . . letting himself wonder how *she* was feeling with that boy pressing and hugging her, letting his gaze rest on the boy's legs, watching his hands move, then being aware that he was aroused and then willing it down as if it were an unwanted fire.

And undressing in the gym and looking at certain boys . . . slimmer ones . . . with well-developed arm muscles . . . Slight thrusts, instant flashes, nothing serious, nothing abnormal, no need to worry . . . He hadn't been influenced . . . infected . . .

But he'd still never even made out with a girl and he ought to start. Once he started he wouldn't have even those little buggy feelings.

He wrote in his writing book. Make out with Ann—*starting now* . . .

In the early evening just before dusk while they were walking by the lake during a not unusual stretch of silence, Ann suddenly thought that a bird had landed on her shoulder.

It was Ron's hand.

They continued to walk. The path by the lake was rocky and his hand was like the Marines having secured a beachhead and her shoulder was like the beachhead shifting constantly to stay secured.

They sat under a designated romantic tree. They sat there in complete silence for a very long time. Her shoulder was becoming numb and his right arm was beginning to hurt and they knew he'd have to do something else soon because they couldn't maintain their position.

Keeping his eyes on the lake and not on her face, he put his head near her and kissed her on the cheek.

Ann, realizing that Ron meant business but was awfully awkward and shy, decided to help him along. She moved closer to him, giving that stiff arm more support by moving her shoulders and back into him.

Ahh, Ron thought to himself, it's going to go better now. It's really going to start going well.

Soon they kissed.

Ron closed his eyes and as he kissed Ann harder and harder and then gently brought his body close to hers he knew that everything would eventually be all right. He could be close to a girl . . . There was nothing to it . . . nothing at all . . . He could do it . . . just like anyone else. He just had to and not think about those other things anymore and gradually he would get all excited just the way Joe and Bill and the rest of them did.

Ann felt a bit empty when Ron walked her home that night. Well, it was a beginning but it still didn't seem like anything . . . Maybe when he puts his hand under my sweater it'll change . . . We'll see . . . Still there's something funny about the whole thing . . .

Ron wrote in his writing book that night. Step number one taken. It was great. Fine. Terrific. Next step: FEELS. STARTING NOW!

Ron's hand started at the side of Ann's breast the next time. Ann was surprised. She'd predicted to herself that Ron would go slower. It all seemed so foreign to him that she was sure it would be a year before he took this step, but there were his thumb and forefinger moving almost at the side of her breast as they kissed in the exact same way as before . . .

But still, it was sort of boring. Maybe if he went a little bit further. She moved her body slightly so that her breast was more squarely in his hand . . .

Here he was, Ann's breast in his hand, and nothing was happening to him. He kissed her harder and even dared to pry her mouth open with his tongue and press her breast harder. Her breasts were large and he should have been very excited, and remembering every detail so that he could share it with the other guys. Oh God, something *was* wrong with him.

In his book that night he wrote. FURTHER. GO FURTHER. STARTING NOW.

The next time his hand went under. Almost immediately Ann reached back and undid her bra strap.

There was no magic in what he held in his hand . . . Joe's popping eyes . . . Bill's dancing cigarette . . . The awe in-

27

spired in them by what he had in his hand missed him completely . . . He wanted to run away, he felt he might start crying. Jesus . . .

Ann liked it. She didn't feel dirty or hurt or squeezed like a sponge, the way some of the girls said. It was sort of like the doctor examining her. She leaned back on the grass and brought him on top of her just as he was about to pull away.

Okay. He rocked gently against her, just the way he did on his mattress. He gave himself up to it, and soon he became excited. Great. Congratulations. They had a terrific necking session. Ann could now somehow think of this boy who sat near her in French, with his greasy slick hair and his big forearms kissing her and taking off her bra.

In his book that night Ron wrote: A REAL LADIES' MAN AM I.

CHAPTER 3

Lenny had been expelled from college and wasn't going to another one. Something "unspeakable" had happened in the shower room of the dorm. He now sat in his room for hours while Blanche and Louis circled around, as though not daring to touch the contagion. There were angry, hissing muted arguments that were shut off whenever Ron was present. They became like two doctors monitoring a disease. They never let the two boys be alone with each other if it could be helped.

Lenny was the only spot on Ron's seventeen-and-a-half-year-old sun. Ron could easily be with different girls, even more than most of his friends. The "other thing" was very minor and would certainly disappear as soon as he got "home" with his first girl and that ought to be pretty soon—they were all getting bolder and going further all the time.

He was president of the class, getting good write-ups for his play on the soccer team, finding a certain magnetism that he had in being able to attract people to him. His friends seemed to need to confide in him and to spark if he approved of what they were doing. He thrived on this. Maybe he'd be a politician after all, not a writer the way his mother wanted him to be. Being elected president made him think of some of those congressmen that kept getting elected and elected right up into their old age.

If only he could make the suffering of his brother go away. He imagined smiling at Lenny full-face in the hall or dining room and by that smile breaking through the awful clouds. But he could only be, of all things, distant and polite, as if his brother were a house guest—a distant uncle that one needed to be cordial with. That was all any of them seemed to want Ron to be, even Lenny was standoffish . . .

One night Ron had had enough of it. He walked across the hall to Lenny's room and knocked on the door.

There was a pause before a sullen voice replied, "Yeah?"

"I've got a new comedy album. This guy Bob Newhart. It's hilarious. You want to come in my room and listen to it with me?"

"No."

At the same moment Ron heard a large book being put down in his father's study and his mother had stopped, in the middle of the bar, playing Tchaikovsky's "June."

Ron persisted. "You've got to hear it. He's got something on Sir Walter Raleigh discovering tobacco that's fantastic . . ."

The door opened. Lenny's nineteen-year-old eyes were saggy and old but he grinned wryly as he said, "Oh yeah . . . I remember someone in the dorm had the record . . . Sounded good . . ."

"Well, come on . . ."

Suddenly Louis was out of his study, just standing in front of the door, and Blanche was at the foot of the stairs peering up at both, hurling silent entreaties at Lenny.

And Lenny half believing that perhaps he *could* damage his kid brother somehow, and not wanting to inflict the kind of driving pain he was going through on Ron, snarled with just a shade of his old confidence and without a further word went back in the room closing the door in his brother's face.

Blanche and Louis, like two sentinels meeting at their check-point, turned and went back to their Tchaikovsky and Whitman (Blanche had been trying to interest Louis in Whitman lately and had herself become more devoted to the music of Tchaikovsky).

But one night Louis and Blanche had to be at a dinner to honor the president of the County Bar Association.

"Why don't you go to a movie tonight with that girl Susan?" Blanche asked Ron as they passed each other in the upstairs hall.

"I've got homework, mom," Ron replied. "Besides, I don't see much of Susan anymore . . ."

Blanche laughed. "My goodness, you go through these young ladies like Grant through Richmond . . . You are a heartbreaker, you are . . . Who are you seeing now?"

"Well, no one in particular . . . But"—he half leered—"I get around."

Blanche leaned over the balustrade and said to Louis, who was walking up the stairs, and loud enough to penetrate into Lenny's room, "You hear that, Louis? Your son's gone through another heart . . . like Grant took Richmond. No more Susan and now he's on to his next conquest."

Louis was having difficulty with his black tie. "Go get 'em, kid, go get 'em."

"Why don't you go out to a movie or the ice-cream parlor anyway? . . . I'm sure we can get your father to give you a little extra on your allowance . . ."

"I've been out almost every night this week and I'm having a history test in two days."

Blanche's lips, at their far corner, jerked up quickly and then came down as if yanked by a puppeteer. It was her reasonable smile, covering up the frustration of Ron's refusal to go out on the town. She quickly went into the bedroom to debate with Louis over the idea of her staying home and Louis going to the idiotic affair, an idea abhorrent to Louis. This one big dinner was too important to be marred by not having his wife by his side the way the rest of them did.

Ron now imagined his brother's eyes piercing through his closed door, controlling everyone from that room—his brother sitting in a lotus position, head bald like a villain in a comic book. The large eyes were growing and getting closer as they grew, he was getting weak and his knees were becoming liquid. He quickly went to the bedroom but left the door open to hear his mother say, "I'm not going. That's all, I'm not going."

"Fuzz, fuzz, fuzz," he heard his father reply.

He'd better study his history, he thought. The hell with it. He started to make notes and confirm dates and events, World War I, the Versailles Treaty . . . He heard noises in the hall, both his parents, not just his father. He looked through the slightly opened door and saw *both* Louis and Blanche dressed formally.

His father had won.

Louis' face was red through to his bald head and Blanche's face was white under her patches of rouge, a clown-like makeup.

Blanche descended on Ron. "I want you to go to bed right away," she said sharply.

Louis surrounded Ron on his other flank. "Right away, son, right away."

Ron nodded in agreement. "Okay," he said, "I've done my homework and I'm tired."

"You're going to turn in?"

"Yes, right away, right away."

"Right away?"

"Right away."

"Come on, we're going to be late," Louis said to Blanche, jabbing her arm with his elbow.

Blanche kissed Ron goodbye, pressing him to her and looking

deeply into his eyes—all designed to give him a protective shield, at least until she got back home. Louis shook Ron's hand very strongly—firmer than Ron had ever had his hand shaken before by anyone and surprising for his father.

I guess that's one reason why dad's a lawyer, Ron thought, he can do that very well when he wants to.

They turned to look back before they left and Ron, wanting them to leave happy, smiled back at them sunnily and said in his deepest Arsene Dupin voice, "Good night, have a good time."

It worked. Louis and Blanche saw a problem-free happy boy. They were reassured and went out to enjoy their evening in the way soldiers and sailors enjoy passes.

It wasn't even eight o'clock yet, Ron thought when he went back to his room. How could he go to sleep so early. He'd get back to his homework. But first he'd like to move the dresser against his door so no one could get in. Dumb. Who'd try to get in?

He felt drowsy. He found himself listening for any stirrings that might be coming from his brother's room. Nothing. He lay on the bed and, unconsciously acceding to his parents' wishes, became drowsy as he gazed listlessly at the ceiling, and fell asleep.

He woke shortly in a quick, eyes-open and alert manner. Something was different. Sounds were coming from the basement. He opened his door and saw that his brother's door was open and the room empty. There was music in the basement—sounded like Johnny Mathis . . . Lenny's favorite. He came out of the room and leaned over the balustrade and heard the sounds of talking and laughter . . . He walked down a few steps and listened closely, especially to the laughter.

It was a girl's laughter. Good. If there was a girl in that basement with Lenny then everything was going to be all right. He imagined telling his parents. There was a girl down there with Lenny . . . His parents would smile and be delighted and embrace both him and Lenny. . . . He walked down further, transfixed by the giggling . . . Yes, definitely a girl . . . There was dancing and talking . . . Someone else besides Lenny and the girl was there, another boy . . . Sounded like Michael . . . Then everything was all right for him too. Ron walked quickly into the kitchen and stood at the top of the basement stairs, still listening . . . He could hear feet shuffling around quickly to fast music. He walked down the basement stairs. No one would mind if he joined them . . . not if there was a girl there. Who was she? Did he know her? He could stick his head in and just say hello and leave if they felt he was intruding . . .

He slowly opened the basement door.

Michael was seated on the floor leaning against the wall drinking beer from a large quart bottle. He looked tired and a bit silly. Ron tried to catch his eye and say hello but Michael didn't seem able to focus very well. Ron saw his brother Lenny lindying coolly, hardly moving a muscle as his partner wiggled and shuffled all over the place. His partner, the only other person there, was a boy . . .

A short, dark-haired boy with little open round eyes and an ugly bulldog face that reminded Ron of a conglomeration of ugly girls all rolled into one. The boy gyrated in a parody of every silly girl he'd ever seen, twisting his hips, rolling his sharp little eyes and shaking his head coquettishly, and *giggling* . . . the giggle Ron had heard upstairs . . . as he danced around Lenny. He stopped his dancing and minced slowly to Ron, and said to Lenny, "Who's this? He's cute."

Lenny walked slowly to Ron and said, "This is my brother Ron."

"Hi," the boy said, lowering his eyes coquettishly. "My name is Timmy."

"You'd better go back upstairs," Lenny told Ron.

Ron didn't budge.

"He's cute," Timmy said. "Let him stay. Do you like to dance?"

Ron didn't know what to do. Lenny watched him carefully as he said again, "Go upstairs."

Then from the corner on the floor Michael said, "Let him stay

. . . Don't be such an old mother hen. . . ." Michael stood up and addressed himself directly to Ron for the first time ever. "Do you want to stay, Ron?"

And Ron said, "Yeah."

Michael walked to him and offered him the beer. "Have a drink."

Ron took the bottle and watched Lenny.

"Have a drink and go upstairs," Lenny said.

Ron quickly turned the bottle up and drank the beer. It was only about the third beer he'd ever tasted.

"It's warm."

"Like piss," Michael said, and Timmy howled, jumping around, slapping his knees.

Was it? Ron suddenly blanched and Timmy quickly reassured him, "It's not. Michael, you're terrible . . ." Timmy took the bottle from Michael and swigged. "Here," he said to Ron. "Would I drink piss?"

"Yes," Michael said, and everyone, even Lenny, laughed at that.

"Okay, good night, kid . . . up to your room."

"Hey, come on. Let him stay," Timmy said. "Tell him you want to stay . . . He's just a big bad bully."

"Yeah, I want to stay," Ron said quickly, looking to Michael and Timmy for support against his brother.

"Come on kid, up to your room," Lenny said in a voice that was approaching anger.

Michael made Lenny look at him and said slowly, "Let him stay . . . if he *wants* to . . ."

Lenny's attitude underwent a subtle change. "What about your studying?"

"I've done it."

"Okay," Lenny said casually. "Just for a little while then."

Michael and Timmy cheered.

Ron had some more beer. Michael put on an Elvis Presley record and Ron danced with Timmy, imitating the cool attitude that Lenny had had when Ron had first come in. Michael and Lenny sat down on the floor mat and soon Lenny was showing Michael how to balance himself for doing one-handed pushups.

Timmy did a lip synchronization of an old Andrews Sisters record of "Rum and Coca-Cola" that sent Ron to the floor with laughter . . . He could just see Pattie Andrews as she sang ". . . both mother and daughter working for the Yankee dollar . . ."

Lenny hardly paid attention to Ron now, and Ron was feeling looser and freer. He danced with Timmy the way he'd never danced with any girls before, doing steps and letting himself move his feet and body to its own rhythm. He drank more beer and he became more uninhibited. He did a Jon Hall imitation to Timmy's Dorothy Lamour sarong native dance, smoking a pipe and seating himself in a white-hunter lotus pose, saying to Michael, "Your daughter is very beautiful, chief."

And Michael said, "She is not my daughter."

"Not your daughter?"

"She is daughter of volcano. Oba-oba."

Lenny jumped up and put his hands up high, a volcano in the process of erupting.

Timmy gyrated around Ron.

Michael said, "Be careful, little daughter, volcano very jealous . . . If you fall in love with white stranger it will erupt and send its deadly lava through our whole village . . ."

"I don't care, father," Timmy said. "He's so cute . . ."

"This whole thing is nothing but village superstition," Ron said, puffing on his make-believe pipe.

Michael said, "Daughter, go to your hut."

Timmy said, "No, I love him." Timmy ran to Ron and threw himself at his feet. "Take me away from this island . . ."

Ron said, "By George, I will."

"The volcano," Michael yelled.

Lenny erupted, chasing them all around the room, his arms waving.

They sprawled on the floor mat with Lenny's arms writhing on

36

top of them. When they'd stopped laughing Michael ached for the bottle of beer and found it was empty.

"No more beer," he said.

"Shit," Lenny said.

"Let's go to Binghamton," Michael said after a pause.

"Nemo's," Timmy said, and Ron saw the rest of them react to the name as if it were the most secret place in the world.

"Yeah, let's go," Ron heard himself saying enthusiastically.

Lenny stood up and looked down on the sprawling boys. The volcano to the little village of huts.

"You're not going."

Ron stood up quickly, and without thinking said to his brother, "I want to."

"Get back to your room. You're not going," Lenny said flatly.

But Timmy had stood up now and he mimicked, "Get back to your hut, get back to your hut."

"Now look," Lenny said, trying to sound reasonable. "You can't go, that's all."

"Let him," Michael said. He was standing too.

Lenny turned to Michael and said, "No."

"Meanie . . . meanie . . ." Timmy needled.

"Shut the fuck up . . ."

"Let him if he *wants* to . . ." Michael said, again looking at Ron.

"You really *want* to?" Lenny asked after peering intensely at his brother.

"Yeah . . ." Ron said, trying to be casual, as if these were his friends and they were arguing about whether to go to the movies or sit in the pizza parlor, but he wasn't allowed to get away with playing it that way. Lenny moved in closer, Michael and Timmy leaned in too.

"Really?"

Ron knew that something very important was being asked of him, so he had to stop acting casual and say seriously, "Yes, I really want to."

"Okay," Lenny said. "But remember, I didn't force you, now did I?"

"No."

"You want to go on your own free will, right?"

"Right."

"You know what's happening?"

"Sure." He hid his instant fear. Did he really?

"Okay. Let's go then."

As they were getting in Michael's father's car Ron whispered to Timmy, "What's Nemo's?"

"A bar," Timmy replied, getting in the back seat next to Ron while Lenny shifted into the front seat next to Michael, who was driving.

A bar? Why did a bar seem so special to them? There were two bars in town. One was attached to the Maples Restaurant where Ron's father's friends slouched over their drinks. And the other bar was off Broadway, very dingy, where men like the school janitor, colored men and farm hands hung out forlornly. Neither seemed attractive or magnetic but the attitude of the boys made this bar . . . this Nemo's . . . different.

During the silent half-hour ride to Binghamton, broken only by the occasional jabber of Timmy, Ron imagined Nemo's. Binghamton was a craggy rock of a city, sharp, tough, and black like a piece of coal. It seemed to exist for the black smoke of it's factories to come to rest on. It was a desert of old asphalt and crooked brown wooden houses. Now, in the middle of this desert existed an oasis called Nemo's. He imagined young men, crowded, whispering to each other. No girls—so that none of the boys had to pretend. They could be themselves, the air soft, the beer mellow, cold, and the boys swaying to some easy kind of unimaginable music, clinging to each other without clammy touching, but touching was there—an almost imperceptible . . . caressing . . .

Ron found himself bulging and without turning his head managed to see that the other boys were not watching him, but then Timmy turned to him and asked a question about school and as Ron answered the bulge went away. Lenny shifted his body in the front of the car to monitor the conversation without seeming to.

Ron told Timmy about the soccer team. Timmy was closer to him, less goofy now, more friendly. Ron found himself liking him very much but being careful because he knew that Lenny didn't want Ron to like Timmy that much.

And Michael drove on, taking in everything that was going on, seeing his friend and lover Lenny playing God, and, after all the talks they'd had on repression, so overprotective, and Ron wanting to bust loose and Timmy, his dirty little mouth salivating, just waiting for Lenny to get diverted with something else. Michael found it delicious and vowed to get Ron away from Lenny as soon as they got into Nemo's . . . The boy was dying to come out if only Lenny would let him alone. But Michael hoped that it wasn't going to be with that awful fag Timmy . . . Certainly there was better for Ron to be found somewhere . . . Michael wouldn't mind himself except Lenny would be furious . . . if he found out, of course . . . Perhaps there'd be someone at Nemo's for Lenny and then Michael could get alone with Ron for a little while in the car or something . . .

They arrived in Binghamton.

Gizzo, Johnny, Ramon and Franky. They were going to kick the shit out of some faggots tonight. They'd found this bar tucked away behind the main drag and had kicked some good action lately. Gizzo loved it. He was tall and skinny like a scythe with his long nose and his protruding belly. He used a switchblade with abandoned viciousness, crouching low and slicing at his opponent's legs, then springing to the midsection. Gizzo, the Slicer, he liked to call himself. Faggots needed to be whipped and robbed, he told the other boys. They liked it, even though they screamed like hell, but then they'd go home and get off on it, remembering every punch and every little slice . . . They loved it, as long as you didn't muss up their permanents.

Johnny had hard fists and he liked to punch. He was seventeen and starting to box but he didn't enjoy wearing gloves. Like getting laid with a condom, you don't get the feel of crunching bones. He loved the old fighters—had pictures of them all over his walls—the way they'd fight with bare knuckles. John L. Sullivan. What a man! Johnny didn't care who he'd hit, faggots, niggers, his brother, Jews, as long as he could hit and feel the bones crack.

Ramon liked to hold the queers while the other boys worked on them. They felt different from other guys he'd held during fights, softer skin, almost like girls—girl-like features, too. He liked to fuck them or have them blow him. And sometimes he'd take one of the queers on the side and put a knife to his throat and make the faggot give him a blow job saying, "Hey, man, one feel of your teeth on my cock and I cut your throat."

Franky was a near-moron, a fat kid whose family had forgotten him and never knew when he was out. Franky worshipped Gizzo and would literally have leaped from a roof if Gizzo commanded. Yet Franky didn't like to beat these funny guys up. They seemed so cute and harmless but he enjoyed Gizzo having such a good time.

Queers were fair game. Even the cops smiled when they heard about them being beaten up. They were an insult to any real man and the boys were doing a public service . . . And besides, they always had good money on them . . . They were smart . . . like Jews . . . and always managed to make money . . . wasn't this better than snatching purses or robbing stores?

The boys waited in a little brownstone hallway across from Nemo's. They liked to get them before they got into the bar and spent their money . . .

Lenny had Michael drive around the block once to make sure there were no gangs around. The last time he'd been in Nemo's Lenny had seen a boy come in with blood all over him and his nose crumpled like an old newspaper. He and a couple of the others had run out angrily to see who'd done it and had caught a brief glimpse of escaping teenage boys as they ran past the end of the block and cut around the corner of an old factory and into the honkytonk section of town where it wasn't safe for anyone to go, much less them.

No one had even thought to call the police. They wouldn't look for anyone who beat up a faggot. The boy was taken to the hospital and Lenny had sat at the bar the remainder of the evening, not socializing with anyone, just brooding over the god-damn injustice of what he'd just seen, his hatred deepening like a nail being driven by a hammer.

Lenny said nothing to the rest of the boys about the danger. He didn't want to alarm them—listen to Timmy's hysterics, feel Michael's shivering or worry his brother. He didn't know whether he was doing the right thing or not by taking Ron along but he wanted to make the experience as good for Ron as possible . . . If he was going to come out he'd learn soon enough about the bad. He directed Michael to park as close as possible to Nemo's. Nemo's was in the middle of a block that contained several two-story ramshackle wooden houses and three or four larger brownstone apartment houses. It said "Cocktail Lounge" not "Bar" and the windows were painted black and there was an Art Deco silhouette of a man in a tuxedo talking to a woman in a gown. The woman was holding a cigarette in a long holder and the man, hair slicked down, was sipping champagne. When Ron saw it through the car window against the backdrop of the large smokestack on the next street it seemed funny to him. Fred Astaire in Factory Town.

Michael parked about a quarter of a block away and they all eased out of the car. The streets were totally deserted and very dark—the lamppost near the bar was out. Lenny hesitated. He didn't like the dark and the quietness. He wanted to see people —a woman with a baby carriage or a man coming home from work with a lunch pail—normal scenes . . . Perhaps he ought to have everyone get back in the car . . . But goddamn it what was that crazy idiot Timmy doing? . . . Shit . . . He was actually doing a stupid Marilyn Monroe imitation walk and Ron was laughing at it and Michael was just smiling.

"Cut it out," Lenny said sharply.

"What's the matter with you, big boy?" Timmy said, giving Lenny some dumb blinks.

"Move quick."

"Walk like a man," Michael said.

"There are gangs around here, you fucking idiot," Lenny said. Timmy started to walk toward Nemo's like a man—a hulking cowboy with guns at his side that were so low his legs were bowed. "Where's the bar . . . I wanna wet my whistle . . ." this with a suggestive leer . . .

"Look at that cocksucker," Gizzo said as he watched Timmy's prancing from the vestibule of the brownstone across from Nemo's.

"They don't look like queers," Franky said. "The other guys look all right." He too laughed at Timmy. He's kind of funny, Franky thought.

"The hell they do," Ramon said. "Look at the one with the black hair. He's a cunt." Ramon was referring to Michael and planning how he would take him into one of the hallways while the guys were working over the rest of them.

And Johnny saw in Ron's round sunny features a chance to mess up one of those nice girlish faces. There was something specially delicious in breaking a delicate nose.

But they all hesitated because of Lenny. He was like a guard in a caravan of harem girls, and his presence made them stay in the hallway an extra second wondering if they ought to let this group go and wait for a lone queer or maybe two instead of four. But it had been a slow night. The beatings had warned many people and Nemo's was almost empty tonight. The crowd had started to congregate at some other bar as they had to once one place was discovered. The boys were frustrated and broke and the weekend was near.

"Well, let's ask them," Gizzo said and stepped out of the hallway onto the stoop. The other boys had no choice but to follow as he walked quickly down the steps across the street.

Ron was the first to see this strange scythe-like pimply-faced boy walking toward them, with the gang behind him, and he yanked his brother's arm.

"Just keep walking," Lenny whispered to everyone and quickly put himself between Ron and the approaching gang.

Gizzo seemed to talk to someone that was above everyone's head as he said, "Hey, you guys see any queers around here lately?"

No one answered, they tried to keep walking but Ramon, Johnny and Franky had moved in front of them and they had to stop.

"We was arguing," Gizzo said. "We thought that maybe you guys was queer. You guys queers?"

"Hey look," Lenny said reasonably to Gizzo, "why don't you just move out of the way and let us go about our business?"

"Yeah, well, this is like a toll bridge, you know. Yeah, we charge the faggots a little toll to go by . . . that's all . . . Give us a buck each, is all. . . ."

Lenny slightly turned to Ron and the rest and said, "Come on." But before a move could be made Gizzo had taken his large switchblade knife out and pressed the little button on the side. The sound of the switchblade was the dearest noise in the world to Gizzo.

"Look, a buck each . . . make it two bucks each . . . Then you can go into the bar and blow each other all you want. Okay?"

He bounced the knife easily in his hand, "Come on, sweeties, pay the toll."

Johnny brought his hands out of his pockets and flexed his fists, staring intensely at Ron's face, almost tasting Ron's flesh on his knuckles.

Ron held onto his brother, wanting to disappear into him somehow. Timmy simpered. Michael turned very pale.

"Don't worry, kid," Ramon told Michael as he took his knife out—careful, however, not to open it yet. "We ain't going to hurt you."

Franky laughed at the sight of Timmy beginning to cry. He removed a heavy chain from his jacket and rattled it in front of Timmy, laughing as Timmy simpered some more when he saw it. Franky thought that Timmy was cute.

"Give them money," Michael whispered to Lenny. Lenny saw Timmy sobbing, his brother clinging and Michael fainting and they disgusted him far more than the wicked freaks in front of him.

At that moment Lenny knew that he wasn't going to live his life paying tolls for being the way he was anymore. That's what they all wanted. His friends and his enemies alike . . . His parents and schools and the whole fucking world wanted him to pay a toll because he was different. Well, fuck them. If he went down bleeding on a dirty street in Binghamton right here and now or if he lived another eighty years, nothing was worth paying that fucking toll.

He growled like a wild bear as his right foot shot out and viciously kicked Gizzo in the groin just a few inches above the testicles that he was aiming for but hard enough to send him to his knees, howling with surprised pain.

Lenny screamed, a wild, Oriental, maniacal scream and took a stance directly facing Johnny, his legs spread apart and his fists held in a karate position.

Johnny smiled and squared off. This crazy cocksucker was guarding the little prince behind him. Johnny was going to crunch this crazy queer and then get his real pleasure out of the kid in the back.

Lenny moved in quickly on Johnny, his arm shooting out straight from his body, aiming at a spot on Johnny's forehead but Johnny was faster than Lenny calculated and was able to duck and come up with a powerful left to Lenny's chest and then a right to the side of Lenny's jaw that sent Lenny to the pavement.

Johnny moved in, set to pound away while Lenny was stunned. When Ron saw Lenny on the ground he knew his life was ending right there and then.

Ramon, meanwhile, took Michael by the back of the neck, held his knife up to Michael's face, still not opening it, moved Michael up a nearby stoop, opened the hall door, shoved Michael in and followed him.

Franky jingled the chain in front of Timmy while Timmy cringed away, sobbing and biting his fingers. Timmy backed off against an iron railing and as Franky moved in on him he moved down a few stairs below the street until two garbage cans stopped him, and he was in a corner as this fat idiot kept following him jingling the chain.

Lenny had kicked Johnny from the ground and was able to face him squarely again, more cautious this time, knowing that he was facing an opponent who was trained in the streets while his training had been self-taught, more than from books, used mostly in gyms rather than with real opponents. And he had to watch the others, especially the one he'd kicked who was now starting to get himself together enough to fight again. And Ron, he had to watch him . . . He couldn't let anything happen to his brother . . .

Lenny and Johnny squared off. There was a body blow that could do a lot of damage, but it had to be in the right place . . . just below the chest, right in the upper part of the solar plexus . . . Should he try it? If it didn't work, this guy with the iron-hard fists might nail him and put him away but he had to do something because the other one was getting up and there was Ron standing right in back of him, frozen.

Lenny feinted with his left hand and Johnny threw his arms slightly up to block the blow. Lenny shot his right fist out at the spot he wanted . . .

"Gimmie your money," Ramon told Michael as he made Michael face the wall. "Come on, gimmie your money. I ain't gonna hurt you."

45

"Please . . . please . . ." Michael pleaded as he frantically reached into his pocket and gave Ramon any money he had. Lenny had taught Michael a lot of things about self-defense but he wasn't going to try them now. He just wanted to collapse. He'd get out of this by doing whatever this hoodlum wanted. This fellow didn't seem to want to hurt him.

Ramon rubbed against the backside of Michael, leaned toward Michael's ear and said, "Suck me off."

Michael nodded. Ramon took Michael by the shoulder and pushed him down till he crouched in front of him, then he unzipped his fly and took out his penis. He had been hard the moment he rubbed against Michael.

As Michael opened his mouth Ramon put his knife, still without opening it, against his throat and said, "If I feel your teeth on my cock I'll cut your fucking throat . . ."

"Hey," Franky said to Timmy as Timmy sat on the garbage can looking at him through his tears, seeming to Franky to be every bit as cute as a neighbor's little dog that he petted. "Gizzo won't hurt you if you give me your money."

"Are you Gizzo?" Timmy asked.

"No. Gizzo's up there. But I'll tell him not to touch you if you give me your money."

"Here," Timmy said, reaching into his pocket for his money, giving it to Franky so eagerly that some coins dropped. Timmy quickly bent down to retrieve them. "Here's my watch too. It's a good one, see . . . a Longine, my mother gave it to me for graduation."

"Yeah . . ." Franky said, wondering if it glowed in the dark like good watches do. He cupped his hand around the face of it and looked in. "It don't glow."

"Really good ones don't glow . . . it's only the cheap ones that do," Timmy explained quickly . . .

Lenny's blow didn't land where he wanted it to but it landed hard enough to send Johnny back against the iron railing, his breath knocked out of him and his guard down. Lenny moved in

. . . He could finish this one now if only he could get to him before the other one with the knife got back into the fight. But now Gizzo came up behind Lenny as he was getting set to chop down on Johnny's neck. He'd picked a place right around the shoulder blades where he was going to start to slice away.

Ron jumped on Gizzo's back and brought him to the ground.

"Hey . . ." Gizzo exclaimed, surprised that this young fag was getting into this at all.

Ron, suddenly on top of this ugly beast, didn't know what to do now that he was there. He almost wanted to apologize. He'd hold him as if he were a soccer ball until everyone calmed down and then Ron felt something cross his leg. It was sharp, like a paper cut, and he quickly looked at his left leg and saw blood and realized that Gizzo had cut him across the leg and was going to do it again. Ron took hold of Gizzo's head and smashed it as hard as he could against the concrete and he felt his leg being crossed again and again as he smashed Gizzo's head again and again, suddenly he heard a strange crack and he saw Gizzo's eyes seem to project themselves out of their sockets as Gizzo screamed, the most agonized scream that Ron had ever heard, or imagined . . .

Lenny had knocked Johnny unconscious and had then gone over where his brother was on the ground with Gizzo, being sliced up by the machine-like strokes and had, with one full stomp, broken Gizzo's hand into many pieces.

Lenny helped Ron off of Gizzo and they hugged each other, both with tears suddenly coming to their eyes.

"Come on," Lenny said. "Let's get the other guys."

Ron went to Timmy, who was sitting on a garbage can talking about the watch to Franky.

He leaped on Franky and got him in a strong headlock.

"Hey," Timmy said. "Don't hurt him . . . He's okay . . ."

Franky broke out of Ron's headlock and viciously turned to Ron, bringing the chain down on Ron's arm with an agonizing thud.

"Okay, my ass," Ron muttered to Timmy. "Let's get out of here."

Timmy ran out past Ron, and as he turned to go up the steps he said, "My watch, get my watch . . ."

"Fuck your watch," Ron told him as he shoved the garbage cans against the slow, chain-swinging idiot and moved away up the steps with Timmy . . .

Lenny opened the hall door and saw his lover on his knees with Ramon's penis in his mouth. Michael's eyes were closed. He was like a pale kneeling corpse. Lenny stepped behind Ramon, who had his eyes closed, sucking the air quietly. He grabbed the arm that held the still closed knife and yanked it strongly behind Ramon's back at the same time taking the other arm and putting a stranglehold around Ramon's neck. He loved the way the space between Ramon's jaw and shoulders fit his arm. He squeezed hard and was delighted to see Ramon's eyes bulging. Michael did not know what was happening yet.

"Michael," he said. *"Michael."*

Michael opened his eyes.

"Bite it, Michael," Lenny said. "Bite it hard."

Ramon convulsed. Lenny twisted his arm harder so that the arm was now up at the back of the head. He expected to hear it crack at any moment. He tightened his stranglehold.

"Hold still, baby," he said to Ramon. "While Michael takes a little bite." And Lenny kissed Ramon softly on the ear.

Michael bit. And when he bit once and felt Ramon squirm and heard him scream he bit again, this time as if he wanted to bite through and bite it off.

Ramon fainted in Lenny's arms.

Lenny let Ramon down gently like a sack of laundry as Michael removed his mouth from around Ramon's penis. Lenny crouched in front of Michael.

"Are you all right?" he asked, touching Michael's face and looking at him. "Did he hurt you?"

Michael shook his head no but avoided looking directly at

Lenny. He started to cry and turned his head away.

"Are you all right?"

"Yes."

"Come on. We'd better get out of here."

Lenny helped Michael to stand up and opened the hall door. Just before he went into the street he said to Michael, "Why didn't you fight?"

Michael shook the question off. He walked toward the car, not even looking around at the other boys.

"Come on," Lenny said to Timmy and Ron as he walked quickly down the stoop. "Let's get out of here before they get more . . ." They moved to the car . . .

Franky saw Gizzo on the pavement holding his hand, muttering. "It's broke . . . it's broke . . . the whole fuckin' thing is broke . . ."

He kneeled down in front of his idol. "What happened?"

"It's broke. The whole fuckin' thing is broke." Gizzo yelled at Franky as if he should have known better than to ask, as if somehow it was Franky's fault.

Franky turned toward the fags and started to run after them. He'd never been so angry in his life. "Hey, who broke Gizzo's hand? Hey!"

"Come on, *run,*" Lenny told the others, and they broke into a fast pace. "You got the key to the car?" Lenny asked Michael. Michael reached into his sweater pocket and held up the key.

They reached the car well ahead of the hulking Franky; Michael opened the door quickly and they all leaped into the car, taking their same seats as before, making sure to lock the doors.

Michael started the motor as Franky approached, his chain swinging menacingly.

"Move it," Lenny shouted.

Franky, his eyes wide with a glazed kind of hatred, leaped on the hood of the car as Michael put it into first.

The car moved. "Oh God, you'll kill him . . ." Timmy squealed.

"Move it," Lenny commanded Michael as Michael hesitated.

Lenny saw past the hulking body on the hood. Johnny had recovered and was chasing the car. Ramon had staggered out of the hall and was leaning against the door, watching, perhaps recouping his strength for vengeance.

Ron wanted to get out of there. He wished he could have shot the fat presence on the hood. "Move it . . ." he echoed his brother . . . Then as his brother said, "Move it," again Ron yelled the same in Michael's ear because Franky was picking up his chain and about to smash it on the car window.

Michael accelerated past the rest of the gang.

"Make a sharp left at the next corner," Lenny commanded.

"No," Timmy screamed.

"Shut up," Lenny told Timmy. He turned to Ron. "Shut him up."

Ron punched Timmy sharply on the arm. "Keep quiet. We've got to . . ."

Michael made a sharp left turn and Franky rolled off the hood, and when Ron and Timmy looked out of the back window they saw him on the ground, rolling around.

"See," Ron told Timmy. "He's all right."

"Fuck him," Timmy said, turning around, facing the front. "I don't care about him. My watch. He stole this lovely Longine my mother gave me and now it's probably all smashed."

They drove warily for a few blocks, as if waiting for some new attack, but when it was clear that it wasn't forthcoming Lenny turned around, his eyes shining. "We take no shit from any of them, do you hear? We take no shit."

Ron said, "Yeah, yeah," and he laughed with his brother.

Timmy chimed in, "Yeah, we take no shit. We knock 'em on their asses."

Michael had begun to cry but even through his tears he laughed too and said, "Yeah . . . No shit . . ."

There was a first-aid kit in the glove compartment and Timmy fussed over Ron's leg. Ron had worn thick corduroy pants, which had helped because the cuts weren't too deep. Michael was having a difficult time driving and keeping himself from breaking down but he refused to let Lenny drive. Lenny shifted closer and talked softly to him, comforting him, letting him know that he understood what happened and he didn't really blame him, apologizing for having been so harsh before.

Just before they arrived back in town Timmy leaned over close to Ron, putting his hand on Ron's thigh. "You feel okay?"

"Yeah," Ron said, suddenly very nervous about where Timmy's hand was. He knew what Timmy was and what he wanted. He knew what his brother was too. He just didn't know what he was.

Timmy's hand slid up his pants and touched his penis. Ron let out a little cry of surprise.

Lenny turned around and said sharply to Timmy, "Hey," and Timmy simply took his hand away and innocently peered out of the other window while Lenny went back to talking softly to Michael, and Ron moved more deeply into his corner with the touch of Timmy's still on him, there, like the feel of soft velvet.

They finally arrived in the neighborhood of the Starr home. Michael parked around the corner. Timmy stepped out of the car quickly. Ron followed him, both of them knowing that Michael and Lenny wanted to be left alone to say goodbye. Timmy stood by Ron in an awkward silence. Ron saw Lenny and Michael as one large presence huddled together in the driver's seat of the car.

"This was some night, huh?" Ron said.

"It sure was."

"You feel okay?" Ron asked.

"I feel great."

"I bet those guys in Binghamton don't feel so great."

"Yeah." They both laughed.

"Your brother is a tornado," Timmy said.

"He sure is."

"You're okay, too. You saved me—that fat pig was going to swallow me up."

"He was disgusting. They were all disgusting."

"Yeah."

"I'd like to see you again," Timmy said.

"Come around . . . I'm usually home."

Timmy stared at Ron, wanting more, wanting what was really there. Ron felt the stare and turned to look at the cute, ugly little clown who was now so serious. Ron felt like he wanted to hold Timmy in his arms and kiss him on the forehead, almost the way he'd kiss a pet bulldog, run his hand through the crewcut, but if he did that then he knew where Timmy's hand would go and he didn't want that . . . The last touch hadn't quite left him yet.

And then Lenny was by his side and Timmy was back in the car and the two brothers watched it pull away, pausing till they saw the red taillights turn the corner before they allowed themselves to wonder about going back home.

Were their parents home yet? And if they were, what state would they be in?

They walked the half block that would take them to within sight of their house in distracted silence. Lenny passed an old tree next to old-man McGraw's rundown once elegant colonial and muttered, "Tree'll die if they don't do something."

Ron nodded. He had an empty fright and his mouth was sand-dry. He couldn't wait to reach the corner so that he could see the house dark, with no one there to ask questions.

But the house was ablaze with light—glowing like a malevolent star—every bulb on from basement to attic. They both stood at the corner a moment. Ron turned to Lenny, silently asking him what to do.

Lenny swallowed. He was frightened, Ron could see that, and his brother's fear had a multiplying effect on his own. But then a new hardness came to Lenny's face, a new kind of defiance that Ron had seen developing all evening and he confidently said to Ron, "Look, we went to Binghamton to see a basketball game—we took the bus and were brought back by some guys from school . . ."

"What about my leg?"

"Don't show it to them. Did you have soccer practice today?"

"Yesterday."

"You got it playing soccer."

Ron wanted to tell Lenny that there was no way you could get hurt that way playing soccer but Lenny was already moving toward the glowing house. Ron stayed in back of his brother . . .

Louis and Blanche were at separate windows and, as on a conductor's cue, on seeing the boys approach dropped the curtains they were peering from into place and appeared, side by side, together as never before, at the front door to await their sons. To Ron, the incongruity of seeing these two people standing together, united, added to the strange feeling that was building in him like a crescendo.

And then they fell on them and all Ron could make out were frantic, angry questions about where they were and what were they doing and Lenny's reasonable voice talking about the basketball game . . . Ron got safely in the house behind Lenny, feeling like a catcher in a baseball game with Lenny as his mitt, face mask and body protector. They were on both sides of his brother now, Louis lawyer-like stentorian, Blanche a frantic little bird with a big crow's voice. Louis' face deep red and Blanche's ashen.

Ron edged toward the stairs and the sanctuary of his room.

Blanche pummeled Ron by the shoulder up the stairs while Louis shunted Lenny into the living room. Ron took the steps two at a time so as to get to the safety of his room as fast as possible. He took one leg up two steps and then in the middle of doing the other he knew he was making a serious mistake, because the stretch accentuated the rips in his pants.

"What happened to your pants?" Blanche asked, freezing the leg midway by deftly catching hold of his ankle. Ron sat down awkwardly on the step as Blanche quickly raised his pants leg exposing the Band-Aids that inadequately covered the three slits on his leg. The iodine that Timmy had poured over the wounds made them seem more gruesome than they were and to make it even worse one of the Band-Aids had come loose exposing a bleeding cut.

Blanche gasped in wide-eyed horror. Ron laughed stupidly because she suddenly reminded him of a movie on TV last week where this old lady sees Frankenstein coming through the moors. It was completely involuntary and the worst thing he could have done. Blanche gasped even louder at seeing her precious boy laughing like a demented degenerate.

Ron tried to say something to her to let her know that the wounds were not bad and that he was all right. But nothing tangible was coming out of his mouth because he didn't know where to even begin so the laughter built. Louis pushed his way past Blanche and stared a moment at the leg, reached down and quickly pulled off the remaining two Band-Aids making Ron yell at the sharp pain of the adhesive being yanked off the skin.

"Those are knife wounds," Louis said with his best courtroom voice. His right arm pointed to it, and he paused as if for dramatic effect to give all the twenty-four eyes of the jury time to digest it.

Lenny laughed too.

Louis in real fury turned to Lenny and bellowed, "What the hell are you laughing at?"

Blanche now clearly saw what she must do. Lenny was a loss that must be cut in order to save Ron from a life of demented grinning degeneracy. It was beginning . . . She saw it as Ron laughed just like his brother. Action must be taken!

"Him! Him!" she screamed, pointing at Lenny.

She pushed Louis in the shoulder.

Louis didn't need much pushing. He knew what he must do also. He saw them together, laughing the same way, going off together now, sharing the same friends . . . It was all starting . . . and he knew where it would end up. They always try to get young boys into the same thing that they do—even their own brothers. God, how he hated them. God, what an offense to any real man his own eldest son was. He moved in closer to the contemptuously laughing Lenny.

Blanche got Ron up the stairs. "Get into your room," she said.

Ron needed no further urging. He raced up the steps and into his room, closing the door quickly and shoving the dresser in front of it squarely.

He heard muffled, intense talking downstairs but he didn't try to hear words as it went on and on . . . didn't want to distinguish voices . . . He just knew that it all made him nauseous and shaky. He sat on the bed and looked at his leg . . . it wasn't bad. He dabbed at it with a handkerchief. They were all talking louder downstairs now. Shouting . . . mostly his parents . . . he didn't hear Lenny. He focused on his leg not to worry about his brother. Lenny could take care of himself.

His penis tingled. It felt like an ear infection he'd had once. Had Timmy's touch infected him? If his parents carried on about the cuts on his leg the way they did, think how they'd act if they saw an infection—there!

Ron dropped to the floor and slid under his bed and he slowly, carefully took it out . . . It felt all right but as he tried to see it he couldn't because there wasn't too much light under the bed. He listened for all the voices downstairs to make sure that no one would burst through the door. He heard all three. Lenny was getting mad now. Blanche was crying and Louis was lawyer-loud again.

He started to worry about tetanus. How fast does that set in? He should get a shot. He could get lockjaw. Lenny was really shouting now. When Lenny was angry his voice became stacatto —like the turbulent parts of Beethoven sonatas. Maybe Ron ought to run down and tell his parents that lockjaw was setting in and they'd run him to the hospital and that would break off the fighting. No. Then they'd really blame Lenny—he ought to tell them that he was okay . . . that he hadn't gotten infected that he wasn't going to turn into one of those . . .

The level of screaming downstairs had become too frightening to ignore. Someone could be killing someone else. Everything in this family had been repressed, muffled and secretive as if each hurt feeling was a stick of dynamite stored away to be blown up in the future—tonight!

Ron began to cry as he looked at the door of his room. Lenny could kill his mother or his father. He could, Ron knew, he was so strong and he had that kind of temper. And his mother could kill Lenny or order his father to do it—like Abraham on the mountain with Isaac. Ron pictured his father with a big sword hovering over his brother with Blanche as an avenging God pushing him, calling him Schmuck and urging him to strike.

Ron stood close to his door wondering what to do and the shouting suddenly stopped. For a moment there was a very ominous silence. Had someone killed someone else yet? Was someone looking over someone else's body while someone else cringed?

Ron opened the door and stepped quickly to the landing. What he saw was to stay with him the rest of his life. Louis and Blanche were cringing against the living-room wall as Lenny paced before them menacingly, his elbow bent with one hand in it as Italian boys did when they were angry. He seemed to Ron as if he wanted to punch them into the wall.

"I'll be the way I want to be and you both can go fuck yourselves," Lenny was saying. "And you know what? . . . If he wants to be that way too I hope he tells you to go fuck yourselves too."

Blanche looked up and saw Ron standing there and knew that he'd heard. She touched Louis and Louis saw Ron there as well.

Lenny turned and saw Ron too.

They all stopped and were frozen for the moment and then as if reacting to the same command Louis and Blanche attacked Lenny. They hit him and they clawed at him and they cursed him and they made him bleed. Ron couldn't believe what he was seeing. Lenny had tears in his eyes but did nothing to defend against his parents who were striking and pushing him.

For the second time that night Ron moved to help his brother. Lenny, seeing Ron coming down the stairs, knowing that it was too soon for Ron to be at his side, knowing that he was at last getting out of this misery and into a new, more open life that he, but not Ron, was ready for, said almost softly in the middle of being pushed and hit, "Get up to your room, kid . . . It's all right. Get up to your room."

Blanche and Louis stopped hitting Lenny. Ron turned, weak and slow now . . . tired suddenly, drained and without looking back woodenly went to his room and finally fell asleep.

Lenny left the house that night for good.

Louis and Blanche were heavily sick with it. They each retreated into their private caves of brooding, not sharing anything but a sullen, secret blaming of each other. Ron never walked over that section of the floor in the living room where Lenny had stood when his parents attacked him, as if to step on it were like treading on an open wound.

And often he imagined himself a character in some huge Shakespearian chronicle, where people were always coming on and saying lines and then leaving, going through some stage business without any real warmth or life, as if he, himself, should have gotten off the stage when his brother did but was left on through someone's ridiculous mistake . . .

He tried to never think too much about his brother. He tried to shut his mind to everything that had happened in Binghamton that night . . . to at least everything he could shut his mind to. Things snuck up on him once in a while. He missed his brother . . . yet it all wasn't too difficult. He was young and college was facing him soon and in college there would be plenty of girls.

CHAPTER 4

L ouis was talking pre-law and Blanche was patiently waiting
for Ron to reject law through his own experience and choose one
of the arts. Ron wasn't a good enough musician, she knew that,
but he could be an actor or a writer. She knew he wrote secretly,
something would develop. Meanwhile let the schmuck think he
had a lawyer.

For father's benefit Ron could be enthusiastic about getting
right into college politics and for mother's he could show her
a course he would take on Elizabethan theater, as if an artistic
calling were sneaking up on him. Blanche savored the future

scene where Ron would tell Louis, "Sorry, dad, I'm going to be an actor—law's not for me."

The college that he was going to start in the fall was a small, co-ed, liberal arts school about an hour and a half from New York City—one step closer to *that* city. Ron was making a journey there, he could feel himself being pulled, but first this campus must be stopped at to prepare him fully. The ideas in the pretty, ivy-covered institution would fill his mind with what he needed to be a New York person. The people would be city-connected people, museum, theater, art, people with Greenwich Village studios. He was ready. His life would start in the fall.

In the fall, on a cold, snappy day, Ron went to the dorm for the first time, laden with papers and luggage. His room was on the second floor. It was awfully small, rectangular, like the building itself, with two thin beds, a nondescript rug in the middle, two pale yellow dressers and small desk boards sticking out of the wall with little bookshelves above them. Two people were supposed to live like that! There was only one window—two people sticking their heads out of one window! Heads so close together . . . Ron turned away from the empty room and walked down the corridor. He was depressed. He wished he could go home.

He passed the community shower room, opened the door and saw the showers very close to one another with no partitions in between.

At the college that Lenny had been expelled from there were things going on in the shower room.

Now Ron became transfixed by the head of one of the showers, a wide octangular head with large holes in it that seemed to be forming like the head of a cobra and angling at him. A large drop of water poised a moment appearing like the tongue of a snake as it drip-dropped in a puddle making a water-hissing sound. The shower head seemed to expand and move more closely to him, the little holes becoming pores in the mouth of the snake. He gave himself up to whatever it wanted to do to him.

Then there was a noise behind him and he saw a huge hand

59

on the door and his heart vibrated and trembled as he snapped out of his spell and backed out of the way of another freshman who was just going to the toilet.

He ran out through the back entrance of the dorm behind a large oak tree, the same kind almost as the one in his back yard, and opening a sheet of instructions he appeared to read them as he just let himself cry, the cry that he'd been choking down.

Nothing was going to happen to him. He wasn't going to be like Lenny. He could live at a dorm and be okay. He wasn't the way his brother was and living at a dorm with community showers and a roommate would prove it.

By this time Ron had read things and heard talk. The Kinsey Report was widely discussed and he'd gone to the town library and assiduously researched everything he could find under Human Behavior especially involving adolescent stages of homosexuality. He was simply going through a stage, a stage that was due to be passed soon, he shouldn't be so frightened of it.

He simply would never do anything overt. He couldn't help the surprise attractions, like ambushes; gazing at someone's hair or body . . . seeing someone and wanting to be with them, wanting to put his arms around certain boys. Often he thought about cute little Timmy—cute ugly little Timmy—and Michael, too. Michael had gone off to college . . . His mind drifted to Lenny and Michael and the gym downstairs.

Soon he could laugh at the idea of being worried about having a roommate. He could look at his roommate, a boy from the Bronx named Mort Mattic (Ron nicknamed him Automatic and it stuck), who had brown, dandruff-filled hair, skin slightly pock-marked, who was perpetually vilifying females, especially froshes because they seemed to prefer upper-classmen. He could gaze at Mort Mattic all day long, balls and all, and have absolutely no problems.

He leaped right into college life and was considered a real comer. He idolized Kennedy and formed a committee of Freshmen for J.F.K., canvassing the town and college with such enthusiasm that more often than not he converted the non-J.F.K. voters he talked to.

He made the soccer team and joined the school paper. He loved the Elizabethan drama course—there were other playwrights of the era besides Shakespeare—Marlowe, Kidd. Sometimes he'd see Lenny as Tamburlaine or the Jew of Malta, glad that he could be with his brother at least that way and not be uncomfortable.

Everything was going beautifully except for the little ambushes. He came to a point in his life where he knew that in order to grow out of the thing that bothered him the most he'd finally have to get laid.

His entrance into the vagina of a female would exorcise this slight disorder that had visited him. It would happen as day would follow night, as sure as there were stars in the sky or whatever other surism existed. It was axiomatic, positive, no questions asked.

Now he just had to go and do it.

By the end of high school Ron had grown expert in making out. His hands knew just where to go and more and more the girls let him, but he'd always stopped before he'd journeyed too far. Not that one or two that he could think of wouldn't have let him . . . maybe they would have . . . but he didn't want to. He'd been content to caress and gently rub against them and then act the way a gentleman should act and stop. Girls became bored with him and they didn't want to see him again. That was all right. There were always girls that would walk with him and go to parties. He was popular, considered a good date; a gentleman, who wasn't bad-looking, could hold a good conversation and who wouldn't get too rough when the lights were low.

But now he had to do it.

It was being done a lot in college, all over the campus—practically, except, it seemed, by freshmen. Whenever a freshman bragged about getting laid no one believed him. Ron cursed the uppity co-eds along with everyone else.

Judy Halbertson was a junior and without a doubt the best girl

61

reporter, maybe the best reporter that the school paper had ever had. She could write up an interview from the most controversial, newsworthy point of view and her copy was professional. She was the local correspondent for the *Times* and had had three items about local happenings appear. She was destined to have a brilliant journalistic career (which she did).

She never thought about sex. She was growing heavier all the time, eating everything that she wanted and smoking at a pace that was breathtaking. She didn't look good and she didn't care. She'd been unvirginated in high school quite emphatically by the custodian's son, an Italian lad who was very well built and couldn't talk English. They'd meet twice a week and go to the workshop in the basement after poppa had gone home and do it on poppa's old couch. Judy remembered how absolutely furious Angelo became every time she'd tear the wrapper off the condom and roll it onto him just before he got into her. She was too smart to get knocked up. Sex was all right, she supposed. It didn't hurt and after a while it didn't even feel too bad but it wasn't anything she'd go out of her way for except . . .

All the kids were talking about it now as if it were something that one had to do in order to be a full person. Girls were admitting they did it, liked it. It made them feel better and look better. Judy studied herself in the mirror and realized that she was going to be graduating before long and looking for a job and if she looked bad it would be harder. Maybe she'd better start doing it again. But goddamn it she just hated to take the time. And the hassle of a romantic thing! When she didn't want to do it anymore with Angelo the dumb bunny had come around to her house and talked in Italian to everyone he could find. He'd wanted to marry her . . . the whole bit. God. How embarrassing when mother had asked her, "Judy, did you have an affair with that boy?" and Judy had had to look at mother wide-eyed and shocked and even make herself turn pale (she was proud that she could do that with special muscle control around the neck) and say, "Mother! My God," reassuring mother completely so that she had the strength to get rid of the boy in her best pidgin Italian.

There was something about this new freshman on the paper that appealed to Judy. Not only was he presentable, acceptable (except for being a freshman) and intelligent, but he lacked the heavy kind of hot-breathing sexuality that had become such a bore with Angelo.

"I want to do a column on happenings in New York City," she told Ron without preamble as she joined him walking to the newspaper office one day. "I don't mean the latest bullshit art show or play on Broadway, I mean significant things that few people are hearing about today but that many will hear about tomorrow."

She paused as if waiting for comment but quickly proceeded. "For instance, there's a movement going on in the Village among kids who use folk songs as a way of getting across messages of protest and dissatisfaction. I want to cover it. Kids are getting interested in it. I convinced the editor that we ought to do one column and see what happens."

Ron was nodding his head. Good idea. Yes. Of course. Why all this to me? Judy tapped Ron's arm.

"Ever do anything like that on that little high-school paper of yours?"

Ron wished that he could lie or at least distort something but he couldn't. He could only shake his head no.

"Well, look, I want to get the thing started but I don't want to be saddled with it. Come with me to New York and let's visit one of the places where these guys perform and we'll see what's happening and work on a column."

"Sure."

Judy's father was a doctor and rich, although to look at the scroungy way that she dressed it would be hard to believe. She owned her own Buick and that night they met to go to New York. Ron had a dark suit on and his best tie and was keenly showered and scrubbed. When Judy saw him waiting for her outside the dorm she cursed herself because although she'd showered this morning . . . or was it this morning? . . . she hadn't done anything to freshen herself or make herself look pretty if that was possible.

Ron slid in the car next to her and said, "Hi."

"Hi," Judy said, noticing Ron's light-colored hair plastered down, neatly combed and brushed. Wet and greasy. He must have poured ten tons of grease on the damn thing.

"Want to drive?" she asked. Men didn't like to be driven by women. She liked to drive though. Shit! Why did she have to go through with this. Was it worth it?

"No, that's okay, you drive," Ron replied. He took in her floppy gray sweater or sweatshirt . . . he really couldn't make up his mind which . . . her black formless skirt and flat shoes. She wore that outfit every day and she hadn't even changed for New York. *That* is sophistication!

As they drove she smoked incessantly. Ron opened the window on his side a crack and suffered through it. They talked about the new President, John F. Kennedy, and how this era was going to be different from the conforming, dull one that they were going through now. She was so rapid-certain and accurate. She talked about civil rights and poverty and leadership in foreign affairs by Americans who will care about the right things for a change. Ron loved talking to her. She felt the way he did about the world and the way more and more people were feeling.

Judy enjoyed Ron's enthusiasm. Personally these ideas didn't do much for her. She could be equally wild about any other point of view. She knew that she used them the way some of the little bitches used tight T-shirts. She'd decided on the car ride into New York that she was going to fuck this bouncy little freshman. It didn't make much difference how she looked. Just plop a boob in a man's hand and they don't give a shit about anything any more. She checked the back seat. There were all kinds of papers and books back there. She should have dumped them in the trunk. She hated to try to fuck in the front seat with that big steering wheel. A headline flashed in her mind. JUDY FUCKS UP.

Ron was stunned by the folksingers in the bar that Judy took him to. Every one of the performers had something to say about the world instead of the usual, "Jimmy cracks corn" type of thing that he usually thought of as folk-singing. They were young, articulate and poetic and their singing was less concerned with tone and smoothness than with force and drive.

Everyone there was dressed more like Judy than like Ron. He felt like a tourist. He abandoned his tie, smoked Judy's cigarettes and then bought a pack of his own and drank a great deal of beer. Most of the audience were college students and they listened intently. Around the room it was whispered that a magical, mysterious young man named Bob Dylan might show up later and at the sound of his name people paused and reflected. He was special. But he never came and eventually Ron and Judy left the bar and went out onto MacDougal Street. Ron had never had a better time in his life.

Two ass-wiggling queens zipped by jabbering intently with each other, their wrists limp and their mannerisms unashamedly feminine.

Ron became queasy. Would he see Lenny that way?

He hadn't heard from his brother since he left. Had he gone to the Village? Could he have become that way? Ron prayed to someone not to let his brother get that way.

"Some pretty sexy dishes, huh?" Judy said.

"Huh?" Was she referring to . . . ?

"In the place, just now. Did you see that redhead? I saw you looking at her."

Ron was relieved to realize that she meant the girls at the bar.

"I don't get excited over just looking. I need the real thing," he said smoothly.

"I bet that's all you ever think about." She hated the inane way she sounded.

"That's right." He honestly couldn't remember noticing any readheads.

She was more and more pleased with her choice. At least she

could be seen with this one and he wouldn't make any big demands like her adorable Italian.

"Come on," she said, taking his arm. "Let's get to the car and knock the shit out of the column."

Definitely I'll be able to do it with her, he thought the moment he heard that language. She's liberated, the kind that does it as casually as a man.

He'd wanted a pretty girl for his first, one that would fill him with desires for femininity. He'd wanted to do it again and again with her, become as insanely excited about her nakedness as all the other guys. He didn't see how he could quite get that way with Judy but still the magical experience of putting his thing . . . there, and coming, while being in . . . there . . . would be the same, wouldn't it? And he liked Judy. She was one of the boys. He could talk to her the way he talked to his friends. She wasn't silly like so many girls.

They worked on the column on the drive back. Long, unjournalistic sentences tumbled out of Ron and Judy edited them as they came at her, like a journalistic gristmill, putting them in their proper place, shortening and tightening them. By the time they approached the college the column was set and all Ron had to do was type it out.

Judy turned the car into the "make-out" section, a large flat area overlooking the Hudson River.

"I just want to check attendance," she said.

"Oh."

Darkened parked cars were nestled into the trees with shadowy heads framed in their windows—sometimes, other times there was no sign of any passenger and to Ron that meant that some boy was on top of some girl. They drove about five miles an hour in silence.

"Goddamn it!" Judy hissed and quickly pulled her car next to a tree about ten yards away from the parked car that seemed to infuriate her.

"What?"

66

"Quiet," Judy commanded. "Get your head down." Ron leaned down.

The couple in the other car had disappeared also.

Judy lit a cigarette. "I bet you that was little Miss Cutesy, goody-goody apple-tits 'I'm majoring in journalism' Shirley fucking Chaplin who just last week got her engagement ring from this jerk in Poke-ipsee and is now flat on her ass with the head of the Psychology Department."

"Dr. Baldwin."

"Exactly."

"He's married, isn't he?"

"Three or four kids' worth."

"Wow."

"She doesn't care about the guy being married. She wants to be seen so that everyone knows how sexy she is. Oh deceit thy name is woman."

Furthermore, Judy wanted to say, if I have to compete for the same kind of job with Miss Apple-Tits who the hell will get it even though she couldn't write a lead for an obit. Men are shit! She brooded silently.

She was just a shadow next to him in the car . . . He could barely make out a feature of her face and the only part of her that he recognized was the grayness of her blouse. He leaned over and put his hand on the back of her head, her curly black hair feeling just a bit sharp in his hand. He kissed her and she slid noisily on the vinyl seat until her body collided with his, her mouth instantly wide open, like a magnet pulling his tongue into it.

She's eager, Ron thought. Does she want to do it on the first time? He kissed her harder, twisting his neck back, forth and around in simulated passion.

All right, Judy thought, enough tongue-kissing . . . Get your hands on the boobs for Christ sake. Angelo would have been slobbering on them already.

Judy pushed her breasts on to Ron and Ron pressed them and cupped them under her blouse. He wished that he could get the kind of excitement they all talked about when he did that but as always nothing happened to him. He just wanted to touch them to let the girl know that he was doing it and move away as quickly and courteously as he could. He liked it better when he could make out with girls underneath their skirt and she soon put his hand there . . .

Jesus, he's fast, Judy thought. I'd have sworn he'd be tentatively trying to unstrap the bra at about now instead of immediately plunging for paydirt. Christ, I thought he was shy.

Ron's hands probed underneath her panties.

Judy felt she was being operated on by an expert surgeon. Cool, calm, collected and detached. Angelo would have been simpering and gasping by now. Ron still held the kiss while his hand was probing as if to camouflage the operation below. Well, Judy felt, everyone's technique is different. Can't expect anyone like my little Angelo all the time. Let's see what this guy's got.

She reached over and put her hand on Ron's penis. It was barely hard. You could cut a diamond on Angelo's!

Ron cringed. This had always been a bad problem when he made out with girls. Whenever they'd want to touch him there nothing happened. The only time anything would happen was when he'd rub against them and close his eyes and just let the good feeling of pumping against their leg come over him.

He wanted to stop. Judy wanted to stop. Neither could really see how what they were doing was going to solve anything.

"Let's do it," Ron whispered.

"Okay."

Ron was so grateful that he was finally going to do it that he put his hand to her breast and felt it. She liked that . . . it made her somehow feel more at home.

"Lemme clear out the back," she whispered getting on her knees and from the front scooping the paraphernalia and dumping it beside her. Ron helped. Soon they tumbled into the back seat.

It was spacious back there in this four-door Buick. Judy could lie flat on her back and spread herself easily without her feet knocking into things. Ron climbed right on top of her and they picked up right where they left off except they were prone.

But it wasn't working. It could get no further. Ron rubbed and rubbed but he was too nervous . . . This meant too much to him now and nothing happened.

Judy had lifted her blouse and undid her brassiere but it seemed to her that Ron was avoiding her breasts as if they were poisonous. She went on though, not being able to conceive of the idea of going this far with a boy and having not one thing happen.

Ron was telling himself that she was too unattractive, that's why nothing was happening. He should have tried with a prettier girl . . . Now he'd have to stop and play the gentleman again . . .

Judy unzipped his fly and gently removed his soft penis from his pants. Angelo had always wanted her to do a certain something but she'd refused, now maybe she could do it . . . just a little anyway to help things along.

She tentatively put it in her mouth.

Ron was startled. He looked down at her dark, curly hair over his penis and for the briefest flash he imagined it was Michael. He let himself close his eyes and lean back and say to himself, "Michael." He became hard. He was deeply ashamed of what he was letting himself think . . . but then he let himself go with it because it was working. His cock was hard! and he could put the fucking thing anywhere he wanted with Michael in his mind!! Let it! Let it be!

Without once releasing the image of Michael, holding onto it doubly tight, even when Judy tore the inevitable wrapper, whose very sound had driven poor Angelo to distraction, he did it with Judy and for the first time had a full manly orgasm inside of a woman.

He felt great. Proud. Happy. Relieved. A real man . . .

CHAPTER 5

Gyla was a curvaceous blond cutie. She swirled around campus in a stream of sexuality. Her corn-blond, naturally curly long hair bounced on her shoulders when she walked. She had a pretty, wide face and a ready bright smile. She was of medium height but of more than medium bust which along with her legs and rear were solidly implanted on almost every undergraduate's unconscious or conscious mind, not to mention grounds-keepers, professors, administrators plus an administratrix or two. She was the campus masturbation image—the embodiment of young American college sensuality—trillions of sperm were propelled nightly in her honor. If she could imagine it she might faint from shame but it's doubtful that she ever could because as is common in such creatures they walk about totally unaware of their real effects.

Ron never talked to Gyla. Actually he never met anyone who talked to her and he never noticed her talking to anyone—she just swirled. She might be an apparition—a ghostly sex symbol—a decoy designed to attract all masturbation fantasies so that the boys' wicked imaginations might leave the other girls alone, he thought. If only Judy were Gyla . . . then it might work. She's so pretty and she has such a beautiful ass. Picture the cheeks of her ass-heaven divided by two. With that in the back seat of a Buick I could get off without any weird imaginings . . . I'm sick of rubbing against Judy like a goddamn cat . . . With Gyla my problems'd be solved . . . especially my problem with . . .

He stopped. Then he let himself admit that he had a problem with his new roommate for his sophomore year, Jeffrey. He was attracted to him. He knew it. There it was.

Jeffrey was a tall boy with jet-black hair that looked like it was window-traced from Li'l Abner, enlarged and put on his head. He also had buck teeth and a big smile like a hillbilly but actually he was a basketball player from Utica, New York, who'd never been down south. He was simple, good-natured, kindly and not overly intelligent.

With Mort Mattic as his roommate Ron hadn't bothered about fixing up his room very much. Everything had been perfunctory. But Ron wanted a home for him and Jeffrey. He talked him into chipping in for curtains and good prints—Renoir for Ron and Sargent for Jeffrey. They bought new lampshades and a modern cover for the grim overhead light. Ron finagled an advance on his clothing allowance from his father and bought a good stereo and classical records, heavy on the Richard Strauss and Stravinsky, and Jeffrey was encouraged to buy the progressive jazz that he liked.

Next he worked on Jeffrey's mind and his consciousness. His father owned a large auto-supply store in Utica and after college Jeffrey was going to go into the business and get married to a girl that his family had already picked for him and that he himself was kind of satisfied with. All that was okay with him—his life was set, all he had to do was to have some fun in it.

Yet he had so much more to offer, Ron knew, and he'd try to talk to Jeffrey about important things, to get him to be aware, but Jeffrey would listen good-naturedly and agree with him about the times a-changin'; Kennedy and all that, but not change an idea. Just before he went off to college his father had warned him against getting involved with all that "college bullshit" and Jeffrey had easily agreed.

"What are you going to school for?" Ron asked him one night.

"To get an education," Jeffrey replied, smoking illegally in bed while Ron was seated at the desk.

"To get an education or to get a degree?"

"I don't care about a degree. I'll never need it. I'm all set."

"Right, go back to Utica in poppa's business and get married and raise a family and that's it . . ."

"Sure."

"You love your fiancée?" Ron asked after a pause in which he debated whether or not to get into this area with Jeffrey.

"My who?"

"The girl you're going to marry."

"Oh Phyllis . . . Do I love her?"

"Yeah."

"Sure, I can't go wrong with her."

"How come?"

"Can't."

"Why?"

Jeffrey liked Ron. He was a funny little guy . . . would give you the shirt off his back, well-meaning and warm. He was going to take him back home to visit his folks during the next intersession. Sure, sometimes he brooded and was very unhappy and tense but he never let it get too bad and mostly he was the only guy Jeffrey had ever met who showed that he really liked him and was interested in him without being mushy or queer or anything.

72

Sometimes Jeffrey thought Ron might be, but he did have a girl and he did get hot over Gyla just like everyone else.

"Look," Jeffrey said seriously, "Phyllis is a nice home-type girl . . . She's steady and she's got a nice pair of tits and her mother's still got a nice pair of tits too which means that Phyllis won't sag or anything."

"Oh, really?"

"Yeah."

"Have you checked her father's balls?"

"No," Jeffrey said indignantly.

"You haven't?"

"What the fuck do you think I am?"

"Did you ever take biology and study genes?"

"I took chemistry."

"If you'd taken biology you'd know that the female mammary genes are crossed with male testicle genes on skipped successive generations. If her father's balls sag then there's an even chance that she'll have a problem."

"Is that a fact?"

Ron laughed.

"Son of a bitch!" Jeffrey said, getting up and punching Ron gingerly on the arm. Ron punched back.

"You scared me for a minute."

"You're an idiot," Ron said, laughing. "All you ever care about is . . . you know." Ron made a motion with his two hands in front of his chest.

"That's not true," Jeffrey said. "There's other parts I care about almost as well."

Ron lay on his bed and said after a pause, "Did you see Gyla today?"

"I see her every day even when I don't see her."

"Can you imagine fucking her?"

Jeffrey leaned back and laughed to himself but out loud.

"What's so funny?"

"Nothing."

"Come on, what's so funny?"

"Can I imagine fucking her? That's funny."

"Why?"

"I can't imagine anything else."

Jeffrey looked at Ron for a few seconds before he said, "I jerked off three times thinking about her yesterday."

"You beat me by two," Ron lied.

In high school masturbation was talked about openly. By the time one was in college you were supposed to be past that stage, getting it all the time. You were supposed to be cool. Jeffrey was not, as many others were not, finding it that way. He felt relieved not to be the only one.

"How do you do it?" Ron asked.

"What do you mean?"

"You know . . . what positions and all . . . ?"

"I don't know . . ." Jeffrey pondered, then said, "You know, I never even got to fuck her."

"What do you mean?"

"I've never fucked her. I never fucked her!" Jeffrey said with mock indignation as if he found out that he was being cheated by the God of Masturbation.

"Really?"

Jeffrey's face was turning a bit red and he had trouble clearing an excess of saliva that was forming around his tongue as he continued.

"Like yesterday you know . . . When I woke up . . . I just thought of her . . . then I popped . . . Just that . . ."

"Jesus . . ."

"Yeah . . . and then I saw her walking you know the way she carried those books up against them like that . . ." Jeffrey made a motion mimicking Gyla propping her loose-leaf book under her breasts.

"Right."

"So then I just ran back to the room and closed the door and thought about just taking those books from her, lifting that

74

sweater up . . . you know . . . and then I popped."

"Jesus."

"And then the next time just taking off her brassiere and there they were . . . and . . ."

"Yeah . . ."

". . . even before I could imagine touching them."

"You know you haven't fucked her once."

"I haven't even touched her."

"You don't know what you're missing."

"Yeah."

"She's a good fuck."

Jeffrey gulped. "Really?"

Ron leaned back in bed. He put his hand on his thigh and said, "With me she puts her little pink hand on my thigh like this and she looks at me with that look of hers and runs her tongue over her lips . . ." Ron ran his tongue slowly over his lips. Jeffrey laughed, breathing hard. Ron put his hand up his pants leg slowly. "She moves her hand very deliberately up my leg and my cock gets hard so that when she reaches it it'll be erect to greet its visitor." God, Ron thought, what porn-shit!

Jeffrey's eyes gleamed. He was looking at Ron's hand slowly going up Ron's thigh getting to believe that it was indeed Gyla's little pink hand going up *his* pants.

Ron was quite erect now. He leaned back in his bed, not looking at Jeffrey. "She touches my thing and she lets out a little soft sigh as she feels it through my pants." Ron had put his hand on his penis . . . "She rubs it ever so gently and she leans down on top of me and kisses me . . ."

From the corner of his eye Ron looked over and saw that Jeffrey had leaned back in his bed too but had thrown his blanket over him, totally heated by the picture that Ron was painting. His eyes were closed and he was gulping hard.

Putting the blanket over him as well, Ron removed his penis and continued spewing every pornographic cliché that he'd ever come across, thankful, ever so thankful, that Jeffrey didn't read very much. "She takes my hand and gently lets me cup her breasts in them . . . her nipples feel hard and erect even under her sweater . . ."

Jeffrey was playing with himself under his blanket. Ron leaned up on one elbow and allowed himself to look over now at Jeffrey who by this time was letting himself go a bit. God, Ron had to hold himself back from going to him and putting his hand under that blanket.

"She leans to me and whispers in my ear . . . 'I want you'. . ."

Jeffrey was coming now; oblivious to the fact that another male was in the room he pumped himself as if he were a piston. The blanket moved up and down as if an animal were caught there. Ron was coming too just looking over at Jeffrey that way and saying almost automatically every bit of gibberish that he could resurrect from his memory.

They didn't say a word to each other after it was finished. They avoided even looking at each other. Jeffrey went to the bathroom first and then Ron afterwards and the first thing they talked about before they went to sleep was their schedule for the next day.

Ron didn't sleep for many hours that night. He found himself looking over at Jeffrey who was definitely asleep, softly snoring. The wicked images raced through him against his will. Yet there was nothing wrong in what they did, Ron kept telling himself, after all it's about a girl. Gyla. I was really getting off on a girl and it just sort of added to the pleasure to help Jeffrey too. Sure maybe I did want to touch Jeffrey there but it was still all over a girl.

But this whole thing was too dangerous. Remember Lenny. Ron's problem was Judy. He really didn't enjoy it with her. He'd have to find a prettier girl. Gyla was out of the question of course but there were other girls he could date . . . plenty of them.

The next morning in his book he listed the names of four girls whom he would start talking to and he told himself he would deliberately forget a movie that he was supposed to go to with

Judy that night and thereby start the definite deterioration of that relationship.

The awkwardness between Jeffrey and Ron grew nightly especially around the time before they went to sleep. Jeffrey anxiously wanted Ron to tell him another bedtime story but he sensed Ron's reluctance.

Jeffrey tried to go back to his old style of masturbation but it was ruined by Ron's much more vivid descriptions. He tried to imitate Ron but he wasn't much good at it. Boy, the way Ron described it he could see her, almost feel her. Finally on the third night while they were lying on their beds reading he said to Ron, "You fuck Gyla lately?"

"No," Ron said quickly, strongly.

Jeffrey went back to reading, hurt by Ron's abruptness. What the fuck was the matter with him?

Ron resented Jeffrey's probe. He did not want to accept the obvious invitation. He'd started to talk to two of the girls on his list and he thought he might be able to date at least one of them. He'd stood Judy up for the movie and neither of them had said anything about it and they had no plans to see each other anymore. He had the idea that Judy was relieved. He certainly was. The new girl Mary Ann was pleasant and had a well-shaped little behind on her, now what the hell did Jeffrey want!

After ten more minutes of tense studying Jeffrey said, "Tell me about Gyla, Ron."

"Tell me about the farm, George," Ron snapped.

"Tell me about plowin' Gyla, George," Jeffrey said, doing an imitation of Lon Chaney, Jr., playing Lenny in *Of Mice and Men.*

Ron put his book down and stood up. "Fuck you. Can't you do your own jerking off? I'm taking a shower."

He took off his shirt and pants quickly and put on a robe.

"Come on," Jeffrey said, looking at Ron in astonishment, "I can imagine it so good when you tell it."

"I'm taking a shower."

"Prick," Jeffrey said, flicking a towel and stinging Ron's leg.

Ron whacked Jeffrey sharply in the arm and ran out.

The shower room was empty. Ron aimed the lukewarm spurt at his pubic area. He soaped and soaped and soaped, then realizing what he was compulsively doing he stopped and said to himself—am I trying to soap it off? Make it drop off, melt, wash itself down the drain. He rinsed the soap and directed the shower to other parts of his body turning the water a bit colder and bracing himself for the chill. What the hell does he want from me with that fucking hillbilly naive act of his? I ought to get him a copy of *Lady Chatterly's Lover* . . . No, that's too literary for the idiot . . . *Fanny Hill* is more his speed . . . or maybe those dirty comic books that we used to read in high school, Tilly the Toiler—the fuckin' moron. Like reading the comics to kids. Now kiddies, as we last left luscious Gyla she was plopping the left one out . . . Jesus . . . He laughed to himself and made the shower colder and stuck his chest into it.

He finished and looked in the mirror to see if he needed a shave . . . No . . . Baby-smooth after having shaved four days ago . . . just a hint of a stubble . . . light blond and fuzzy . . . His features seemed too regular . . . round smooth face . . . too-smooth skin—almost like a girl's. He wished he had hair and roughness like Jeffrey. He put his hand through his thin, blond, short hair and wished it were dark black and thick . . . Lenny's was dark black and thin but Jeffrey's was thick . . . thick and knotty like a dark, hot jungle. Maybe he'd shave anyway so that he wouldn't have to go back to the room so fast. What the hell did Jeffrey want from him? Why had he been acting so peculiarly these last three days? Hadn't he been walking around the room bare-assed more lately?

Provocative? Ridiculous. No one hated "queers" more than Jeffrey. He was vehement about them. If someone would even suggest to him that he was acting provocatively Ron was sure that he'd punch and roar.

Ron decided not to shave and he went back to the room.

When he came back he didn't see Jeffrey. Suddenly he felt himself being grabbed from behind in a tight half-nelson. Jeffrey's muscular arm was around his neck and he squeezed Ron's throat semi-hard. He threw Ron on Ron's bed and put his knee in the small of his back.

"Come on, tell me about Gyla," Jeffrey demanded.

"Let go," Ron said. He felt Jeffrey's bare knee and the cloth of his robe. He must have taken off his pants and just had his robe on.

"I'll break your arm," Jeffrey said mock-menacingly.

Ron became angry. He jerked his body trying to tumble Jeffrey to the floor. Jeffrey held him strongly and leaned down on Ron's back hard. It hurt. Bastard! Son of a bitch! Ron hated being treated like a bundle of hay by a dumb hillbilly.

Jeffrey leaned down closer to him. "Come on . . ." he whispered hoarsely, the vibration of his hoarseness reverberating through Ron. All right, you fuck, you're asking for it, right? No, not asking. Begging. Pleading. Fine, you're going to get it.

"Okay," Ron said, "get off me."

Jeffrey immediately stood up and Ron turned around and saw Jeffrey breathing hard and beginning to grin. Ron stood up and said sharply, "Lay down."

Jeffrey went toward his own bed.

"No," Ron said, pointing to *his* bed. "Here."

Jeffrey obeyed immediately. Ron enjoyed commanding him that way.

Jeffrey lay on his back on Ron's bed, breathing in anticipation.

As Ron looked down at Jeffrey he felt something in himself like superhuman power. It was as if the Great Goddess Spirit of Gyla had entered and had taken possession of him, making him as wickedly confident of her powers to manipulate and toy with this mortal as any goddess might be.

There was no comic exaggeration or defensive parody as his low soft sensuous voice came out of him and said, "She came to me last night in this very room. I was lying right where you are lying now. You are me . . . You've sent me away so that you can be alone with her . . ."

"Yeah . . ." Jeffrey approved of that move.

Ron locked the door.

"I don't want us to be disturbed." Ron walked to the bed and sat on the edge of it by Jeffrey's feet. Jeffrey's eyes were closed and his hand was placed gently on his upper thigh, his robe covered the slight bulge that was making the robe move as if it were draped over a little animal.

"I've come to give you every pleasure that your little heart desires . . . I'm taking off my blouse now button by button . . . and as I do you can see that I have absolutely nothing underneath, can't you?"

Jeffrey sucked in some air and his hand disappeared under his robe. Ron put his hand on his chest and could feel his chest expanding slightly and his nipples becoming active . . . "My breasts are like two magic globes . . ."

The harsh light of the ceiling bulb introduced on Ron now. He wanted his breasts to be silhouetted for Jeffrey in the moonlight. "I'm going to turn out the light . . ."

"Yeah . . ." Jeffrey murmured, his robe open now, and softly, uncharacteristically gently, for Jeffrey, playing with himself. Ron, as if in a trance, walked over and shut off the light and sat back down on the bed.

"The moonlight streams through the window silhouetting me just for you . . . My nipples are hard and erect waiting for your touch . . . your lips . . ."

Jeffrey became excited.

"No . . . no, don't get too excited, you dear boy, don't let yourself go too fast . . . there's so much pleasure . . ."

Jeffrey slowed down.

"That's better . . . Mustn't be selfish . . . Little Gyla needs her pleasure too, doesn't she? My tongue wants to taste your body." Ron slowly moved his left forefinger to Jeffrey's ankle, ready to stop if Jeffrey objected, or freeze with an apologetic joke or quip or manly punch if it went wrong. Ron touched Jeffrey's ankle and his foot jerked a bit as if a small electric shock had been put there but he became still more excited and his eyes were still closed and he even moved his ankle along Ron's finger. Ron wet his finger with his tongue and Jeffrey accepted it as Gyla's tongue slowly traveling up his calf and then his thigh. He saw her traveling up him and whispering things like "I want you inside of me . . . I want to taste you and have you . . ."

Ron's finger touched Jeffrey's penis.

Jeffrey removed his own hand and put it behind his head.

Ron ran his finger around Jeffrey's penis slowly as if it were a tongue. Then he stopped and got on his knees before Jeffrey.

He looked down at Jeffrey's body. He poised for a moment.

Jeffrey felt the silence, the steadying as well . . . Nothing touched him now, his eyes were closed ready . . . waiting for . . . there it was, he felt the lips on his penis.

Ron just stayed there that way for a moment. He, for the briefest, zaniest second, wasn't Gyla anymore but a royalist Frenchman with his head in the guillotine waiting for the knife to slice his head off.

This is Gyla . . . this is Gyla . . . Jeffrey pictured her fully, hovering over him . . . her breasts like two marvelous, inverted hills brushing his thighs as she had his thing in her mouth moving it up and down . . . up and down and he started to move it up and down too.

Ron wanted Jeffrey to come into him. He vividly saw the semen coming out like little white garden snakes marching in tandem. Jeffrey was pumping harder and harder and Ron was feeling it go deeper and deeper down his throat . . . fearing for a panicky second that it would choke him but then deciding not to care . . . not to care at all . . .

The moment before Jeffrey was about to come something snapped in him and he realized what was happening.

The next thing Ron knew was that everything was pulled away from him and he was dumped roughly on the floor and he was being choked by a Jeffrey gone berserk with wide-eyed frothing rage.

"You queer fuck! You queer fuck!" Jeffrey kept hissing and squeezing. Ron was getting dizzy . . . he didn't know how much breath he had left. He jerked and gripped Jeffrey's arms trying to get Jeffrey off his throat but those big hands seemed locked there like steel bolts. Ron could feel his tongue out of his mouth and his eyes popping but still he couldn't quite believe this was happening to him. He was still the Goddess Gyla. His body and his mind were mostly where they just were and his inner core felt a sense of peace and contentment even as he was getting choked to death. He was going to die . . . all right he knew that . . . here it was . . . He couldn't breathe, he was kicking and gasping and he could see that this crazy wasn't going to stop.

Jeffrey stopped himself from killing Ron. He thought about Phyllis and his father and the auto-supply business. You don't kill queers anyway, you beat the shit out of them.

Jeffrey let go of Ron's throat and instead smashed his fist as hard as he could into Ron's face, aiming for the nose so that it could be busted and make Ron look like a man.

The blow caught Ron on the upper cheek and Ron felt that his entire face had been caved in.

But Jeffrey was off-balance now and Ron jerked out from under him and rose shakily to his feet. He snapped on the light switch.

"Keep your goddamn hands off me." He gasped, putting his hand to his face where Jeffrey had hit him and feeling it start to swell and ache.

"Queer fuck . . ." Jeffrey said, getting up ready to spring on Ron again.

"Am I the queer fuck? Who forced me? Who made me get into that whole thing? You're the queer fuck!"

Jeffrey seemed to explode from inside. He lunged at Ron but Ron was able to dodge him and unlock the door and run into the hall down the stairs and onto the grounds behind the big tree in the back.

When it became apparent that Jeffrey wasn't out chasing him and that everyone was asleep he started to cry, feeling the swelling under his eye as he leaned against the tree. He took the tree in his arms and cried on its shoulder.

It was cold out there and Ron wanted to go back and go to sleep. He picked up a loose brick from the path and walked in. He belonged in that room just as much as Jeffrey did. The dorm was totally asleep as Ron walked in. The night lights cast a dim shadow as he walked up the stairs. The brick was ready. Then his door was in front of him and he braced himself for Jeffrey's presence. He opened the door and he found Jeffrey seated on his own bed, stock-still, eyes wide open waiting for Ron. Jeffrey had a baseball bat on his lap.

Ron closed the door behind him and held up his brick.

"Listen," Jeffrey said, "I don't want any more fighting. I just want you to change your room. You go and ask for a room change and we'll forget the whole thing."

"Me?"

"Yeah."

"You go."

"Bullshit."

"I'm not going."

Jeffrey became red. He stood up and his baseball bat became poised. Ron lifted his brick.

"I suppose you still have hopes, huh? You son of a bitch, I'll kill you—"

"Who started it? Who forced me?"

"I always felt you were that way . . . the way you are with guys . . . so *warm* and *friendly* . . . The other guys say so too. But you fooled us because you had girl friends and you talked about them like the rest of the guys . . ."

"You set me up. If I'm queer, you are too."

"Bullshit. I'm not ashamed of what I did. I didn't suck no guy's cock. I'm going to tell. I'm going to tell how you got me going with those stories and then worked on me. Everybody in the school's going to know that you're a fucking faggot."

Is this what happened to Lenny?

"I'm going to go to the administrator and tell the whole thing unless you go tomorrow and give them whatever bullshit you want to get the fuck out of here. I will."

"I don't want to stay here with you. You don't have to force me to move. I want to move."

"Then you'll go tomorrow?"

"Yeah. I'll go."

"What'll you tell them?"

"I don't know. It shouldn't be too hard. There's room over in the North buildings . . ." They had both lowered their weapons now. Ron sat down on his bed very sad and very tired. He wondered how his eye looked.

Jeffrey sat on his own bed and laid the baseball bat down.

Ron looked in the hand mirror that was on his desk. The left eye was red and purple.

Jeffrey was reminded that his knuckle was bruised and hurting. He wanted to go to the bathroom and run water over it but he didn't because he thought Ron would want to go and run water over his eye and he didn't want to be in the bathroom with Ron. He'd wait till tomorrow. It didn't feel too bad. He went in under his covers and closed the light and almost instantly fell asleep. He was very tired.

Ron leaned against the wall and thought about going to the administration room tomorrow and requesting a room change with his eye swelled like that. Would they suspect? It didn't matter. He'd think of a logical explanation tomorrow. He was good at that sort of thing but right now all he wanted to do was go to sleep. He was so tired.

The room had been changed. The eye had been explained as a soccer accident. Jeffrey did not exist for Ron. If he saw Jeffrey on campus he ignored him.

84

In a week there was intersession and he went home for Christmas. He was supposed to have spent the vacation with Jeffrey's family up in Utica. What a laugh! Who the hell wanted to spend all that time with dumb car-parts people anyway and meet his big-titted fiancée Phyllis.

CHAPTER 6

Michael saw Ron on Ron's first day home for Christmas. He pulled up in his car as Ron was walking down the main street, opened the car window and said, "What happened to your eye?"

"Soccer," Ron said. The lie that had come so easily with everyone else scared him with Michael.

Michael grinned cynically, snickered, rolled back the window and drove off.

The next day was Saturday and Ron was posing for his mother out in their back yard. Blanche had taken to painting. Grandma Moses had become famous as an old woman and Blanche wasn't old yet. Never too late. She barely touched the piano anymore and hardly shopped so that Louis became the housekeeper, complaining mildly, yet secretly grateful to utilize all the free time he now had. Since Lenny's leaving he'd become more doddering and the firm managed to give him a great deal of time off. He was preparing lunch inside.

"Ron in Winter" . . . Blanche was painting her darling boy against the backdrop of a snow bank and a wintry tree. She made him keep his face at an angle to hide that horrible black eye. The boy shouldn't play soccer and get hurt like that. Still, he was a real boy, wasn't he?—a real man really. Men get hurt being athletic —not sissies, she thought.

They could only be out there for a half hour or so at a time before it became too cold. Blanche imagined that painting out in the cold weather would help to get the iciness into the picture that she wanted, give it that real touch of coldness . . . Yes, but now her fingers were beginning to chill . . .

"Mom," Ron asked suddenly, "where's Lenny?"

Lenny hadn't been mentioned in the house for almost two years. Yet today Ron had felt his presence there as he had at no other time, as if Lenny were a giant magical bird that could hover and be inside at the same time. His closed room seemed to vibrate like an old magnet with a fresh charge.

"Ask your father," Blanche replied quickly, not pausing in her stroke.

Louis Starr, in the only religious act he had performed in all his adult years, had gone to a Brooklyn rabbi and had declared his son dead. He had said kaddish and he went each year to this synagogue in Williamsburg on the anniversary of his son's death and said a kaddish prayer for him.

Blanche despised him the most when he made that trip. Last year she had just squished all her paints together on the palate in a pictorial essay that she called "Despise."

"Father wouldn't tell me even if he knew . . . and I don't think he knows," Ron replied.

"He's dead." Ron became frightened. Was that really true?

"You mean as far as father is concerned not . . ."

"No, of course not, he's not really dead. He should be dead. He's put a curse on us all and his death would be the only way to remove it. But people like Lenny don't die so fast. He's probably in a penitentiary someplace or a hospital for insane people. He's very insane. Or maybe he has some form of leprosy . . . his skin eating itself away . . ." She stroked a bit harder.

"Mother," Ron said sharply yet softly. Mother could get into spells like that, her hatred could run away with her and make her cut through things in the kitchen unless she was softly restrained.

Blanche finished an icicle that she was very particular about before she signaled that she wanted to go back in the house. Ron hoped that father had lunch ready for them as he was hungry and cold.

As they were about to walk in Ron saw Michael leaning against his car trying to catch his eye. He stopped. Michael flicked his head, smiling at Ron. Ron hoped that Blanche wouldn't spot Michael as he said to her, "I'll be right in, mom."

She didn't seem to hear him as she just went into the house. Ron quickly trotted to Michael.

"He wants to see you," Michael said.

"Th-that's great . . ." Ron said.

Michael laughed outright.

"Come up to my house this afternoon and I'll give you the details."

Ron just stood there wishing the car would disappear before anyone saw Michael. Ron had seen very little of him since two years ago and now Michael seemed so swishy, with his eyes rolling a lot and his shoulders moving too much . . . In Greenwich Village he'd seem normal but here he was like a sore thumb.

"Okay?" Michael said, rolling down the window. "This afternoon?"

"Sure," Ron replied through his dry throat. "I'll come on by."

Michael zoomed off.

Ron went in for lunch.

88

Louis was beating an egg, slowly, with great concentration, fluffing it up so that he could make an omelette. His bald head was egg-shaped and he was making oval motions with his stroke and as Ron saw him there it seemed that his father was turning himself into an egg, an egg that would start all over again, redo what had been done . . . give it all a new beginning, a fresh middle and a great end . . . that's what eggs do, after all.

Blanche stopped in the middle of the kitchen, not two feet away from Louis and said, "See Michael. You remember Michael, don't you? He would know where Lenny is . . . if anyone would . . . Michael has been assigned by Lenny to watch over us. He comes around sometimes and asks about you . . . Then he sends carrier pigeons to the insane asylum and lets him know how we're all doing."

Ron couldn't believe that she was talking about Lenny in front of his father. He stared at Louis bracing for some emotional outburst.

Louis kept fluffing for the omelette. Blanche stopped and looked at him too.

"Look at the way that fluffs there," Louis said. "Get you and your mother a plate and some silverware, son. It'll be ready in two shakes of a lamb's tail."

That afternoon, right after lunch, Ron took a stroll three-quarters of a mile up the old East Road. Icicles, like animals' teeth, hung from the trees and ridges of the little hills. Ron batted down the ones that hung from the trees as he walked. They were little and easy and they tinkled as they fell. Then he challenged the larger ones hanging from the ridges and they didn't budge from his pushes. Then he kicked some low-hanging ones from a nearby pine and laughed contemptuously at them as they gave in, stomping them and seeing them crumbled. Then he nudged the tough icicle with his elbow like an old buddy and said to it, "Hang tough, buddy . . . fuck 'em and hang tough. Only the sun can melt you, all the bastards in the world can kick you and push you but only the sun can get you, and when he does you melt gracefully like a ballet dancer doing a pirouette and you change into a stream and you find your way back into the earth. Hang tough, hang tough." Ron slammed the icicle with the butt of his hand and continued his journey.

Sheriff Pollard's house came up on the left as a bad surprise. It had grown decrepit, paint peeling off the siding, yard littered like a junkyard, a commode filled with snow, a dirty bathtub, tires, auto parts. Ron hadn't seen the house in perhaps three years and he remembered it as being an okay house. Hadn't it had some foliage? There seemed to be none now.

The man who answered Ron's knock couldn't be Sheriff Pollard. This bedraggled, skinny, wasted, drunken man had to be a poor relative from Tennessee or something.

"Is Michael home?"

"Lawyer Starr's younger kid, ain't you?" Ah, yes, the voice was that of Sheriff Pollard but he wasn't sheriff anymore, Ron suddenly remembered. He'd been defeated in the last election.

Ron nodded. "Out back," Sheriff Pollard said. "Go 'round the house."

Ron walked around the house stepping around an old filthy bathtub and a rusty car transmission. There was a large garage in the back and Ron recognized the back of Michael as he was delving into the motor of an old car. He heard the back door of the house open and he saw Sheriff Pollard, beer in hand, come out and sit down on the back porch. He sat as if it were a summer's day. Funny how people in this town today . . . his mother, Sheriff Pollard, are staying outside and getting the bite of coldness on them . . . Funny, he thought.

"Hi, Michael," Ron said. Michael emerged from the motor and smiled at Ron. He leaned back, took a breath and brazenly checked Ron out toes to head. Ron was wearing an old three-quarter-length gray overcoat and a maroon scarf. He brought the overcoat into himself and buried his chin into the scarf.

"Look at him. He lost the election, you know," Michael said, indicating his father with a contemptuous toss of the head. He was a bit spacy and his eyes shone. "He blames me, you know. Dirty rumors. He's on county welfare now. Mother is sick . . . probably dying . . . That's the only reason I'm still here, to take care of her. Do you know that mother used to answer the police calls when poppa"—he pronounced it the fancy way, Pa-pa— "was drunk. Would you like to go skating with me later on?"

"I can't," Ron replied. "I have a term paper I have to work on over the holidays."

Michael was back under the hood of the car even before Ron had completed the last sentence.

"How's Timmy?" Ron asked.

"Timmy?"

"You remember that night . . ."

"Oh yeah, Timmy. That little fag . . . I hate little fairies like that. I don't know how he is . . . I couldn't give a flaming shit."

Michael was out of the motor of the car again. "Who hit you?"

"An accident."

"Was he cute?"

Michael rolled his eyes at Ron. It made Ron nervous with Sheriff Pollard drinking beer not thirty feet away and staring at them like that.

"How's Lenny?" Ron asked.

Michael laughed sardonically. What the hell was wrong with him?

"How do you like our baby?" he asked Ron.

"Baby?"

"Our baby junkyard . . ." He walked out into the yard with his arms spread out at the pieces of junk.

"Fine."

"Hear that, poppa?" Michael said to his sullen father. "He likes our little baby junkyard . . . It's going to mature into a real man junkyard one day and who knows, it may be President . . . Every male baby in America has a chance to be President, right?"

Sheriff Pollard crushed the beer can with one hand and threw it hard at Michael, missing his head by just a little bit.

Michael laughed and walked back to Ron.

"Come on, let's go ice-skating this afternoon . . ."

Sheriff Pollard had gotten up and gone into the house.

"I can't . . . How's Lenny?"

"It's cold," Michael said. "Let's go inside a bit . . ." Michael walked into the barn and Ron followed, closing the door as well as he could with the car sticking out of it. Through the opening in the door Ron saw that Sheriff Pollard had come outside again with another beer in his hand.

Michael smiled derisively at his father. "God, look at him. I don't think he trusts me with you. I don't blame him." His voice deepened. "You've grown lovely since . . . since I knew you years ago, Linda . . . Why you've grown up to be a real . . . a real woman."

He laughed almost uncontrollably. He seemed drunk to Ron but without the smell and the slurry speech that Ron associated with liquor.

"You guys have this stuff up at school," Michael said, taking a little bottle of pills from his coveralls.

"What's that?"

"Speed. Want?"

Ron declined.

"I called Lenny last night and I told him about you . . . about the eye and about you and he wants to see you."

"Great. I want to see him too."

"Bullshit. Why haven't you tried in almost two years?"

"I wrote him," Ron said. "All the letters came back from the address he gave me . . . See . . ." He produced a packet of letters that he'd written to Lenny. Lenny had called the house when he first left and had been hung up on by Blanche and Louis until Ron had answered the phone and then he'd only had time to give Ron an address in New York that he could be written to. The letters, written with college return addresses only to prevent them from being seen by Blanche when they came back, were long and chatty. Ron wrote about home, the kids in town, school, all the news that he felt that he would like to know if he were Lenny. As he wrote he knew they'd come back but writing them was still important to Ron, a way of keeping in touch with his brother. When the letters had come back marked "Addressee Unknown" Ron had opened them and looked through the pages as if Lenny had really read them and had put a little mark on them somewhere to let Ron know that he had.

Michael hardly glanced at the letters. "Why didn't you see me? Wouldn't you think I'd know where he is?" Michael smiled knowingly, opened the car door and moved into the back seat stretching himself comfortably.

"Love me, love my friends I always say. It's all right. He knows everything. He's not bitter about you. He knows what you're going through. He is all-wise and wonderful. He watches over you all through my eyes . . . I pass by your house . . . Your mother knows, right?"

Ron nodded.

"It's too bad what's happening to them, isn't it? They're cooking in their own juices. Ha! He's doing fine! He's thriving! He's magnificent! And you . . . Come in the car . . ."

Ron didn't move.

"You're getting weird. I told him. You're an event that won't let itself happen. A shooting Star-r-r that won't let itself shoot. A statement that won't say itself. Come in the car."

Michael quickly opened the car door and it hit Ron in the stomach. "Hey."

"Get in."

Ron slid into the back seat and pressed himself tightly against his corner. He made sure that he had Sheriff Pollard in his vision all the time.

"Can you go to New York this afternoon?" Michael asked.

"I guess so."

"You can talk to me about what you're going through, you know," Michael said more kindly now. "Don't you think I know?"

"If I'm going to New York I've got to catch the bus and go home and tell my parents and all . . . We'll get together next week and talk more."

Ron looked at Michael with a reassuring look.

"You're not like him at all, are you? No. You'd be a good businessman or a politician, something like that. You're full of good social bullshit."

"Fuck you," Ron said.

"Ha."

"Do you want to give me Lenny's address or don't you?" Ron said, putting his hand on the door handle to get out.

"Bravo," Michael said. "A burst of fire to please me. Oh, you're good. You're so good you even fool yourself."

Ron had had enough. He was going to leave. Michael reached into his coveralls and drew out a slip of notepaper and gently laid it on his crotch. "Here it is . . . Come and get it, big boy."

You don't intimidate me, you weird fuck, Ron thought. He quickly reached for the paper. As he snatched it Michael gripped his wrist tightly and pressed his hand to his rapidly rising penis. Ron's fist remained tightly clutched. He stared at Michael coldly as Michael moved Ron's hand on him and gyrated slightly. They stared at each other—Ron cold and hard, Michael taunting and seductive. Ron with the paper securely in his palm and Michael with Ron's wrist securely in his.

Then Ron remembered Sheriff Pollard. He looked out of the back window and almost screamed from fright to see the face of the sheriff plastered against the rear window.

Michael saw it too and laughed. Sheriff Pollard just glared into the car, a stone gone mad, but in the deepest part of his eyes burned a little fire of the purest blue-red hatred.

Michael took a screwdriver from the seat of the car, put it in his mouth and moved his face close to his father's . . . he made gurgling spitting sounds in between his laughter.

Ron slid out of the car and moved away from the sick scene, saying to himself as he walked back down the East Road . . .

sick fucks, sick sick fucks, sick . . . sick . . .

Ron knocked on the jamb of his father's slightly ajar study door. He had to knock very loud before his father looked up. Louis put his newspaper down, smiled at Ron, gave permission to come in.

"Dad," Ron said as he walked into the room, "I have to go into the city, New York City, to do some research at the Historical Museum for this paper on sociology."

In the middle of this Ron realized that he was by rote asking his father for permission. Just the way it should be. His father wasn't passive. He was the man in the house who made all the major decisions. No patterns of homosexuality—passive father, aggressive mother making boy play with dolls and all that stuff.

"Soc., huh?" Louis nodded. "That's a good pre-law major."

"I know."

"I majored in history." Louis thought a bit. "Was it history? No, that was my minor. What the dickens was my major." Louis didn't shave much on weekends anymore and his scraggly gray beard made him seem like an old desert prospector trying to recall his last gold strike. "No, it was history . . . fascinating . . . history is fascinating."

"Dad, I've got to catch the bus soon and I may have to stay overnight. I can stay at friends'. Do you have some bus fare and spending money you can let me have."

"Sure," Louis said affirmatively. "Blanche, Blanche," he yelled.

Like an Oriental servant Blanche appeared at the door. Yes, Ron thought, she always listened to dad . . . Oh sure, there have been bits of hostility but no one could say that mom was the aggressive domineering one.

"Yes," Blanche asked.

"The boy wants to go into New York to do some research on a history project. Pre-law."

"Ahh," Blanche said, very happy all of a sudden, "New York, maybe you can see that marvelous new playwright from England, Pinter . . . I think is his name. His plays are full of foreboding

95

silences, and menacing, funny pauses. Louis, give him money for the theater."

"Oh sure," Louis said, reaching into his pocket. "Maybe you can take in a nice movie. What do you need?"

"Oh ten dollars should do it, dad."

Louis gave Ron ten dollars. He always handled the family money. Just like a father, Ron thought. He looked at Blanche going on about the theater. She was always a typical woman . . . music, art, poetry and theater.

"Bring me back a playbill . . . I love to collect old playbills."

"I don't know if I'll get a chance to go, mom."

"I haven't gone to the theater since I can't remember when," Blanche said. "Louis, we have to go to the theater one of these days . . . Let's go to New York and make a weekend of it . . . maybe next weekend, all right?"

She was asking, not telling.

Louis reflected, "We'll see, Blanche, we'll see how we feel next weekend. We'll see . . . "

"All right," Blanche said, smiling in agreement.

As Ron left the room, Blanche turned to him and said very loudly, pleasantly yet significantly. "Please give my regards." She knew where he was going.

Lenny lived on West Eighteenth Street between Ninth and Tenth avenues. It was late Saturday afternoon that Ron found the five-story, dirty red-brick apartment house and moved up the stoop.

STARR and RESNICK the names on the doorbell said. Sounds like a vaudeville team, Ron thought. He rang the bell and almost immediately, as if the other person was waiting, the ring was returned and Ron opened the door.

Apartment four was on the second floor and Ron, rushing through his nerves, bounded up the stairs and knocked hurriedly on the door.

The person who opened the door was not Lenny.

"Yes?" the man said. He was a thin man with light blond hair in a ridiculous little pompadour with delicate features and a blond stubble of a beard . . . like mine . . . Ron thought. He must have been about thirty, airy fairy but dirty, like a picture of a flower on dirty paper.

"Is Lenny home?"

"Who wants to know?"

"I'm his brother."

"Oh, how nice."

The man examined Ron a moment and Ron stonily submitted to the examination.

"Ahh yes, there is a slight favoring . . . around the cheeks and the mouth . . . Yes the mouth . . ."

"Is he home?"

"He's working. He should be back soon. Do you want to wait for him?"

The man moved back from the door and invited Ron in.

"I don't have that long to stay in the city . . . I'd like to at least let him know that I'm here. He doesn't expect me."

"I'll let you know where he works. You can see him there if you like."

"Okay."

"Come in."

Ron stepped just inside the door while the man moved, his ass wriggling in his tight slacks ever so slightly more than usual now that a pair of eyes could be watching it. He brought back a business card and handed it to Ron.

"Here, it's not far from here . . . you can walk in no time."

The card said, "West Side School of Self-Defense" and in addition to an address and phone number it had a picture of a fierce Oriental in a karate stance.

"Have you come all the way from upstate?" the man asked Ron.

"Yes."

"Oh what a long journey . . . Why don't you sit and rest awhile. Lenny'll be working for another couple of hours anyway. Saturday is his busiest day. I can make you some tea, or would you like something to drink . . . ?"

Ron turned to leave, and the man was right next to him saying, "I hope to see you again sometime . . . Will you be around?"

Ron shook his head no.

"I never introduced myself," the man said, sticking his hand out suddenly. "I'm Hal Resnick." The handshake was clammy. Ron was afraid that Hal would hold his hand and try to do something.

"I'm Ron."

"Nice to have met you," Hal intoned, his voice going higher as he became more coquettish. Ron disengaged himself and walked quickly down the stairs. As he reached the bottom he looked up and saw Hal's grimacing smile under his little blond pompadour.

Ron was slightly nauseous. He wanted to go home. Little pompadours, sickly smiles, sneaky hands . . . what the hell was this? Lenny would be this way. A seedy, sneaky, faggotty, sickly queer —no manly grace left to him. Ron would go home rather than see Lenny that way. But then he looked at the business card, at the fierce Oriental, and he decided to go.

The school was in a storefront on Seventh Avenue. He tried to peer inside from a gap in the white cloth front but he could discern nothing.

He opened the door and went in.

Lenny was instructing a class of pre-teen boys and he strode around the mat in, if anything, a more masculine manner than before. He barked instructions at the boys in that staccato way of his that now sounded like an Oriental getting punched in the stomach. Ron waved at him as he walked in. Lenny nodded, acknowledging him. There were parents of the children on the side of the large room with big white mats and they seemed to watch with admiration. Ron wanted to tell them that the instructor there in the middle was his brother.

He waited just a little while before Lenny dismissed the class and then followed his brother to the back of the school into a small locker room. Lenny held his arms out and Ron came into them enjoying the rough squeeze and the hardness of his brother's muscles. Lenny then tilted Ron's head toward the light and peered professionally at his eye. "You really got some shot there, huh?"

His voice was still gruff, no eye-rolls or limp wrists or silly wiggles.

"Want a beer?" Lenny asked, letting Ron's head go.

"Sure."

Lenny strode to a small refrigerator and took out two small bottles of beer without once taking his eyes off his brother. He was drinking him in, getting used to the sight that he had been so used to for most of his life. His little kid brother, Ron, there talking to him, the family treasure. And he, Lenny, the family pirate.

Some time ago, in a bar over on Hudson Street, he'd been talking for hours with this queen from Louisiana who kept telling him in lilting, southern tones how great it had been to come to an understanding with his family. He'd convinced Lenny that Lenny was too hard and bitter and that it was affecting his other relationships and all that crap. Lenny had been hung up on enough and thought he'd gotten over it so he didn't want to try again but he'd had a lot to drink so he impulsively went to the pay phone and called upstate. As the phone was ringing he wondered why he was bothering to do this . . . Imagine home, family and apple pie coming from this old southern cocksucker's mouth. Well, maybe he was too hard on people. He did want to floor anyone who didn't immediately accept him for what he was and he guessed that that kind of stupid attitude wasn't doing him any good.

It was Blanche who answered the phone, "Hello."

"Hello, mother," Lenny had said, waiting for Blanche to recognize his voice.

"Leonard?" Blanche said, her voice rising.

"Yes."

"Leonard, how are you?" She sounded genuinely glad to hear from him.

"I'm fine, mother."

"Where are you?" Blanche said hurriedly. "Are you all right? Leonard there's nothing wrong is there? Is that why you're calling?"

"No, mother, I'm fine, fine . . . I'm not sick or anything."

"Oh, Leonard, why did you wait so long to call? . . . Leonard, where have you been? How are you?" Blanche was sobbing.

"Never darken your doorstep again and all that kind of stuff, remember, mother."

"Are you all right?"

"Fine."

"I'm painting now."

"Good."

"Oh, I must show you my work . . . I'm going to form an Art League up here . . . They don't really have one you know."

"Great. And father?"

"He's not doing well . . . you know this whole thing weighed heavily on him. Leonard . . . I don't know if I should tell you this . . ."

"You're going to tell me anyway, mother."

"It wasn't me, you know . . . I hate him for this. I despise him."

"What happened?"

"He went to a synagogue in Brooklyn, Williamsburg, and he declared you dead . . . He says kaddish over you . . . you know what kaddish is, right?"

Lenny looked through the dirty glass of the phone booth at the bar where the queen from Louisiana was placidly sucking on a cigarette, checking the action through the reflections in the mirror, and he wished that he could have let him hear what Blanche had just told him. Love, family, apple pie. I'd like to snap one of your fucking fingers, he thought, concentrating on the queen's long fingernails. "Yes, mother, I know what kaddish is, a prayer for the dead. I'm glad I helped father find his way back to religion."

The queen looked over and smiled at Lenny with a mischievous gleam in his eye. Lenny smiled back. You're going to get some hard fucking tonight baby, he thought . . . you're going to bleed from that tired old asshole of yours.

"Lenny," Blanche said, her voice taking on a new resolve, "I don't care what he says . . . what the schmuck says . . . you're my son and I want to see you again."

Lenny pulled his focus away from the scene in the bar and on the black of the phone. "Do you mean that, mother?"

Blanche was crying. "Of course I mean it . . . You're my son and I love you . . ."

"I love you too, mother . . ." Lenny said and almost started to cry, not caring if the queen did see. "Mother, I'd like to come home . . . just for a short visit . . ."

"Oh, no, we, you'd better not for now . . . he won't take it well if he sees you . . . Let me come and see you. Where are you, in Greenwich Village or something?"

"Nearby. I'll give you the number."

"All right, let me get a pencil and a piece of paper. Hold on." Blanche put down the phone.

Lenny leaned back in the phone booth and wondered about Ron. Michael had been able to give him only skimpy reports. He hadn't even been able to be sure of what school Ron went to. If Lenny knew, he could visit the kid.

"Go on," Blanche said when she returned.

Lenny gave Blanche his address and phone number and then said, "How's Ron? What school's he going to?"

The phone seemed to freeze in Lenny's hand as if a lightning streak of ice had zipped through the telephone lines.

"I think your father is coming now. I'd better hang up."

"How's Ron? Where is he?" Lenny said, raising his voice.

The queen was turning around watching everything now. The cocksucker.

"I have to go now. I plan on being in New York soon to go to the theater . . . I'll call you . . . We'll have lunch or something in one of the charming Greenwich Village cafés."

"Where the fuck is Ron?"

Everyone at the bar could hear and they all turned in mid-drink, in mid-feel, mid-smoke and looked at Lenny shouting at his mother.

Blanche had hung up.

"Growing a little thin," Ron said, indicating Lenny's slightly receding hairline and the thinness that was beginning to make its way through the rest of his hair.

"Father's revenge."

They laughed.

"Your time'll come too," Lenny said.

"Bite your tongue."

"I'm going to shave the whole thing off one of these days . . ."

"Like Yul Brynner?"

"Like Yul Brynner."

"Wow."

"You better believe it."

"I wouldn't do that."

"What would you do, wear one of those toupees?"

"No."

"I bet you would."

"No . . . but guys like Bing Crosby look good in them, even Bobby Darin wears one."

"If I catch you wearing one of those things I'll burn it right off the top of your head."

"You summon me to your presence, then you give me commandments. Just like old times."

"How did you get that eye?"

"Soccer," Ron answered casually and finished the beer. Ron stood up and threw the beer away. "Aren't you going to take me for a tour?"

So little brother wants to play it cool, Lenny thought, wants to check out the territory first . . . "Well, okay, let's go."

They walked through Greenwich Village on an early Saturday evening. Lenny was dressed in a white turtleneck sweater and a navy blue pea coat and dark sailor-type pants. Ron felt insignificant and invisible beside his brother. On almost every block someone would nod to Lenny—not all of the ones who nodded were "types." For instance, a very distinguished executive-looking old football player came by and smiled at Lenny.

"Ahhh," Lenny said, as they passed him, "the ol' Silver Fox is back in town, huh?"

"Who's he?"

"A weird fag. When he gets drunk he likes to concoct danger. He's the president of a large transportation company. Old-line, everything. His goddamn teeth go back to the *Mayflower*. But then he picks up the most nancy types and goes to all his uptown, East Side haunts . . . hand on ass . . . teeheeing all over the place . . . All the while he's scared shitless because if they find out they'll scandal his ass right off the board . . . That's his kicks."

Ron looked around at the man. Hard to believe. "Weird."

They passed one with makeup on and he smiled at Ron and Ron smiled back, feeling safe to do so with Lenny there.

"Tourist attraction," Lenny said, referring to the nods and gawks of some of the married couples and college kids who'd seen the obvious one that had just come by. "That's only a small part of the story down here. The real story is about people whose asses don't wiggle and whose wrists don't go limp. There's something happening down here and one day it's going to explode all over the country. Come on, I want you to meet some other "types" over at a bar on Christopher Street . . . Regular people . . . not freaks . . . Guys who are bookkeepers, accountants, lawyers . . ."

Ron excitedly interrupted him. "Let's have a beer over there," he said. "Dylan hangs out in that bar sometimes. Maybe we can see him."

"Dylan?"

"Bob Dylan. You never heard of him. Me and my girl come down here all the time and write about him and others too . . . Come on . . ." Ron led the way to a bar in the middle of the block and continued jabbering. "The whole folk-music scene is where it's at. I'm surprised you're not up on it. I write a column for the college paper now and I cover it. It's great."

Ron really wasn't sure if it was the rather nondescript bar they were headed for or another one further down that the mythical Dylan was reputed to hang out in, but it didn't really matter. Lenny was following him in and not insisting on going to the "other place."

Dylan was not there. Ron settled down at a table by the window and Lenny joined him and they were brought beers. They sat awhile in silence. Ron had assessed the territory and hadn't liked it. He didn't want to meet any swishy accountants or lawyers. He was glad he'd seen his brother. Hello and goodbye. He'd ride this visit out. Thank you.

Lenny said, "Now, I'm going to make a bit of a speech to you. You don't have to say a word—that's okay. If I'm wrong, then I've just spoken for nothing and that's no big deal but if I'm right then maybe we can get somewhere.

"The reason I wanted to see you when I heard about the eye from Michael is connected with the fact that you weren't too eager to keep in touch with me." Ron opened his mouth to protest, reaching for ten letters in his pocket as proof, but Lenny stopped him imperiously.

"Save it. Whatever you did you could have done more. I don't blame you. I understand it." Lenny leaned forward now and whispered but Ron had no trouble hearing what he said. "I think you got that eye fucking around with the wrong guy or the right guy in the wrong place or a combination of the two. Now you can tell me I'm full of shit and we can play our little masquerade of brother visiting brother or you can tell me what's going on and we can talk more openly or you can just be silent and let me talk at you."

Ron couldn't say a word. At that moment he didn't even remember anything about the eye.

Lenny continued, "I know it's hard to talk about. I went through it and I didn't get anyplace until I met Michael and we were able to share our feelings.

"It doesn't have to be weird and sick. It often is because of repressing it . . . being so afraid that it never sees the light of day. If you get to know who you are and how you are you can build your life around it any way you want to . . . Remember *Father Knows Best?*" Lenny said, smiling a bit.

"Sure."

"Still watch it?"

"No."

"That's the American ideal. The erotic American dream. Three wonderful heartwarming children, the insurance business, middle-American comfort and at night can you imagine them going down on each other after twenty years of marriage . . . A wild sex life. Ol' Jane Wyatt coming thirty-eight times. Ol' Robert Young waking her at three in the morning for another round."

Ron was laughing, relieved now that Lenny was being this light.

"That's what we all would like. Complete acceptability and complete sensuality. But some of *us* who are a bit different have to get our model from another show. You still watch *I Led Three Lives?*"

"No more."

"Well, remember Philbrick, Richard Carlson?"

"Sure."

"He had no doubt about his identity. He was a rock-bottom true American. He worked for the F.B.I. and posed as a dirty Commie, right?"

"Right."

"Now he'd be very confused if he didn't have this rock-bottom identity knowledge. Sometimes he'd think he might be a real career F.B.I. man or maybe even a Commie who was infiltrating the F.B.I.—anything. But he never gets confused. He knows who he is."

"Right."

Lenny leaned in closer to Ron. "Just like a guy who likes to suck cocks . . . He can do whatever he wants, adopt any disguise that pleases him. He doesn't have to wiggle his ass in the Village. He can be right there in Middle America. He can be on the football team or be a Boy Scout leader. As long as he doesn't lisp or wiggle he's okay and then he can have whatever pleasure he wants. There are plenty of takers, more than you can begin to know. They're out there ready to lead three lives too. The one clue, like with Philbrick, you've got to know who you are. You can't fool yourself. You just have to fool others."

"Look," Ron finally said, "I know what you're telling me but it doesn't apply to me."

Ron saw something old and familiar in the way Lenny's mouth tightened, and he quickly removed his hand from the table before his brother could grab it and twist or something.

"Bullshit. How did you get that eye?"

"I told you."

"Come on, let's get out of here."

"No, I want to stay."

"I'll grab your fucking earlobe and squeeze it off right here in public if we don't leave."

"Where we going?"

"Don't worry about it."

"You better not start anything."

Lenny stood up. "Come on."

Ron stood. He contemplated just running away from Lenny. He was always faster. He could run to the subway . . . No he'd better not do that . . . If the train didn't come Lenny would have him. He could just go off and get lost in the streets . . . He had to . . . He knew his brother was getting crazy and was going to take him someplace and start something.

"You're not going to run," Lenny whispered as he paid the check at the counter near the exit. "If you try I'll get you, don't worry . . ."

Just then two "showy ones" walked by and seemed to look in significantly. Ron suddenly became very frightened, positive that Lenny ran a network of sinister fairies—mad hags who were posted in key spots around the Village and who wouldn't let him escape. The horrible image of being gobbled up by screaming cannabilistic queens shook him.

He found himself walking passively with his brother toward Washington Square Park and then saying, "All right, it wasn't soccer. I had a fight with my roommate in college."

"Over what?"

"A girl."

Lenny didn't react to that. "What was his name?"

"Jeffrey," Ron said the name softly as if the hovering fairies of his imagination were waiting to hear it and chant it deridingly the way children do . . . "Ron loves Jeffrey" . . . "Ron loves Jeffrey . . . Ha, ha, ha."

"You liked him?"

"I like a lot of guys. That doesn't mean anything, does it?"

"I don't know. That's what I'm trying to find out."

"Well, it doesn't. I make it with the girls you know. I have a girl friend, Judy. Would you like a testimonial?"

The wind was out of Lenny's sails with that. They were in the park now and Ron was comforted to see it loaded with winos. He felt safer and he strutted a bit ahead of Lenny so that Lenny had to catch up with him.

"Look," Ron said, "this guy Jeffrey wanted me to make up stories about this sexy chick so that he could get it off with himself."

"Stories?"

Ron laughed. "Corn-porn shit. Things like the-moonlight-shone-on-the-white-globes-of-her-breasts kind of shit."

"Oh yes, a nice technique."

The word "technique" bit into Ron.

"You didn't like me to use the word 'technique'?"

"No. It was no technique. I didn't use any techniques."

"Who started the stories."

"I forgot."

"I bet you did. He sounds too dumb. Go on."

They were headed toward an exit of the park under the arch on the Fifth Avenue side. Ron didn't want to leave. This was his sanctuary.

"Let's sit on the bench."

"Okay," Lenny replied easily. They sat on a bench, with one black wino at the far end groggily looking about and huddling in a dirty large overcoat.

"A lot of winos coming into the Village, huh?" Ron said softly to Lenny so as not to offend the one on the same bench.

"Go on."

"All right, well I wanted to stop because I could see that it was leading to trouble. He kept bugging me to continue."

"You really had him turned on."

"It wasn't me, it was the girl. You should see her . . . She might even get to you."

Lenny got Ron's earlobe in his fingers and squeezed. Ron winced.

"Get this, kid. I can fuck anybody I want to fuck. If I wanted to, I could. I could fuck her ten times better than ten of the best jocks you could name. Save your shit."

Lenny let go. Ron peered at the wino who had seen what was going on and had smiled dreamily at it.

Ron stood up and walked away. Lenny was by his side.

Ron was almost crying the way he always did when Lenny bullied him. He wished he could go to the winos and complain the way he had to his mother when Lenny had acted up.

"Don't treat me this way," Ron said vehemently, "I'm no goddamn kid. I didn't have to come here and take this shit."

"Then why did you come?"

"I don't know now. I don't know."

"You came to find out. You came to put your toe in the water to see if there was any warmth to it before you put your body in."

Ron stopped and faced Lenny.

"Look, I'm tired of your stupid analysis—"

"Okay," Lenny snapped. "Get the fuck out of here. Goodbye."

"Huh?"

"Goodbye." Lenny stuck his hand out stiffly for a handshake. "Nice seeing you again. Regards to the folks and piss on you all." Ron just stared at the outstretched hand and Lenny turned and walked away.

As Ron watched Lenny's back he thought of his mother's talk about sending carrier pigeons to the insane asylum. There were so many pigeons in the park.

"Hey," he yelled loudly at Lenny. Lenny just continued to walk. Ron ran after him and caught up. "Hey, come on, I don't want to part this way."

Lenny stopped and looked at Ron as straight in the eye as he could. "I don't want to force you to be something you're not. I just want you to be able to talk to someone. Can you talk to mom? Pop? Michael? Anyone? I don't want to turn you into a Greenwich Village fag. I just want to find out where you are. But then, you're such a hard case I don't know if I want to bother."

"Okay. Let's talk."

Ron turned back in the park and Lenny walked alongside of him.

"All right, I knew that the whole thing was leading to trouble so I tried to stop it. I stopped telling the stories but he insisted . . . He even forced me . . . twisted my arm and made me do it . . . like . . ."

"Like the way I used to force you to do things."

"I guess . . ." Ron said. "Used to? You still do."

"All right, all right. Just tell me what happened."

They had passed the place in the park where old men concentrated on chess games. Lenny's sudden outburst had made one of them look up. Ron walked ahead faster, wanting to get more toward the middle of the park. There was a group of people gathered around two men who were having a loud political argument. The worst of it was over. Maybe they could go and listen to the argument afterwards.

"So I went on and we both got kind of carried away and that led to the fight."

"How did you get carried away?"

"Well you know, we touched . . . each other . . . and then he got pissed and he hit me."

"You touched his cock."

"Yes."

"He touched yours."

"Yes."

"Then he hit you."

"Yes. He called me a fucking queer, then he hit me and started to choke me and everything. He was crazy."

Ron wanted to suggest that they go over and hear the argument now. It seemed like a good one with both antagonists getting quite heated and attracting many of the younger students who were hanging around, but he waited until Lenny reacted to what he had just told him.

They walked a few more paces.

"Some guys get crazy over this kind of thing," Lenny said. "The further they are from any idea of their own feelings the crazier they get."

"Yeah, I know."

"You know a lot of strictly heterosexual people have done what you did and it doesn't mean there's anything wrong. You were thinking of this girl, right?"

"Yes, she's really stacked like a brick shithouse."

"You make it with the girls do you?"

"Sure. I have this girl Judy at school and remember Susan . . . back home . . . ?"

"Susan . . . I remember her . . . Cute kid. Her?"

"Sure."

They stopped. Lenny turned to Ron, a soft smile on his face. "I guess you're going to be the family's Robert Young."

Ron laughed, "Jane Wyatt, here I come." He suddenly felt very happy.

Lenny looked at his watch. "Big doings in the ol' town tonight. Saturday night. I've got to get back home."

"I've got to catch the bus."

"I'll walk you to the subway."

They started to walk out of the park.

"My only advice to you then is to jerk off alone."

Ron was elated. He laughed loud, relieved and free. "Don't worry," he said, "no more joint ventures."

"Nice pun." Lenny laughed along with him.

They were out of the park and onto the street. As they passed a small alleyway Lenny stopped and peered into the small dark opening. He signaled for Ron to come close to him and see what Lenny was looking at and Ron walked by Lenny's side and then suddenly he was propelled into the alleyway and he was up against the wall pinned there as if by steel stakes unable to move. One of Lenny's arms was up against his throat.

"You like it this way so I'm going to give it to you this way. I want to hear the fucking truth. Now if you don't tell me I'm going to snap your little pinky. Pop. Do you still play the piano? Hard to do those soft little runs with a snapped pinky."

Ron jerked convulsively but he was pinned dead to the wall. He could feel two of Lenny's fingers around his pinky ready to snap it as if it were a twig.

"Now what did you do to Jeffrey. *Tell me.*"

Ron closed his eyes, mumbled, "I . . . sucked his cock."

"What?"

"You heard."

"What?"

"I sucked his cock."

"Louder. They've heard that here. This is the capital of it."

111

"I sucked his cock."

"Louder."

"I sucked his cock."

"Louder."

"I sucked his cock." And then Ron broke down and he cried and he put his head on Lenny's shoulder . . . and sobbed as he kept telling Lenny . . . "I sucked his cock . . . I sucked his cock . . ." And then Lenny released his grip on Ron and he took his brother in his arms and held him while Ron sobbed and sobbed. Ron was amazed that he felt good, as if dirty, filthy vermin-infested water had been dammed up in him, rotting him, and now the water was draining out, emptying him, purifying him. He loved Lenny very much at that moment and he unashamedly kissed him and held him.

They calmed down and then in three or four sentences Ron simply told him everything that had happened with Jeffrey. When he'd finished he said, "Am I . . . queer, Lenny?"

"I don't know. You might be. You might not be. The only thing is you must stop hiding from yourself or you'll turn weird. Understand?"

"Yes."

"How do you feel now?"

"Better."

"Want to go back now?"

"Yeah."

"Come on. I'll walk you to the subway."

They walked. Ron's legs felt wobbly.

"What do I do now?" he asked.

"Want to see a psychiatrist?"

"Have you ever?"

"For a little while. He couldn't understand how one man could do it to another. He found men hairy and disgusting."

"I don't know. I couldn't see one now if I wanted to. I'd have to wait till I was on my own."

"They're not worth shit anyway. If they're straight they try to convert you and if they're not they try to fuck you."

"Well, what do I do?"

"Don't do anything. Watch yourself. See how your feelings run. Try to get someone to talk to, male or female . . . Doesn't make any difference as long as you can talk."

"You."

"I'm going to Japan soon. I'll be studying with an eighty-one-year-old man who's a ninth-degree black belt. I might be away at least a couple of years."

Ron felt abandoned. He would have to open up to someone else now. He couldn't. Why the hell did Lenny have to go away?

"We'll write," Lenny said, trying to shore up Ron. "I'll send the letters to Michael so that they don't give you any shit at home. Maybe you can talk to Michael."

Ron turned away.

"All right, Michael's too weird. I know. Isn't there anyone at school?"

Ron shook his head.

"If I had money I'd give you money for a goddamn psychiatrist," Lenny said loudly. A young couple was startled. Lenny turned on them. "You can't find anyone to talk to in this fucking country!"

They giggled and walked away fast.

"Listen," he said, stopping Ron and pointing his finger at him, "you've got to find someone. You're supposed to have a mother and father but in our case forget it. Our father's a lawyer, a counselor. Joke. Forget it. Get a buddy. That's your responsibility. You have to open up to people. Do you think you're the only one? There are millions. Do you think it's a small closet? No, it's a big closet. You go to college, there's smart people there—fucked up but smart. I'll break your fucking head if you don't find anyone to talk to. Okay?"

"Yes, all right," he said, calming and quieting Lenny down. "I'll find someone to talk to. I promise. Now that it's out it'll be easier."

"Promise."

"Promise."

The subway was in sight.

"I have to go away," Lenny said as he spotted it. "You have no idea what I'm going to learn from this man. He's—"

"All *right.*"

"Ahh, good. Don't take any shit from me . . . Tell me to shut up. That's good. I get to be a bully sometimes, don't I?"

"Yes. You're a fucking pain."

They reached the subway station. People were congested around the station. It was a busy spot. They moved into a doorway of a store that sold records. Cello music, a mellow solo played by Pablo Casals came to them. They listened a moment to it.

"I'll be all right," Ron finally said.

"Mom still play the piano?" Lenny asked casually.

"Not very much."

"And pop—is he still buried in his study?"

"More than ever."

"How're they doing?"

"Not too well."

"Yeah, well, so it goes . . ."

"You ought to try and see them."

"Fuck 'em."

"Mom at least. I think she'd be open. I can bring it up to her."

"Are you kidding? You'll give her a heart attack if she knows I saw you. She's so afraid I'll corrupt you. The only reason she'd think to see me would be to bug the lawyer."

"Keep me out of it. I'll tell Michael to approach her. She can take a bus into the city . . . Tell pop that she's seeing a play or something."

"You'd better go back."

The reunion was a closed subject.

They walked out of the doorway, both feeling sorry about leaving the Pablo Casals solo before the end.

"It's good," Lenny said. "What is it?"

"Shalom by Block . . . on Jewish music . . . I've got to get the record."

"Me too."

Just before Ron went down the subway stairs he turned to his brother. He wanted to shake his hand goodbye but he couldn't just do that. He felt like crying and embraced Lenny, and Lenny embraced him back.

"Lenny," he said. "I love you."

"Yeah, I love you too . . . Now goodbye . . . I'll see you."

"Okay, I'll see you. I'll be all right."

"I know you will."

Ron turned quickly then and walked down the subway stairs.

CHAPTER 7

In Ron's senior year he enrolled in a playwriting course, under Professor Gerard Lavalle.

Professor Lavalle didn't seem very Gallic. He was fat the way a turnip is, with a very small head and very small twisted feet and an enormous ass that stuck out like a bustle. He had thin brown hair, a beak nose and buck teeth and when he talked he made a metallic, clicking sound at the back of his throat like something that ought to be coming from a cigarette-rolling machine. As he sat and lectured his class he drank coffee interminably from an ancient thermos and would often get so carried away with his idea that the coffee would pour down his hand, at which time he would casually wipe it on the long-suffering lapel of the jacket he was forever wearing and continue on.

There was little doubt that he was a brilliant scholar and critic. He told his students about the viciousness of some nameless people on campus who accused him of turning in all his "fellow traveler" colleagues during the McCarthy era and causing whole-sale removals. "There are some who say that my full professorship, earned at an age when most are happy to be getting a Master's, was the result of my snitching on my pals. This bit of venom ignores the fact that I've published on Shakespeare, Milton, play-writing and poetry. The combined published works of a lifetime of all the instructors and professors of this department do not equal my output in my twenties. My thirties are not quite finished, if any one of you has any curiosity, and the output continues. I stopped traveling with my fellows long before McCarthy and those who would link my advancement to certain headrollings are merely peddling the familiar party line that I myself had been guilty of peddling in the forties. No, my dear undergraduates, I dropped out of party affairs long before the purges, recognizing, as it were, that the people involved had merely found havens for their particular neuroses, not any real Utopia—as I'd originally thought. So let's clear the air, you are not dealing with a rat-fink, no, you are dealing *avec moi,* Professor Gerard Lavalle, who will teach you what it is possible to teach anyone about the art of writing for the theater."

Ron found him enormously attractive. He picked the intelligence and sensitivity from the grossness of the flesh like diamonds from mud.

Since he'd seen Lenny, Ron had suspended himself, monitoring his feelings as if they were blips on a radar screen, yet not allowing himself to get involved with anyone—male or female. He dropped out of the newspaper, really not interested in journalistic writing anymore. He kept on with the soccer team but his playing had lost much of its old spirit and he never made the first team the way he seemed likely to when he first started. He had planned on running for the student council, but decided that because of his cut-down in social and political activities he probably wouldn't win anyway, and much to his father's disappointment he sat on the side as far as school politics were concerned. His spirits were damped but at least he was trouble-free.

The playwriting course had been little more than taking the easiest two-credit course he could fit in. Ideas of being a writer had been given up. It would be law. He planned on becoming a lawyer for the poor and disenfranchised. He concentrated on marks, getting straight A's now, delighting in flexing his intellectual muscles for the first time, realizing that he was smart—really smart. He'd be a great lawyer. It would be better if he had no attachments. He could practice without worrying about making money and raising a family, his total devotion would go to his work. He'd emulate great lawyers like Darrow and Lincoln, married men for sure, but essentially lonely, isolated giants. This need of his to be political, to be well liked (from his mother's favorite play *Death of a Salesman*); to change himself like a chameleon to please whoever he was with . . . He became aware of that as he watched the radar screen of his emotions. He didn't like it anymore. He was not going to be that way. Smart people, really smart people like Professor Lavalle did not need to be that way.

And of course the other thing was there. He could feel the attractions now more openly. Yes, he was more comfortable in letting himself know what he was feeling as he was feeling it, Lenny was very right about that. And he could handle it the way these things get handled, secretly, at night, like any other boy his age. He allowed once-forbidden images into his mind now. He played and replayed Jeffrey, playing the scene differently than it had occurred and then playing sequels as well.

He mentally snickered at Jeffrey when they passed on campus. If that pseudo-macho latent fairy hillbilly idiot only knew what I did to him last night and he to me, he thought, he'd probably love it if he let it happen . . . Poor Phyllis, one day Jeffrey will tire of your blubbery boobs and he'll go off to some men's room in Utica to find what he probably really wants and where will you be then . . .?

And Gyla, he saw her now as she paraded around campus in a different way. Now he didn't have to stoke flames that weren't there. He could watch the boys salivate over her and enjoy it.

Yes, Lenny was right. This was better. Except—what could he do with it? What could he do about it? There was no one to be with. There was no final safety in it. Let it pass . . . Watching it blip across the screen of his emotions he wished it would blip off the screen and never come across again. It will, it will, it will . . . One day he'd wake up and it'd be gone. He knew it. He had a faith that it would.

Meanwhile . . .

"As your first assignment," Professor Lavalle intoned, "you will activate the following situation. Character A wants to get into or be part of something that Character B is in charge of. That is your premise. Make it live. Now remember drama consists of action, conflict, resolution—not just on the part of one of the characters but each must have an action toward the other that results in a conflict that cries out for a resolution. All too often we see a situation, and I'm talking about plays that are on Broadway or even in world literature, wherein someone tries to persuade someone else to do something—all action is in some sense just that— and all the other person wants is to be left alone. God, how dull Hamlet would have been if the ghost had said to Hamlet, now avenge my death and Hamlet had said, look, why don't you just leave me alone. Hamlet wants to find the ghost out, test the ghost. The ghost wants Hamlet to seek revenge and Hamlet wants to get at the truth. Cross-purposes. See? Now make the scene as simple as possible. Don't give me Macbeth, not yet anyway. By the time this course is over I will have my Macbeth from you." He looked around the class slowly, clicked his device in the back of his throat and said, "Well some of you." Paused again and said, "One of you?" Everyone laughed.

"Seriously, class, writing for the theater is the only writing that absolutely can be taught. There are guiding principles to be mastered that can enable even the most mediocre talent to put on the stage a work of genuine theatricality. I will demonstrate how to construct first a scene, then a one-act play and then if some of you are so inclined, a full-length three-act work. I will show you the way great masters instinctively followed the principles that I have formalized. Now lest anyone come from this class and corner one of my many detractors on and around this campus and say, 'Oh, ol' Lavalle is telling us that he's going to make us Shakespeares by some formula that he's come up with,' let me hasten to inform you that all I can do is provide guiding principles, axioms, but the writer has to breathe the fire. There's no formula for fire." But then he leaned into the class and Ron was caught up as Professor Lavalle said, "But there is fire in all of us. The most humble peasant or the most jaded theater critic has a passion and a humanity that cries out for expression. Everyone has something of value to give all of us. Everyone, even undergraduates."

Ron went back to the dorm in an excited daze. In his mind he pictured a minimum-security prison for women that had just been built near his home town. Louis had laughingly told him that they couldn't find enough ladies to populate it because women had been committing more serious crimes these days so that some buildings were empty. Ron dreamt up an old lady who'd been forced to give up her little farm and had no place to stay and he worked on a scene in which she went to the prison to see the warden and ask him if she couldn't stay in one of the empty rooms. She was a piquant old lady, kindly yet very firm, and the warden was very stern and official. He enjoyed writing the scene, working very hard on the warden so that the character wasn't just saying leave me alone and get out of here to the old lady. When Ron found something that the warden could want from the old lady the scene swung out and came to life (he wanted her to scout the courts and talk to the judges about sending prisoners to him before his budget was cut).

A few days after he handed the play in, Professor Lavalle took a pile of work out of his worn, black leather case, thumped it on the desk and addressed the class. "I see I have my work cut out for me." He scornfully looked at the twelve students there. "I have flights of whimsy, poetry, fancy—illusions and disillusions of grandeur and depravity. God, some of the subjects you undergraduates deal with . . . But there're no taboos anymore . . . So be it. Yet I could hardly find an action in most of these little things. Most of you don't seem to know what I mean when I say action! I don't mean John Wayne chasing Indians, nor do I mean, as one student no doubt thinks I mean, a twelve-page description of the life and times of this procurer whose main action it seems is to sit around and justify what he's come to all day. How does he have time to supervise his charges I'd like to know. Nevertheless, class, what is an action?"

One student raised her hand and said, "It's wanting something from someone else."

"No!"

"It's getting something from someone else."

"No. It's not wanting or getting, it is *doing*. By their fruits ye shall know them. You may *do* without wanting. You may *do* without getting. Chekhov's people do things all the time and they don't seem to get or even want a goddamn thing." He slammed his hand on the desk. His thermos shook and coffee leaked out. His face was red and he was furious. "I would like to have one of these works read in class and then hear your comments." He held up Ron's script. "Here is one titled 'The Would-be Convict.' Mr . . . uh . . . Edelman, Larry Edelman, would you come here in front of the class and read the character called Warden Rogers and Miss Syzliski . . . Anita . . . is that right? Yes? Amazing, I'm usually terrible at such names, would you read the only other character, called the Old Lady?"

Ron listened to his playlet as if in a frozen block of ice. Words that had sounded so funny and charming to him sounded flat and dull especially as read by the seemingly semi-illiterate, skinny, frightened Anita Syzliski. Larry Edelman was good as the warden.

He picked right up into the character and Ron was grateful that Larry was there. But Ron wanted to hide—leave the room, anything, as the class and the professor listened stonily to the scene. Why did it seem so long? Let it be *over*, already.

When it ended Professor Lavalle said, "Well?"

No one in the class said a word. He glowered at them, his eyes frothing with malicious fury. Finally Larry Edelman raised his hand, swallowed and said, "I think it was good."

The professor boomed, "Why?"

"They both had actions and they had reactions to each of the other's actions . . . I liked it."

The professor thumped on his desk very hard. The coffee jumped out of the thermos cup onto the back of one of the scripts. "You are goddamn right it's good work. The only goddamn good work I saw." He looked down at the script, "Who is Ron Starr? Stand up."

Ron stood up.

"Is that Ronald or Ron?"

"Ron."

"Have you written plays before?"

"No."

"What have you written before?"

"Sketches . . . some journalism . . ."

"You have a talent for theatrical writing, young man. As part of this course we choose some of the best work and present it in a production later on in the term. Polish this a bit and I think I'd like to use it." He tossed the script to Ron with a nod and a half smile. "Now, on the other end of the spectrum I should like the following to be read as a prime example of what not to do . . . this time however I shall mercifully allow the playwright to be nameless."

"And mom, two of my plays are being done and I'm acting in one of the other plays that was written by my friend Larry Edelman . . ."

Blanche clapped her hands in a joyful prayer-answered attitude. "Oh God . . . the theater . . . the theater . . . I want to come and see the plays."

"Well, you can't for this time, mom. No audience except students . . . It's just a workshop thing. But at the end of the term Professor Lavalle is talking about having a whole program of one-act plays . . . the best from the workshops to be presented to an audience and then I want you to come."

"Oh yes . . . Yes . . ."

Ron was home for Easter vacation and the family was finishing supper. Louis had listened taciturnly to the rhapsodic duo between his wife and son before he commanded attention by loudly clearing his throat. When that didn't work he, for a moment, contemplated tapping his knife on a glass the way it was done at Rotary meetings but he decided to just come right in rather than go that far.

"Now, son, I'd like to get the benefit of your thinking as far as law school is concerned. This is April and you graduate in about two months. That doesn't give us a lot of time you know. Have you got any definite ideas about which school you'd like?"

"I've been thinking about schools, St. Johns . . . Columbia."

"Keep away from New York schools. They're not really what you want. I've been thinking about some of the Midwest ones. I got a lot out of the University of Indiana, you know . . . Fine school."

But the idea of going to school in New York was more attractive to Ron than going to school. Off-Broadway was there. Professor Lavalle had talked about little theaters where young playwrights could get their start. Of course, Ron was still going to go to law school but he wanted to be near; a subway ride away from that magic place.

"Well I don't know, dad. I mean, New York has some of the best law schools in the country."

"Oh yes, academically they're all right. They rank high. But you know you want to get out there in this country and meet the real people. There's a bunch of strange characters in New York. You would do well out in the Midwest. They'd like you and you'd like them. You're their kind of person, you know . . . You're not like a New Yorker . . ."

"Well, what's the matter with New York, Louis?" Blanche said. "My goodness, we're from New York, aren't we?" She giggled.

Louis watched her giggle. And as he watched she giggled uncontrollably. Louis then, as if to prove a point, said, "There are strange people in New York."

"I-I really had my eye on Columbia. My marks are good enough and—"

Louis threw his napkin down on the table, one of his dramatic movements. "I do *not* want you to go to a New York school." He glared at Blanche and his voice became deep, lawyerish as he said slowly, "There are strange people flitting . . . floating, whatever they do, around New York City."

He stalked out of the room.

Blanche moved to Ron and sat next to him. She stroked his hair and looked closely at the curves and corners of her son's face. "You're so handsome, baby . . . I bet the coeds can't keep their hands off you . . ."

Ron leaned back and allowed her hand stroking his face to feel like gentle waves against his cheeks.

"He's such a schmuck," she cooed as if lullabying a baby. "Denying his religion, denying his son, denying you your city . . . Such a schmuck . . . such a schmuck . . ."

"Mom," Ron murmured, "I want New York . . ."

"Don't worry," Blanche lullabyed. "You'll have New York . . . If you want New York . . . you'll have New York . . ."

Ron put his arms around his mother's neck, embraced her and kissed her cheek. She kissed him back and continued to stroke his hair . . . "Son . . . you like girls don't you . . . ?"

"Sure . . . Of course . . . Is that what he's worried about?"

"I think so . . ."

"I wish I could tell you about some of the things we do with girls but you *are* my mother, you know . . ."

Blanche giggled. "I bet you're terrible, aren't you?"

"Yes mom, I am terrible."

During the vacation Ron debated with himself as to whether or not he should see Michael. He'd written a long letter to Lenny in Japan openly talking about how he felt about what they'd talked about. He wanted to see if there was any mail from Lenny, but he was afraid of Michael. Michael would want to fool around, and maybe he would want to too . . . And then Michael would start coming around the house to see him, and his parents would get all excited. *No.*

So Ron waited till the next to last day before he went to visit Michael. If anything happened then Michael wouldn't have time to come around.

Michael's house was more junkyardy in the spring than it was in the winter. There was more junk and less snow to cover it.

There was no answer when Ron knocked on the door.

He went around to the back of the house.

The barn was empty.

Ron came back down the old East Road with an empty and disappointed feeling but then he thought about the outline he'd presented for his full-length play to Professor Lavalle. He knew the professor would be impressed—knew it, knew it, and he sort of hugged himself as he walked home. Professor Lavalle would want to see him in his office about the outline. He would. Ron knew he would.

It had gone exactly the way he thought it would. After class that morning the professor had wiggled his finger at him, Ron had approached his desk and the professor had said, "We'd better talk about this outline of yours at greater length. Can you come to Room 1327 at two-thirty this afternoon?"

"Yes."

"Excellent."

Ron very tensely sat in Professor Lavalle's leather chair in the professor's office in the English Department waiting for the great man to enter.

The professor arrived at 2:45, his shadow covering the frosted glass door of his office as he clumsily opened it, arms loaded with papers and books and his coffee thermos stuck under his arm. When Ron was about to rise to help him the professor shook his head no and dumped the papers heavily, noisily and sloppily on his desk muttering Shakespearean curses to the printed matter and then quickly turning to Ron with Ron's outline in his hand saying, "Quite an ambitious project you've got for yourself here, Ron."

The professor's tone was warm and relaxed with no trace of the pedantry found in class. He also used Ron's first name which he'd never done before. It was a pleasant surprise.

"I guess it is . . ." he replied.

"Think you can come up with a first draft by the end of the term?"

"I-I don't know. I wrote some of those one-act plays in two days."

"Ah yes but a full-lengther with all these characters might not lend itself to such speed. Have you written any scenes?"

"I've begun. You're right. When you have to think about what's going to happen in the third act it's not so easy to write the first one . . ."

Professor Lavalle leaned back and crossed his legs and lit a cigarette. The white cylinder seemed out of place, very small in his hand. He offered Ron a smoke but Ron declined.

"Non-smoker, hey?"

"Well, once in a while . . ."

"Ahh, then join me."

Ron took the cigarette from Professor Lavalle and lit up.

"You're a senior?"

"Yes."

"What are your plans after graduation?"

"Law school."

"And you, of course, have the youthful ambition to be one of the rare exceptions who will practice it with honor and social conscience, correct?"

Ron was tongue-tied with Professor Lavalle. He badly wanted to be witty.

"What are you planning on doing with your talent?"

"Talent?"

"Yes, your talent for the theater, Ron. You have it, you know."

Ron took a deep drag on the cigarette and exhaled the smoke. He didn't want to reply—this is what he'd wanted so much to hear but now that he'd heard it he felt wary, frightened.

"Well, I don't know . . . My father wants me to go to law school."

"Do you want to go?"

"Yes."

"Well, then there's no dilemma, is there?" The professor squashed his cigarette in a nearby ashtray as if he were squashing an idea. He handed Ron the outline and said, "Do what you can on this play in the available time. I don't think you're going to finish it before the term is out, especially since you've got to polish the two one-acters for the end of the term. Whether you complete it or not you're assured of an A in the course."

"Thank you," was all that Ron could find to say.

The professor smiled at Ron and said softly, "I can't recall when I've enjoyed working with a student more."

He put his hand out signaling the end of the interview and said as Ron clasped it, "Good luck to you, Ron."

As Ron left the office he was very disappointed. He'd wanted Professor Lavalle to try to talk him out of law school and into the theater. If the professor really thought he had talent, wouldn't he have done just that? . . . "Absence of a dilemma"—*not* true . . . Ron knew there was a dilemma but it scared the living hell out of him.

The play was called *Farm Hand.* It was about a widow who ran a little farm with her teenage daughter. The widow reminded Ron of a woman who did run a large farm upstate and who had had his father's law firm do some work for her. She was gentle but fiery underneath—with a kind of rustic regality that, as he wrote her, he found he admired greatly. He called her Janice Shea. Her daughter was a regular little bitch, Debbie, and Ron saw Gyla in that role. A young boy comes for a job. He's shy, handsome and sensitive. They're both very attracted to him in their own way. His name is Tony and he comes from a wealthy family. He's supposed to take over the family business but he wants to find himself first before being buried in that sort of thing. Perhaps the land—working with his hands, getting back to the roots of his forebears who were originally farmers.

The play was set in the middle of a heat wave and the main action involved the growing involvement and attraction that the characters have for each other and the rivalries and jealousies that develop, particularly around both of the females' suitors, who don't view Tony's presence kindly.

Ron finished the first act by the end of May. He would never finish it before school was over. Larry Edelman, much to Ron's jealousy, had been invited to join Professor Lavalle's inner circle, a group of students and ex-students who met at the professor's New York apartment to read aloud from their writings. Larry couldn't even write. His playlets were little thuds. But he was an actor and very useful as that. He was quick if not perceptive in his reading a role cold, but most of all Larry possessed the one thing that Ron didn't. He was going to make the theater his career. That was the one criteria, aside from talent, needed for the inner circle.

Ron could taste belonging. If only he could, at least over the summer. He'd finish the play before law school. And if not he'd work on it during law school. He could do it, he was organized enough to do both. If only . . .

He turned in the first act and received an immediate response. Professor Lavalle was waiting for him in his office this time and before he'd even had a chance to sit down in the old chair the professor said, "I won't beat about the bush. This is good. Damn good. Do you know what the sirens were?"

"Yes."

"This has a siren sound to it for me but I'm tying myself to the masthead of the ship and jamming corks in my ears. You come to me as a senior with this kind of writing talent? Where the hell were you for the other three years? Journalism—you say? That's not writing, that's arranging words. Then you tell me you're going off to study law in the fall, five short months away. Very well, it's not for me to talk you out of a law career. Your father is a lawyer, is he?"

"Yes."

"He would sue me and probably win. Fine. Study law. As previously said, you have an A in the course . . . no, an A-plus. Go with God young man and do not darken my doorstep with this kind of work anymore unless you can commit yourself to finish it." He tossed the first act in Ron's lap and turned to other work, leaving Ron just sitting there. Ron read the notes, scrawled in large red pen on the front page.

Hate the title—sounds like middle-brow pornography. Love the concept and the feel of the first act. Hotness is an appropriate symbol for this play. Love Mrs. Shea. Debbie's a marvelous bitch but we're going to have trouble with Tony—too ethereal. Also Mrs. Shea's suitor is absolutely made of wood—a convenient plot device. Not so sure about Debbie's boyfriend but he might give us trouble as well. The action needs clarity. Too much exposition about Mrs. Shea's husband. I'll show you how to handle the details of that without it seeming like exposition.

All and all it's a beautiful, inspiring beginning. I feel that I'm there, that I know these people and that I want to know more about them. *Marvelous.*

Ron gazed up at the hulk of the professor's back. He was supposed to get up and leave now, get out of this overstuffed chair, accept his A, then off to law school.

"I want to work on this play," he stated at the professor's back.

"I don't give a damn about law school."

Professor Lavalle turned around and gazed sweetly at Ron, a smile on his lips. He gently squeezed Ron's arm. Ron put his hand on his wanting to squeeze but not . . . Professor Lavalle's hand slid off Ron's arm, lightly brushing his leg . . .

To Ron, Professor Lavalle's large New York apartment on Central Park West seemed like a museum with not enough space. There were massive, dark works of art everywhere—gargoyles on the walls, huge beams of old carved wood on the ceiling, huge paintings with enormous baroque frames, and that was only the foyer. In the dining room, where the inner circle sat around a long, heavy wooden table, there were relics of the Crusades crowding each other—medieval weapons on the walls, old chairs, rubbings, chalices and even a knight or two in old, dull, somewhat rusted armor.

Ron had come with Larry and they were greeted by a Professor Lavalle bedecked in an embroidered silk robe with a pinkish chiffon scarf fluffing from it. He was smoking an ornate Sherlock Holmes pipe giving off smoke that filled the air with an exotic aroma. As he led them into the dining room he pointed to a small, sorry-looking suit of armor that had an ax stuck in its left hand and said, "Meet Sir Rusty, he axes the one with the worst scene at the end of the session."

There were three other people standing about as Ron entered with Larry, but Ron immediately focused on just one. He was a tall, graceful, slender young man in his mid-twenties who was very handsome and bore a striking resemblance to a young Errol Flynn, except that instead of the Flynn rakishness there was a tender softness around the eyes. He was quite beautiful and Ron had a sickening sense of inadequacy to even be in the same room with him—like a puny knight against a magnificent one competing for the favors of the king, in this case, Professor Lavalle, who upon their arrival signaled for his court to be seated.

Something happened when they all sat down. Ron found himself on the right of the professor, who of course was at the head of the table. He'd been subtly shunted there. The beautiful lad had awkwardly seated himself diagonally across from Ron. There was a slight, tense pause, some paper shuffling . . . Ron intuited that he had replaced this lad. He started to feel good. He unsheaved his play. It felt powerful in his hands, like a sword off the wall.

Professor Lavalle began. "Now Sean," he said casually, leaning back and peering levelly at Ron's almost vanquished rival who was getting his material prepared. "I assume you have reworked the problem of the third act on which we spent the entire time last week?"

Sean nodded. He seemed paler now to Ron than before, as if the imaginary wound that Ron felt he'd inflicted was starting to take its toll. Good, Ron felt.

"Very well. Assign your roles and let's get started." Sean, Larry and a girl named Marsha, an intelligent-looking woman in her mid-thirties who was fashionably dressed and who smoked cigarettes from an ivory holder, set out in the middle of a poetic drama set in Ireland.

Ron felt hit back as he heard Sean read. Sean had an Irish lilt to his voice. Lavalle sat back and closed his eyes as Sean read. Sean's face had more color now. Ron was certain that his own was draining.

But the play went on and on. Ron couldn't get a sense of what was happening, it all seemed poesy to him. When it was over there was a long pause. Ron looked at Professor Lavalle and then past his head to see someone pass by quickly in the hallway . . . A head of flaxen hair with large glasses perched on it . . . A woman's head . . . Who the hell was that?

Professor Lavalle said, "Well, dear boy, what do you think of this?"

"Well," Sean replied, "I think there's more focus than last week. I mean, I understand now why the village priest turns the way he does."

"You understand?"

"Yes."

"That's marvelous. What about us?" Sean swallowed. Ron licked his lips. "Do you think as audience it's important for us to understand? Or should we come away from this theater experience, after getting a baby-sitter, parking the car, paying outrageous prices and say to our spouse—well you know the playwright understood what was going on. We are writing for an audience. That is our *raison d'être*, is it not?"

Sean had been knocked off his horse.

Ron leaned forward for the kill.

"Shakespeare combined poetic imagery and dramatic action. He was a dramatist first and a poet second—at least at his best. His people got up there and did things. By their fruits ye shall know them. Action is character and character is action. There is no one who wishes to restore the beauty of language to the theater more than I do. My god, today they speak in the theater as if all theater-goers were *Daily Express* readers . . . but Sean, my dear fellow, your initial promise as a dramatist is quickly fading . . . Perhaps pure poetry is your forte. We ask here for dramatic action and each week you come by with more imagery. Good god, man, would you have us believe even in Ireland that people sit around and spout imagery all goddamn day. They must *do* something. Do you know what your characters do?"

Sean then looked weakly at Ron, a very slight smile on his lips. He didn't blink as Professor Lavalle slammed his hand down on the dark wood of the table and boomed, "They do shit!"

Sean stood up, gathered the papers that were right in front of him and walked out of the room, without bothering to get the other scripts from Larry and Marsha.

Lavalle relit his pipe, looked around the room and said, as if nothing at all had happened, "I want you all to hear the opening scene of a play that Ron here is working on. Have you brought sufficient copies of the script to hand around? . . . Good, I especially would like you to see how the imagery is felt rather than stated. I want you to see how the characters deal with each other in that they have wants and desires that are derived from their life on this planet Earth . . ."

Dear Lenny,

Why haven't you written? I want to talk to you very badly. I'm involved in a whole new thing. I'm writing plays. I'm studying with this professor at school who really likes my work. It's exhilarating . . . marvelous. I'm working on a full-length play and I swear he told me that when it's done . . . if it keeps going the way it's going he's going to show it to his agent. Will you come back to see it open on Broadway?

I'll send you free tickets . . . even plane fare. I'll be rich!

Nothing is happening with anything else. Nothing. Nothing. I think the professor wants something to happen but I don't know . . . It's scary. I wish we could talk. Write!

I've been accepted at two law schools both in the Midwest. Wisconsin and pop's old school, Indiana. He won't hear of me going to any school in New York, afraid of bad influences.

Mom is thrilled at my writing plays . . . She's like a new person. Everytime she hears me going at the typewriter upstairs she sings.

Do you ever miss them?

They miss you, they really do. It comes out in funny little ways, especially pop. I saw him handling the gym equipment the other day, flexing what's left of his muscles on the flexer. I could tell he was thinking of you . . . And mom talks about you in front of him now very openly . . . He just never wants to hear it.

I could talk to her about a reconciliation if you gave me the word. Enough time has passed. Yes? No?

Meanwhile I've just graduated and law school looms in the fall. And I don't care about law school. I eat and sleep this play. I've just finished the second act and sent it to the professor. If I can get it done in the summer and into the agent's hands then I can go to law school and not have to fight with pop. He'd disown me if I didn't.

I really want to go to law school. You can't count on the theater for a living. Or can you? I'm confused. Write, you bastard.

How are you doing? I'm babbling about myself endlessly . . . but I'm mad at you. In the Village that day it was like finding someone that I could be myself to . . . talk to about what was bothering me . . . everything . . . the way we'd never even talked when we were kids and then you went away from me . . . Come on, Lenny, don't be such a bastard all the time . . . I hope you're doing well and all that but I'm sure you are, so I'm not even going to ask you about yourself. So please write, please . . .

So?

Ron

Ron checked himself in the apartment-house mirror before he took the elevator to see Professor Lavalle. The professor had sent him a note to come in today and talk about the second act. It would be the first time that Ron would be alone with him and Ron had shaved and showered to look as fresh as possible. He'd worn a T-shirt that showed his chest and arms to good advantage. He'd selected his best-fitting slacks.

When he rang the bell of the apartment, the door opened slightly and an eye, blue-green and strange under flaxen hair, peered out at him. It was the woman he'd seen on his first night of the inner circle. Was it the professor's wife? Mother? Maid? Sister?

"Yes?" Her voice was young.

"I'm Ron Starr. I'm here to see Professor Lavalle."

The eye disappeared and the door opened and Ron stepped into the foyer. He was eager to get a look at her but found only dimly heard footsteps down a part of the apartment that he'd not been in during the inner-circle meetings. Ron heard tapping on a door and her voice saying, "Gerard, Monsieur Starr *est là.*" Then to Ron, commandingly, "Very well, come."

Ron turned the corner of the foyer toward the command and she was gone. The door to a room to the left was ajar and Ron walked toward it. The apartment was different during the day. Slivers of sunlight were allowed into the large hall making the objets d'art seem dusty and tired. The sun robbed the lighting of its effects on the large paintings. They seemed like playboys who came to life at night and who looked disheveled, dreary during the day. Ron entered Lavalle's study, which was a great surprise, decorated in a totally different fashion from the rest of the house that he'd seen. It was almost completely Oriental. The walls were dominated by rows and rows of pressed butterflies, delicate Oriental screens and embroideries. The desk and the bookshelves were constructed of bamboo. The floor had a closely woven Oriental mat and surrounding the two windows were two large Buddhas of faded gold, one with an enormous belly who resembled in no minor way the good professor himself.

The only unOriental thing in the room was what Professor Lavalle was lounging on—a lounge that he associated with Madame Dubarry or any of the famous courtesans. A Hollywood vamp lounge in the Louis XIV style. He had on a light-blue Oriental robe and at the foot of the lounge there were thongs for his feet. He wore the robe loosely and a good deal of his flesh, smooth and surprisingly firm, showed. On each side of the lounge stood incense burners emitting a sensuous aroma. A box of French chocolates was nearby. He dropped one in his mouth and closed his eyes as he savored it. "Ahhh . . . I know that I shouldn't do that but we all need a weakness or two to keep us human."

He signaled Ron to sit on a large light-red pillow placed at his feet. Ron thought he carried it all off well . . . Not afraid to be himself . . . to be as eccentric, as free as he damn well wanted to be. God, he hoped he liked the second act.

Lavalle looked at Ron. The boy understood him—seemed pleased to see him, no doubt about that. There was no turning away, no dissembling to hide disapproval.

The boy had something. He'd found himself lecturing in class and in the inner circle to this boy, fielding the rebounds of his words. He loved that. It was so rare. He'd spotted Ron the first day and had prayed that *this* one had some talent . . . And when he'd read his first effort he'd felt happier than he'd felt in a very long time.

Law school indeed. This wonderful-looking, vibrant young man who seemed to tune into every word of his could really write . . . And now the boy was seeing more of the real Lavalle. And without a word being spoken he knew that the boy did not just tolerate it, did not just go past it, but saw it for what it really was. Great minds need great excesses. He looked down from his lounge and was pleased to see that Ron wore short sleeves so that his muscular arms were apparent. Yes, and the lotus position was just right for those snug-fitting slacks. Were they worn on purpose for today's visit? If so they were effective, though really unnecessary . . . He'd liked what he'd seen from the beginning . . . But he'd better be careful, not to be too flagrant and scare the boy away . . . It was too early to move . . . Ahh, but the anticipation . . .

Professor Lavalle reached under his lounge and picked up Ron's second act. "Splendid. Absolutely splendid." He tossed the script to Ron. "I've made some notes but let's discuss the main things. First, the two women are alive and well . . . You are giving them total credibility and their behavior toward Tony is very clear and altogether delightful . . . Both mother and daughter working for the Yankee [he gave it a slight West Indian accent *à la* the Andrews Sisters] Boy. As the second-act curtain descends my mouth waters for their inevitable confrontation in the third act . . ." He slid off the lounge onto a pillow opposite Ron, joined him in a lotus position, his robe draped over his thighs. Ron tensed against reacting to this. And wondered if the professor was wearing anything under that robe?

"Now we come to a potential trouble-spot. The boy, Tony. You see, writers are blocked on the character that's closest to their own. The confusions of the author appear in the confusion of the character, who becomes too passive or sentimental or whatever. Perhaps Tony is you?"

"Me? I've never been in a situation like that."

"That's not the point. What is Tony?"

"What is he?"

"Yes. What's his sex life like?"

"I-I don't know . . ."

"You don't know Tony's sex life? I bet you could write in great detail the way Debbie and her boyfriend go at each other in the back of the car or even the way Mrs. Shea made love to her husband, but your main character's sex life is a mystery to you?" A playful smile. "Does Tony like boys or girls?"

"Girls, of course."

"Oh? Here's a scene early in the second act where this cute little Debbie is swishing her behind in Tony's face and he's off talking about how he feels like digging a hole in the ground . . . Come, come . . . No one's about, why doesn't he grab a little feel? . . . Hey?"

"Well, he might be afraid that someone is coming or he really might be more attracted to the mother . . ."

"Might? If you don't mind, let the *audience* experience the ambiguity, not the playwright. When you wrote that scene did you feel how Tony would feel looking at Debbie alone in the house?"

Ron was feeling a little sick now. It was no good. No good. Professor Lavalle was right . . . He didn't have a clear idea in his head about Tony, the character was bloodless, sexless—

"What's the matter?"

"Nothing," Ron said, turning away.

Lavalle moved closer to Ron. "Tell me, dear boy." (Ron could smell the cologne.) "The character needs a little work, that's all. He needs clarity. We need to define his action."

"How can I define his action?"

"You need to define yours. When you free yourself from your own confusions about certain things then your character can be free too. He can go at Debbie or her mother as a young boy should go at attractive women or perhaps go at Debbie's boyfriend, if you choose to have him go that way. Do you understand?"

"Yes, I guess . . ."

Lavalle put his hand softly on Ron's shoulder, gently running his finger on Ron's collarbone. "You're a bit shook up, aren't you? Scared that your work isn't good and that I'll drop you?"

Ron nodded.

"You sweet boy, I wouldn't drop you . . . You have genuine talent . . . promise. I love this work. I'm anxious to show it to my agent. It has, dear boy, found great favor with me. I reward you . . . I knight you . . ."

Ron lifted his head. Lavalle had gotten to his knees. He leaned over Ron and gently kissed him first on the left shoulder then on the right then softly and lingeringly on the forehead. The robe had fallen away, revealing his long, graceful penis, rising . . .

Ron, unthinking, took the professor's left hand and kissed his fingers as if he were kissing the hand of the monarch who had just knighted him. Lavalle let out a small sigh and looked down at his grateful subject kissing his hand. He moved his still rising member to the boy and when it touched Ron's arm he let it stay a moment before he moved it gently onto the boy's small vaccination mark. Ron kissed it. The royal scepter. Professor Lavalle put his hands on his hips and slightly spread his legs, feeling every bit like Henry the Eighth in his prime, surveying his kingdom.

So he was one. He finally knew it. It felt natural, wonderful, exciting, full—in short, everything.

After he left the professor he took a subway down to Greenwich Village. He walked around saying a silent hello to every homosexual he passed, paying a silent homage to them now, apologizing and promising amends for past shunning. God, they're beautiful, he thought. I'm beautiful. I am one of them.

Dear Lenny,

You'd better write me now! I'm in love with a wonderful *man*. My professor, Gerard Lavalle—the one I told you about. He's helped me find out *who* I am. The confusion, the game is over. Yes, dear brother, I tell it to you loud and clear—*I am one.* I'm also happy. Hell, I'm joining the ranks of some of the world's greatest—Shakespeare, Marlowe, Whitman . . . Lenny Starr! All problems solved. Lost identity discovered.

Busy working on the play, minor revisions in second act and on to the third act and it's going well. I'm going to finish it soon and then . . . I want to work in the theater . . . Be a playwright and live openly as I am—as *we* are. I'd love to live with him. But law school? . . . Pop? Mom? What to do?

WRITE! WRITE! WRITE!!!

LOVE

RON

The next time as they lay naked on the soft floor, Gerard stroking Ron's body, he said to Ron in a near-whisper, almost in rhythm to his hand, "This kind of love, unencumbered by the compulsion of procreation, is surely the purest kind of affection in the world . . ."

Ron lay on his stomach.

"*Our* only goal is to give to each other pleasure . . . the means itself being the end . . ."

Ron felt something soft and jelly-like being put in around his anus.

"Don't tense up the way you did the last time, dear boy," Gerard said, kissing him gently around the neck and ears. "The pain is like the frustration and ache before you get a line or character or scene just right. We grow through pain . . . So relax as well as you can, soon it will bring true pleasure."

He was inserting himself into Ron's anus.

Ron winced. The first time Gerard had stopped, but now he was going in all the way. Ron wanted him to, but, oh God . . . it hurt, hurt badly. He was almost crying. "Gerard . . ." he said, fighting back tears, "Gerard!"—it had been the first time he'd used Lavalle's first name—"I love you but . . ."

Lavalle reached in front of Ron to reward him, stroking his penis. "Of course you do . . . Of course . . . Just move into me a bit . . . please . . . Yes . . ."

Ron moved. The pain was so bad that he had to bite his lips hard to keep from screaming.

Lavalle suddenly started to push quickly and deeper, moving his hands wildly over Ron, "Oh yes . . . Your sweet little ass was meant for me, dear boy . . . It feels so good . . . so good . . ."

The room was spinning for Ron. He was beyond pain. It was his own damn fault. He should have relaxed more. But he wouldn't stop. He wouldn't scream or say a word. His teeth were sinking into his lips.

He felt Professor Lavalle convulse into him, and when it was over he finally let himself break down and cry in Lavalle's arms.

"Was that really your first?"

Ron nodded.

"The pain will be forgotten. We can't remember pain or reexperience old pain. That's a blessing. But you will always possess the pleasure that the pain has helped make possible."

They lay silently for a while before Lavalle asked, "Other than the pain, how was it?"

"Wonderful," and settled into those huge protective arms.

Dear Mr. Enthusiasm,

Sorry. Just because you've found yourself and your life, what's to get so excited about? An everyday thing.

Seriously—beautiful. I mean it. Sounds great. I knew that's where you should be at from the beginning but I knew that you couldn't be pushed. That you'd have to find it your own way and you did.

Now for some brotherly advice. Don't get too carried away. Experiment a bit. You don't have to worry about being unfaithful or anything. I bet he's got a wife, hasn't he? (The woman with the flaxen hair had turned out to be a wife. Ron had asked once and Gerard had simply stated the fact without further comment —that was that.) Sometimes these older guys try to use kids ... I'm not saying this is true with your friend, but it never hurts to experiment.

As far as mom and pop are concerned, *don't* come out like I did. You'll kill them. Let them be. Law school? I don't know. Delay it if you're not sure.

You know, in your last letter you were so self-involved that you didn't ask me about a family reconciliation. I've got another year or two here in Japan. After that maybe. I've learned a lot here, learned about my own ego and how large it is. You can't get your body and your reflexes right without conquering your mind as well. I'm beginning to understand myself and the whole family a lot better now. The kind of thing they had to face with me wasn't too easy for them. We'll see about a reconciliation.

Meanwhile. Keep writing and I'll try to write more often myself and of course you'd better send me free tickets and plane fare for the Broadway opening.

Love

Lenny

In the Starr home the click of the typewriter in Ron's room combined with the blast of heroic German classical music transmitted new energy. Blanche was in love with everything now, seeing beauty in every leaf, playing the piano again, painting and even being kind and warm toward Louis.

And Louis, even though his son was making weekly trips into that hellish New York, was content too. The boy had been accepted at law school and would be starting in the fall. The University of Indiana, his old alma mater. Louis hadn't been back there for years and now in September he'd drive Ron there, father and son across half of America. He'd visit around a bit. There'd be a few old professors still around and of course there'd be the town and the campus. He'd gone to AAA and had a road map carefully marked, mentally driving the car with Ron almost every night before he went to bed.

One morning, at breakfast, listening to the clicking of the typewriter Louis said to Blanche, "Isn't the boy looking good lately?"

"Yes," Blanche said, letting it burst out as if it were a song. "He's looking marvelous."

"Do you think he's in love?" Louis asked her.

"Ohh, I wonder." It was the first time she'd thought of it.

"Why don't you find out? Who knows, we might be having a marriage on our hands?"

Blanche giggled. "He's too young."

"He'll be twenty-one soon. They issue licenses at that age you know."

Blanche leaned back on the chair and sipped her tea slowly. She felt warm and good all over. "Marriage . . ." she said.

Louis, seeing the Blanche Rosenzweig in the law office twenty years ago, smiled at her. "Grandchildren . . ." he said.

She saw the young balding lawyer of years ago too, and she repeated, "Grandchildren . . ." She'd never thought of that either.

Louis gently put his hand on hers, and she turned her palm up and gently squeezed it.

Their hands went back to their teacups, and as they finished the rest of their breakfast in silence they each, in their own way, thought about Lenny. Their other son.

When Ron finished his second-act revisions and the third act he sent them off to Gerard. After waiting a few days he called and he waited to hear the verdict.

"I think it's ready."

Ron nearly choked.

"I want you to bring in copies and have the entire third act and parts of the new second act read at the coming meeting."

"All right."

"How does it feel to have finished your first draft of your first full-length play?"

"Good."

"More than good, it's marvelous."

He was on his way!

The inner circle had been developing a foster-parent feeling about his work, as if they were nurturing a baby. Ron loved carrying her (he thought of the play as a "she"), being asked about its progress the way a pregnant woman is asked questions about the life inside her. Now when they'd finished reading the play there was an awkward silence. Everything had sounded bad tonight, Ron felt, but he'd thought that before and everyone had loved it, yet tonight . . . Lines and words came off at wrong angles, people fidgeted . . .

Professor Lavalle lit his pipe slowly. "Comments?"

Marsha, replacing a cigarette in her ivory holder, nervously said, "What happened?"

Ron felt as if Marsha had jabbed him.

"It's off."

Someone else said, "Yes." It was a new member from school named Paul. Ron never liked him—a smart-ass intellectual.

Professor Lavalle nodded and turned to a girl named Celia, an actress that Larry knew who came along to read the role of Debbie. "What's your impression, young lady?"

"Something seems to have gone wrong . . . I don't know."

Professor Lavalle turned to Larry. "Seems fine to me," Larry said adamantly. He never seemed more Roman.

"Seems fine to you?"

"Yes."

"Paul, what say you?"

"It's as if the third act doesn't belong with the second act, which I felt hardly belonged with the first act."

Ron wanted to say something but his throat was closed. His

143

mind too. Why didn't the professor mow them down, slam his hand palm down on the table and tell them what idiots they were?

"They're right, you know. It's off. I've seen it from the moment of the opening of the second act. It can be set right, though, by simply remembering a few of the basic precepts of drama. Watch." He mimed rolling up his sleeves to go to work. "Marsha, who in your opinion is the main character of this play?"

"Debbie, the daughter." She answered as if the question itself were absurd.

The professor nodded and turned to Celia. "Celia, who is the main character of this play?"

Celia was looking at Marsha as if Marsha had said the most ridiculous thing in the world. "It's the mother, of course. Mrs. Shea."

He turned to Larry, "Mr. Edelman, who is the main character of this play?"

Ron knew what Larry would say before he even said it. "Tony."

"Tony." Lavalle looked at Ron to see if he was getting the message. He wasn't, he was dizzy and beginning to tune out what was happening.

Lavalle turned to Paul. "Paul, who do you think is the main character?"

"At first I thought there was no main character. I took it as a sort of group psychodrama with all the characters moving in accordance with the seasons of the land—the planting, the harvest . . . that kind of thing. I liked that concept. Then in the second act I thought it was the boy, then the mother, and then I didn't give much of a fuck anymore because it was only degenerating into a battle of who was going to fuck who and I didn't much care."

"Ron, who is the main character of this play?"

"Tony."

"Then why is the audience so confused? You've let the action get muddled. By having too many focuses you've wound up with none."

Well, all right, then he'd go to law school and that would be that.

The professor was droning on . . . "Even though the main character needn't be the one the audience is necessarily sympathetic toward he must be the one who carries the action, who involves us . . . Ron, do you know what you have to do?"

Ron nodded, feeling numb. He was a fool to think he could just bang out a play and have it on Broadway and have his life, his glamorous life in the theater, all set. He had no real talent. What the hell did he have to say anyway?

When a meeting was over it was the custom of everyone to file out and say good night to Professor Lavalle by the door. Ron had usually been the last but now he was the first. He wanted to shake the professor's hand in a perfunctory way, get out and back upstate and away from this awful crunch. But Lavalle held Ron's hand tightly, and wouldn't let him get away. He said goodbye to everyone else as they filed past him, holding Ron prisoner in his huge, surprisingly strong hand. Ron just leaned against the wall as they went past him, feeling like a court-martialed soldier as he bowed his head and looked down. Usually they all waited at the elevator for each other.

"You'll call me in fifteen minutes?" Lavalle said. Ron couldn't talk. He just turned away. Lavalle squeezed his hand and gently caressed his cheek. "Call me . . . please . . ."

Ron nodded. And then Lavalle sent him to join the others at the elevator. The ride down was painful. Marsha touched his arm and Celia tried to catch his eye to show sympathy. Paul clearly was pleased. Ron felt like socking him. Larry's loyalty, or stupidity, was almost audible.

Downstairs he turned away from all of them without saying goodbye. He found an outdoor phone booth and immediately dialed the professor's number. His wife answered.

"I'd like to speak to Professor Lavalle."

"He's retiring. Call him tomorrow, please."

"I-I can't. I'd like to talk to him now . . ."

"I'm sorry, it's rather late. I'll inform him that you've called."

"All right . . . I'll try to call tomorrow . . ."

"Yes, good night."

"Good night . . ." but as Ron was about to put the phone down he heard a click on the other end and then the voice, "I'll take it. Ron?" She clicked off.

"Oh, I thought . . ."

"Come up."

"I was going to go home."

"Come up. Now. I'll let you in."

"All right."

"I'll wait."

"Goodbye."

"Goodbye."

Lenny was right, Ron thought on the way up. Old guys who try to take advantage of young ones. Talk about the casting couch. I'll put your play on Broadway, young man. Just you come on over here on my little ol' Oriental mat . . .

Lavalle was waiting for him. Ron walked past the open door and straight into the study. There was no incense or soft lights tonight . . . There'd better not be.

He turned and glared at Lavalle as the door was being shut.

"Loaded for bear, are you? Do you have anything to say to me?"

"No."

"Are you going to give up?"

"I'm going to law school. If I have time maybe I'll work on the play. Maybe not."

"When did you decide that?"

"It's what I'd decided all along. I lied to you . . . to get into the inner circle. I always intended to go to law school. I'd hoped to have the play completed by then."

"You were just using me, then?"

"Yes, I never really thought that I'd make a career in the

146

theater. It's too rough and I don't know if I have that kind of talent. I'm sorry."

"De rien. It's happened before."

"Yeah, that's life. Well, I'd better be getting back."

Lavalle's eyes never left Ron's face. He went to the door and put his hand on the knob. Ron walked toward it, turning his face away. Lavalle didn't open the door. He took Ron's shoulder with one large arm and brought Ron into him, kissing his head and hugging him gently. Ron tried to jerk away but couldn't. "Gerard, let me go, damn it . . ."

"Don't be a fool. You have enormous talent." He kissed Ron's cheek. "Why didn't you tell me it was going off?" Ron said, suddenly looking directly at him for the first time, not caring about the wetness that could be seen in his eyes.

"Because then you wouldn't have gotten it all out. Trust me, I know how to work with writers. You had to get a first draft out. And you have to be able to take that kind of rough criticism in the theater. It's your baptism by fire. Now we can go to work on what's there."

Lavalle kissed him and they moved impulsively into each other. Lavalle gently put Ron on the mat, helped him take off his clothes. They made love, this time not as king and subject but as two equal, sharing partners.

It was only days before the scheduled trip to Indiana for orientation. Ron had not been able to find a way to approach his parents. Louis was up on every detail of his entrance into school and the trip. He'd written an old teacher who was now a dean and had been invited to stay over for a few days at the dean's house. He checked and rechecked his son's papers and transcripts to make sure there were no errors. He hadn't had all the cash for tuition and he'd borrowed money. He was proud that he could make this sacrifice. There was a sharp new vibrancy to him now so that the firm began to throw more business his way and things were "coming along in fine style."

Mother was an enigma. She talked a bit derisively about "the lawyer" but seemed content that Ron was going to law school. Ron appeased her with talk about the theater. He also wanted her to confront him, make him reveal his real hunger for the theater and thereby carry the news to his father. It wasn't working. Where the hell were her artistic pretensions now that he needed them!

He'd been practicing the piano a good deal lately and sounding pretty fair. It struck him that he was doing it to further motivate his mother and laughed at his own deceitfulness. Except he enjoyed it too. He was playing Beethoven's "Rondo in C" and wondered if Gerard had a piano somewhere in that cavernous apartment of his . . . Yes, probably on the wife's side. He thought of it as sides, His and Her towels. He'd like to play for Gerard. He visualized his lover listening to him in silent appreciation, pleased to discover a new dimension in him—a soft touch on his shoulder. Blanche sat next to him on the piano bench. "You played that like a man in love," she said.

Ron stared at her.

"You don't think your mother knows, huh? You can't hide these things from mothers, especially mothers who believe in looking under the surface."

"Mom, I am in love but it's a problem. She's in the theater . . . and I don't want to leave her . . ."

"Oh, but law school?"

"I know."

"Oh dear . . . Well, these things work out. Write to her, of course, and there's intersession and holidays—"

"Mom. There's more."

"You've gotten her in trouble?"

"No. It's not that. I want to be with her. I want to *be* in the theater."

Blanche didn't seem to hear him. She seemed to be absorbed with looking at the music of the Beethoven Rondo. Ron had to repeat himself. She turned to him. "You're having a full relationship, aren't you?"

"Of course."

"What's her name?" Blanche asked suddenly, as if interrogating.

Celia. No, that's Larry's girl. "Marsha," Ron said quickly, hoping that his hesitation didn't show.

"Marsha is a nice name. I always liked that actress Marsha Hunt. I wonder what ever happened to her. Sophisticated, yet so pretty and delicate."

"Yes." He had to head her off at the pass. "You see we're talking about marriage and children and everything but it's too soon. We don't know each other that well yet."

"Of course. Mustn't jump into anything."

"But you see, I'm so involved in my play and Professor Lavalle is almost ready to show it to his agent . . . He's a Broadway agent, mom . . . I just have a few revisions that may take a little time . . ."

"Do you ever hear from Lenny? I heard from him." She seemed again to be talking to the Beethoven Rondo. "He wrote me from Japan. He wants to see me when he comes back . . ."

Ron went to her, got on his knees in front of her and put his hand on hers. She turned to him and looked intently at him.

"Mom," he said, "Marsha and I want to get married, be a husband and wife in the theater. She's in advertising, but she's a director and a writer too . . . And she wants a family and so do I—"

"A family?" It was all right then. This one was all right.

"Yes, mom, a family." And at the moment, as Ron looked at his mother, he wished to God that what he was saying were true, because he really loved her very much . . . He hugged her, and she hugged him back.

"All right," she said, "tell me what you want."

Just like writing a scene. What one character wants from the other, he thought, good technique. Action, conflict, resolution.

He told her. A delay of just one semester, an allowance to live in New York and work full-time with Professor Lavalle on the play without having to take some energy-wasting job like driving a cab or waiting on tables.

Yes, all right, she would talk to his father. They'd work something out, just leave father to her . . .

The scene had gone well. Mother reassured of her son's heterosexuality, son ending with a strong ally . . . And son feeling very damned shitty about the whole thing. Talk about contrived . . .

For two days the house was filled with muffled thunder. His father was a stormy pale shadow to Ron, a hurt, wounded old man who wouldn't even look him in the eye. Explosions of words would come out of his parents' bedroom, abruptly stop.

Ron concentrated on the play. He started back with the second act and became Tony against this new world he'd found himself in. It actually began to feel better, more life seemed to be coming into it . . .

One night he looked up from his typewriter and saw his father standing in the doorway, watching him. He didn't know how long he'd been there.

"Can I come in?"

"Sure."

Louis sat on the edge of his bed.

"I've never been an arbitrary man, you know that don't you, son?"

"Yes, dad."

"Not one of those fathers who insist that the son follow in his footsteps . . . be a chip off the old block, that kind of nonsense. Not me. After all, let's face it . . . I haven't had the most brilliant career in the law, my brother who manufactures sweaters and never finished high school could buy and sell me. You know that, don't you?"

"I know about Uncle Morris."

"Even my sister, a schoolteacher and married to a guy who

150

works for the State Motor Vehicle Authority, Irving . . . You ever meet Irving?"

Before Ron could answer Louis said, "A jerk. But they probably could buy and sell me too. They have every nickel they ever made. But look . . . I think this thing with New York and the theater and that professor is the *wrong* thing for you—that's all. It's just not the kind of life you're suited for."

"You might be right, dad, but I just want to try it for a while before I start law school—"

"I *understand* that . . . Look, I'm disappointed but I understand. But can't you just stay home and write, the way you've been doing all summer? Then go into the city for your classes with the professor?"

"Dad, I know how you feel and I'm sorry, really sorry, I'm disappointing you. I know how much you looked forward to going back to your old school and me going there and being a lawyer and—"

"It's not important what I feel."

"Sure it is. I may eventually be a lawyer, but right now I'm sort of driven by this thing and I've got to work it out . . . I can't go to law school feeling this way and do it justice—"

"I know."

"Look, dad, I know I could stay up here and write but that would be the long way around and frustrating as hell. Professor Lavalle will work with me every day. I need that. If we can just get a few scenes right my play will go to his agent and then I can do whatever I want."

Louis didn't say anything for a very long time. Then: "This Professor Lavalle. He's very interested in you?"

"He's interested in anyone with some talent."

"Doesn't he teach at college?"

"Yes. He teaches two days and commutes to the city."

"Where does he live, in the Village?"

Ron thought, Thank God, he doesn't. "No, he lives up on Central Park West." Ron wanted to throw in somehow that he

151

had a wife but he didn't want to seem too anxious.

"Married?"

"Yes," Ron said, grateful. "His wife is a well-known art critic, writes for magazines. Mom has heard of her."

"Oh good, good . . ." Louis leaned back against the wall. "Got a girl, have you?"

"Yes."

"Thinking about getting married, I hear."

"Well, it's a little soon yet."

"How long have you known her?"

"Just a few months."

"Sure it's soon. Kids today aren't like we were. I mean in the sense of . . . having to wait until you had a full kind of thing with each other—right, son?"

"It's different, yes."

Louis' forehead and scalp had reddened a bit. "You and your girl . . . ahh . . ."

Ron saved his father further embarrassment. *"Sure,* dad."

Louis nodded, peered at Ron. "You know what I mean?"

"Yes, dad, I do. I tell you, there are no problems along those lines." Ron made sure that his father and he were looking directly at each other. "Dad, I know what you're worried about so please let me tell you that there is *nothing,* absolutely nothing, to worry about."

Louis smiled, stood up and walked about the room. He picked up a hair brush from the dresser and dropped it, ran his hand over the wall poster of Kennedy that Ron had left up after the last election.

"So you want to live in New York and write and work with this professor and see about law school later."

Ron stood up too. "Yes, dad."

"Why don't you bring this young lady up here for dinner or a weekend soon?"

"Oh, well, I don't know, dad . . ." Ron laughed. "I mean she's so busy and all—"

152

"Well, she's probably not busy weekends . . . Love to meet her. Mother would too."

"Well, I don't know . . . We're not quite at the meeting-of-parents stage yet . . . When I live in the city and I see more of her then we can come up here for a weekend."

Louis had turned mean, suspicious now. With a tension in his voice that Ron had rarely ever heard, he said, "No, son, let's meet her *now.*"

Before any decisions were going to be made about New York, Ron realized he'd better have a genuine Marsha. "Dad, we're really *not* at that stage yet—" Ron started to say but stopped. Louis was clearly furious. He went to the door, looked at Ron with the same kind of contempt that he'd looked at Lenny, with the same kind of contempt that the hoodlums in Binghamton had looked at them all, with the same kind of contempt that everyone had for him and "his kind."

He knows, Ron knew. He may not even know that he knows, but oh my god, he knows.

Louis opened the door and said in a very loud voice, "I am not going to support anyone living in New York. I do not like New York and I never will. I do not, I repeat, I do not care a damn about what your mother says. I will not put myself in debt for writing *plays* in New York. Write here, son, to your little heart's content."

There was a huge silence in the house. He yelled, "Blanche!"

The door of the bedroom opened. Blanche stuck a head out of the door and Louis screamed at it.

"My decision is final. Goddamn it, no!"

Then with one last look at his son, he slammed the door and marched to his study, where he closed the door and hammered himself down into his overstuffed chair.

CHAPTER 8

"**W**hy don't you pull over to the side and come in the back seat. You seem so far away."

"I can't."

"Why not?"

"I'm on duty now. I'm driving."

"You can pull over. Leave the clock running if you like."

"I've got to be in the garage by eleven o'clock."

"What's the matter with you? Who are you kidding? I can tell, you know."

"I have somebody."

"So do I. But so what?" The man with the British accent

154

moved into the jump seat of the cab, put his face as close to Ron's ear as possible and whispered, "My mouth waters for you. Let me *do* you . . . That's all . . . It'll only take a second . . . I *guarantee* that."

Ron turned his head slightly to look back at the aquiline nose and elegant face of the gentleman he'd picked up outside the Waldorf. The man resembled a British actor, Michael Wilding, or was it Michael Redgrave? Anyway, he didn't find the offer attractive. It seemed sleazy, somehow . . . This elegant man from Britain strolling out of the Waldorf, looking so distinguished and then propositioning a New York cab driver after five minutes of rambling, idle, forced chatter.

Besides, after he brought the car into the garage he was going to see Gerard to give him his third rewrite of the third act, and he was sure they'd be able to spend more time together than they had been lately.

He badly needed to talk to Gerard.

His mother had had to cut down drastically on her allowance to him thanks to a long siege of doddering his father was going through, which cut down the entire family's income considerably. He had had to move from his one small but private room to a large railroad flat on the West Side that he shared with three other men, all having their own room and sharing common kitchen, toilet and living room. The shared space was a mess and Ron had given up talking to the others about it. Privately he called his three roommates Depression, Paranoia, and Alcoholism—and no symptom of any of the diseases involved cleanliness. He wished for a neurotic-compulsive cleaner. Driving a taxi cab was even worse—the ugliness of the men at the shape-up, the slogging through New York streets, the way he was treated by passengers and in turn the contemptuous way he was beginning to treat them. He hated the way he was changing. The people of his New York world seemed in eternal darkness, their common ground their alienation. One could match neuroses, touch base on grievances, but only those—he even began to see what his father meant by hating New York. He longed for hometown simplicity and friendliness and he was even beginning to think about going back to that existence. A year of this life was enough.

Yet he wanted Gerard to talk him out of it and encourage him the way he had all that year. Besides, when Gerard saw how unhappy he was he'd make sure to satisfy him.

The Britisher whispered, "Let me bless it for you."

"Bless it?"

"Yes, your lover will thank me. There'll be a spiritual depth— an extra dimension that wasn't there before . . . He'll feel it. I'll wager he'll even tell you."

Ron stopped at a red light and turned around to see if the man was kidding. He couldn't tell, there was a weird playfulness about him. He had never followed his brother's advice on experimenting and he really didn't want to, but this guy was getting him very curious. It was night in midtown and he could just pull over next to one of the large quiet office buildings . . .

He did.

Making sure that the man in the back knew who was in command he said sharply, "Come in front."

"There's more room in the back."

"In front."

"Very well." The Britisher quickly got out of the cab, making sure that his scarf and coat were secure to protect him from the brisk October wind. He slid into the front seat and immediately moved close to Ron, his hand fumbling at Ron's crotch.

Should I stop him? Ron asked himself. No . . . the hell with it . . . It hasn't been all that great lately . . . not great at all . . .

The man had a nice touch, as elegant and crisp in its way as he was. Ron felt very responsive. As the man bent over him Ron noted that he hadn't even taken off his hat, a distinguished black homburg. Pretty damn droll.

He removed the hat and in so doing brushed the scarf away and saw the high stiff white collar. He quickly moved the scarf, revealing a *minister's* collar.

156

"God," and had no sense of the irony of his expression, only the shock he felt. Hearing Ron's exclamation, the man looked up, totally revealing his collar. "I'm not a priest, you know, with their vows of chastity. I'm Church of England." Proudly.

Ron, like his father, had grown up to look upon that collar with more reverence in a way than the followers of the religion. It stood for the keeper of the Protestant spire, gentile respectability, down-home friendliness . . . He moved quickly into the corner of his seat and zipped himself up. "Look, it's okay . . . I mean you being a . . . Well, I have to get into the garage . . . I'll call you later . . . Give me your room number . . ."

The man didn't seem to hear him. He patted his wispy gray hair in place, carefully put on his homburg and fixed his scarf. "What do you have on the clock?"

"Just two twenty-five."

He reached into his inner jacket pocket and brought out a billfold, gave Ron a five, waiving the balance as a tip. A very nice tip.

He put his hand on the door handle. "Do you know of any good places?"

"Not really. I never go. Let me take you back to your hotel."

"No. I'll walk or get another cab on the corner."

"Look, seriously, give me your room number and I'll call you."

The minister opened the door and stepped out; before he closed it he said to Ron, "No. You don't mean it. You just want to make me feel better for the moment. If I give you my room number I'll only sit alone waiting for your call which will never come. Your someone is a lucky man. Goodbye."

Ron hurried to his "lucky man."

The worst, he thought, is to be like that. He said he had somebody so why was he cruising? Goddamm it, I'll never be that way. If you have someone you stay with them like any normal couple instead of degrading yourself. So many of them are just always reaching their hands out to touch anyone's cock. Not me. Not ever.

Except I was in the front seat with that man. I say that's different, but that's what everyone says. I better get things straight with Gerard . . . I don't like the way I'm turning . . . I don't like the way this is turning me . . .

As Ron was walking into the apartment building he passed someone vaguely familiar. He went to the elevator and stopped just before pressing the button.

Was that Sean?

He'd only seen Sean once, at Sean's beheading so to speak, but still . . . And it had been about a year ago . . . but still . . .

He quickly walked back out of the building, looking to his right in time to see the man turn the corner.

Ron followed quickly, the October wind clipping his face sharply. He broke into a run, inexplicably needing to know if this really was Sean.

The man had gone into the subway station. Ron followed him. Prepared to go on the platform or into the train if necessary.

It wasn't necessary. The tall man was fumbling for change at the turnstile, and Ron saw him plainly.

It was Sean—except it wasn't. He couldn't be sure. There was a rugged young man where before at the inner-circle meeting there had been a delicate ascetic one. Had the delicate features been roughed and aged, or was it just that this wasn't the same person? Ron hoped this wasn't Sean because if it was and he was seeing Gerard then Ron was in deep trouble and he felt sick because this man who had now found his change and put it into the turnstile was beautiful—goddamn achingly sickeningly beautiful.

He went back to Gerard's apartment house and up the elevator. When he rang the bell it was Mrs. Lavalle who opened the door and peered out of the crack. He hadn't seen her in months. Actually he'd never seen her—fully that is; through the year that he'd been coming there he'd seen flaxen hair, an eye here or a foot there, a hand or an arm as it answered a door or closed one; mostly, though, she was a voice, mellifluous yet piercing. He'd

158

teased Gerard once, suggesting that perhaps she didn't exist at all —perhaps she was the product of a special-effects department of a movie studio that the professor had influence with, her purpose being to prevent Ron from asking to move in and share quarters. That had been received coldly. They never talked about the "other presence" inhabiting the recesses of the large apartment like the inevitable mad relative in old Gothic novels.

"Is Gerard in?" he asked.

A thin arm slithered quickly out at him, the veins like scraggly streams of dirty water running through an ugly wood. It scared him. He'd never seen this much of her before. She must be tall, he thought, even through his fear.

"Is Gerard in?" he repeated to the reed-like fingers.

"He's retired for the night. He left instructions for you to leave your material."

"No. I want to see him."

"He's retired for the night. He left instructions . . ."

"No."

The arm slowly withdrew.

"Wait," he said to it—stopping it. "Here." He put the manuscript carefully in the palm, fascinated, as though watching a cannibal plant fold in on its food, watched the fingers grasp the manuscript, the arm withdraw and the door close.

On his way back down he found himself thinking of the most felicitous way of committing suicide. One of his roommates, Depression, had been talking about it yesterday. Ron felt as depressed as he was sure Depression was. Almost everyone he'd been talking to in New York these days had tried it at least once.

He tried to rid himself of the feeling by going to the Village. He'd no longer practice a fidelity that no one expected or cared about. He'd gone about the Village a great deal the past year, talking to, getting to know a great many of the men who hung out outside of the bars and in the little parks. He always brought extra cigarettes—he'd taken to steady smoking for his nerves now that he was a full-fledged cab driver—and extra money to give out.

In its way New York was a small town too. He'd stayed aloof from any other liaisons, though, taking a good bit of needling about his unnecessary fidelity.

But tonight he wanted someone. Why did he stop the Englishman? To hell with fidelity. To what? Gerard and Sean? Ron could picture the scene, that bastard letting his new old lover out and then turning to his ghost wife and saying . . . "Oh, when Ron what's-his-name calls just take the manuscript and send him on his way . . . Tell the dear boy that I'm retired for the night, or any other little thing you want . . ."

Ron wondered if his wife knew. Were they kinky? Maybe he went into details with her and she got off on it. Sick. Did they laugh at him? Did he and his new-old lover Sean laugh at him? Sean was great-looking, he'd like to fuck him himself . . . Maybe he'd ask Gerard to stage an orgy. Gerard should like the job—the great director . . .

Was that Sean?

Maybe he was being paranoid—like one of his roommates—it was catching. Depression first—now Paranoia . . .

No, that was Sean. Gerard had been obviously cold lately. He was getting tired of him. Well, it was mutual.

It started to pour and everyone went inside. Ron was going to go into one of the bars but he stopped. He had very little money. He'd go back to his apartment and calm himself.

When he went back there were a girl and a boy in the hallway outside of his door that he'd never seen before. They were very involved with each other. No sneaking for them, he thought, they could go into strange halls and pump against each other to their hearts' content.

He went directly to his room and sat on his cot and reached under the bed for the bottle of Scotch that he kept there, and without pouring it into a glass swigged hungrily.

Alcoholism too? he reflected as he lay down to sleep. I've caught them all, I guess. Rock bottom.

The next day he called Lavalle at 9:30 in the morning, ready to disguise his identity to get through if Mrs. Lavalle answered and tried to block him. It wasn't necessary. Lavalle picked up the phone.

"Hello, Gerard."

"Ron, how are you?"

"Fine."

"Just got up and having my coffee."

"I'd like to see you this morning, if you have time. About my play."

"I haven't had a chance to read the new third act—"

"That's all right. What I have to discuss doesn't involve the new third act."

"Well—"

"It's important and I won't take much of your time. I promise."

"Oh well, of course. Come up in about an hour then. Ron?"

"Yes?"

"Are you all right?"

"I'm fine."

He showered and carefully combed his hair. He put on the one suit that he'd taken with him from upstate and was glad that even though he'd gained some weight it still fit him well. The tie and the shirt he selected were sharp-looking and when he was finished he looked at himself in the mirror with satisfaction. When he put the papers together into the black attaché case that he'd brought with him from upstate and then looked in the mirror again he could have been the epitome of the young Madison Avenue executive.

Gerard opened the door himself, and Ron walked in confidently. He was delighted to see the stare as he was being looked over. Like what you see, Gerard?

"Well, well. Look at you."

Ron smiled, said nothing.

"Coffee?"

"Yes, please."

"Go right into the study and I'll bring it right in."

Ron, instead, pretended he hadn't heard the invitation and casually walked to the dining-room table. Lavalle checked himself from repeating the invitation, noting that Ron seemed to be in some sort of state and from experience knew it was wisest to let such states run their course—although seeing Ron this handsome and fresh-looking certainly gave him a morning appetite.

Ron sat at the large rectangular table facing Sir Rusty as Gerard was getting the coffee. He hadn't been in this room for a long time. He'd dropped out of the inner circle because he'd been working so closely with Gerard and had lost contact with Larry, everybody, including Sir Rusty. Who's going to get the ax today, my squeaky knight?

As Gerard brought the coffee in it occurred to him that Ron in his suit and with his attaché case looked like a salesman ready to make a presentation. He recalled the time someone had come to sell him land in Florida, or was it a burial plot? Anyway, it had been quite a challenge, the man had been quite charming and they'd wound up nicely in the study.

Ron sipped the coffee. "You certainly know how to make good coffee, Gerard."

Gerard nodded. Salesmen use flattery too, he thought . . . The boy had been drinking the coffee for almost a year and never said a word.

He waited.

"Gerard, over a year ago I started to write a play about a boy who's confused and who winds up on a farm with a mother and daughter. I thought I knew what I wanted to say. Wasn't quite sure but I had an idea. Since that time I've rewritten it so many times I've gotten lost in it. I've written a play about a daughter who tries to seduce her mother's lover. Then another one about a mother who tries to seduce her daughter's lover. Then one about a boy who's not quite sure if he wants to seduce the mother, daughter or the daughter's boyfriend. Recently I began thinking from the perspective of the mother's middle-aged suitor, making him the main character, and I contemplated having him—that poor small-town drugstore clerk—want to kill the lot of them. I finally stopped myself. I'm caught in a hopeless morass of rewrites and rewrites of rewrites and tangled perspectives. Now before I get totally lost, or start writing it from the point of view of their cow, or something, I'd like you to call your agent and introduce me and I'd like to hand him this manuscript, which is in the best state I can put it, and hear what he has to say."

"My agent? I don't have an agent."

Ron felt sick.

"I fired the son of a bitch almost a year ago. He's suing me. The ingrate! Can you imagine. I was negotiating my own deals, publishers didn't want to deal with him so I let him go. He was a thief . . . But you could try producers directly. I have a listing of them. Make sure, though, that you copyright the play first . . . Yes, you *should* get on to something new . . ."

Professor Lavalle put his hand over Ron's and squeezed it.

"What's the matter?"

Ron just shrugged.

"I think you should definitely put this work aside, yes, start on something new . . . You'll come back to this in a year and it'll all open up to you . . . Come back into the meetings . . . The contact will do you good. All new people, quite stimulating. Do you know that Noel Coward wrote over thirty plays before his first success?" He stood up and whispered into his ear. "Come in the study, Ron . . . come . . ." He stood and let Gerard walk him into the study, caressing him.

Yes, Gerard will do his damnedest to satisfy me today, Ron thought—he really likes the way I look . . . the image . . . He likes unbuttoning my *business* suit and taking off my tie and now my shirt, button by button. He'll go into every crevice of my body that he knows gives me pleasure . . . Yes, there he is now . . . He knows what *that* usually does to me and yes, it's doing it . . . He's encouraged at my reaction, getting his own clothes off in a hurry now . . . God, you've gained weight since we've started, Gerard, your skin is losing its firmness. Are you forty yet? Why didn't you say earlier that you had no agent? The thought of that makes me soft . . . You look up, wonder why. You're so fucking insensitive, you going-to-fat bastard. Eat me some more. I'll play the king now.

Ron got on his knees and put his hands on his hips *à la* Henry the Eighth. Gerard enjoyed it. He would play slave.

Do I taste good, serf, Ron thought, looking down on Lavalle's thinning brown hair. Getting bald too—and look at you, one ear is twisted convex and the other concave. I never noticed that before. You are indeed one ugly serf. How do I taste, serf? As good as Sean?

Ron stood up abruptly, pulling himself out of Gerard, who looked up at Ron as Ron looked down on him. Ron put his right foot in the professor's face, and shoved as hard as he could. Lavalle fell over with a grunting thud.

Well, there was something new and exciting in playing the punished serf to Ron's furious king. He crawled to Ron. Ron pushed him away. He was putting on his pants and grabbing his shoes and shirt. Lavalle tried to wrest them away. Ron pushed him hard, made a fist. Gerard giggled nervously and came at Ron in an attempt to hold his escaping king.

When Ron opened the study door and was about to run out in his disheveled manner, pants and shirt barely on . . . shoes in hand . . . Lavalle finally realized that the boy was in earnest and truly angry. He grabbed his own robe and, without bothering to do anything but place it loosely in front of him, followed Ron into the hallway.

Ron ran past the dining room. He passed the black attaché case with his play in it and was going to go in and get it, when the front door opened and Mrs. Lavalle came into the house.

She stood in front of him for the first time as a whole person, took in his semi-clothed, panicked state and her husband's semi-naked pursuit, which had terminated at her presence.

Ron was shocked by the way she looked. He'd expected her to

be a witch-like ugly woman with awful teeth and sharp features; instead she looked regal, attractive, and totally self-possessed, her expression slowly changing to disgust, revulsion. And at that moment Ron thought the hell with the play . . . the hell with the whole thing . . . He just wanted to get out, and brushing past Mrs. Lavalle was finally *out* of there.

As he put his clothes on in the hall he had one thought—at least she'd caught darling Gerard . . . Now he hoped she'd cut his balls off.

In Brooklyn there is a section of the Belt Parkway that borders on the cold waters of the Bay. It is well protected from suicidal motorists—whether consciously so or not—by a substantial gate. Ron was more than idly thinking about suicide now. For days he'd driven his cab up and around that section, imagining his cab smashing through that gate and diving with deadly grace into the water. That's the way to go—the way we come—from the water and then back into it.

Sometimes he was whimsical about his depression. Lenny had written from Japan saying that he was finding it very difficult to go on—money and ego problems; the Western ego found it tough to subject itself to the rigors of Eastern martial arts. Ron had also been up to see his parents a few weeks earlier and found his father very slumped, though mother remained indomitably batty.

Yes, perhaps he'd take all the men in the Starr—*Starr* . . . some joke—family on a suicide taxi ride. Throw the clock and hunt down a place that he could bury them all in the water. A single fare for the whole crowd.

Or if not that, then what? Law school? He didn't want to be a lawyer. At least he knew that now. Back to a new play? Remember Noel Coward . . . Except there was no new play in him and was he really any good?

Gerard hadn't gotten in touch, hadn't sent the manuscript back—obviously hadn't even cared about why he was so upset. Maybe he was scared. Maybe his wife had put him on ice. Maybe he was just waiting for Ron to call him . . . So what if that was Sean . . .? One could care for more than one lover at the same time. Everybody said so.

Finally one day he doubled-parked his cab on Second Avenue in the middle of the morning rush hour, went into a bar, dialed the professor's number.

It was Mrs. Lavalle, sounding bright and cheery, who answered. "Hello," she sang out.

Ron muffled his voice. "Is Professor Lavalle home?"

"Hold on, please."

In a moment Ron heard the professor pick up the phone. "Hello," he said crisply.

Ron paused before he could get the words out . . . his throat was very dry. "Gerard," he said, "this is Ron . . ."

Silence at the other end of the phone, then the click of the phone coming to him in a deadly andante.

Cars and trucks were blaring their horns at Ron's double-parked car. Zombie-like, he moved out of the bar and slowly slid into his seat. Someone ran to him and yelled, "Free?"

He didn't reply and the man opened the back door and instantly became part of Ron's team as he yelled back at the horns.

Ron heard a vaguely familiar voice from the back say, "Those sons of bitches. Empire State Building."

He headed out into the traffic. But there was something strange happening to him . . . A hand was on his shoulder and someone was repeating something to him . . . It sounded like his name . . . His shoulder was being shook as if someone were trying to wake him up . . . "Ron . . . Ron . . ."

Perhaps this guy was trying to rob him. He'd never been held up as a cab driver . . . although almost all the drivers at the shape-up had been at one time or another. It seemed to be something that you had to go through at least once.

But it wasn't a hold-up man. It was Larry Edelman.

"Where the hell have you been? I've been trying to get in

touch with you for months now. You moved from your last place and they didn't know where you were."

Ron stopped at a red light and turned fully around to inspect what to him appeared to be a new Larry Edelman in an old body. Larry was very sharp-looking; he had on a bright plaid suit and a solid blue tie and crisply collared shirt. His hair was neatly cut and slicked down in just the right style for him, and he carried a genuine alligator attaché case. More, there was a new vitality, an alertness to him. He didn't seem much like the dumb handsome Roman soldier anymore.

"Are you still writing?" he was asking. "Still studying with Lavalle?"

The shrug and the nod didn't answer the question, but Larry hurried on . . . "Listen, I have to see you, let's make an appointment."

An appointment? Strange word.

"I'll give you my new address, come on up any night," Ron found himself saying.

"At seven o'clock, or would eight be better?"

Ron shrugged. Anytime. It made no difference. He had no place to go.

Larry took out a leather-covered appointment book and jotted down Ron's address, then leaned back in his seat. "We'll talk more tomorrow. I've got to study these figures. I'm meeting with the president of a very big corporation this morning."

Sure. Go ahead, Larry. Ron watched in the mirror as Larry peered at some papers. He'd never studied a script with such attention; he was different, all right. Ron liked him better this way, he seemed to be so alive . . .

When Ron reached the Empire State Building Larry pushed two bills in his hand and dashed out of the cab with a quick, "See you tomorrow, then."

Ron watched him run into the building and then turned to the traffic, his depression free to come back in full force now.

The next evening at seven o'clock sharp Alcoholism tapped shakily on Ron's door.

"There's a guy here to see you."

Who? Ron asked himself.

It wouldn't be Gerard. Gerard wouldn't come here. I doubt if he knows my address. Maybe it's Lenny? Dad? Someone in the Village? No. No one in the Village knows my address. And that's the way I want it. "I don't want to see anybody."

"This guy says he has an appointment with you."

An appointment . . . Oh Jesus, Larry Edelman.

He rolled out of bed. He'd allowed himself and his room to get as dirty and sloppy as everyone else's. He didn't want Larry to come in here. He should put on some clean pants and a shirt and clean himself up before he saw Larry, but somehow he didn't have the energy. Well, Larry was an old friend, he'd just have to understand.

He made his way to the living room, where Larry was standing, beaming at him.

"It's good to see you, Ron," Larry said and shot out his hand. His shake was firm and reassuring, yet strange too . . .

Larry sat on the couch and waved Ron over to sit next to him.

"Ah," Larry said, "I see you've got a piano here. Have you been playing much? Boy, I remember when you played that beautiful Beethoven thing in school . . . you know the one, for Elissa."

" 'Für Elise.' "

"Yeah, it was beautiful."

Ron mumbled thanks and looked at Larry again, closely. Larry had never been like this. Was this put on? It didn't seem so. Except it must be.

Finally Larry cleared his throat. "How are you doing?"

"How am I doing? Larry, I'm doing pretty bad. I don't believe in myself anymore. As a writer or a person. I don't know what the hell I'm going to do . . . I don't want to go to law school . . . You know the other day I drove my cab around and around the Belt Parkway in Brooklyn . . . You know that stretch of road that faces the Bay—and thought of just driving myself into it."

There it was. It was all out of him, unexpectedly. He hadn't planned this. He'd never confided anything to Larry before. Their friendship had been on the surface, but he felt better spilling it out. He needed to have someone to talk to at least.

Larry nodded his head as Ron spoke and listened very carefully. When Ron had finished Larry said, "Um-huh, I mean, how are you doing *financially?*"

"Financially?"

"Yes, for example, are you saving money the way you'd like to . . . ?"

Ron felt nauseous. He was going nuts.

"Ron, are you all right?" Larry was shaking his arm gently.

Ron snapped his head and focused his eyes on Larry. Larry was talking about finances, and he wanted to talk about suicide. Well . . . maybe Larry was right. Look how well he looked. He must be doing something right, no doubt . . .

"Uhh," Ron started, slogging through a dry mouth and almost punch-drunk brain, "I'm doing all right. I pay my rent and I eat . . . you know . . . I'm doing all right."

"That's fine. There aren't many people who can even meet expenses these days . . . You're to be congratulated. But are you saving any money for long-range goals?"

" 'Long-range goals'?" Larry was opening up that alligator attaché case, and Ron almost expected to see large teeth as the jaw of it opened. Instead a blue vinyl book was withdrawn with a large "M" implanted on its face.

"Yes," Larry continued smoothly, "long-range goals like retirement, saving for the future education of children . . ."

Children? Retirement? Good lord, Larry was trying to sell him something. It was ridiculous, and yet something strange was happening . . . He was feeling better. He was listening, reacting to Larry . . . *Wait,* am I attracted to him? No, not that way. Larry never did anything for me and he still doesn't. Then what the hell is it?

"Ron, if I could show you a plan that would guarantee your saving goals, guarantee that whether you lived, died, quit or became disabled you'd achieve what you set out to do, how much could you save each week toward that plan, assuming of course that you agreed that it was the finest plan you'd ever seen."

Ron searched Larry's face. There was no hint of con. To the contrary, there was an almost religious sincerity. Ron wanted to feed on it. "I guess I could save any damn amount you want." He felt euphoric.

"Could you?" Larry's face was beginning to light up.

"Sure? What do you need? What do you want?"

"Look, you've got to have something to live on, right?"

"I guess . . . whatever . . . I don't care."

"Well, can you save ten dollars a week?"

"Sure."

Larry opened that marvelous vinyl book and said, "Now Ron, how old are you?"

"I'm twenty-three."

"When will you be twenty-four?"

"Next August."

Larry turned a page of the book and there were bright red and blue figures on the page. Huge dollar signs in gold next to the figures. There were pictures of old men, young men, wives and children with bright shining non-suicidal faces reaching for huge pots of glowing gold. Larry talked, and talked, and pointed animatedly to the figures. Ron didn't care what he said, he was carried away on the wave of Larry's enthusiasm.

Finally Larry was writing information about Ron on a piece of paper, and then he put the paper in front of Ron and put a pen in his hand and asked Ron to place his name where the line was X-ed and Ron did so. Gladly.

Then Larry said, "Now, Ron, could you give me a check for the first monthly deposit into this savings plan or cash would do just as well."

"I don't have a checking account."

"Cash'll do just as well."

"How much?"

"Forty dollars."

"Forty dollars?"

"Yes, just forty dollars."

"I don't have it now."

"Oh?"

"Well, you know I have about eight dollars and I'm a few days behind on my rent. I-I haven't been paying too much attention to making money lately . . ."

"You know, you mustn't let routine daily problems divert you from your goals. You know, Ron, I bet if I asked you what you were worried about two years ago you wouldn't be able to tell me, right?"

Larry was so *right.* His unstoppable positive could roll over any negative in its way.

"I'll work some extra days and I'll get the money for the rent *and* the money for this plan—"

"Super!" Larry bounced on the couch.

"Only—"

"Only what?"

"I don't want to drive this goddamn taxi anymore."

"Good, you're too good for that crap, anyway . . . Wait a minute . . ." Larry was so excited that he stood up and paced up and down the small room, then sat back down on the couch. "Ron, how would you like to make money and have the same kind of tremendously rewarding experience that I'm having?"

"Doing what?"

"Being an agent for the Meridian Life Insurance Company. Doing what I'm doing. And loving it. You'd be a natural, the way you are with people. And when you sell for a while you go into management, you could get to be a vice-president—all the way to the top, old buddy. You're a natural."

Ron leaned back in his seat and from that view he saw that Paranoia was watching the entire proceedings from the kitchen table. Well, the same way he knew he wasn't going to drive a cab anymore he wasn't going to be living with the likes of Paranoia, Alcoholism and Depression either.

"Larry," he asked, "what made you quit acting?"

"Well, I didn't quit really. I'm in a play at the Jewish Center where I live—"

"I mean as a profession."

"I remember going on one of those cattle calls for a summer-stock job and looking up and down the line seeing that each and every one of the fifty guys waiting for this little job seemed better-looking than me, seemed to have more training, spoke better, moved better, had more experience than me. That was pretty bad. But you know what the worst thing was?"

"What?"

"None of them would get the part either. You know who'd get the part?"

"Who?"

"The boyfriend of some fag director. Now you may think that this is rationalization but I'm going to tell you something, Ron —if you're going to make it in the theater, whether as an actor or even a writer, you've got to be a fag. And I am no fucking fag! Now, when the chance came for me to be in the life-insurance business I jumped at it. Right away I loved it. I was good at it. I could win more than once in a while. And if I sold a guy I didn't have to worry about another salesman coming around and blowing the guy and taking the sale away from me. If I could motivate the guy he was mine. And I could act, be theatrical as hell— everything I'd always wanted to be and still be successful."

God, he believed it, it obviously had worked for him . . . Ron wondered if it could do the same for him . . . Could he be saved from his shit by selling life insurance? Selling—then management —then a vice-president of a Big Insurance Company. Up the Protestant spire, dad!

Larry was leaning in closely to Ron. "You know, I want to tell you something. Are you still studying with Professor Lavalle?"

"No. No, I'm not."

"Good. I couldn't stand what he did to your play. It was damn good. I mean it wasn't Hemingway or anything but damn good. The way he was twisting it and turning it made me sick . . . That's one of the reasons I stopped coming to those inner-circle things . . . I wanted to tell you but the girl I was going with at the time, Celia, she told me not to because you were so into the whole thing that she thought you'd never listen and just get mad. And do you know something else?"

Larry leaned very close to Ron now and whispered. "I think that fucking Lavalle was queer." He paused. "I mean, not that he ever tried anything with me but I got a feeling about him, that's all. Did he ever try anything with you?"

Ron looked at the big "M" on the blue vinyl book, the alligator case on the broken coffee table, the bright shine on Larry's shoes, the peering eye of Paranoia at the kitchen table, and he whispered softly back to Larry, "Are you kidding? If that fucking queer had ever tried anything with me I'd have knocked him right on his fat ass."

BOOK **2**

WHAT THE MIND
CAN CONCEIVE

CHAPTER 9

Doris Spadaccini gazed at her picture of Paul Newman and absentmindedly removed one corner of the tape that held it on the wall next to her bed.

"You fuck!" She heard her mother scream at her father a moment after she'd heard the sound of a beer can being opened. Her older brother Carmine slammed the door and left the house, whistling past the curses. She thought of him getting into his new car and driving it as fast as it could go up and down the Bronx River Parkway. He'll get killed one day, she knew it. Crash and he'll be dead. She could see the funeral. He was just the kind it happened to and there was nothing she could do about it. She'd tried to talk to him but now she'd given up, was resigned . . . Just the way she was resigned to the nightly scenes of her father drinking beer and her mother first cursing him, then hitting him as he blocked her blows with a drunken idiotic smile on his face while trying to watch television and then . . . If her presence got in the way of something very interesting and if drunk enough, pushing her, or shoving or kicking her out of the way.

Resigned. Because she was nineteen and she'd get married soon and get away and everything would be fine . . . Of course she wouldn't be married to Paul Newman . . . She took off the second corner. She really didn't have a crush on him anymore. That was a schoolgirl thing. Now she had a real thing with Jimmy McDonald. Maybe she'd marry Jimmy. He was real cute with his freckles and his red hair and the way he shifted a toothpick from one side of his mouth to the other . . . Only . . . well, only he'd better know that he'd have to wait until they got married before they did anything. If he really had good qualities he'd wait and if not . . . ? Well . . . she didn't know. Modern girls were supposed to be different and she was a modern girl, after all. But still she'd rather wait. She hoped he would . . .

The new assistant manager, Mr. Starr, would if he were the one. Doris felt very warm as she visualized his face.

He'd wait, he was such a gentleman . . . That's what the word meant, gentle-man.

Doris looked closely at Paul Newman as she removed the other corners of his picture and silently said to him, oh, he isn't good-looking the way you are, Paul, but he's got a real nice sort of face . . . Sweet, almost like cupid . . . His hair's getting a little thin and I'm sure he'll be bald by the time he's forty and he's eating too much . . . Needs a woman to put him on a diet. Oh, not me. He'd never go for me, although he looks at me sometimes in that way of his . . . So sensitive, sincere. He's a college man, and real smart. They say he's going to be a vice-president some day. He's the most dynamic man in the office without even raising his voice or anything. They all come to him with their problems because he's so sympathetic and he's always interested in helping people. And he never does numbers on the girls or makes dirty remarks the way the other guys do. Married men too, Paul. They're disgusting. He's a bachelor and Nancy says he's not seeing anyone and he does look at me but he's hardly ever said two words to me . . .

The picture of Paul Newman was off now. Doris put it on top of her small neat dresser and noticed the pale spot on the wall where the picture had been and wondered if she could take one of the pictures of Mr. Starr that appeared in the *Meridian Monthly* when he won a sales contest and put it there but she wouldn't because her mother would ask about it and her sister Theresa would too and Carmine would make dirty cracks.

The phone rang, and Doris jumped off the bed and ran into the living room to answer it before anyone else. But she was too late. Her sister Theresa, who was staying with them for now because she'd had a big fight with her husband of eight months, was there first.

"Get the fuckin' phone," Mr. Spadaccini yelled from his side of the living room. He was watching a police show. "Talk in the hallway."

Theresa picked up the phone. "Hello." She was tense, expecting it to be her husband or the lawyer she'd left a message for. Doris was expecting Jimmy McDonald. Her father wouldn't even let *her* pay for a phone extension in her own room. He couldn't afford one, he'd said, and he'd be damned if he'd allow one of his daughters to pay for it and show him up.

Mrs. Spadaccini stuck her head out of the kitchen and said to Theresa, "Yeah, talk in the hallway . . . After all, it might just be important and you don't want to interfere with the television."

Theresa handed the phone to Doris just before either of them could manage to shield the transmitter from Mr. Spadaccini's "Fuck off!"

"It's for you," Theresa said, rolling her eyes in apology for not shielding the phone. Doris nodded in understanding. "Hello."

"Hi, kid."

"Hi, Jimmy."

"How you doin'? Whaddya know, whaddya say?"

"Fine."

He was so cute. The way he talked like the old thirties gangster movies, but he rarely called at the house because she never encouraged it. He usually called at the office.

"How's about I pick you up after work tomorrow about five okay and we go out to a nice place to eat . . . Maybe Cookie's or something."

"Sure."

"Listen," Jimmy said, clearing his throat, "you know my friend . . . I told you about with his own apartment in Flushing? You remember I told you about him?"

"Oh sure. I remember."

"You know he's going away for about a week or so and he said I could use his place if I want to. He's got a great collection of records and things . . . Broadway shows . . . *My Fair Lady, Guys and Dolls* . . . you know, things like that that you like."

Doris almost shook, steadied herself against the wall. "Oh sure."

"Yeah, well maybe we can drop there after we eat and stuff."

The last time they'd been together in Jimmy's car she had let him get very far and when he wanted to go all the way she had stopped him and told him, "Not here, not in the back seat of a car."

She meant it. Maybe she could resign herself to giving herself before marriage but not against cold vinyl upholstery. There was something degrading about that. She knew that Jimmy had been about to suggest a motel but he'd stopped himself before he said it. Much to his credit, because if he had she'd have broken with him right there and then. She really would have.

Now he had a friend's apartment . . . Broadway show albums. She couldn't refuse that, could she? She was nineteen and a modern girl in the business world and all. But she wanted to let him know that just because she'd go over there with him that didn't guarantee him anything. She'd do that tomorrow, though, because she heard rumblings from the living room. Theresa was beginning to carp at her father and her mother was joining in and pretty soon the screaming was going to start, so she said quickly, "Okay, but look, I've got to go now. I'll see you tomorrow."

"Okay, kid," Jimmy said, very happy to clinch his deal and eager to call his friend in Flushing and tell him to get lost for the evening and leave the key under the doormat.

The next day was a strange one for Doris. It was the deadline of a sales contest and the office was hectic with last-minute processing of applications. The agents were nervous, snappy. She didn't mind that because then they didn't flirt, but she was really on edge about this evening.

And further, Mr. Starr was, well, very strange. He kept walking out of his office and looking at her. Yes, she was sure it was her. She couldn't understand what was going on. Maybe she was imagining things, but when she went down with Nancy, a heavy-set girl who was one of the other clerks, Nancy said to her, "What's going on with you and Mr. Starr?"

"Did you see it too?"

"Yeah. He keeps coming out and lookin' at you. Did you get him mad or anything?"

"No . . . I don't think so."

"Well, you know he always has an eye for you but today it's like he's on fire."

"Yeah . . . It's strange."

Nancy put a cigarette in her mouth and before they went into Chock Full O' Nuts she said, "Well, at least you don't have to worry about him lechin' after you like those other guys."

"Yeah," Doris agreed. Except what did she mean, that there was nothing to worry about? She asked Nancy.

"He's a fairy."

Two people got up and Doris and Nancy sat down. Doris ordered the clam chowder and a cream cheese on raisin bread and Nancy ordered three sandwiches and a chocolate drink.

"What are you talking about?" Doris whispered to Nancy. "He's not a fairy."

"Can't you tell?" Nancy said as she took the first half of the first sandwich in almost one gulp.

"He doesn't lisp or walk like Jack Benny or anything. And his voice is deep . . . You're crazy."

"Did you ever see the way he talks to guys compared to the way he talks to women? I mean he really gets into guys and he doesn't care about women . . . except you."

Doris was very confused and suddenly not hungry at all. "You mean he does things with the men at the office?"

"No. He wouldn't fool around with anyone at the office. He's the type of guy that roams around in Greenwich Village or puts on women's dresses and bras at home and looks in the mirror. Weirdos."

Doris forced herself to eat the raisin bread and cream cheese. "Well if that's so what about the way he looks at me? In case you haven't noticed, I'm a woman."

Nancy laughed and wiped her mouth. "You're more like a cute little boy. The way you dress, always flat-looking, with business suits and bow ties."

Doris was not going to have lunch with this fat slob ever again. She was going to get her schedule changed. She was very feminine, she told herself. She looked good in her page-boy haircut and her styles were very classy. She wasn't busty . . . She just wasn't, and she was not going to wear any padding and this style suited her best . . . Nancy was jealous because the men in the office flirted with her—that's why Nancy would dare to call Mr. Starr a degenerate—a fairy! She couldn't wait to finish her lunch.

Just before she did, she turned to Nancy and said much louder than she intended, "You know, Nancy, you are *really* messed up, you know that?"

An old lady sipping coffee next to Nancy turned around to tune in on the conversation. Doris didn't care. "If a man isn't trying to get something from a girl, if he isn't trying to make out and grab something you think he's a fairy. You know there *are* such things as gentlemen."

Nancy's mouth was open and the ham from her sandwich was hanging from it.

"I'm going back to the office," Doris said, getting up. "I've got a lot of work to do. Coming?" she asked, knowing that Nancy was not about to leave her other sandwiches.

Nancy shook her head and Doris stalked off . . .

The Daily wasn't done yet and it was close to five o'clock. The Daily was the regular report of the day's business that had to go to the home office at the end of each business day. Doris was in charge of it and Ron was hovering over her, checking the figures, especially the ones of the men he was responsible for. He was a new assistant manager and his job was to recruit salesmen. If they did well he did well. So far she was proud his men were doing the best. They seemed to do it for him more than themselves, and he'd get happy for their success.

The general manager Mr. Parkinson—named after the disease, Nancy had said—would insult the men and put them down if they didn't do well, and when they did he'd begrudgingly give them a cigar or an off-hand compliment.

But Doris noticed that Mr. Starr was fussing much more today than usual. He made her double- and sometimes triple-check the figures. Did all this really have something to do with her?

She was finally done at five to five. Jimmy would be here soon. She hurried to the ladies' room and reinforced her makeup, slight as it was, and felt a little sad because now that the day was almost over and the Daily was finished Mr. Starr would go back, as usual, into his office and she wouldn't see him again until tomorrow . . . And tomorrow she might not be the same person that she was today.

When she came into the office she saw Jimmy McDonald was already there and Mr. Starr was talking to him. Jimmy was taller and Mr. Starr was just looking up at him, very much interested in what Jimmy was saying. The toothpick in Jimmy's mouth was jumping from one side of his mouth to the other at a rapid rate.

Doris remembered what Nancy had said and became frightened for the moment and then saw the I-told-you-so look on Nancy's face and she sailed right into their conversation.

Mr. Starr had been asking Jimmy what he did for a living. He talked to everyone he met, Doris noticed, trying to get them to become agents for Meridian Life. He was very enthusiastic about the career it offered, which was, she felt, why he was becoming so successful at it.

Doris didn't believe that Jimmy would make a good salesman at all. He worked with his father, who was a painter, and he had an application in for United Parcel, which he expected would be coming through soon and that was fine with him.

Ron shook Jimmy's hand. "Well," he said, "if that job with United Parcel doesn't work out, come and see me and maybe you can try things out here."

With his free hand he pulled a business card from his jacket and gave it to Jimmy.

"Thank you, Mr. Starr," Jimmy said, disengaging his hand and taking his wallet out to carefully put the card away.

"Call me Ron."

"Okay, sure. Ron."

Ron looked directly at Doris. "Good night, Miss Spadaccini."

"Goodnight, Mr. Starr," Doris said, and watched as he turned to go back to his office. She felt scared, like a little girl being left alone in the dark, and she looked at him in a way that caught his attention. He stopped and looked at her, and for the briefest moment they both felt a strong link. She knew she'd connected with him, but by then he had turned completely and had gone back into his office.

Feeling numb, she went to her desk, covered her typewriter, put the odd papers into her drawer and locked up. Jimmy waited for her near the office entrance and she joined him, feeling as if going to her own execution. The rest of the non-selling staff had already left. She was the last one to leave and had to lock up. As she was getting her keys out she heard his voice saying softly, almost in her ear, "That's all right, Doris. I'll lock up."

He'd come back. He hadn't left her alone. He even used her first name. God, she'd never even been sure that he knew it.

She looked directly at him and she let him know how grateful, no, how happy she was that he'd come back out. "Thank you" —she wanted to say "Ron" but couldn't; instead she barely got out "Mr. Starr."

His stare frightened her, yet also made her feel an instant kinship that she couldn't begin to interpret. It was over quickly. Jimmy had her by the arm and was escorting her, pulling her to his car.

Whatever else Mr. Starr's look meant, it was definitely strong and meant he was aware of her. No question about that.

After dinner they drove out to Flushing. Their conversation had progressed from forced to stilted to agonized as they approached Flushing.

Doris was thinking that she might as well. Even if he didn't want to marry her she might as well. She was so old-fashioned, what good did it do? Her mother had been one and look what she wound up with. Her sister Theresa had been one and after eight months of marriage she was back home. None of her girl friends were anymore. One by one they'd fallen—there I go again, thinking about it as if it's some big sin, which it isn't anymore. I've been going with Jimmy now for about six months and he's nice and the guy deserves a break . . . And then Jimmy was gone and in his place was Mr. Starr, except she shouldn't think of him as Mr. Starr, he was probably around Jimmy's age. Ron. She liked that name. There was a nice ring to it. Doris Starr, nice, like a movie star . . . Joke . . .

"What're you smiling at?"

"Oh, nothing, just something at the office."

"Oh."

They had arrived.

Doris pretended that she didn't see Jimmy quickly bending down to scoop the key from under the black rubber welcome mat to his friend's apartment.

"He's got a nice place," Jimmy said as he escorted her in, put the lights on and helped her off with her spring coat.

The apartment was small and surprisingly neat for a bachelor. Doris had half expected to find crushed beer cans and dirty underwear on the floor. And of course right there on the coffee table near the stereo were albums of *My Fair Lady* and *Guys and Dolls* and some others. Pleased, she went to them, sat on the couch and began to look through them.

"Want a drink?" Jimmy asked from the kitchen.

"Yes, okay. Seven and Seven if he has it."

She put *My Fair Lady* on the record player, waiting eagerly for Rex Harrison.

"Here," Jimmy said, handing her the drink and sitting next to her, very closely, drink in hand.

She wanted to hear "Wouldn't It Be Loverly?" before she let Jimmy try anything. That was her personal favorite in the whole show, although she realized it probably wasn't the best tune.

When it came on after the "Why Can't the English Teach Their Children How to Speak?" number she realized that she'd never be able to concentrate on it with Jimmy fidgeting so much and pretending that he was listening to the music, so she leaned back into his arms and he kissed her and immediately put his hand on her little nub of a breast.

By the time Julie Andrews was finished with the last refrain of "Wouldn't It Be Loverly?" Jimmy had landed where he was the other night in the car, and was pressing her very hard.

She decided to stop being a prude. Her legs relaxed enough so that Jimmy could get his entire finger there and Doris closed her eyes and started to enjoy the hot probing. This had happened to her before on dates and it always felt nice so wouldn't the real thing feel even better?

"Let's go in the other room, okay?"

"Okay," Doris said. She stood up, put the *Guys and Dolls* album on top of the automatic record changer so that she could hear that next, and was escorted into the bedroom by an even more fidgety Jimmy.

They kissed and rubbed against each other on the bed and then Jimmy carefully started to take her clothes off. She'd never been completely naked with a boy before and she didn't want it to be a groping experience so she excused herself and went to the bathroom.

She undressed behind the closed door, folding all her clothes neatly and putting them on the toilet seat. She was going to be very calm. This was not going to be a big girly-girly crying deal. It's part of life and waiting until one gets married is too stupid.

She put a towel around herself and emerged from the bathroom, making sure to turn out the light quickly.

Jimmy was tucked under the sheets now, his clothes strewn on the floor and next to the bed. On the dressing table, where he knew Doris could see and be reassured, was a box of rubbers.

She quickly slipped in with him and in a moment they were pressed against each other, the towel being quickly discarded by an eager Jimmy.

Oh God, she thought, in the middle of Jimmy's gropings, I wish he'd leave my breasts alone . . . It's as if he wanted something more to be there and he keeps squeezing and sucking and biting as if he were trying to make them grow. That's all there is, Jimmy . . . That's all there is . . . I'm like a boy . . . Remember what Nancy said . . . Am I like a boy? . . . is that it, Jimmy?

Well, it's not going to happen. I'm nineteen and it's not going to happen.

Then suddenly Jimmy was straddling her and she heard the rip of the rubber package being opened. She saw the shadow of something being slipped onto Jimmy's penis as he straddled her and she wanted to run but she stopped herself because she was being foolish . . . foolish . . .

Jimmy tried but Doris knew that he couldn't get any place

because she was dry and closed up tight. Jimmy started to play with her breasts again. You jerk, she thought. *He* wouldn't do that . . . He'd understand . . . He'd know . . . Dumb Irish freckle-faced jerk . . .

Now Jimmy's mouth was on her nipple and Doris had a vision . . . it came to her like a revelation. She knew what Mr. Starr . . . Ron . . . had been trying to tell her at the door. He wanted her. He, Ron Starr, wanted her for himself. And he wanted her to be pure. He wanted to be the only man in her life and he would love her and understand her for what she was—not for what he wanted her to be.

She knew at that instant that she loved him and that this thing with Jimmy McDonald was all wrong.

She shoved him off so hard that he fell to the floor with a grunt and twisted his ankle.

Exit Jimmy McDonald.

CHAPTER 10

Ron had pushed himself hard in the year and a half since he'd met—and been hired by—Dudley Arthur Parkinson, General Manager, Greeley Square Branch, Meridian Life Insurance Company. He didn't know it at the time, but more than a little of Larry Edelman's recruitment fervor was motivated by Larry's need to get a new man in the field before he'd be brought into management by the general manager. Ron became a "walking talking" salesman. He could always just talk to people, and he now did it with a vengeance, with waiters, store owners, his dentist, people he'd meet in the elevator or whatever, to sell sell sell. He made it a kind of simple game—he carried twenty jelly beans in the right pocket of his jacket, meaning he was to talk to twenty people a day about insurance. After he spoke to one he'd transfer a bean from his right to his left pocket and he wouldn't quit at night until twenty beans were in his left pocket. He worked seven days—one hundred forty beans—a week.

And the work was working. He saw *results*—not like the damn play. He sold. He loved it. *Yes* was bliss. Especially after all the no's in his life.

In the beginning of his second year he set out to be the number one new agent of Meridian's greater New York area. He put thirty beans in his pocket. He'd do it if it took forty, but he really didn't need that many. He'd built clients who liked him and were recommending this energetic, warm young man to their friends and relatives.

He sailed into number one. *Numero uno.*

One day he was working alone in the "bullpen," a very large office with drab secondhand steel desks, grimy black phones and an unwaxable vinyl linoleum floor, where management placed new agents in the hope that the depressing surroundings would motivate them to do better and earn themselves private offices. Ron hated the place, coming in only to do some paperwork, trying to shut his eyes to the sight of his fellow agents stewing in their anxieties. One of the newer men, whom Mr. Parkinson had just fired, came into the bullpen and began cleaning out his desk. Ron had been introduced to him months ago and could never remember his name, only that he drank, looked disheveled and didn't sell very well.

A moment later Mr. Parkinson walked in and sat down on the edge of Ron's desk. "How would you like to come into management?" he asked without preamble. Parkinson prided himself on his ability to spot talent.

"Management? What about Larry?"

"We're transferring him."

Ron put his pencil down. "I don't know." He had been expecting this offer and he was inwardly delighted with the way he'd shown surprise, and now doubt. I am utterly convincing, he thought.

"You don't know? When I hired you, you told me that's what your goal was."

Ron lowered his voice, not wanting the outgoing salesman to hear. "I'm making so much money now, I don't know . . . management is a cut in income . . ."

Mr. Parkinson hoped Ron was "playing the game." A successful salesman isn't supposed to want to go into management because he's supposed to be making too much money and enjoying his independence out in the field. So he expresses doubts about being tied down and having to play politics and taking a cut in income. Then he waits to be coaxed. If the coaxing works too easily, he's frightened of the field and that will always be held against him. If the coaxing takes too much effort, it shows insufficient motivation for management.

Mr. Parkinson was the front-line coaxer and it was his job to determine if the game was being played or if Ron sincerely didn't want management. Ron would eventually get coaxed pretty high up, probably by the vice-president in charge of marketing, and if Parkinson was wrong it could be embarrassing. It wasn't wise to make powerful enemies at his age, only a few years away from a comfortable retirement. He lit one of his dollar cigars.

Ron lit a Marlboro, wishing the guy across the room would leave. Mr. Parkinson seemed to enjoy the situation. "There's money to be made in management" he was saying expansively. "And satisfaction—teaching what you know to other people, bringing salesmen through . . ." The man had gone back, dejectedly stuffing his useless business cards into a cardboard suitcase, probably thinking what a prick Parkinson was.

Ron had been mentally rehearsing his hard-to-get act but he'd always imagined it happening in Parkinson's office. He was a little off-balance here and kept lowering his voice. "The thing is, I've found a lot of satisfaction in the field, helping people . . ."

"There's satisfaction in management too," Parkinson boomed, "if you get good men, that is. Sometimes you get bums, but mostly you get good men and you get a lot of satisfaction with overrides."

The man was finally packed up. He walked over to shake Ron's hand. "Mr. Starr, let me wish you all the luck."

"Oh, are you leaving?" Ron asked.

"Yeah, I'm leaving," he said. "Just couldn't make it."

"That's right," Parkinson let slip. "He's leaving. He just couldn't make it."

"Mr. Parkinson," the man said, "fuck you, you know," and walked out of the bullpen.

When he was gone, Mr. Parkinson turned to Ron, laughing. Ron laughed with him.

"You know," Parkinson said, "if he'd shown that kind of spirit in the field he might have made it."

"Maybe he would now. Maybe he's been holding that fuck you in so long that it's been eating him up."

"Maybe."

Ron stood up. "It might be worth another try."

"If you were in management, would you bring him back for another try?"

"You better believe it."

"I'll be right back." Mr. Parkinson was up and out of the office surprisingly fast for a man of his age and girth. Ron followed him out to the front office and saw Parkinson catch up with the man at the door. "Hey, come back in here a minute. I want to see you."

Ron could see the man fight the urge to repeat his "fuck you." Then, uneasily, yet with visible hope, back into Mr. Parkinson's office.

As Mr. Parkinson closed the door he winked at Ron. They both knew that this kind of thing was a hell of a lot more enjoyable than selling policies.

And Mr. Parkinson knew that Ron was playing the game.

Ron went to the home office to keep a luncheon appointment Mr. Parkinson had made for him with Colonel (USMC, Retired) Thomas J. McCloud, the regional vice-president of the greater New York region.

In college Ron had voiced his share of the fashionable cynicism about American business, but he'd inherited too much of his father's awe of WASP Establishment life and each of the three or four times he'd been to the home office on Madison Avenue since the year he'd started selling he was simply stunned by the cathedral of a lobby that extended all the way from Madison to Park Avenue, by the lofty arches, sepia expanses, subdued shadowy lighting and huge open marble spaces. If he had someone with him when he entered through the revolving door, he lowered his voice automatically, as if to avoid interrupting a service.

Here he wanted to be one day—on the thirteenth floor where wrinkled executives held sway. He didn't connect his ambition with his father. Actually, as part of his TURNABOUT he was fighting introspection. He was already good at keeping his anxieties at bay with the plethora of positive mental-attitude techniques that were rampant in the business, and when these didn't quite work he'd take to drinking more heavily. He knew what he was doing, though. When the TURNABOUT was completed, when all those terrible attractions were completely gone, he could stop, and he knew he would not turn into an alcoholic. He didn't have that basic weakness, and he was going to make it in this new life . . . If a drink or two helped through rough times, that was the price he had to pay. Everything has a price.

I *am* making it too, he thought as the wood-paneled elevator carried him up. Here I am being courted by the superstuds of American business. . . . He laughed at the thought, maybe too from the drink he'd had before coming. He felt relaxed and cocky. Parkinson was seducer number one, leading him up to the grand seducers on the thirteenth floor. Ron loved it; it was almost sensuous being looked over and admired, touched with their eyes, beckoned into their private chambers.

Colonel McCloud and Ron were handshakers. They'd met casually twice before at sales meetings and they'd enjoyed their first hand contacts. Ron was the kind of handshaker who gets snugly into that space between thumb and forefinger, squeezing warmly but firmly while leaning into people and looking up at them, crouching a bit if need be to let them feel taller.

Colonel McCloud swung into his handshakes as if putting a curve on a soft ball and doing a do-si-do at the same time. He greeted people as if his entire day had been filled with tiring frustrations alleviated by the arrival of that person. The hand that got shaken by Colonel McCloud belonged to a friend, a bright face in an otherwise dark world.

McCloud was in his early forties, in top physical condition with the kind of iron-gray hair that went with his previous rank. Yet he seemed too gentle and vaguely puzzled by life to have been a colonel in the Marines, or even to be vice-president of an insurance company. He was like a simple farm boy who'd wanted nothing more out of life than to snuggle against the banks of the Mississippi like Huck Finn, fishing rod dipping lazily in the water, contemplating his next meal and his next meal only. Instead the world had showered these big titles and large worries all over him and of course what could he do but handle them . . .?

When Ron came into his office they had an orgasm of handshakes and proceeded to the executive dining room, with McCloud serenading Ron all the way. It was wonderful, Ron's record was . . . great to have a man who could get out there and talk to the people . . . In the small town where he came from it was all eyeball to eyeball selling—no telephones . . . No reason why we couldn't have more of that in the big city . . . He'd like Ron to give the new men a talk on walking and talking . . . Who said New Yorkers weren't friendly? . . . Doodlewash . . . Friendliestpeopleintheworld if you approach them right . . .

They entered the executive dining room where it seemed to Ron as if people moved to some kind of minuet. The browns and sepias of the lobby were carried over here, though more airily.

They were shown to a table for two and immediately a parade of dignitaries waltzed over shaking Ron's hand, trying their technique on him just as he worked on them. They'd heard of him, they all congratulated him on his record. He felt enormously flattered, like a ballerina acknowledging bouquets thrown by an ecstatic audience.

By the time the coffee came he was too euphoric to even think of holding out when McCloud, like a sneaky man putting his hand on a knee, whispered the question about coming into management, and Ron, like an eager lover pining for the hand, smiled and nodded yes to Colonel McCloud and to himself yes . . . yes . . . a thousand times yes . . .

He tried never to hire anyone he was attracted to, but in Gil Sloane's case he had made an exception because Gil was going to be terrific. Gil had been a male model before coming into the business. He was tall, with a blond crew cut, all-American-boy features, a sunny smile and a beautiful body.

Ron was right; Gil became wonderfully successful and Ron had been able to control any feelings except that one time when they went to the men's room together.

They'd been talking about a sale. After he finished urinating, Gil turned to Ron, his gorgeous cock in his hand, shaking the drops out, and Ron suddenly thought he was going to faint. He quickly turned away, leaning against the sink and washing his hands, inwardly furious at Gil for doing that to him.

He made a mental note never to go to the men's room with Gil again.

Some days later they were sitting in Ron's office and a new girl walked by. Gil stuck his head out of the office door and signaled for Ron to follow suit. When Ron got to the door Gil pointed at the receding backside and said, "Look at the ass on that . . . Boy I'd like to fuck her right up the ass . . . jam her right against one of those fuckin' desks and . . ." He made a forceful gesture with his fist.

Gil was always carrying on that way. He was like Jack Armstrong, all-American boy, gone pervert.

And Ron had said, without dissembling, spontaneously, "Yeah . . . me too . . . I'd like to fuck her too."

And they laughed lewdly, two men leering at the ass of a woman. A woman! Ron almost cried, he was so happy. Was the turnabout turning about, was the goddamn attraction for women that he should have been having all these years finally starting? Yes, God, please God . . . please let it be . . .

That new young girl was Doris. There was something there. He felt sure enough to make his first move.

The day after Ron had talked to Jimmy McDonald out front he passed Doris in the hall and asked her to step into his office when she had a chance. Ten minutes later, during her coffee break she came in shyly. "You wanted to see me, Mr. Starr?"

"Yes," Ron said. He'd been nervous waiting for her and had tried without success to lose himself in some sales literature. "Sit down please."

She sat at the chair by his desk.

"I wanted to talk to you about Jimmy McDonald. Is he your fiancé, or boyfriend . . .?"

"No, he's not. As a matter of fact, I'm not seeing him anymore."

"Oh?"

"I broke off with him as of last night."

Ron felt there was some special meaning that he was supposed to pick up. "I see. I thought he might be good for the business."

"Oh, he wouldn't be. I can tell the kind of salesmen who'll be successful, and he isn't one of them. He just wants a steady salary and job security, that's all."

"A civil-service mentality."

"Exactly."

"I see. Well, no harm in trying. You seem to have an idea of the type of man we're looking for. Do you know anyone else?"

"Well, some of my girl friends are getting married or starting to get serious with fellas . . . Most of the guys want to be cops or are in construction."

"Oh?"

"I don't know . . . the people I meet here seem to come from a different planet than all the ones I know in the Bronx."

"Which planet do you prefer?"

"I like this one. You're all so alive. You and the men . . . even though they're pretty fresh . . ." She blushed.

"That's how men who sell are . . . I'm sorry, though, if any of them offended you."

"Oh no . . . that's all right . . . They're like little boys, most of them . . . I don't mind . . . I don't pay them any attention . . . Thanks for apologizing anyway . . . that's sweet." She stood up suddenly. "I'd better go back now. Could I just ask you one thing?"

"Sure."

"Well, sometimes I've passed by the conference room while you were having a sales meeting and I heard things you were talking about . . ."

"Uh huh."

"Things like positive mental attitude and changing your circumstances, making your life better by changing the way you think . . . I heard you say that one day to the men."

"Right."

"Could that apply outside of sales?"

"Sure."

"I do want to think in a better way . . . and I'd like to learn about things like that."

"Well, maybe I can help you."

"I don't want to be a bother or anything . . . or take up any of your time . . . but if you can just suggest something . . ."

"Well, look, it's no bother." He reached over to his bookshelf and took out one of his favorite books, *The Magic of Belief,* and he handed it to Doris. "You can change your life by changing the way you believe. I've . . . I'm doing it." Yes, definite attraction

197

while she stood there. He'd like to just stand up and hold her.

"I'm going to read it tonight," Doris said, holding the book against her chest with both hands the way she held the Bible at Holy Communion.

"Good. Let me know what you think about it tomorrow."

"All right. I have to go back now."

The next day Doris came in to see Ron on her morning coffee break. Ron invited her to sit down.

"Well?" he asked eagerly.

"I've never read anything like it in my life," she said. "I finished it."

"Really."

"I stayed up all night and I finished it."

"Wow . . . But you shouldn't read it that fast . . . You have to think about each chapter . . . each paragraph . . ."

"I started it all over again this morning on the subway."

"Good."

"And do you know what? It works . . . I tried it already."

"How?"

"I never get a seat on the subway you know . . . I just never do and it's awful . . . people pushing you around and guys getting away with things they shouldn't and all. So I took the idea from the book that if you really believe, and make that belief go into your unconscious, and then forget about it and then act as if you completely expect it to happen, it will happen. I did all that this morning with the idea of getting a seat on the subway and it was like a miracle. Like magic, this woman stood up right in front of me and I sat down . . . the first time in all the months I've been working here."

"Wonderful."

"It's like a whole new life."

Her voice, even though excited, was in a very low register. Her Bronxese wasn't too bad. He wondered how it'd feel to run his hand up her leg. He had the start of an erection. He envisioned cupping one of the cheeks of her neatly turned ass and he was getting a full erection.

"You know what you'd love? I have a record that I listen to every morning before I get out of bed and every night before I go to sleep. It inspires me through the entire day, and it seeps into my unconscious before I drop off."

"Oh I'd love to hear that."

"It's by Earl Nightingale . . . This man started with nothing and retired before he was forty. He is fabulous . . . the sound of his voice, what he says . . ."

"Oh I'd love to hear that."

There was a pause.

"I'd love to hear that."

"I-I have it at my place."

"Oh I'd love to hear that."

He was as tongue-tied as she was. "Well, maybe," he shrugged and mumbled, "sometime . . ."

"Yes," she said, sensing that it was time to go. She stood up and said, "I have to go back now."

"All right."

She left. Ron slowly put his hand on his penis . . . yes . . . it had gotten hard. The Magic of Belief.

Gil Sloane walked in just after Doris left, a big leer on his face.

"You like little boys now, huh?" He grinned. Ron's heart jumped. "Huh?"

"When I first saw that chick's ass . . . I couldn't wait to check out the front but when I did I just kept waiting to see the ass."

Ron leaned back and winked wickedly at Gil. "Didn't you ever hear of an ass man?"

Ron made Gil's obscene fist gesture. Gil guffawed with Ron. Ron had an even tighter erection than he'd had before. He suddenly wished he could share it with Gil. Have Gil feel it, acknowledge it and in turn feel Gil's . . . He checked himself angrily.

"Get the hell out of here and sell insurance."

Gil laughed and left.

At the Chock Full O'Nuts lunch counter that afternoon, Nancy looked at Doris over a raisin-and-nut-bread sandwich. "What's with you and cupid?"

"I wish you wouldn't call him that," she replied, sipping her tea. She should have changed her lunch schedule.

"Well, he's just like a little cupid with his round face, and he's getting a little stomach."

"He is not."

"Has he tried anything?"

"You are gross."

"I bet he hasn't."

"Why?"

"You know why."

"You're crazy."

That afternoon Ron wanted to ask Doris to his apartment to listen to the Earl Nightingale record. Doris wanted to be asked. They avoided each other until five o'clock, when the salesmen had gone and the office staff was locking up. It was a good time for Ron to ask her, while she was alone at her desk putting her things away. He'd never been this way before —with anyone. Why the hell was he so shy now? He didn't want to think about it so he just walked back to his office. He'd try another time. He wished he had a drink. He'd wanted to put a bottle in his office but that was bad form. He sat at his desk and pretended to read while he listened for the front door to close.

Doris was at his door.

"I-I just came back to say good night Mr. Starr." She'd never come back to say good night before.

She pulled a book out of her handbag, *The Magic of Belief.* "I'm going to read it on the subway."

"Um-huh."

"Then I'm going to spend the whole evening with it. Better than watching dumb ol' TV."

She looked so fuckable with that book held like that, he thought, and that black little pageboy hairdo and the big bow tie. He *was* getting an erection again.

"Would you like to hear the Earl Nightingale record tonight?" he said.

She swallowed and said, "Oh, I'd love that."

"Can you come over now? Maybe we can have supper afterwards."

They hopped a cab to Ron's apartment in the east seventies. Ron had hoped that José the doorman would be on duty now to see him going into the apartment with a real dress-wearing girl, but no one was on duty at all. Doris didn't notice. "Oh, I love this building. And I love the location. The East Side . . . the seventies . . . The lobby is like a thirties movie."

"It's called art deco," Ron said as he pushed the button for the elevator. When it came Doris said, "It must be very expensive to live here."

"I'm just beginning to afford it now."

She laughed.

"But now that I can afford it I have to move out."

"Why?"

"It's too easy to become complacent. You've got to move yourself ahead financially so that you don't stop growing." They reached Ron's door. "I want to let you read *Think and Grow Rich* by Napoleon Hill when you've digested *The Magic of Belief.* You'll see what I mean."

Inside the apartment, Ron switched on the light in the vestibule as Doris said, "That's why you tell the men to spend money on nice cars and nice clothes and have their wives spend, because it keeps one growing."

"It sounds horrible but it's not. You've got to live as if you expect success, and if you do, success will happen. You read that in *The Magic of Belief.* "

"Oh yes," she said, walking around, getting the feel of the apartment.

She liked it. It was New York and classy. East Side seventies. Not a bit of the Bronx here. The living room had a huge oriental rug, a brown suede couch, and contemporary chairs placed tastefully in the corners. There were chic modern lamps that came out of the walls and very nice paintings that looked like the ones she'd seen in the Museum of Modern Art. The kitchen was one of those cute New York ones, small yet neat, set off with a folding louvered door. Off to the far right corner was another room that she surmised must be the bedroom. She wondered when she'd see that.

The apartment was spotless. She knew it would be.

As she walked about, Ron was saying, "I put a deposit on this apartment with my first commission check from Meridian. It was absurd. The rent in this place is enough to choke a horse, but I vowed to myself that I'd make it . . ."

"And you did . . ."

"And I did, so now I'm going to move. Would you like a drink?"

"Do you have a bit of wine?"

"Sure."

"Too bad you have to move. It's such a nice place."

"I want to be number one assistant manager in the entire country, and I feel myself getting too comfortable."

Ron poured Doris some white wine that he kept in the refrigerator and mixed himself a strong Scotch and soda. When he gave her the glass his fingers touched hers, a soft sensation. He sat opposite her on the brown suede couch. She crossed her hands in her lap, and could have been a little schoolboy with a bow tie and pageboy haircut, sitting in class, hands folded, paying strict attention to the teacher. He was getting hard again and he leaned back not minding if she could see it bulging inside his pants.

"That's wonderful," she was saying. "People I know are so frightened. They're always in debt anyway but it's not debt to

grow from . . . you know . . . it's debt that makes them afraid
. . . I don't know . . ."

"Of course," he said, moving a bit closer to her, "people are
frightened to take their lives in their own hands, frightened to
think . . . so life takes hold of them instead of the other way
around."

"Yes. I mean they don't plan to go into debt the way you do
. . . It just happens to them and they're miserable."

"People don't plan to fail; they fail because they don't plan."

"That's wonderful."

Her voice was so deliciously low. Even when it went high it was
sort of baritone-ish. He moved even closer to her.

"Earl Nightingale says . . . Maybe I shouldn't tell you this because you're going to hear the record, but I want to anyway . . ."

Doris leaned closer to Ron, instinctively making her voice as
low as possible. "I'd rather hear it from you than from the record
. . . although I'm sure the record is great . . ."

"He says that our mind is like a fertile field with rich, marvelously rich soil . . ."

"Yes . . . I can see that . . . I can see a rich fertile field . . ."
They were very close now.

"You can plant anything you want in that field and it will grow.
You can plant weeds, which most of us do, or you can plant the
most beautiful, richest, greenest plants . . . you can plant gold and
it will grow . . ."

"That's wonderful, I'd love to hear the record but it'll never
equal coming from you."

Ron kissed her softly on the lips.

Fairy my ass, Doris thought as they got into more heavy kissing.
I wish that fat Nancy could see this. Oh God, what is this? I feel
it right up against my appendix scar . . . Ha, some fairy. And his
hand is naughty . . . Oh he likes my behind . . . I could always
tell by the way he looked . . . He's not going for the chest the way
most of them do . . . That's good . . . I don't like it when they
go there because they always seem disappointed . . . He won't

squeeze and squeeze as if he were trying to make something grow. . . . It's not a fertile field . . . tee-hee . . .

I wonder if he's going to try to go all the way. If he does, should I let him? I wouldn't mind. I would have with Jimmy and I care for Ron more than I did for Jimmy, still it's just the first time and I shouldn't. I don't know, he's so gentle the way he's kissing me . . . I trust him. If he wants to go all the way . . .

There came a time when they both thought that he ought to have a go at her chest, for all that there was. It was obligatory. She led the way by putting his hand there. He faked excitement but they both felt his erection draining down like water in the sink when the plug is pulled.

With divine sexual instinct she turned herself around on the couch, jamming herself gently into him and reviving everything. She lay on her stomach while he climbed on top of her and they resumed their heated petting.

Ron didn't want to chance going any further. It was too good to ruin now by scaring her away. He gently disengaged himself. "I think we ought to stop now," he said.

"You are a very kind man," Doris replied as she gently stroked his face. "*Whatever* you say is all right with me. I trust you completely."

"Rome wasn't built in a day," he said, smiling in that sweet way of his. She loved him so much at that moment. "After all, I promised you the Earl Nightingale record and you shall have it."

CHAPTER 11

Dear Ron,

I'm back. I'm here in Los Angeles and maybe I'll check out Frisco or possibly go the other way down further to southern Cal. Don't know . . . just kind of kicking around and loose.

I'm sorry I haven't written you very much this last year or so. I've sensed that you needed me but things were too heavy over in Japan for me to do you much good. I learned a lot there, mentally and physically. They sure know how to kick the shit out of the Western ego.

I'll be all right, though. I like it here on the West coast. There are more guys like us and people aren't so much into giving us bullshit.

Would you consider coming out here? Ha, I just wrote a pun. I'd like to open a self-defense school but I don't know yet . . . I'll see . . . we could do it together. I know you've got a good head for business and you could make enough money to write plays to your heart's content.

How *is* your writing?

Any chance I get to see the New York papers, I search for your name. Are you doing well? Can I expect to hear about any productions? Come on and write me. Tell me *something*.

How are they? Mom and dad. Do they talk about me at all? Mom at least? Times are changing . . . there's more information going around these days about us. I sense an assertiveness, an aggressiveness, happening amongst us gays that I can swing onto with great vigor and happiness. We're going to sweep this country and give it a new and startling awareness of who we are and particularly who we are not.

Jesus, will you look at me going on with a polemic in a letter to my own little brother . . . How are you with that? Do you still have that professor? Have you been experimenting? Coming out? Problems?

I can't wait to get your letter.

Ron—see what you can do about mom and dad . . . I'll beg, borrow or steal plane fare to see them and talk to them. It's not right for me or for them either. Goddamn it I'm not a criminal and even if I were a murderer or something they'd still at least acknowledge me.

See what you can do?

Love
Lenny

Louis Starr had had a heart attack. Heavy pain had struck him one day at the office. He knew exactly what was happening as he fell to the carpet and his terrified secretary dialed the hospital. As he lay there gasping he thought that he was going to die and never see Lenny. He hated his heart so badly then—to hit him this way before he could work things around to be in touch with his son again. He writhed on the floor, fighting the evil that was trying to kill him. He was not going to die before he made it up with Lenny.

He fought and won.

Recuperating in the hospital, he made friends with a black orderly who was obviously gay. Herman conked his hair, swished, lisped and rolled his eyes. He was kindly, efficient and willing to talk about how he was. Louis started by asking roundabout questions about Herman's life. Herman gently confronted him, "Are *you* in the closet, honey?" Louis laughed and found he could admit to Herman that he had a son who was . . . that way. It was the first time in years that Louis had actually spoken about Lenny and that in itself lifted a weight that had been heavy on him.

They talked. Herman came by on his own time to educate Louis and bring him literature from the groups that were becoming more open and active: Gay Liberation, Gay Task Force, the Mattachines. Louis found it all a relief. It wasn't his fault. It didn't mean that he had been a namby-pamby Casper Milquetoast of a father. It didn't even mean that Lenny was sick. He could be that way and lead a productive life. Louis was amazed to find out all the great men who were, famous name after famous name. He'd always thought of them as real men. Herman corrected him—they *were* real men. Louis couldn't understand at first. I'm a man, Herman explained. Well, technically, Louis countered, but you're a man who wants to be a woman.

"Bullshit, Mr. Starr, I don't want to be a woman. I'm happy

with the equipment I got. I know I have my little mannerisms but that's just my way, the way some so-called straights have, some swagger and some sway, and some tippy-toe. We all have our own style you know . . . Now that son of yours sounds like a real man to me."

"Oh, that boy could tear this place apart without raising a good sweat," Louis said proudly.

"Yes, he sounds like a holy terror. I think I'm in love."

Louis was shocked, then he laughed heartily.

He kept all this from Blanche. Not that he hadn't mellowed toward her as well. Many of his friends had bitchy wives who made big money demands on them, which Blanche had never done. Still, if he started talking about Lenny her first instinct would be to try to make him feel guilty and responsible. No, it'd be better if he were coaxed. If you're coaxed you're not blamed. He decided he'd respond when she started mumbling about Lenny again, instead of ignoring her as usual.

But when he finally went home from the hospital he realized that Blanche wasn't going to resume her hints about Lenny. She'd be afraid of aggravating him. Ironic. He'd speak to Ron—the boy must know where his brother was. Ron would then suggest to Blanche that Louis could be persuaded . . . Yes, Ron was the one. The boy was a master salesman. Thank God he was out of that faggoty theater thing—of course, he knew that it wasn't as bad as he'd first thought it was, but even with his new attitude he was damned glad that Ron was okay.

One evening when Blanche was out he tried to call Ron at his New York apartment. The operator told him that the number had been changed and was now unlisted. Louis wondered about that, but he had no trouble reaching him the next day at the office. "Hello, son. How are you?"

"Fine, dad. How are you? How do you feel? Are you taking good care of yourself?"

"Coming along fine, son. Just fine. How are you doing?"

"Well, dad, I'm almost doing great."

"Almost?"

"I want to be number-one assistant manager of the company this year but I'm not there yet. When I am, I'll say I'm doing great."

"That's great . . . Oh, before I forget . . . I tried to call you at your apartment last night but you've unlisted your number . . . What's that all about?"

"Oh, in New York you get all kinds of crazy calls."

"Ahhh sure . . . Well let me have it . . ."

"I haven't memorized it yet. I'll drop it to you by mail."

"Oh, sure . . . Listen, son . . . I-I've been wanting to talk to you about something that's been on my mind a great deal lately. I've been doing a lot of thinking and a lot of soul-searching about the past and . . ."

"Dad, look, I can't really talk to you now. I'm late for an appointment with one of my men on a very large case . . . Look, I'll call you back, okay?"

"Oh?"

"Okay?"

"Well, sure, son."

"I'll speak to you, dad. Give my regards to mom."

Dear Ron,

Please tell me I'm crazy. Tell me you're not avoiding me. When you didn't answer my last letter I naturally assumed that you hadn't gotten it. I called the phone number of your last apartment and some drunken-sounding jerk gave me this East Side address. So I looked up your number and I called you. Now goddamn it I'm sure it was you who got on the phone and told me that I had a wrong number. I know your fucking voice! I called back but the line was busy, and the next day the number had been changed and unlisted.

You don't owe me any money you little bastard and if I'm not crazy and you *are* doing these things I'm going to fly to New York and jam my fucking fist down your throat!

If I'm wrong then I apologize and I'd love to hear from you, okay?

Love
Lenny

Time was a-wasting. Louis was doing fine, and the doctors told him that if he watched himself he'd outlive them all, though you never know . . . he might not be so lucky the next time. Of course Ron wasn't avoiding him, but the boy didn't answer his messages. Of course, if you're doing that well you have to be busy. Still . . . a personal visit is the best way to handle these things.

One morning Louis took the bus into New York and went to the Meridian Life Insurance Company's Greeley Square office. He walked slowly up to the logo on the front door; lines circling the globe—insurance companies have all the money, nice fancy logo, pale blue and modern . . . yes, very classy. He liked the building that Ron's office was in. It was older and had more architectural character than those glass look-alike things uptown. When he got to Ron's floor he was greeted absentmindedly by a fat pimply-faced girl at the switchboard.

"Yes? Can I help ya?"

"I'd like to see Mr. Starr?"

"Do you have an appointment or anything?"

"No, I don't . . ."

"Well, okay, I'll see if he can see ya." Nancy buzzed Ron's office, figuring that this old guy just came in off the street to try to get a job selling insurance. Sad, he's too old and weak to start this game. "Who shall I say is calling?"

"Mr. Starr," Louis answered, having a little fun.

"Yeah, but who should I say is calling him?"

"His father."

"Oh hello," Nancy said, all smiles now. Louis laughed and sat down in the reception area.

Doris, whose desk was near the switchboard, looked over at

Louis and smiled at him when she heard his name. Louis smiled back. Friendly girl, he thought.

Doris saw in him the image of Ron as he was going to be years from now, and liked what she saw—a gentle-looking, balding man with just a hint of the devil in his smile at the girls and a non-arrogant intelligence about him. She knew he was a lawyer, but like Ron he seemed so untypical of his profession.

"Oh sure, show my father back to my office," Ron told Nancy over the intercom as he slowly put down the phone.

Nancy was about to tell Louis where Ron's office was when Doris tapped her shoulder and said, "I'll take him back."

"All right," Nancy whispered. "Make your points with the family."

As she led Louis down the hall, Doris wondered if Ron expected his father today. She wished he'd talk more about his family. She'd just have to be patient—about a lot of things.

"Nice offices you got here," Louis said.

"Oh yes," she replied. "Wait till you see your son's office. He just had it decorated."

Nice ass on this little girl, Louis noticed, like swaying parentheses—wouldn't mind putting an exclamation point there—ha! Should get into New York more often. Upstate the best you can see is at the local football games, the cheerleaders show a lot of ass and leg but not much boob. Here in New York, especially in the spring like this, you see a lot of boob. Ha! Haven't thought about asses and boobs in a long time. I must be feeling better.

When Louis was shown to his son's office, Ron stood up and shook his hand warmly. "Dad, why didn't you let me know you were coming? Come on, sit down, rest a bit . . ."

"I'm all right."

"Can I get you something? Some coffee?"

"No—that's okay . . . I had some tea before I stopped in."

Doris, standing by the door, asked, "Can I get you some coffee, Ron?" The first name had slipped out. She usually didn't do that in the office, but to Doris this wasn't business, it was family.

Ron didn't seem to notice. He was flustered and confused and he just nodded. Doris went down the hall to get him coffee.

Louis hardly looked around the newly decorated office with its fiberglass drapes, neat light brown contemporary furniture and fabric wall covering. He made for the nearest chair but Ron headed him off. "Let me show you around, dad."

"Okay, but later," Louis said, plopping down in a chair by the corner table. "Let's chat a bit first."

"I really don't have that kind of time. I wish you'd let me know."

"Won't take long, son. Sit down a minute."

Ron paced the carpet. Louis cleared his throat to start. He'd thought about openers all the way on the bus ride. "Ron, I've been thinking a great deal about your brother lately. I wanted to talk to you about it." No, I should use his name. "Ron, it's about Lenny. I've been going over it again and again in my mind" . . . Better . . . but I don't want to seem that I'm already committed to a reunion. I want it to seem that I'm in doubt and that he and his mother ought to gently persuade me. "What do you think, Ron? Was I too rough? Too harsh? I mean, what he turned out to be was awful but still . . . was I too harsh?" The open door constrained him. He motioned for Ron to close the door but Ron didn't seem to notice. He was pacing and lighting a cigarette, and when someone whizzed by he shouted, "Danny. Danny, come in here a minute, will you?"

A small, dark man with curly hair and large, slightly crossed watery eyes stuck his head in the doorway. "Danny," Ron said, bringing him by the arm into the office, "I'd like you to meet my father."

Danny's eyes fixed themselves on Louis and his body just seemed to follow his stare. Louis stood up and shook hands with Danny. He felt slightly hypnotized by the crazy eyes. "Are you this man's father?" Danny asked.

Louis laughed, breaking the spell. "Depends on what he's done. I might take the Fifth when I find out why you're asking."

"I'll tell you why." He had a Mediterranean accent and a soft voice. "Because this is a great man. This man here is a great man, and if you are his father then you must know that you have sired greatness."

Louis hadn't been prepared for this. He smiled happily. Well . . .

"Talk about greatness, dad, Danny Carpagian's only been with the company three months and he's already in the President's Club. He's going to be the best damn insurance man in the world."

Louis Starr could see how . . . the man had a way of mesmerizing that was uncanny.

"Do you know what I was doing a few months ago when he found me?" Danny said, putting a hand on Ron's shoulder. "I was washing cars . . . he found me washing Cadillacs and he said to me that I could be driving one."

Danny produced a piece of yellow paper from his jacket and immediately opened it for Louis. "Do you know what this is?"

Louis fumbled for his glasses but Danny stayed his hand, telling him, "This is an order for my first Cadillac. You have a great son there." He took Louis' hand again.

"I have to go out in the field now. It has been a great honor."

Danny was gone quickly, and they needed a moment to recover because Danny created his own atmosphere when he was in a room.

"Terrific guy," Louis said. "Was he really washing cars?"

"He'd just come over to this country when I saw him. He was the best damn car washer you ever saw."

Louis headed for his chair again. "Ron . . ."

"You know how much money I predict he'll make this year?" Ron said.

"Uh . . . no."

"He'll make a hundred thousand."

"Go on."

"He will. He'll be the greatest."

"Amazing. And you'll make overrides on him."

"Oh yes. I'll lead the country because of him, primarily. Just wait."

"That's amazing."

It popped into Louis' head at that moment that he ought to visit his brother and sister while he was down in New York. He wanted to tell them all about what Ron had just said . . . They were always talking so much about their children, successful lawyers and doctors and one a big architect, designing those glass monstrosities uptown. But first down to business.

"Son, will you close the door a moment."

Ron went to the door but instead he reached into the hallway and pulled someone in by the arm.

This one really looks like Jack Armstrong, the all-American boy, Louis thought. He felt as if a television commercial were walking toward him with perfect teeth, hair, clothes.

"Dad, I want you to meet one of my top men, Gil Sloane— meet my father."

Gil's handshake was just right, not too firm but not too soft. "Are you Ron's father?"

"Guilty as charged."

Gil laughed. Louis felt a bit seedy standing next to someone like this.

"Are you in from upstate? What do you think of Manhattan?"

One of the secretaries whizzed by—all boobs, Louis noted. "I like the scenery here fine."

Gil leaned out of the doorway and peeked down the hall. "Especially the hills and the valleys, huh?"

"Oh yes, I'm a great lover of those."

"You know, talking about nature," Gil said, "I can see that the apple doesn't fall very far from the tree. Your son is a big scenery watcher too . . . hills and valleys and apples . . ."

Louis inexplicably felt joyous and Ron did too. They laughed with each other and they had what probably was one of the best moments they'd had together. They laughed so much that tears started to come and Louis had to sit down. Gil, taken aback by this burst of hysterical laughter over a bit of typical male banter, excused himself, thinking that there was a weirdness in the room that he didn't want to get involved with.

"You've got some characters here," Louis said. "Fabulous guys."

"Gil used to be a male model. Oh, but you should see, he's got a million girl friends."

"I bet. How are you doing in that department?"

"Okay."

"Going with anyone?"

"Sort of. Playing the field. You know."

Louis stood up and started to push the door shut himself when Mr. Parkinson chugged in, out of breath.

"I'm late for a meeting at the home office but I heard you were here," he said to Louis, grabbing his hand and pumping it like the tie rod on the wheels of a locomotive.

"Dad," Ron said, "this is Dudley A. Parkinson, my general manager."

This one didn't impress Louis. Reminded him of a fat judge in Binghamton who'd always squinted at him from the bench and had picked on him for no apparent reason.

"Is that the meeting on pensions?" Ron asked Mr. Parkinson.

"Right."

"I have to go with you," Ron said.

"How come?"

"Danny just got involved in a big pension case and he needs my help." He turned to Louis. "Dad, I'm sorry but this is a very big case."

"I can always give you the information," Mr. Parkinson said. "After all, your father's in."

"No, I have to go. My father understands."

Doris was back in their midst with Styrofoam cups of coffee.

"Oh, Doris, I'm sorry, I have to go to the home office," Ron said to her, lifting a handsome lizard-skin attaché case from his desk. "Are you going back upstate, dad?"

Doris said to Louis, "Sure you don't want this coffee, Mr. Starr?"

Louis was too flustered to answer.

"You've met Doris here?" Mr. Parkinson said to Louis. He had been matchmaking Doris and Ron from the beginning, clucking "Fine girl" whenever he noticed Doris in Ron's presence. He knew there was something tepid going on and he wanted to heat it up. He rounded Ron and Doris up in his arms and said, "These two are a bit of an office item."

Doris blushed. She could have embraced Mr. Parkinson at that moment.

"Oh?" Louis said. "I was going after her myself."

Ron moved out from Mr. Parkinson's arm and he put his hand tentatively on Doris' elbow. "No chance, dad," he said, "she's all mine."

Yes, I am, Doris thought, I wish you'd take me already.

Ron and Mr. Parkinson started to leave. Louis said, "Ron, wait a minute."

"Dad . . . I've got to go."

"Oh, we can be a bit late," Mr. Parkinson interceded, "they don't do anything for the first few minutes but blow hot air." He gave Louis his train-wheel handshake. "Nice meeting you. See you out front, Ron." Doris followed, smiling as sweetly as she could at Louis.

As they departed, Louis walked to the door and closed it, turning around to Ron.

Ron braced himself.

But it was the wrong moment for Louis now. God knows when someone else would knock on the door or his son would pull someone else in. He had a better idea. "Son, that was a nice girl there . . . Doris was her name?"

"Yes," Ron said quickly.

"Why don't you bring her upstate for the weekend? Meet your mother, have some nice food and a bit of rest . . ." And more leisure to talk, he added to himself.

Ron, in a great burst of relief, said, "Yes, dad, sure . . . oh sure
. . . she'd love it . . . she's always asking about the family . . . Sure,
great . . ."

"This weekend then?"

"Fine. Great."

Ron was pumping Louis' hand. My own son, he thought, it
must be an occupational thing, like black lung.

"What the hell are you so happy about?" Blanche said sharply
to Louis the following Saturday.

"Put on a happy face . . ."

"He sells insurance . . ."

"He doesn't sell, he's an assistant manager."

"What difference? He sells insurance and he brings a dumb
little guinea from the Bronx and you're happy?"

"Quiet."

"I'm going outside to sketch. You entertain them until dinner.
I can't take either of them."

"Blanche . . ."

"Where the hell did he get her from? She looks like a boy that
someone put a girl's wig on . . . she's got no figure and she's got
no brains. What happened with that Marsha?"

Louis escaped into the living room with the drinks. He'd made
Ron's a bit weaker this time—it was his third.

"You played soccer?" Doris asked Ron when Louis showed her
some old pictures. Ron nodded. He was plinking at the piano,
wondering if Doris would ask him to play something, but she and
Louis were totally absorbed with those stupid old soccer pictures.
He played a run but he was rusty and his fingers tripped all over
the keyboard. Then he played, rather well, the opening bars of an
easy Mozart sonata. Neither his father nor Doris looked up.

He was getting testier so he went into the kitchen and made
himself another drink.

Louis noticed that he was having another, but Doris had
learned to not pay attention to Ron's drinking. She saw a picture

of Ron in a baseball uniform when he was ten. "Oh, he played baseball too?"

"Oh sure."

"Who's this with him? I've seen him in other pictures too."

"That's his brother Lenny," Louis replied as Ron returned with his drink.

Ron's hand shook. The drink spilled over his knuckles. Dad is talking about Lenny! Words are coming out of his mouth about his brother!

Doris looked at Ron and said, "Are you all right? You never told me you had a brother. Is he younger or older? He looks older."

"He's older," Louis replied.

"Where is he now?" Doris asked.

"I don't know," Louis replied. "He's away. We don't hear from him much any more."

"Well, so it goes with families," Doris said. "My father has a brother in Italy that never writes and my father and him haven't been in touch for ten years . . . yet my father talks about him all the time and I never can understand why they don't write or anything . . ."

In spite of the drinks he'd had, the edge on Ron was getting sharper and sharper.

"Want to see our rooms?" he asked Doris. "Mine and my brother's?"

Doris smiled. "I'd love that."

"Go ahead," Louis said, standing up and putting the photo album aside. "I'm going to go out and watch mother paint a bit . . ."

Ron allowed Doris to precede him up the stairs and reached up to playfully pat her behind.

She giggled, bade him stop in innocent-girl tones. She'd never seen him like this. Almost like the other men at the office.

When they reached the top of the stairs Ron kissed her and she moved close to him. Ron had his hand on her slight breasts, moving them about. She welcomed it, he never did this. God he was roaring hot, she told herself. Why didn't he get that way in the apartment? He always stopped himself there.

"Come on," he whispered. "Let me show you the rooms . . ." He led her through the door on the left of the landing and closed the door behind them.

"Is this your room?" Doris asked.

"No, it's my brother Lenny's . . ."

"Where's your room?"

Ron drew her roughly to him with his hand on her behind. "I like it here."

He kissed her, putting his tongue as deeply as he could into her mouth. She wasn't used to him going so fast, and besides, this setting . . . his brother's room and his parents right outside . . . Something was happening—she didn't know what—and she certainly wasn't one to miss an opportunity.

She moved herself into him . . . yes, he was very hot. He put her on Lenny's bed and climbed on top of her . . . on top this time like it should be, not the way it always was with him behind her and all . . .

She reached down and felt him and shivered to feel how hard he was. He, not her this time, decisively unzipped himself. He was more erect and taut than he'd ever been.

"Ron," she whispered, "your parents . . ."

"We can hear them if they come up . . . There'll be plenty of time . . ."

He lifted her skirt roughly with both hands, slipped one hand deftly under her panties, pushed her legs apart and put his finger into her vagina.

She suddenly wanted to cry. It was going to happen and she could feel everything in her body tense and harden. She was feeling like a dirty slut, getting fucked in a musty old room with the family downstairs. Not even his room, his bed! This was no fitting time . . . no romance, bells, soft tenderness to soothe her aching. He's taken his pants off now and pulled the panties off oh so roughly . . . She'd never seen him this way . . . he scared her . . . He was on top of her again now, kissing her very passionately and wetly . . . He's like an animal . . . Oh God, if it's going to happen I want all our clothes off, to feel him body to body . . . His goddamn sweater itches my jaw . . . I want to tell him to stop . . . I should tell him to stop . . .

But then if she did she'd halt the momentum of this great thing that was happening, she knew. Let it happen the way he wants it to happen. I love him. I love him. And whatever is going on with him will be okay, in time, as long as he's with me . . .

She felt the head of his penis nudging into her vagina and in an instant of panic she hissed, "What if I get pregnant . . . ?"

Ron pushed more deeply into her. "It'll be our baby. We're going to get married."

Doris sobbed and closed her eyes. There was no pain, absolutely none, as she lost the virginity that she'd been trying to lose for all the months she knew Ron. She moved into him and held him close to her and when she at last felt him come she sinned against her entire religious upbringing by thanking the Lord but she didn't care. There was something beautiful and holy about it and she didn't care.

When they left Lenny's room Ron sneered at it as he closed the door. There was a new, manly strut to him as he escorted her down the stairs through the living room and kitchen. In the back yard he informed his parents that they were engaged.

Louis and Ron took a walk after supper—leaving Doris to weigh heavily on Blanche.

Ron felt prepared when Louis said, "Ron, I'd like to talk to you about Lenny."

"Sure dad."

"I've been thinking a lot lately, reading some . . . What do you think? Do you think I was a bit too harsh. I mean what he turned out to be was pretty awful and I felt in a way that I had to protect you, but I don't know . . ."

"Me. There was never any danger with me, dad."

"I can see that now."

"Did you ever doubt it?"

"Kids are impressionable and you always looked up to him so much."

"Well, those things are basic. I've always gone with girls."

"Ron. Have you heard from Lenny at all?"

"No. Not for a long time. He went to Japan to study with some Japanese black-belt master and I haven't heard from him since."

"How long ago was that?"

"About three years ago."

They walked in silence some more.

"It's starting to get dark," Louis observed.

"Yes."

"We ought to start back."

They turned and started to walk back to the house.

"Did he ever talk much about me . . . us? Was he bitter?"

"No, he wasn't bitter. He never said much about it, but he understood. The same kind of thing happened to most of them too."

"I suppose it's common among them, huh?"

"I think it is."

"A hell of a life they have to lead, huh?"

"I'll say. A hell of a life."

On the following Thursday night, Lenny stood across the street from his old house for several minutes. It was dusk and the few people who walked by him seemed not to notice the young man in a light gray jacket, corduroy slacks and an open-necked shirt, slightly balding in the same spot as the master of that particular house, Louis Starr. One could almost take him for a statue from his motionless, rock-solid presence. But Lenny was scared.

Why the hell was he bothering? They didn't give a shit about him. Why did he care about them? He knew he couldn't make them understand, even though he understood about them. Why come all the way across the country for this?

He wanted to turn around and go back but then he told himself, you spent all your money for plane fare so you might as well go ahead. If they turn away in disgust it won't be any worse than it has been . . .

He went ahead.

His third step up the porch brought forth a startling squeak, almost turning him back. He paused on the next step . . . Maybe no one was home. The house seemed empty, not the way he'd remembered it with Ron banging away on the goddamn piano and their friends coming and going.

He rapped with the big brass knocker and waited.

He heard someone on the other side of the door. Who was it? God, what if his father saw him and dropped dead? What then?

But it was his mother's voice, "Coming . . . coming . . ."

The door opened and she was facing him. Lenny saw her eyes crinkle with tears, sorrow and gladness and fear crossing her face all at the same time. She cried out and almost leaped at him and they hugged each other, kissing each other's cheeks, mumbling inconsequential yet terribly meaningful things to each other.

Lenny heard his father's voice from the study. "Who is it?" Louis walked out of the study and looked over the landing at the front door.

There was no answer. Lenny and Blanche were by the front door, their arms around each other, watching Louis come slowly down the stairs. There was absolutely no expression on Louis' face. Lenny braced himself for the slap his father was going to give him and decided he was ready to turn around and go back to California now. His mother's greeting had been all he needed.

Louis came right up to him and peered very closely at his face, then calmly extended his hand to Lenny. They shook each other's hands and then Louis' hand went on Lenny's and Lenny's on Louis'. Lenny wished he could embrace his father, but to his surprise Louis took him by the back of the neck and hugged him.

Then Blanche and Louis put their arms around their son's shoulders and took him into their house, gently closing the door behind him.

Early the next evening Lenny took the bus into New York City. In the bus station men's room he folded his gray jacket and put on a black leather one over a tight maroon T-shirt and a purple scarf. He shaved closely, doused himself with cologne and took the subway to Greenwich Village. It wasn't long before he had tried someone against a mail truck on Christopher Street, snorted a bit of coke, and had run into his old friend the Louisiana Queen.

After a drink or two together, Lenny said, "You know something, assholes are more flaccid in California than they are in New York."

"It's the heat . . . loosens everything up."

"Oh?" Lenny replied, absentmindedly drinking straight Bourbon and feeling more ornery by the minute. "But cocks are tauter out there. Can you explain that?"

"Tauter?"

"Yes, definitely tauter."

"Closer to the sun. The sun stretches things."

"Both ways. You can't have it both ways."

Lenny plunked some money on the bar. "I'm going."

"Where?"

"Visit."

"Who?"

"My rat fuck bastard brother on the East Side in the seventies."

"The East Side in the seventies? Disgusting neighborhood."

"That's right."

"Do me a favor sweetheart, tear the son of a bitch apart."

Lenny laughed mischievously.

José the doorman spotted Lenny rounding the corner and prided himself on knowing immediately that this was a maricon. He'd worked in an apartment house on Fifth Avenue where guys like this would sneak in while the rich guys' wives were away. This one had a different swagger and arrogance, though—almost like a toreador. José was shocked when the maricon made for the apartment-house lobby. This was a straight building; who the hell would he want to see here? Somehow this guy looked familiar.

José stood squarely in Lenny's way. "Who you want here?"

"Ron Starr."

Oh Jesus, it figures, José thought. "I got to announce you."

"Listen, I'm his brother from California. I want to surprise him."

"It's almost midnight. Some time for a surprise. I have to announce you, that's the rules."

"Hey, come on. Don't you believe in surprises?"

"How do I know you're his brother?"

"Can't you see the resemblance?" Lenny engaged José's eyes. "Come on," he whispered.

"He's up there"—José hesitated conspiratorially—"with his girl."

They snickered. For a wild moment José imagined this out-and-out maricon breaking in on his masquerading brother, and the scene delighted him. He almost wished he could give this guy the key to the apartment and be there to see the action.

"Listen," José said, opening the door for Lenny. "If it ever comes up, you got in with one of the other tenants and I wasn't here . . . okay?"

"Okay. Thanks."

"Nada."

The buzzer woke Doris first and she moved Ron's shoulder gently to awaken him. He'd drunk too much this evening and had fallen asleep before they could even do anything. Yet she didn't want to complain. It had been getting better. Sometimes it was great and that gave her a glimpse of what it was going to be like if she persisted. One of the stories that she had come across in the positive-attitude books, one which was a constant source of inspiration to her, was the three-feet-from-gold story where the prospector stops digging after years of work to later find out that when he'd stopped he was just three feet from a strike. And someone else came along, dug the three measly feet and found all the gold.

So when he made love to her as if it were a dirty chore, when he made her lie on her stomach and not face him, she thought of the story and of the other times when they would make love fully, with him on top, kissing her just the way it was meant to be. When the good times happened she often felt sure that he was going to finally set the date, but something always held him back and it would go bad for awhile. He'd get nasty and sarcastic. But it was all right. Men were like that. They start feeling trapped. It's common. The woman just has to wait it out. Ron will be much better when he just lets himself set the date.

"Ron, there's someone at the door."

Without a word he rolled out of bed. He scooped his robe from the bedpost, pulling it on over his pajamas, and walked into the living room. Doris slipped on her slacks and the over-size white T-shirt that Ron liked her to wear as a pajama.

"See who it is first," she said as she saw him unlocking the door without even looking through the peephole.

But he didn't care who it might be . . . Any diversity in this relationship—be it earthquake, tidal wave or the fires of hell—would be welcome. Sometimes Doris hung over him like a lead blanket, burdening and smothering him, and no amount of Scotch could hide it. Why didn't he break it off? Because other times it was all right—better than all right. He loved going to company functions with his "fiancée." She was interested in his career, and they could talk about this man or that—what made him successful or not. She was learning the business. Ron shared experiences with her. She had a good sense of who would make it and who wouldn't, which vice-president he would do well to cultivate and which to avoid. When they were clicking along together that way he could make love to her fully man-woman, and he knew that if there was any hope it was going to be built along those lines. And when it wasn't clicking along that way he could use his imagination easily enough with her. It would work out. He had to be constantly on guard and sometimes he just couldn't find the spirit to go on, but he knew that he must. He should set the date, but he'd wait a bit longer, at least until things were all right a majority of the time instead of a minority. Tonight he didn't give much of a fuck who was knocking on the door.

He swung the door open and Lenny strutted in. "Hello, little brother."

Lenny walked past Ron and right up to Doris. "Introduce me to your friend. Tom? Dick? or Harry?"

Ron closed the door and said, "This is Doris. Doris, this is my brother Lenny."

"Oh," Doris said. "I'm so glad to meet you."

Ron was pale. For a crazy moment Ron considered running, then relocked the door and leaned against the wall.

Lenny swished around the apartment inspecting it. "Oh how lovely," he said at this piece of furniture or that painting.

"Can I get you anything?" Doris asked Lenny.

"Yes darling . . . You're so kind . . . Anything with alcoholic content please . . ."

Doris opened the louvered doors to the kitchen and fixed Lenny a Scotch, deciding not to make one for Ron.

"Where did you find her, darling?" Lenny lisped at Ron. "She's absolutely perfect."

Lenny sat on the brown suede couch, leaned back and seemed to relax as Doris brought his drink. But Ron knew his brother. When he appeared to relax was when he was the most treacherous. Ron moved off the wall a bit less shaky now.

"Aren't you having one?" Lenny asked.

"No."

Doris was pleased.

"What about you?" Lenny asked Doris.

"All right," she said, stepping back to the kitchen. "I'll get a little white wine. I can't really drink. Your brother drinks a bit too much—you should scold him."

"Oh, he never used to drink," Lenny said. "Something bothering you, little brother?"

"He works so hard. There's no other assistant manager in the company who puts in the kind of hours he does. Any time one of his men needs him he's available—day or night."

"Oh, that's lovely. I bet they're a charismatic bunch, aren't they?"

"Oh, some of them are pretty good-looking. We have one fellow, Gil Sloane, who used to be a male model. He's beautiful . . . if you like that type I mean . . ." She came back in with her wine.

"My God, I'd love to meet him. Do he and Ron work very closely with each other?"

Ron interrupted, "Doris, don't you have to go home now?"

"Oh, I can stay," she said, and sat down again. "I've been dying to meet your brother. I love it when families get together especially after long absences." She turned to Lenny. "I was talking to your father about my uncle in Italy. Were you upstate to see them yet?"

"Yes," Lenny replied, with a significant look at Ron. "I've been upstate."

"Oh? How did it go?" Ron asked, mentally rehearsing all the things he was prepared to say—never received the letters or the phone call, changed his phone number because of . . .

"Went great," Lenny replied. Blissfully Ron saw he wasn't pursuing it.

"Family reunions are so special," Doris went on. "My father is going to Italy to see his brother who he hasn't ever written to in ten years. Ron, it is too bad you weren't there."

"I'm sorry I missed it."

Lenny said, "If your number hadn't been unlisted, you might not have. Why did you have your number unlisted? Crank calls?"

"Sort of."

"Homosexual overtures?"

Doris was looking at Lenny.

"Do you know what a homosexual overture is?" he asked. She

227

stared at him. "When a fag writes opening music for an opera, that's a homosexual overture."

Doris thought a moment longer and then laughed. "You've got a funny brother, Ron."

"Yeah," Ron said. Hilarious. "How long are you in town for?"

"Oh, I don't know. Not long. I'll be going back out to California soon."

"California must be wonderful," Doris said. "So sunny."

Ron said, "Listen, you can stay here for the night, I've got to take Doris home and I'll be back soon. If you're up we'll talk. I want to hear all about what happened upstate."

Lenny said to Doris, "See any good movies on TV lately?"

"No. We don't watch that much TV," Doris replied, ignoring Ron's reach for her arm. Why was he trying to get rid of her? His brother was so colorful, she thought, people in California seem to all be like that. She wedged herself deeper into the pillows of the couch. "Have you?"

"I saw one the other night called *Pinky*. It was made in the late forties or early fifties I guess. It was with Jeanne Crain . . ."

"Oh yes," Doris said, sipping her wine. "She's one of my favorites. Whatever happened to her?"

Ron went to the counter of the kitchen and poured a Scotch over three ice cubes. He leaned against the counter and watched the two of them as if they were actors in a play—*The Copperhead and the Rabbit* by Ron Starr . . . his play . . . He could have been writing it . . . Usually he played the part of the rabbit but this time it was Doris . . . Well, he was too in a way, that's what made it interesting. He could watch and be eaten at the same time. Yes, Lenny was the snake, beginning to hypnotize his prey, his eyes engaging hers, and she was becoming fascinated. When he sipped his drink his tongue flicked over the edge of the glass. And as Doris, the perfect little white rabbit, set herself up to be gobbled Lenny sent a shadow of a smile obliquely at Ron—acknowledging, as a good omniscient snake should, that he knew that Ron knew what was going on.

228

"It's about this Negro girl, Pinky, real pretty, real light-skinned, who's passing for white. Big problems. She falls for this nice white guy, William Lundigan . . ."

I've worried about this moment so much that now that it's here I can enjoy it, Ron thought as he tasted the Scotch. They're about five feet apart on the couch. I bet he moves closer and closer to her and she to him so that when he strikes . . . snaps her up—it'll be quick and deadly. She is so inane. Everything's fine by her. Lenny is doing me a great favor to get rid of her. God knows I couldn't do it. Thank you brother copperhead, thank you.

"Well, anyway, they wind up getting married and having big problems. Will he ever find out? Will they have pickaninny children? That kind of thing."

"Yes," Doris said thoughtfully, sipping her wine, alert to the deadly charm of Lenny's face yet inching a bit closer to him on the couch. "Well, it's wrong to hide that kind of thing, I think."

"Well, she was afraid she'd lose him. She loved him."

"Still—it wasn't fair. When people get married they should be totally honest with each other."

When he does it, will he do it so badly that she screams in pain, Ron wondered. Should I deny it? Of course—that goes without saying.

They were about three feet apart on the couch and Lenny's tongue seemed to dart as he talked. "Well, then we're all agreed. Total honesty in marriage, even between families. For instance, I'd want to know if my brother was getting into a family with Mafia connections."

Doris smiled. "My father keeps saying that he'd like to run into the Mafia and get some of that racketeer money that everyone thinks Italians have—but he's only kidding, of course."

What if Doris is so upset that she tells people in the office, Ron thought. Her porky girl friend Nancy, for instance. Nancy would spread the word in a minute. I never thought of that. Doris wouldn't do it, she's not that type, yet . . . who knows . . . When you're hurt you sometimes lash out.

"We have secrets in our family," Lenny confessed, lowering his voice. "For instance, I'm a homosexual." They were about two and a half feet apart now and Lenny's first strike had been delivered deftly, skillfully—Ron admired it enormously. Doris looked blankly at Lenny, then turned to Ron, but he maintained an inscrutable stare—after all, he was just audience.

Doris chose not to reply.

"What do you think of that?" Lenny prodded softly.

"Think of what?"

"What I just told you."

"Is it true?"

"Yes."

Doris turned to Ron. "Is it true?"

Just audience, darling, Ron thought, and forbade any expression to appear on his face. Ahhh, he knew what he would do . . . He'd come in tomorrow and talk to Parkinson and Gil and everyone else about problems he was having with Doris . . . She didn't turn him on anymore . . . That would counter any rumors. He'd invent a new girl friend, someone in this building, big bazooms . . .

"I-I'm sorry," Doris told Lenny.

"For what?"

"For your affliction."

"How Catholic you are." They were two feet apart now. "That is a Catholic word—affliction."

Lenny moved even closer to Doris. She was mesmerized. The strike was coming and Ron waited for it suspended . . . suspended . . . suspended while it came with great deliberate speed . . .

"Ron is one too."

Her face was framed in Ron's mind. Ron wanted to be able to remember the change of the eyes, the mouth, the complexion. Now that Lenny had struck, the audience would see the rabbit squeak and squirm.

"One what?"

"A homosexual."

Doris said firmly, "No, he's not."

Lenny crouched and even more firmly said, "Yes, he is."

"No, he's not. I know."

The copperhead had struck, but the rabbit had dodged. The copperhead ought to have realized that the rabbit had carnal knowledge of me, Ron thought. What are you going to do now, Mr. Copperhead? He watched Lenny lean back a bit and take a breath for the next strike.

"Look," he said reasonably. "I understand that this comes as a bit of a shock. I'm telling you so that you and my brother don't make a tragic mistake. It won't work. It can't work . . . even though he may be able to be, at this point, what you might consider normal. I know where his heart is. He really is homosexual."

Lenny drained his glass and waited. Doris sipped her wine.

"Do you think that because he fucks you that he's not queer?"

Wince, Doris, wince, Ron thought. God, she's impassive.

"I could fuck you if I wanted to," Lenny continued quite reasonably. "You're absolutely adorable in that T-shirt . . . I love the flat look. Now do yourself and Ron a favor and get yourself lost back in the wilds of the Bronx. You're over your head here."

She's not turning color, not starting to cry, she's just peering evenly at Lenny, Ron observed.

Lenny slid very close to her. He lifted himself slightly above her by putting his knees on the couch so that she was looking up at him as he whispered venomously, "That man there—your Ron—he has put men's cocks in his mouth. Fucked and been fucked up the ass. Those lips . . . guess where they've been. If you marry him he'll wind up plunking little boys, lurking around men's rooms—all the sick crazy things you hear about he will do. He will be treacherous and nasty . . . the way he was to me and my parents by blocking our reunion so that he could hide me. That's what happens to people who hide themselves this way. They can't help it—that's just what happens. In other words, Doris, listen to me. Your future husband, your Ron, is a cocksucker. Do you understand? A cocksucker."

Doris half smiled at Lenny and then turned to Ron and said, "You know, he's just like my brother Carmine. I mean, you know, Carmine curses a lot and he tries to shock people. I think it's a way of calling attention to himself or something." She faced Lenny. "You know, you ought to realize you don't have to talk this way to get attention. You seem to be a nice intelligent man. I think you ought to let your brother give you some of the books that we've been reading . . . Ron, I think *The Magic of Belief* would be good for him, don't you?"

Lenny jerked back, like a copperhead shot with a gun. Ron roared to himself—she is magnificent. Magnificent!

The rabbit had eaten the snake.

They were married in two months.

CHAPTER 12

Ron worked in five-year plans, like the Russians. He set goals moment to hour, hour to week, week to month, month to year, and year to five years. Anything beyond that was a pipe dream.

In the five-year plan he had set down for all to see (part of the success of a plan was showing it openly so that the pressure of other people would help achieve it) the following predominated:

Having a baby. It had to be a girl. He gave himself mind treatments and made Doris do the same.

Getting his own office as a full manager and establishing it on a very solid base. He was too young by most standards but he didn't abide by standards.

Buying his own home. He'd picked his area, Jamaica Estates in Queens. The quiet elegance, old-fashioned small-town rich-section feel of the area spoke to him.

Unwritten was the goal calling for the complete elimination of all urges, drives, etc., that could cause problems. The written goals were achieved. The unwritten one not quite.

There were times when months, or was it weeks, well days anyway when he felt nothing for anyone . . . well almost nothing, but it was controllable, always controllable . . . never any danger of *that*.

All that however was minuscule compared to the greatness of his life now.

First and foremost was his baby girl Valerie. He worshipped her. He'd named her Valerie because when he was a child he'd seen an English actress named Valerie Hobson in old TV movies whom he adored for her intelligent beauty, wit and warm sophistication. He'd imitated her in the mirror: "Really darling, we can't have Lord Bore here for tennis, not with Janet about." Ron could stay in Valerie's room silently watching her sleep or toss about in her playpen, contentedly, the way one can watch waves coming in at the beach. He took countless pictures. He bathed her, lingering more than necessary in the folds of her vagina—marveling at it—it was a part of him, wasn't it? That part—that feminine part that had been his plague but also had been his salvation.

He knew that what made him successful was the warmth he had for men, being able to be with them, take care of and mother them. In these folds was the so-called "sick" thing that he'd made work for him in business yet was forced to hide and try to do away with. Through his daughter it could live somehow in a good, sound, healthy way. It couldn't be explained without sounding sick or weird but he knew it wasn't. He could grow up with her, be a little girl, a teeny-bopper, then a young lady and a mother. He could laugh at the antics of boys showing off, cry openly when hurt, skip down streets, neck with boys, have a "friend," make love and have a baby . . . all through Valerie without distorting

234

her. Perhaps that would prove enough. He fervently hoped so but if not . . . well he'd had her. He could love that part of himself openly and freely now . . . openly and freely, he'd think as he rinsed away the soap, cleaning it, toweling it, powdering it.

For Doris he had no five-year plan. Their relationship had nowhere to go because it was where he wanted it to be; so did Doris, who wanted whatever he wanted.

That Doris could give him something so precious as Valerie; that she could preside over his Jamaica Estates home, be his hostess, his business partner and his wife—all this made her supremely content. She suffered no sexual frustrations but was troubled that Ron often did. He was moody and withdrawn and needed to do things in strange ways. If she could only calm him, let him know that that whole thing wasn't all that important. It was how you lived that mattered. Building a great business and having a beautiful home and a child and leading a useful productive life. If he could only be as happy as she was. My God, if she never did it it would be all right with her, although she certainly enjoyed it when it was done right; like going to a good play or seeing a nice movie.

On Ron's way home some nights he drove past a street corner where young men smoked cigarettes in doorways, pretending to be just hanging out while warily looking out at the street waiting for cars to pull up to the curb.

At first he was amazed to see this kind of thing uptown, in the open this way. It was shocking, uncomfortable to have it this close to his office. For a while he chose different ways to go home, then he forgot all about it. But in time his car seemed to head itself for that street. He was less shocked now and more curious. The young men, boys mostly, weren't attractive—life was treating them too harshly. Ron went through a "there but for the grace of God and the insurance business" syndrome. He could have evolved to that. He wondered if Lenny ever did, but he tried never to think much about his brother anymore. They were three thousand miles, a million light years apart, except for an occasional token visit when Lenny came to visit upstate (that was weird to Ron—his parents actually looked forward to those visits) . . . He didn't want to think about any of that.

Soon though he felt safe enough to imagine himself in their midst. He could see himself joking, bumming cigarettes, pot, pushing playfully, dancing . . . being glad or jealous when a car pulled to the curb, opened its door and swallowed one of them up.

He hated the customers and hoped that the boys fleeced them. They were fucks, cheating on their wives or lovers. The boys were mostly transients, though there were some steadies. Ron contrived to have coffee at the diner across the street, or drive around, watching. He started to play favorites, identify regular customers, note techniques. It was an interesting game and he'd have loved to share it with someone the way some of his agents liked to watch the way the female prostitutes worked. But of course sharing this kind of thing was out of the question. Meanwhile he watched a game at which he could be both spectator and, through his imagination, participant.

There was one . . .

He fascinated Ron. Not that he was Ron's type—not at all. Ron would have run from that—a streetcorner prostitute not a mile away from his office—talk about self-destruction, Oscar Wilde would have nothing on him. This one had balls, chutzpah, style, pizzazz—yet he was as funky as the times, dressing in a cheap tan Stetson hat over a speckled Indian band, ragged imitation leather boots with dark jeans and white U.S. cavalry stripes sewn on a white T-shirt with a peace sign and an overdone buckskin leather jacket. Mix 'n' match. He had long stringy blond hair that straggled down nearly to his shoulders. He had pimples around his mouth, which was his worst feature, but the rest of his face was quite ingenuous. He was such an insane mixture of everything. He had the best-selling technique of all because he just didn't seem to care. Ron had some agents like that, where the prospects almost have to plead with the man to sell them. He loved that quality of poised elusiveness, the ability to control a situation without seeming to care about the outcome, perhaps because it contrasted so much to his own ever-churning enthusiasm. This lad never peered hungrily into the streets, yet Ron knew that he was more aware than the others of what went on. The men who would drive up often had to beep for him or even get out of their cars and almost plead with him. He spurned customers until the price was made attractive enough.

Ron wanted to talk to him . . . find out what made a kid like this tick . . .

One evening he went home, ate supper and returned using Doris' Ford instead of his own Mercedes which everyone in the office knew. He put on dark glasses and a hat as he pulled up to the curb where the boys were. He double-checked his car doors to see that they were locked, since some of them were brazen enough to jump in and try to hustle. He had prepared himself for a cool reception from his young mix 'n' match and was amazed when the young man boldly strode to his car. Ron jabbed at the button to lower the power window on the passenger's side, opening the back window by mistake before he got the front one down.

His mix 'n' match stuck his head through the door, the roof of the car knocking the Stetson back. "Hi ya'll . . ." he said. Ron hadn't expected this phony, almost vaudeville western accent. "Can I come in?"

Ron pushed the button for the power doors and the lever on the passenger side shot up. He slid into the car.

"What's your pleasure, friend?"

"No pleasure," he said after a moment of clearing his dry throat, "I just want to talk."

"I'm a businessman, mister, just like you, I'm sure, or you wouldn't be ownin' the most expensive model that Mr. Ford makes . . . Costs more than a Caddie I betcha . . ."

"That's right."

"Tape deck, back and front speakers, all power . . . you like to push them buttons, huh? Now if someone takes you away from your lucrative business you couldn't afford all this, now could you."

And it's only my wife's car, Ron thought, as he asked, "How much?"

"Thirty."

"That's expensive."

"Cheaper than all this here drivin' around you been doing and drinkin' bad coffee and eatin' in dingy diners."

So he'd noticed.

Ron produced a twenty and a ten and watched it disappear in the left side pocket of the cavalry jeans.

"I don't want to do anything though."

"It's time not flesh you're payin' for."

"How much time?"

"Not much."

"Okay." Ron jerked his head to the left, saw there were no cars coming and quickly pulled away from the curb. He was more at ease by the time he stopped for the first red light and was able to look at his new passenger.

"What's your name?"

"Gregg," the young man said. Actually his name was Bedřich.

"Where you from?"

"Tennessee." Bedřich was from Pennsylvania.

Ron activated the tape deck with the thousand strings of Mantovani.

The light changed and he went on. He was feeling calm now, glad that he'd started this adventure.

"Want some coffee?"

Gregg tersely shook his head no.

"What do ya'll want to talk about?"

"You."

Ron parked the car on a nearly empty street close to a darkened office building. He shut off the headlights but let the engine idle. He offered Gregg a cigarette from a compact gold-plated cigarette case. He lit the cigarette for Gregg with his lighter, noting the

pimples on the chin and the unattractive mouth with some reas-
surance because the intimacy of Gregg's presence had just started
to affect him.

"I'm always willin' to talk about me."

"Mainly I'd like to ask you what you are doing with your life?"

Gregg peered closely at Ron and said, "You ain't no religious
nut 'cause they'd never pay thirty dollars to you to preach at you.
Them fuckers collect, they don't pay."

"No, I'm no religious nut. I'm just a businessman, but if I
hadn't wised up I could have been doing what you're doing now."

"Is that so?"

"Could have been."

"You think I ought to change my ways, huh?"

Ron laughed. "I guess it sounded that way didn't it? How old
are you?"

"Nineteen." Gregg was twenty-three but nineteen had more
appeal.

"Run away from home?"

"My folks didn't like my ways and so it was best I left and got
out on my own." Gregg did that line with practiced ease—the
repressed hurt, bitterness and anger seeping through. He was
usually able to get an extra ten for that because the fairies could
cry with it. Actually his parents had split up years ago.

Ron lit a cigarette and leaned back. He removed his sunglasses
and looked directly at him. "You want to know something? I
think you're full of shit."

"Huh?"

"You heard me. I think you're full of shit. Your accent. Your
act. It's phony. It's all part of your technique."

Gregg laughed. "You sure are smart."

"More technique."

"There's no stoppin' you is there?"

"I'd just like to talk to you. The real you. Not your technique."

"Well, I appreciate that but I've got to be gettin' back now,
so if we could kind of get down to business . . ." Gregg suddenly

slid closer to Ron and put his hand on Ron's knee. Ron quickly shoved it off.

"I told you I just want to talk," he said sharply, the touch not quite leaving him.

"You got a few more minutes," Gregg said, leaning back on the seat and listening to Mantovani's version of "Lover." "But after you done talked yourself out you're goin' to want to do something and there ain't goin' to be time."

"You don't believe that I just want to talk. That I want to get to know you—that I don't want to do anything."

"Hell no."

"Want to go back now?" Ron asked.

"Your pleasure."

Ron pulled away from the curb and started back. He put his sunglasses on and looked sideways at Gregg—hoping to catch a look of surprise or wonder. Gregg was stone-faced, humming.

Ron stopped at the curb about a block from where he'd picked Gregg up.

"You can get out now if you like," he said.

"You mean you really don't want nothin'?"

"I told you."

"No refund or nothin'?"

"No."

"Okay."

Ron released the door lock. The lever shot up.

"I would like to get to know you though. And really talk to you about yourself."

"You know where you can find me."

"Where do you live? I'd like to get in touch with you aside from here."

"I got to be goin' now."

He opened the door but before he got out he swiftly leaned over, put his hand on Ron's thigh and kissed Ron's earlobe softly, flicking his tongue below it on the neck and sending surprised shivers up Ron's spine. "Bye ya'll, hear."

240

And then he was gone.

That night at home Doris got it full front for a change.

"You know what I don't like about you?" Gregg said to Ron the next time they were parked next to the same office building. "You're a phony."

"Why?"

" 'Cause you just want one thing . . . maybe two or three but you come on like you don't."

"If I want it why don't I get it then?"

"I don't know. Why don't you?"

"Maybe I don't want it."

"Ha."

"If you thought better of yourself you might believe that I'm interested in you as a person."

"I had a psychiatrist fella who told me the same thing. He wanted to treat me . . . get me on his couch."

"How did you meet him?"

"Same way I'm meeting you."

"Weird."

"Only difference is he got his money's worth."

"Did he want to treat you for your homosexuality or for your hustling?"

"I ain't no homosexual."

"Ha!"

"Catch me being a goddamn queer!" Gregg jammed his cigarette out and said to Ron, "You goin' to do anything tonight?"

"My time's not up yet."

"You know something. You pissin' me off."

"Why?"

"Forget it."

"You want to know my name?"

"Not particularly . . . All right what the hell is your name?"

"Ron."

"Is that your right name?"

"Yes."

"Now look Ron—if you goin' to do somethin' this time you'd better start, 'cause I want to get back. If you don't I'm goin' to tell you something and then you gonna take me back, okay?"

"Okay."

"Okay what?"

"Tell me something."

"I ain't no goddamn queer! I just happen to have a cock that comes up whenever it's around any human hole that's warm and fuzzy and cozy enough to house it. My preference is young ladies if it's any interest to you but young ladies ain't in the habit of payin'—least not the young ladies around St. Marks Place . . ."

"Oh, you hang out in the East Village?"

"Yes, I hang out in the East Village."

"Where? Maybe I can meet you down there and we can have a drink together."

"Fuck off. Take me back. We don't drink much down there."

"Doesn't matter."

"Take me back please."

Ron brought the car back to the corner and released the door. Gregg turned toward him. Ron was ready to block any advances.

"You give me another tenner and we can do something real quick . . . right here . . . won't take but a minute."

"Why the bargain? Do you enjoy it?"

"Sure," Gregg said seductively.

"That makes you queer."

Gregg's face became red. "I'm going to punch you right in the mouth, you know that. You're the fucking queer!"

"I haven't touched you."

"You're still a goddamn queer!"

"I used to be. I straightened up. I'm not that way anymore. Listen," Ron held Gregg's arm and said forcefully, "I'm a married man. I enjoy a full, open, and complete sexual union with my wife. I have a child, a beautiful wonderful child. I have a career—a great career. I turned myself around from the same kind of road you're on. It can be done. You can do it. You've got to believe you can and you will. You've got so much on the ball and you're not like the rest of them . . ."

"You better believe it."

"Then what are you doing out there?"

"It's the easiest money in New York."

"Bullshit, it's the hardest."

"Goodbye. See you."

"Where's your accent?"

"Fuck you!" Gregg slammed the door as he left.

"You know you got to me the last time—you know that?"

"Good."

"Was you ever a hustler?"

"No."

"Then you don't know what it's like."

"No, tell me."

"Never mind."

They both smoked silently for a while, listening to "Night and Day" on the tape.

"There's this freaky kid down the East Village named Donna . . . from Idaho . . . freaky but real nice . . . She's my girl you know."

"Yeah?"

"Yeah. We been thinking of getting a place of our own and living there . . . gettin' a job . . . that kind of thing . . . me gettin' off the streets . . . I'm gettin' tired of it, I really don't need all the money that I make . . . I piss it all away, you know . . ."

"You make good money, don't you?"

"You better believe it."

They smoked a while.

"You're a nice guy," Gregg said.

"Thank you."

"You really don't want nothin'."

Ron just shook his head slightly.

"My name ain't Gregg you know . . . it's Bedřich."

"After Smetena? Bohemian?"

"Lithuanian. I'm from Pennsylvania. Never been to Tennessee. Can I ask you something?"

"Sure."

"Can I get a job?"

"Why not?"

"Doin' what you're doin'?"

"Sure."

"You would hire me?"

"Sure. But you don't even know what I do."

"No . . . but I bet it's good."

"I'm in the life insurance business. I'm a manager. I hire and train agents to sell insurance."

"Hell, I could do that."

"You're a little young. Nineteen . . ."

"I ain't nineteen. I'm twenty-four—well I'll be twenty-four soon. You would hire me? You wouldn't be afraid that it'd get out the things you told me about yourself . . . where you met me and stuff?"

"You wouldn't tell, would you?"

"No."

"I trust you."

Gregg chuckled and lit another cigarette from the one he had. He leaned back into the soft brown leather of the car seat and relaxed. "Pipe dreams."

Ron put his cigarette out and said, "It doesn't have to be pipe dreams. I've hired people who've been dropouts from the human race in every way. I've taught them to get a belief in themselves and run with it."

"I'll think about it. I have to get back now."

Ron was disappointed but he didn't want to push too much. He was making progress and that would be enough for now. "All right," Ron said. "I'll take you back." As he turned around to check traffic he felt Gregg's hand on his upper thigh. "Ron,"

Gregg whispered, "come on, let me do you."

Ron gently but firmly took Gregg's hand away from his thigh. "I told you I don't want that and I mean it."

"But all that money . . ."

"It's okay."

Ron drove. Gregg had moved closer now and it made Ron uncomfortable. The whispered proposition still reverberated through him. He was shaky and unsure, and during the entire ride he didn't dare look sideways at Gregg.

When they were at the corner where Ron usually let Gregg off, Gregg just sat there as if he were about to cry.

"What's the matter?" Ron asked, and he put his arm around Gregg's shoulder.

Gregg reached into one of the pockets of his buckskin and brought something out, shoving it affirmatively into Ron's hand. It was a wad of money. Ron knew that it was ninety dollars, the amount of money he'd given Gregg since he'd known him.

"What's this?" he asked.

"It's your money. I don't want it."

"Take it, it's yours. It's all right."

There were tears in Gregg's eyes. "Look, I ain't had nobody genuinely interested in me since I can remember . . . maybe nobody ever was or ever will be 'cept . . . you . . . I ain't gonna take no money off you . . ."

"Okay," Ron said, letting the money fall on the car seat between them. "You'll let me help you then?"

"No," Gregg touched Ron's cheek. "You don't understand. I-I can't do straight things, nine-to-five plastic things . . . you know . . . I mean, I can't hack that stuff you know . . . ?"

"Bullshit, you can . . ."

"No, look, let this be goodbye, okay. When you come around again I ain't going in your car . . . thanks for the offer anyway but I can't hack it . . ."

Gregg reached for the door handle. Ron was suddenly furious.

"Take your fucking money then—you *are* nothing but a prostitute." Ron picked up the money with one hand and grabbed Gregg's arm with the other. "You are a prostitute and you always want to be one, right? Here." Ron attempted to stuff the money in Gregg's jacket pocket. They scuffled a bit. Ron's palm rubbed against Gregg's chest. He held him with one hand around the shoulder and the other on Gregg's chest but Gregg's squirming made it impossible to get the money in. He then tried to put it in the pocket of Gregg's jeans, but somehow his hand fell on Gregg's penis which was fairly bursting from its tight denim prison.

The years. The years without it. Why? Why? The moment that Gregg flicked something on his waistband and Ron felt the heat of Gregg's penis in his hand and on his face he knew that he'd missed this oh so much—too much—he could have it both —millions did it. He deserved it . . . he needed it . . . and most of all he wanted it . . . with a great, desperate, dreadful, palate-gnawing, beautiful hunger. When he experienced the wet, shaky explosions he felt like a human puzzle into which the last missing piece had just been dropped. He savored every drop, licking the skin, fondling, knowing that he could never hide this part of himself from himself, ever again.

When it was over Gregg deftly picked up the wad of money and said to Ron, "Now who's the queer?"

Ron chuckled weakly and lazily watched as Gregg opened the car door, pulled his hat cockily down on his head and with a sure step once more went to his corner.

CHAPTER 13

Ron shuffled his feet in the shadows at the farthest end of the small, dark, woodeny off-off Broadway theater on the Lower East Side. He was edgy. For the fifth night in a row he had seen David Corday, and now he was determined to approach him. The play was closing and this was his last chance. The other nights that he'd waited with the small crowd of people, most of whom were friends of the actors, he'd felt like a canoe above a waterfall and he'd stopped himself, haranguing himself. God, he was developing a crush on an actor whom he'd never even spoken to—insane! He'd have to stop. Yet he was back again. He was sure that David had noticed him by now . . . he was sure they'd talk.

David appeared from backstage carrying a little Air Canada traveling bag. He wore a navy blue pea coat and dark Levis with pale white tennis shoes. As on stage he moved strongly, lithely with just a touch of fey. Ron's throat was caught up and tight as he made himself emerge from the shadows and say, "Hi."

"Oh, hello," David replied, his voice miraculously having that same effortless ease that Ron had loved on the stage.

"I just wanted to tell you how much I, well, enjoyed really isn't a good enough word for it . . ."

David laughed. His laugh was very natural and spontaneous. "Thank you."

David had stopped and Ron noted that he was taller than he seemed on stage. His side right teeth were crooked and chipped, making his beauty seem more human but probably hurting his chances to get TV or movie work. Ron felt a crazy impulse to tell him right there and then that if he wanted to get his teeth fixed he'd pay for it. "Can I buy you a drink?" Ron asked.

David paused for a second, his deep, dark brown eyes slowly scanning Ron's face before he smiled and said, "I'd like that."

He likes me. Ron knew it and he felt delicious chills all the way through him as David walked with him up the aisle toward the exit. Ron was proud to be beside him. They went out into the East Village street, and all the overflowing garbage cans and the refuse strewn about didn't dim for Ron the glow that he felt.

"Do you know a place?" Ron asked.

"Sure."

They walked in silence, each huddling into his coat against the brisk early spring air. Their silence was exploratory, not in the least uncomfortable.

Soon they were seated cozily in a dark bar where Ron saw some other people from the cast. Around him were words and phrases about the theater that he hadn't heard since college. Strange, he thought, they all look different now—beards and no bras, lots of hair—but the phrases and the cadences seem about the same.

Ron ordered a martini and David some red wine.

"I gather you enjoyed the play," David asked.

"*The Importance of Being Earnest* is probably my favorite play ever. When I studied theater in college our professor used it all the time to illustrate all the important playwrighting principles . . ."

"Oh, you studied theater?"

"It was a long time ago and like so many people I don't do anything anymore . . ."

"What did you do?"

"I wrote."

"Plays?"

"Yes, but that was fifteen, sixteen years ago. They weren't very good and I don't do it anymore . . ." Ron mumbled. He wanted to escape from that. "You are so *good*, do you know that?"

David laughed heartily. "Thank you. That is great to hear."

"There was no one else on the stage for me. I mean there was Jack and of course Lady Bracknell and dear Cecily but from now on there'll never be another Algernon for me. Never."

"I don't suppose your lady friend, the one you had with you the first night, shared your enthusiasm. She hasn't come back with you, has she?"

Ron played with his martini glass.

"That was no lady friend, that was my wife." They laughed together.

"Oh, you're married?"

"Yes, father of a lovely nine-year-old girl too."

"That's wonderful . . ." David leaned back and sipped his wine before he said, "The girl that is . . ."

Ron said nothing.

"Was I out of place?" David asked.

"No," Ron replied. He lit a cigarette.

"Having the girl is wonderful. The wife and the rest of it, well sometimes that's hard."

"I can imagine. I've always wanted to have children."

"Do you come from a large family?"

"Four. I was the youngest."

"I was the youngest too."

"How many in your family?"

"Just me and my brother."

Ron finished his drink and asked David if he wanted another one. David declined.

"Are you hungry? Come on, it's on me . . . or rather the company expense account if that'll make you happier . . . a big fat insurance company."

"Well, now that you mention it, yes, they have the finest cheeseburgers in town here. And their quiche is marvelous . . ."

Ron found himself lost in David's face, traveling the rolling gentle hills of the cheeks and nose as if in a pastoral idyll.

They said very little as they ate. They enjoyed the food and, more importantly, they enjoyed each other enjoying the food. They shared. They sipped each other's re-ordered drinks . . . When they finished, Ron called for the check and they went out into the cool night air.

"Do you live far from here?" Ron asked.

"Over on the West Side about Fourteenth Street."

"Oh, my brother used to live around there . . . Chelsea, right?"

"Yes. I share with a friend . . ."

"A friend?"

"Just a friend. Would you like to come by?"

"Yes. I'd like to . . . I'll get a cab . . ."

"All right."

During the cab ride to David's place Ron said, "I used to drive one of these, during my writing days . . . I hated it."

David touched the large tiger's eye ring that Doris had given him for his thirty-third birthday. "Nice."

David's finger lightly caressed Ron's knuckle. Ron was very aroused. He wanted to hold David in the cab and he knew that David felt the same—though why or how he couldn't imagine. David was so beautiful. He could get anyone he wanted. Ron was balding and pudgy, in his mid-thirties and not very handsome anymore, yet there seemed to be something that David felt for him.

"I've been going to the theater a great deal lately," he said. "The Broadway scene is much too commercial so it's been off-off for me. Sometimes you get to see some awful stuff but other times it's marvelous. This is your first New York role, right? At least that's what it said in the program."

"Yes."

"What now?"

"Auditions."

"Do you have an agent?"

"No, not yet. They're hard to come by."

"But they're important, right?"

"Oh yes."

I'd get you one, Ron thought. With your talent and looks, if you had the right clothes and someone with the kind of visionary persistence that I have, you'd have an agent and you'd start getting the right roles . . .

Easy Ron, you've just met him and you're already beginning to take over his life.

They walked five flights up to David's place. Ron was puffing and out of breath and on the third floor David stopped and said, "Let's rest here."

"No," Ron replied, walking past David. "It's okay . . ."

Ron loosened his tie and collar. He wished he hadn't worn a suit . . . it made him seem so out of place in these surroundings. He ought to get in shape though, stop smoking, cut down on his drinking. For the first time in a long while he thought about Lenny out in California with his self-defense school on the beach . . . Lenny must be in great shape.

David rented a room in a friend's large apartment. No one was home when they entered and Ron just followed David through some darkened rooms and into David's neat little bedroom. The place was immaculate—bed neatly made and everything precisely arranged on the dresser. There were no chairs in the room, only a bed, a dresser and a table for the small TV and a radio. David took Ron's overcoat and hung it in a small closet, then removed his own pea coat to reveal a faded cotton work shirt. Ron sat on a corner of the bed and David sat on the opposite corner. "I'm sorry I have nothing to offer you to drink or anything."

"That's all right . . ." Ron replied.

They felt tongue-tied and awkward.

Ron wanted to smoke but there was no ashtray in the spotless room and he didn't want to offend David. Finally David said, looking away, "I saw you and that lady in the audience on that first night . . . and I was hoping you'd come back. I sort of played to you. Somehow I felt you would . . . and then on the second night you were there again. It lifted me. That was a bad night, I remember, everything was going wrong . . . God . . . then I saw you waiting for me and I wanted you to come over but you didn't . . . I figured that you were shy . . ."

"I'm not usually . . ."

"You can smoke if you want to."

"You know me very well, don't you?"

"I think so . . ."

"I don't want to smoke."

"Good. You gave me a lot of anxiety you know . . ."

"I'm sorry."

"If you hadn't said anything to me this time I'd have said something to you."

"I just didn't think someone who looked like you and was like you could be interested in someone like me . . ."

David leaned across the bed and put his hand tenderly on Ron's cheek. "You have so much. I feel a wealth in you . . ."

Ron drew back and looked away from David.

"What's the matter?"

"I want to run," Ron said, amazed at his own frankness yet so glad that for the first time in his life he could say what was on his mind. "I'm afraid . . . I-I was in love once . . . and it hurt a great deal . . . Now for years it's been casual things . . . No"—

he turned and looked directly at David—"not casual things . . . That makes it sound better than it is . . . It's been prostitutes . . . It hasn't been very good, you know . . . but it's been better than getting hurt the way I was hurt . . ."

David put his hand on Ron's. "Do you want me to reassure you that I won't hurt you?"

"I-I guess I do . . ."

"I can't do that . . . except to say that I'm not that way."

They were very close now.

"You know," Ron said, "it's really crazy . . . I don't know you, you don't know me . . . but I can tell you things that I've never been able to tell anyone in my entire life . . . things that are even news to me . . ."

"I know . . . I'm not usually this forward . . . you must think I'm a vamp . . ."

"No . . ."

"I'm usually so shy and backward . . . but I feel so safe with you . . . Ron?"

"Yes, David—I love the sound of your name. You know I've been saying it to myself for five days now . . . David Corday . . . David Corday . . . It's like a Brahms sonata . . ."

"Or the lady that killed poor Marat."

"Remind me not to take baths with you around."

"Ron, can you stay for the night? Will you get in trouble?"

"No. I'll be all right . . . I can stay over . . ."

"Good."

They moved into each other and from the first touch and the first kiss Ron knew that his life was changed. David was taste, spark, warmth . . . Now he felt that he was alive.

CHAPTER 14

He was watching Merv Griffin on television with Doris on the sofa near him and Valerie doing her homework on the carpet. He'd heard somewhere that Merv had been an actor as a young man. Had Merv wanted to play Hamlet? Ron wondered idly. Or in his time was it Biff in *Death of a Salesman?*

During a commercial break he said to Doris, "Whatever happened to my old plays?"

David had asked him to bring them the next time they were together. Ron had demurred—they weren't any good and besides he couldn't find them if he tried . . . they'd probably been thrown out. He wished he could be with David tonight. There had been three times since the first time and he could think of nothing else, could hardly sleep or concentrate on anything but David. It was to be tomorrow night but he wished it were tonight. He'd had four Scotches already but the edge was still on him—at this rate he wouldn't sleep tonight, either . . .

"Huh?" Doris replied a few seconds after the question, still intent on the commercial.

"Never mind," Ron said, and walked into the kitchen to get some wine. Wine might make him sleep. He poured some red from the refrigerator into his highball glass and sat down again. Merv was introducing another guest and Doris was totally absorbed.

"You have some plays, daddy?" Valerie asked, looking up from her homework. His little china doll, he thought. Her eyes were slanted, her cheekbones high, her face narrow and her complexion dark—a funny face yet it all worked. She was all sharp triangles, from the angle of the eyes, the nose, the brow to the high forehead—even her ears. There were times when he played games with her to see how many triangles he could locate on her face. She never wanted to share the game, however, as she wasn't particularly thrilled at looking so sharp and oriental. She'd have preferred the rounded circles of her father's features.

Valerie stopped whatever she was doing and thought for a minute.

"What's the matter?" Ron asked.

"I didn't know."

"Didn't know what?"

"That plays were written. I thought they were spoken."

"Well, they're written before they're spoken."

"Why?"

"So that the actors know what to say when they get up on the stage or on television."

"Otherwise they wouldn't know what to say?"

"No. And don't ask me why."

The commercial break was over and Merv was introducing the

next guest. Doris shushed both of them. It was the guest that she'd been waiting for all evening. Neither Ron nor Valerie liked that.

Ron continued: "Did you think that the actors just got up and said whatever they wanted to say? You've been in school plays. You know that you've read words that someone else had written."

"Can I see?" Valerie asked.

"See what?" Doris said.

"Daddy's plays?"

"They're put away." She didn't recall any plays, and if they were really stored away and not lost she'd be hard put to guess where.

"I want to see them," Valerie insisted, hoping to capture daddy's attention.

Doris could have snapped her head off. Sometimes her daughter seemed to enjoy taunting her. Valerie didn't seem to come from her. Sure, there was a resemblance, but more and more Valerie reminded her of that awful brother of Ron's, even beginning to look like him around the mouth and nose especially. Ron didn't seem to be picking up on the child's nonsense so Doris felt safe to ignore it.

Merv was going off the air now. Ron wondered if Merv still kept within reaching distance any old scripts that he'd worked on —as keepsakes, remembrances of what he once was or might have wanted to be . . . a marked Hamlet script? Ha! Merv as Hamlet —hilarious . . . good sense of humor, Ron ol' boy . . . My old plays never had much humor . . . or did they? That storekeeper from town . . . in *Farm Hand?* Weren't there some funny lines in that?

"Where *are* my old plays?" he asked Doris.

"Probably in the garage," she replied, reaching for the *TV Guide* to see what was next and to indicate to Ron and his little snake of a daughter that she was not interested in any rummaging through old things.

Ron stood up and walked through the kitchen. He pressed a button on a wall panel and the door leading to the garage slid open. Valerie slipped through behind him.

Ron looked over the shelves packed with old suitcases and large cardboard boxes. There were three from his old apartment which probably had things from his college days. He was feeling vital and energetic. He did not want Doris to do this for him the way she usually did things around the house. He moved the Mercedes out of the garage, set up the stepladder and went through all the boxes, but all he could find was his old Olivetti typewriter. He was getting angry. Now that he was after it he was after it. He didn't want to get Doris in on this but he had to—goddamm it he depended on her too much!

Valerie knew it was coming and she anticipated it by saying, "Shall I get mother?"

"Yes, get her."

She skipped into the living room, delighted to sidle up to Doris in the middle of a movie, and say, "Daddy wants you in the garage."

Doris turned the TV off with the remote control, and followed her daughter to the garage. She'd lost.

"Where the hell are my plays?" Ron snapped.

"They're not in any of those boxes?"

"No."

"I never remember seeing any plays. What did they look like?"

"They looked like plays."

"Huh?"

"Manuscripts."

What the hell would they look like? Her dumb goddamn family had helpfully packed all this stuff away—what the hell would they know from manuscripts, they'd probably use them to wipe their asses. He was getting madder.

"They might be in the crawl space in the attic," Doris said. "Carmine packed some stuff away and I didn't get a chance to really look at it."

Ron shoved past Doris and took the attic stairs two at a time with Valerie running after him. Doris followed, saying, "You'd better not move around that crawl space, Ron—there's no room up there. I'll call Carmine and get him to come over here tomorrow. He'll take the boxes out and we'll find them."

Ron whirled on the stairs, stopping the procession. "I don't want your brother Carmine over here, thank you."

This has been a rough year so far, Doris reflected. I wish we could have mind treatments now the way we used to. I think they would calm him but he doesn't want any . . . he won't even let me ask him. I just have to be patient and provide the stability, especially for Valerie. She has a tendency to pick up his vicious ways but if I show her that they don't bother me she'll grow out of it.

I wonder if he doesn't like my family . . .

By the time he had drawn the attic ladder down and climbed up to see how packed and cramped the crawl space was, he was in a fury. "How the hell can you move up here?" he muttered. "Did you throw my plays out?"

"No."

"Let me look for them, daddy," Valerie said. "I can move around up there."

"No. It's too dangerous."

"She can," Doris said.

Ron moved off the ladder and Valerie climbed up the five rungs and disappeared into the opening with just her bare toes sticking out. "What should they look like?" she said.

"I don't know, just move the boxes over so I can take them down."

He found them rather soon, untouched since that day many years ago when he'd simply packed everything in a cardboard box. He took out one of the many versions of his old play. It was yellowed and had a musty odor. Yet . . .

FARM HAND
by
RON STARR

258

There it was . . . it felt so funny . . .

"It's old," Valerie said reverently, touching it lightly.

"Yes, it's old," Ron replied. "Why don't you go to bed now. Thanks for helping me."

Valerie, seeing that her father wanted to have the play to himself the way she might keep a leaf or a stone that had special meaning for her and no one else, flicked a kiss at her father and went to her room to get ready for bed.

"Leave the boxes for tomorrow, Doris. I'll put them back . . . I'm going to the study."

Now that the play was in his hands he became queasy. He'd never show it to David. David wouldn't laugh of course, he'd be polite or something . . . but still there were one or two parts that weren't bad. He turned on the desk light in his study and started to read.

He meant to read only the first act and then go to sleep, but it carried him forward. He wanted to find out what happened next or what this or that character was up to. He hated the young girl with a passion and fell madly in love with her mother, and Tony was crystal clear to him, especially when he pictured David in the role. And it was funny. The mother's suitor was a riot and even the daughter's boyfriend was funny—it was a lighter play than he'd remembered . . . a tender, human comedy . . .

When he'd finished, Tony's departure choking him up a bit, he dialed David's number. David's roommate answered with sleep in his voice.

"Is David there?" Ron asked.

"Hold."

Ron waited three or four minutes before David came on.

"David, it's Ron."

"Oh . . . hi . . ."

"Listen, can I see you tonight?"

"Tonight?"

"Look, if it's too late or you're going out, forget it . . ."

"I'm not going out, I'm going to sleep."

"Are you alone?"

"Yes."

"Look, I just want to show you something and then I'll go if you like . . ."

"If you come I'll want you to stay . . . but . . . will it be all right at home?"

"David, I do what I want at home. I don't have to report."

"All right."

"You're talking from your roommate's room and you can't say much?"

"Yes."

"Do you really want me over tonight? I mean, I can come tomorrow as we planned. It would be all right."

"Please come. Now that I've heard your voice I want you over."

"About an hour?"

"Sooner if you can."

"Goodbye."

"David . . ."

"Yes . . ."

"I'll see you soon."

"Okay."

They hung up.

Ron walked hurriedly into the bedroom. He didn't even look over at Doris who was lying in bed reading a book with a regular nightgown on. She wouldn't try anything tonight. It wouldn't work. He was too nervous.

He was getting dressed again to go out and it was ten-thirty. What had happened infrequently in the past was happening regularly now. She kept her voice casual as she asked where he was going. He didn't reply. She watched him put on a pair of beige slacks with a maroon sport shirt and checkered jacket.

"That combination doesn't work, you know."

"It's all right."

260

"Is it that same agent who's depressed tonight?"

"Yes."

"He should see a psychiatrist."

"I'm trying to get him to see one." Ron leaned over and kissed Doris perfunctorily on the cheek. "I may stay over at his place and be back in the morning."

"All right." Ron started to go. "Ron." He turned. "You'd better wear a topcoat. The black one with the maroon lining would be good. Black goes with anything."

"Okay."

Ron lay naked in bed next to David as David read *Farm Hand*. He must be crazy—he was letting himself in for an awful beating. This scene of almost domestic tranquility, lying next to David this way, not trying to check his feelings about David, all in direct contrast to where his outward life was. If he were one of his men he would be telling himself that he was setting mines in the field of his mind—self-destructive—the whole bit. He knew it when he saw others do it and he recognized it in himself. It would be great to have David as an occasional lover, but showing him the play like this and getting so used to the idea of being with him reading together side by side—insanity!

David finished the play.

"Ron," he said softly.

Ron looked at him fully and held his breath.

"It's good, Ron, really good."

"Come on, no polite shit . . . !"

"No . . . really . . . I wouldn't be polite about a play . . . I mean really . . . it's good . . . *you're* good . . ."

David put his hand tenderly on the back of Ron's head. "You're good. It's beautiful. Oh, I'd love to play Tony."

"When I read it again tonight I saw you in the part. It's as if I wrote it for you years before I even met you . . ."

"Except how could you ever expect me to be attracted to that bitchy daughter . . . oh wow, who could make it with her?"

"You mean you don't think the character would be attracted to her?"

"Oh no . . . no . . . the character would—I believe that. I'm just saying that the actor would have to work hard . . ."

Ron put his hand on David's bare thigh. "I would play her in drag . . ."

David slid his hand up Ron's leg and kissed him sensuously on the mouth. "Now that's more like it . . ."

"Wait a minute," Ron said, tapping David's ascending hand. "Come on, what do you think of the play?"

David laughed. "Literary criticism at this hour? All right. I think it's splendid, really, but not for these times. It's a fifties play, well made with good turns of plot, good characters, nice humor. It's like a young Inge. I love Inge—*Picnic* and *Dark at the Top of the Stairs.* But not a copy of him. It's got its own feel for character and place and events. Look, what I'm trying to tell you is . . . you can write, Ron, you can really write."

David wanted to say something else but he just squeezed Ron's arm.

"What do you want to say, David?"

"Nothing."

"Do you want to ask me why I stopped?"

David shook his head no. Ron was prepared to tell him everything—Professor Lavalle, his goals, his accomplishments, his reasons for not being ashamed of giving up his writing, but the way David looked at him, begging him not to, telling Ron that he didn't *need* to, made Ron realize that the way he was was all right with David. Ron's play had given such pleasure tonight. It had found its audience. Ron had found his perfect lover—a lover who accepted him the way he was with his little belly, his complicated justifications and his split-up life.

So Ron stopped himself and just made love to David in a deeper way than he'd ever made love to him before.

Soon Ron found David a nice little one-bedroom apartment in the Village and they furnished it and decorated it together. He had David's teeth capped, bought him clothes and actively worked to find him a theatrical agent. He could see David when he pleased and not see him when he couldn't. If David saw other people—and Ron was sure he did—he was discreet enough to hide it.

Ron dwelt in this little apartment even when not there. It was his "mind" home and David his "better half," as they say. Everything else seemed like an errand he had sent someone else to do while he stayed "home." During his business day, and with Doris, he could amuse himself by imagining that he was lying in bed with David watching himself go through the paces as if on TV, commenting during commercials on the ironies of this or the stupidities of that. In that life—the one David and he watched—he hired decorators and electricians to fix his house or office, but here in his real dwelling he'd do it himself, with David. Like Tony in his play, he had an itch to do things with his hands. He built shelves and put up some paneling in the living room and wallpaper in the kitchen and bathroom. Together they sanded the floor so that it could be revarnished. They picked out every bit of furniture and worried together about mistakes, mismatches and slipcovers that didn't fit. They bought cooking equipment and Ron started to get into Chinese and French cooking—woks and sauces.

They felt safe joking about living together permanently because they knew it was impossible. When Ron had to leave and spend a few nights at home it was as if he were a traveling salesman going away on a road trip. David bade him be careful of driving too fast—watch out for those motel meals, sometimes the food's not well cooked. And Ron cautioned David to make sure that the doors were locked at night and that the checkbook was balanced before writing each check—or better yet let me write the checks when I come home, here's some cash.

Ron could drive past street corners where boys were and not be one of the men who stopped their cars. It made him feel terrific that he didn't have to do that anymore. Months went on. David still loved him and he loved David. Doris wasn't upset. Valerie was doing well in school. He had what he wanted. He wasn't toppling into an abyss. It was great, only . . .

There's always an only . . .

They weren't coaxing him into the home office. He waited for it, but the home office simply smiled, shook his hand and said nothing. He began to entertain more at home—frequently making little "soirees," as David called them, of home-office people, agents and managers, letting the drinks and the food flow freely, creating an easy atmosphere where everyone could get a bit drunk and talk about the people in the business it was safe to talk about. Soon these soirees became sought after and more important people from the home office heard about them and wanted to be invited.

Ron cultivated one of the younger managers, Marvin Brock, whom he thought of as the company courier. Brock knew everything about everyone, and his gossip was invaluable and entertaining. He was also a protégé of the now executive vice-president in charge of marketing, Colonel Thomas J. McCloud (USMC, Retired). Brock was at every one of the soirees and would entertain with stories about those accepted targets in the business— the known failures or alcoholics or bullshitters, who were kept on because it is the nature of large companies to keep these men on as it is also their nature to taunt them.

McCloud had expressed an interest in coming, so Ron invited him. This Tuesday night was going to be a good one— all the stars would be there, Carpagian, Edelman, Brock and a few others who'd proved entertaining, successful men all basking in their own glories . . . a creative melting pot, a kind of super-charged sales atmosphere that would let McCloud see what someone like Ron could spark. Around him people became witty and charming, more dynamic, more creative, and this was his real talent. McCloud had seen it before but now he needed a reminder. Were they waiting for Ron to ask? No way. To ask was to settle for a lower-rung vice-presidency, goddamn it he was going to get coaxed as he should be.

The phone rang that Tuesday night just as Ron was taking the hors d'oeuvres from the refrigerator and thinking that it was amusing that here "at work" he ordered hors d'oeuvres in and "at home" he made them. Valerie, very involved lately in answering telephones, was ahead of Doris. She said very maturely, "Hello." Pause. "Yes, he is. Hold on please." Then she beckoned Ron and said, covering the mouthpiece with her hand, "He sounds funny."

It was David. He'd never called here before. There must be something wrong—Ron was shaky and scared.

"What is it, David?" he whispered, bringing the phone into the living room so that he couldn't be overheard.

"Is it all right my calling there?"

"Yes. Of course."

"Was that your daughter? She sounded lovely."

"Thank you. What is it?"

"Well, nothing much . . ."

"Are you sure?"

"Only look . . . I'm leaving tonight . . . I was going to write you a note and all, but I don't know—I can't do that so I thought I'd call you and say goodbye and explain and everything . . ."

"Where are you leaving for, David?"

"For Toronto, Canada. I have a flight tonight."

"How long will you be staying?"

"Ah, well that's what I wanted to explain in the note."

"You're thinking of staying for good?"

"I was going to explain in the note . . ."

"For good? You're giving up?"

"I wish you'd let me read you the note."

"When's the flight?"

"Ten-thirty."

It was seven-thirty.

"I want to see you."

"I can't."

"Where are you calling from?"

"The apartment."

"Take a taxi. I'll pay for it. There's a diner a few blocks from my house. I'll be there in a half hour. That's as long as it should take you. I'll meet you there. Do you have a pencil?"

"I . . ."

"Do you have a pencil?"

"Yes."

Ron told him the name of the diner and the street where he was to tell the cab to go.

"What about the plane?"

"I'm sure you're packed. Bring your bags and I'll give you fare to get out to the airport from where you meet me." He would have added—if you still want to go—but he knew enough about selling to know when to take the pressure off. "There'll be plenty of time."

"All right," David said. "Ron, you're not angry, are you?"

"Of course not. Now get out there and get a cab and I'll see you soon. Come on."

"All right."

"Where are you going?" Doris asked as Ron pressed the button that made the hall closet slide open and took out a mismatched sports jacket. "They are going to start showing up soon."

"One of my men has to see me. I'll be back soon."

"The same one."

"No. A different one."

"But Vice-president McCloud is coming tonight."

"He'll be glad to know that my men come first," Ron said with his hand already on the door. "Just pour them drinks the moment they walk in and they'll hardly know I'm not here. I'll be back soon."

As Ron left, Doris said something about the jacket not matching the pants. He paid no attention.

The diner was near the subway. There'd be no danger of being seen there because Ron's guests would be coming by car or taxi. He sat in a corner at the end booth next to the window, sipping coffee and keeping a sharp lookout for David's taxi. It was early. The place was called the Baseball Diner and on the far wall was a large mural depicting a baseball game. There was only one bored, middle-aged, waxen-haired waitress on duty and about eight male customers scattered about, all reading a different section of the *Daily News*.

He checked his watch. Almost eight. No problems. They wouldn't start coming until eight-thirty or nine. David would be here soon and it would take him ten minutes at the most to talk him out of this nonsense. The boy gets into these things. He goes along on course for a period of time and then suddenly veers off into something self-destructive with great impetuousness, like a ship hit by a strong wind. Then the captain, yours truly, has to take hold of the rudder and veer the ship aright. Ron knew that they were three feet from gold. David was up for a good part in what seemed like a very promising off-off Broadway play at a good house. If he got it Ron was sure he'd hook up with a good agent. Three feet from gold and the silly boy is talking about going back to Canada. God!

David alighted from a cab and Ron was appalled to see how out of place he seemed in this middle-class block. People here trudged gracelessly about, David floated. Teenagers passed him as he walked into the diner and they made the traditional sign that people make to denote "fairy." It was the first time Ron had ever been with David away from their apartment and the Village. As David walked to the back of the diner Ron wanted to hide under the table. David was so obviously gay. He blared in the Baseball Diner like a pink trumpet.

David slid next to Ron on the dirty maroon vinyl of the semicircular booth. Ron lit a cigarette. He wished that he could order a drink.

The wax-haired waitress approached and Ron turned to David. "Tea? Something to eat?" David shook his head no.

"I'll have a bacon, lettuce and tomato on toast," Ron said, not really wanting it. "And bring tea please."

She left, getting the chef busy.

"All right," Ron said. "So what's happening?"

"Please . . ."

"Please what?"

"Stop being so angry."

"I'm not angry."

"You are. Did I cause trouble at home? By calling?"

"No." Ron put his cigarette out. "You're right. I am coming off angry. I'm sorry."

"It's all right."

"I have a gathering tonight."

"McCloud?"

"Yes . . . I'm tense about it, I guess."

"Of course . . . I'm sorry."

"No. What's happening?"

"There's a new company being formed in Toronto . . . They're going to do repertory from classics to moderns to originals. They've got funding and everything. They want me as the assistant stage manager."

"Assistant stage manager? You're an actor."

"Yes, but I can stage manage. I studied it in college. I think I could like it. I might want to move into directing."

"Directing?"

"Yes."

"David, you're not a director. You're an actor. And one of the finest I've ever seen. David, please hear me, it's not that I don't want you to have a good opportunity. It's not that I want to keep you with me. If you got a good part in the movies on the Coast or a road company I wouldn't stand in your way, but you can't direct. You can't tell anyone to go anywhere or do anything. You're afraid you'll hurt their feelings, that's the way you are. On stage, my God, you could play Caligula and kill hundreds, but in real life I've seen where you were afraid to shoo a fly. Directing is real life. You tell people where to go and what to do and how to do it and you call electricians and yell at costume people and fire actors who aren't right for their parts. David, can you do all those things?"

David, like the batter in the mural, was ready for the pitch.

"Well," he said, "I've thought of that . . . I might be able to work into getting some roles, though."

"Have you heard from that part you were up for?"

"Didn't get it."

Ron suddenly knew. He means it. There are the keys to the apartment in his hand. He's making the sharp edges hurt his fingers. He's going to give them back to me soon. That's going to be very hard for him. He's loved me as deeply as I've loved him but . . . I should have known that it couldn't really last. Boys like David are so damn unstable. All right, take the keys and say goodbye, and that'll be it. I'll keep the apartment and someone else will come along . . . or maybe he'll be back . . . who knows . . .

The waitress brought his bacon, lettuce and tomato sandwich. Ron pushed it away. His insides were beginning to go amok. He knew he shouldn't have let himself go like this with David. A zoo of insane animals were beginning to run around inside him.

"Ron," David whispered. "What's the matter?" He moved closer.

"Nothing. I'll be all right." Ron swallowed hard to keep it all down. He wished David would leave. He didn't want to look at him anymore.

"Look," David said, "if it doesn't work out I'm liable to be back."

"No." Ron turned swiftly and vehemently. "If you go, go."

David turned away and just stared at the tea in front of him. "I should have written a note," he mumbled.

That fucking BLT stared at Ron. He wanted to smash it on the floor. He was beginning to pop and boil inside in the most uncontrolled, alarming way in his life. "Just leave."

"All right," David said.

Ron turned and moved closely into David and held his arm. "Why are you doing this?"

"Ron," David murmured, "calm down, please. Look where we are."

Ron looked. The men in the diner were immobile as figures in a waxworks. "Let's take a walk," David said.

"All right." Ron tried to slide out but he had no power in his thighs. His ass refused to slide. He was afraid that he would sink to the floor of the diner like the batter in the mural if he'd been beaned. He stopped David from getting up, and pulled him close to him. "Why are you doing this? What do you want?"

"I don't want anything."

"I thought you loved me."

"I do."

"Then how can you do this?"

"I don't know . . ."

Ron touched David's face with his hand. "Please, David. If you're going to do it, do it, but you must tell me why."

"I don't know . . . there's no reason."

"Anything I've done?"

"No."

"The way we live?"

David hesitated. "No."

"The way we live then—that's it."

"No. This is the only way it can be."

"Nothing is the only way it can be. There are always alternatives."

"Like what?" David asked.

"I don't know, but if you leave there's no alternative."

David took Ron's hand. "Ron, I have to go, please . . . Look, here are the keys to the apartment . . ." The metal felt cold in Ron's palm.

"No," Ron said, pulling David to him and pushing the keys back in David's hand. The keys dropped. The waitress turned around, her eyes wide with open contempt. "You can't leave me, goddamn it. I love you . . ." A couple of the customers looked over at them, and from the corner of his eye Ron became aware of a figure which had emerged from the subway. That figure, which Ron hadn't bothered to define before, was standing at the window of the diner. It was Brock, Marvin Brock, staring at them. Brock had been there for a long time.

Once when Ron was a boy playing soccer he'd been banged on the head by someone's knee and had sat on the field watching the world whirl around, the pain starting from the place of the blow and rippling through his entire body. It was that way now, the swirling world went around and around, finally settling into place as Brock moved away from the window toward his house. Brock was going to his house—couldn't make sense of that.

David sensed the new presence outside the diner, and, taking it as an opportunity to avoid a further painful scene, picked up his slim luggage and walked out of the diner.

To Ron it seemed that Brock and David were in a bizarre slow-motion race to see who could get away from him faster. Something told him to stop David, but he'd been beaned too hard and was totally immobile.

David and Brock passed each other at the corner. For some reason Ron felt surprised when they didn't acknowledge each other. Then they were both gone and the waitress brought over the check. It said, Thank You Come Again.

He stood up after he felt some strength back in him and paid the check at the cash register. Outside he breathed deeply. The baseball diner had been like a coffin. He knew what he could do. He could go to his house. Brock would be sitting there drinking his booze—Beefeater martini on the rocks. Doris, ol' girl. He could call Brock aside and just tell him to go to hell, then he could get his car and let the other bastards sit in his house and drink each other to death and go out to the airport—would it be La Guardia or Kennedy? Kennedy of course—it was Canada. He'd find David and tell him that as of tonight they'd move in together. He'd separate from Doris. He could get away with it as far as the company was concerned, as long as he stayed in the field as a general manager. He'd never told David that. They look away from people in the field as long as the business gets brought in. Going in the home office was a different story, of course . . .

He opened his front door and went in. There was a hum of voices in the living room, nothing distinguishable. He pressed the button to open the sliding door of the hall closet, then pressed it again compulsively. The door slid back and forth.

He'd always wanted to show David these buttons. He'd have loved them. Buttons for everything in the house—closets, stereos, TV's that came down from the ceiling, beds that tilted and vibrated. David would have gone wild. Ron had often thought about having him over when the family wasn't home. Once he'd given David a box wherein one pressed the button on the side, the top opened, an elegantly gloved hand emerged and slowly found its way to the button, pressed it, and made itself disappear back into the box. David had said it was the most philosophical toy ever invented. We exist to press ourselves into oblivion, he'd said. He'd played with it endlessly. Ron suspected that it was less philosophy and more button pushing that attracted David.

As the door was in the middle of a slide, Doris emerged from the living room. "Ron, they're all here."

He plunged into them. Hands were shaken, hearty greetings exchanged. Brock was seated on a large, oversized chair near the mock fireplace sipping a martini and talking to Danny Carpagian. He didn't greet Ron.

If it was a nice piece of ass, Ron thought, a foxy lady, with long legs and big tits, Brock would have shunted me off to the side and asked to be filled in on all the details. Good blow job? How were her tits? Her ass? Her pussy? Any friends? Share the wealth, ol' buddy! . . . Ron found himself getting so furious at the back of Brock's head that he had to leave the room to go in the kitchen and spill a lot of Scotch into his glass. . . . Meanwhile McCloud is standing there at parade rest, still as a bored colonel, probably unhappy over my being late to my own shindig. McCloud is never late to anything. Brock certainly couldn't have told him anything, there hasn't been time . . . Oh God . . .

When it hit Ron he quivered and then he giggled skittishly. Doris came into the kitchen and said, "What's the matter?" But Ron just stepped away from her and faced the refrigerator.

Brock babbling. It was too good for him to pass up. Brock would be on the phone first thing in the morning. Guess who I saw with the gayest-looking fag you'd ever hope to see—hand in hand, practically kissing, going through the whole scene. Ron Starr. Ron Starr. I always thought there was something funny about him, you know, my wife always had a feeling . . . and there it was. It's true.

Everybody. McCloud. Shit, would Brock even wait till tomorrow morning? Wouldn't put it past the fuck to start it at my own house.

Ron walked back into the living room. Brock hadn't moved. He was chatting loudly with Larry now, and Ron doubted that Brock would say anything to him. They'd gone to school together. Maybe Larry was one too, he'd think.

Ron giggled out loud. Making love to Larry Edelman—once Larry had been handsome and slim but still unappealing because he'd been so dull. Now he was fat and dull. You think we make love to anybody, right Brock? You think we're just fucking degenerates who want to stick our cocks into anything.

Ron wanted to smash Brock with the bottom of his Scotch glass. Just go over and hit him on the head. Instead he just drank in gulps. There was McCloud now, talking to Danny Carpagian. I hope that Danny can loosen him up a bit. God you could walk on him, he's so stiff. Should I ask Doris if he and Brock have had a chance to talk yet?

He found himself standing between Brock and McCloud as if to intercept any communication. When he realized it he giggled to himself, but it wasn't to himself, it was out loud and he was looked at. Then he circled around Brock, as if he were a band of Indians and Brock a wagon train. Meanwhile he was drinking a lot and giggling skittishly at no matter what was said. His Scotch brimmed over onto his hand, onto the rug.

Danny had picked up on Ron's strange conduct this evening and started to tell the story of how Ron recruited him into the life insurance business. They'd all heard this many times but it had become a great legend told by a master storyteller and they all settled in to hear it again.

Brock surreptitiously glanced at his watch as Danny began. He wasn't listening. Why don't you listen? Ron wondered. See what I did? I took a car washer and made him a millionaire. I help people, and you want to mess me up. Why don't you listen, learn about the man you're going to bury? McCloud's listening and loosening up, and all you do is politely sit there and glance at your watch! What the fuck were you doing at that subway anyway? Where was your car?

"Ron," Danny said. "There's something I never told you about those days . . ."

"Huh? What?"

"I used to worry about you. I mean there I was washing cars every day, the craziest Armenian car washer you ever hoped to see bending over those cars, and I'd look up and see this guy staring at me . . . I used to worry."

They all laughed, except Brock and Doris.

Brock told someone that he had to be getting home; he had an early recruiting interview and he was tired. His car had broken down and he had come by subway, but he'd be taking a cab this late at night. He shook hands with McCloud, then Danny and Larry. He called Doris in from the kitchen and said a reserved goodbye to her . . . he usually kissed her goodbye and made risqué remarks about stealing her from Ron, but not tonight. Doris expressed polite disappointment at his leaving so early. Ron watched as if he were at a movie seeing a hazy dream sequence —as if he weren't part of it at all.

Ron said, "I'll get your coat," and followed Brock to the front hall closet. Brock looked at the panel of buttons, trying to figure out which one belonged to the hall closet. He still hadn't said one word to Ron.

Ron reached over Brock's shoulder, careful to not touch him, and pressed the hall-closet button. Brock ran his hand along the coats trying to get his. Ron spotted it first and neatly scooped it from the hanger and held it in his hand.

Brock turned around and put his hand out for it but Ron pulled it away slightly. You're going to have to look at me to get this fucking coat.

After a long moment Brock looked into Ron's eyes.

And now that he had him he didn't know what to do with him. Don't tell on me? Why not? Could he be so sure that he wouldn't tell if he were in Brock's place? What past favors or old debts could he invoke? What special friendship had they shared? Did Ron even want to have a shared secret with this man? Have this kind of closeness with someone in this part of his life?

Ron slowly and gently let Brock's eyes go. For the second time that night they parted, and Ron watched Brock briefly as he walked down the street. He was thoroughly drained.

CHAPTER 15

Ron stopped giving soirees, sending out feelers, and even stopped coming to the office any more than he had to.

He hid. He became a family man—a sensuous Robert Young. The missionary position was indulged in. Doris, at last, found in him what she'd always dreamed of. He was handy around the house and even cooked (where did he learn all those things? she wondered). He became a good father to Valerie, and disciplined her for a change. The three of them took vacations and outings, like a real family.

The ache of David was easing and of course he wasn't going to go out again. He was finished with it. He was going to learn to *adjust,* goddamn it! He had to learn to appreciate what he had. He threw himself back into his work. He was amazed to find that he still had it, could still inspire the way he used to—maybe even better now because he felt a new understanding and depth which, coupled with the old fire, formed the essence of sales manager mastery.

Maybe he could start the feelers again . . . Several months had gone by . . . you never know . . . Three feet from gold, Ron.

He'd pay some calls at the home office, drop in to say hello to McCloud, get some positive rays going out. Who knows, maybe Brock had kept quiet, or if he hadn't, maybe no one believed him.

One morning he went to the home office. The elevator let him off on the executive floor. He suddenly told himself that it would be nice to pay a short visit to the vice-president in charge of mortgage investments, Morgan B. Gerhard.

Vice-president Gerhard was, like Ron, one of the secret men who lead double lives, like spies, who wear business suits and have wives, children, grandchildren . . . men who tell dirty jokes, get drunk, play golf and leer at women just like any other business-men. They are impersonators, denying the other life that they secretly lead—that they secretly love. These men drive their cars to certain streets, or go to men's rooms in certain places, or sneak into certain movies where they could gently put their hand on some shadowy young person's knee. The core of their lives is in those few moments that they spend with some anonymous penis or anus, when all the hiding, all the sly role-playing, all the dis-honest heterosexual intercourse that they lived through for nine-ty-nine percent of the time seemed worthwhile. And when it was finished . . . when the last bit of semen was expended and the denim pants of the young man were zippered up and they were parting, usually without a word, the spy resumed his cover again . . . looking around to see if he'd been seen, forming his opening gambit to his wife, buying the next toy for his grandchild . . . able to go on a bit longer now . . . able to be more comfortable in his impersonation, his fix obtained . . . not allowing himself to want

or need more because to do so would upset the balance of his life
. . . a beautiful life really . . . a life that had everything that anyone
would want . . . except for tense questions like . . . what if
sometime someone saw? Is this one of those men's room traps?
Remember Bobby Baker. Well, there's always a price.

Secret men sometimes know each other, not by any club-tie-
Masonic sign but by a brotherhood of furtiveness. Vice-president
Gerhard's Mortgage Investments Department was in a different
area of the company from Ron's, but once years ago, when they
were at a company luncheon, they looked at each other and
instantly knew how each of them was. Ron had managed to talk
to Gerhard after the luncheon. There's never a question of sexual
intimacy when secret men get together. They're not interested in
each other and they never talk openly of their real lives. They take
soundings of each other's insides to judge the degree of erosion.
Gerhard was older than Ron. He had soft wrinkles, a modest
toupee and seemed kindly and comfortable. An old spy in a safe
berth.

Gerhard had invited Ron to stop by his office for a chat.
Gerhard comfortably chatted away mostly about being in the field
for the company for many years. "There's competition in mortgage investments too, you know," he had told Ron. "We've got
to put our money in the best place under the most favorable
circumstances. Lots of people out there trying to do the same
thing."

Ron had studied the pictures on Gerhard's desk. There were
a wife, children and grandchildren. Gerhard had talked easily
about them . . . they were scattered all over the country and
Gerhard and his wife visited them frequently. Gerhard went on
about how he'd become familiar with various cities across the
country. Yes, when Ron became vice-president and traveled, he
would get to know where to go fast enough. Every city has its
spots. Balance of nature—nature provides for all its creatures.

When the chat was over, Gerhard had risen and escorted Ron
to the door. He shook Ron's hand warmly and their eyes found

278

each other—for a moment they'd let down their guard.

"It's really a good life," Gerhard had said softly. "A fine life . . . well worth it . . ."

"Yes," Ron had said, nodding, seeing that it was . . . that here was a living example of the kind of success that he really wanted. The soft wrinkles, the large office, the grandchildren and genteel safety.

"You just have to be careful, that's all," Gerhard said.

Just have to be careful. No big deal. We all have to be careful. No matter what we are. We all are something. We all have to be careful . . .

Ron reached the desk of Mr. Gerhard's old-maid Irish secretary, Ellen Kearny, who as always had a nice greeting for him. "And how are you, Miss Kearny?"

"I feel very well today."

"And mother?"

"Not well, but holding her own. You know when they get old like that it's not easy." Miss Kearny's mother was ninety-three and lived with her.

"Is he in?" Ron asked, not wanting to get too involved with tales of mother.

"Oh, no, he's in San Francisco all this week," she said regretfully.

Frisco, Ron thought, good pickings.

"Tell him I stopped by to say hello then," Ron replied.

"Oh I will, he'll be sorry he missed you."

Ron left. Next step McCloud.

His secretaries were usually very young, not distractingly pretty but fashionable. This one was a black girl, with severe makeup and a morose, almost hostile expression—McCloud's civilian version of military effectiveness.

"Is he in?" Ron asked.

She looked at him inquiringly.

They both knew who he meant and the pause in Ron's voice let her know that he was aware of her little game. "Vice-president

McCloud." He should have added, Who else?

"Who should I say is calling?"

"Ron Starr. Just want to say hello if he's not too busy." Ron wanted to slap her and his fury scared him.

She buzzed. "A Mr. Starr here to say hello if you're not too busy."

Practically the next moment McCloud was out of his door, walking very fast with several sheets of paper in each hand.

"How you doing fella?" he said almost breathlessly, veering away from Ron toward the corridor door. "Listen, I'm headed for a meeting I should have been to ten minutes ago . . . How are you?"

Ron approached him. McCloud held on to the sheaves of paper.

"Fine . . ." Ron said. "I just stopped up to say hello . . . that's all . . . Nothing to talk about in particular . . . just hi . . ."

"Well, then fine . . . hi . . . back to you ol' buddy, and thanks for stopping. Boy it's good to see a face from the field once in a while . . . they're nuts up here . . ." McCloud was on his way out of the door. "How you feel? Okay?" he said.

"Sure." Ron replied.

"Fine."

McCloud disappeared. Ron's hand felt unshaken.

He had to get out of there before he ran into somebody else.

He got down the elevator and out into the street as fast as he could. He took a long deep breath . . . What was the matter with him? Should he see a shrink? Nothing had happened up there, absolutely nothing and he'd had a silent fit. He walked a block or two. What the hell was he doing out here? He had other people in the home office he should drop in on. Three feet from . . . fuck it.

Even if McCloud is thoroughly convinced that I'm one of "those," he would never openly refuse to shake my hand. I don't believe it. Or do I?

Will no one shake my hand in the home office? Is there a confidential home-office directive?

He laughed to himself and two or three people passing him on the street looked at him peculiarly. Worst thing they can do to a fella in the insurance business is not to shake your hand—like taking a tit away from a baby or the silent treatment at West Point. We'll take your business but not your hand, like pimps collecting from their whores in polyethylene, sanitized bags. Fuck it, he needed, really needed, a drink.

He was near a bar called the Nautilus, located off the lobby of a midtown businessman's hotel. He'd passed it before, and although he'd never been inside, something about it always vaguely reminded him of something else. It came to him. Nemo's—the Nautilus and Captain Nemo. He'd never gotten to Nemo's. He wondered if it were still there in Binghamton.

He went in and ordered a Beefeater martini straight up . . . that would give him an immediate lift and then make him sleepy afterwards. Perhaps he'd just check into the hotel and sleep for the afternoon, eat out by himself afterwards . . . He didn't want to go home . . .

He took the first sip and looked around. The circular bar was almost empty, but there was someone diagonally across from him behind a pole whom he couldn't fully see, and there was a young, dark-haired man in a suit two seats away. The man smiled slightly at Ron as Ron glanced his way. Ron smiled back. The man smiled even more. Was he coming on? If so, okay. Perfectly safe. Two businessmen chatting in a straight bar. Ron said something and the man answered in a deep southern accent. Ron moved into the seat next to him and they talked. Minnesota Mining, in for a few days on business—staying at the hotel—live in Memphis, weather was getting warm in New York—saw a good musical last night—city was a great place though it gets a bit . . . lonely. Their knees touched and it lasted longer than it should have. Ron was getting excited. Why not? He ordered another drink for himself and one for Minnesota Mining. He looked Minnesota Mining over lustfully, full mouth, teeth a little big and buck (hope he knows how to han-

dle that). Nice build, tight-looking ass . . . Ron's erection was up
and he opened his jacket to let it show as they talked. Minnesota Mining saw it and he smiled and talked some more.

Ron had a painful need to pee. "Stay right here now?" he told
Minnesota Mining as he excused himself, carefully folding his
jacket over his protrusion for the walk to the men's room.

"I will," Minnesota Mining grinned back, his fearsome teeth
flashing in the darkened bar.

He went into a stall to pee. God, he was hard—getting it up
for Doris lately had been like thumping on a dying horse and now
it felt like a rocket taking off. He was almost coming. He wanted
that hillbilly fag out there so much. It still wasn't down as he put
it back in his pants. Fuck it, let it stay straight up like a periscope
on a submarine . . . the Nautilus. He washed his hands quickly
and checked himself out in the mirror; no beauty he, but the fire
of the moment was in his eye. Oh yes.

He stepped out of the men's room, and as he walked back
around to his stool saw the other man at the bar. It was Jack Gray.

Jack Gray had been let out on mental disability years ago. He
had been one of Meridian's leading managers, a man of class,
distinction and intelligence whom Ron admired and even idolized. Jack had suddenly gone disastrously to seed over a two-year
period, was eventually declared mentally disabled, and hadn't
been heard from since. No one, not even Brock, knew how or why
he'd gone off the deep end.

Avoidance was Ron's first impulse but he realized that he had
nothing to hide. "Jack," Ron said loudly. Jack didn't move at the
sound of his name. Ron took in the statue-like profile under the
yachting cap, the short-sleeve shirt showing muscular arms
flecked with soft white hair, a blue Popeye-like tattoo on one
forearm, sea-blue eyes set in one of the most beautiful Christian
Executive faces Ron had ever seen, soft wrinkles, the majestic
angle of the chin, facial features now sun-blessed, the wrinkles
deeper yet softer than he remembered.

Jack looked marvelous! Mental disability is certainly cosmetic.

Ron's hand itched to be shaken, and he began to extend it, but stopped as Jack turned and coldly appraised him.

"You want to know how it's done, don't you?" Jack said.

Ron knew what he meant but ignored it.

"How you doing, Jack? You look wonderful. How do you feel?"

Ron wondered if Minnesota Mining could hear him. He couldn't see his face from this vantage point.

Jack's steady look told Ron to "cut the shit."

Ron decided to cut this short and get back to his new friend. "Give us a call will you? You know my number. Doris'd love to see you again, looking marvelous, take it easy ol' buddy."

Ron started to circle back to his seat but he heard Jack say something that sounded like, "You're not going to get it . . ."

He came back to Jack. "Not going to get what?" he asked.

Jack had some spiritual relationship with the shot glass of whiskey directly in front of him—untouched absolutely, whiskey to the very top.

"The home office," he said finally.

He's crazy, Ron thought. He's been away for years. He knows nothing—has been in touch with no one. Crazy people sense things, though, unconscious barriers are lowered. They pick up things that sane people filter out. He sensed my whole home office thing in a moment. "How do you know I'm not going to get it?" he asked.

"Because you're a little gay," Jack said evenly, without rancor or feeling.

Is it spread around so much that even people like this know it? Ron could kill Brock. He felt queasy and he had to lean on the bar . . . He peered at the decor of the bar, the portholes and the ship's rope. He was seasick on a rollicking boat . . . He sat on the bar stool next to Jack. He could see the elbow of Minnesota Mining—a patiently waiting elbow, proof of the pudding right across the bar.

A young Irish-looking bartender swaggered over to him as if on the rolling deck of a ship. He too had tattoos on his arms. Ron glanced out at the Manhattan street to make sure he wasn't really at sea.

"Sir?"

Ron had a drink over by Minnesota Mining but Jack was lightly touching Ron's arm and saying to the bartender, "Give him one of these . . ." meaning the shot glass in front of him.

The bartender nodded. Ron imagined he was about to say, "Aye, aye sir."

"And another one for me, too," Jack said, pouring the whiskey from his shot glass onto the bar.

The bartender wiped it up routinely with a bar rag and poured a refill from an unmarked bottle, carefully placing the shot glass exactly where it had been before. He poured one for Ron and placed it in front of him in perfect line with the other one.

"Thank you," Ron said, his voice controlled and natural in the midst of this surreal seagreen madness.

Did Minnesota Mining see what had just taken place? Ron leaned to look and Minnesota Mining grinned at him—a big, toothy cock-biting grin, as if he, too, were part of this mad play.

The next line must be his. An inside director was nudging him, giving him his cue. "H-how have you been?" dribbled out of him inanely.

"Don't waste time. I wasted two years. Two years that I could have had on the other end . . . the end that I'm happy on."

Ron moved his shot glass a fraction of an inch on the bar top. He knew he wouldn't be able to lift it without spilling the whiskey. "Had a bunch of the boys over the house recently and we talked about you." In fact, they hardly ever mentioned Jack. It made them all nervous. "Brock, Edelman, McCloud . . . he's in charge of marketing now, you know . . . You keep in touch with him? You were in the Marines too weren't you?"

Jack looked sadly at Ron, as if he were watching a weak fish trying to get upstream. Ron swallowed and asked, "Where did you hear that from?"

Silence.

Angry now, Ron hissed, "Who have you seen recently?"

"You're not ready yet."

The bastard's off rhythm. Not responsive. He's really flipped out, hasn't he? Why the fuck am I paying attention to him? Get me out of here—the hell with Minnesota Mining . . .

"You're not ready yet," Jack repeated. "But you will be. I always felt you'd be one of us, Ron."

Jack stood up and put one hand on Ron's shoulder, the other out to be shaken. Ron's hand, hungry for a safe, warm berth, automatically went into Jack's. Jack's eyes were soft and hypnotic. "I never had anyone to guide me, no philosophical or spiritual mentor. I can be yours. I want to be yours. I want to say, 'Welcome aboard mate, . . . and I will, I will . . .'"

Ron was dizzy, feeling suddenly at ease, at home, wanting to stay and be part of the deep mystical comforting secrets that Jack represented. Yet . . .

"I have to go now," Ron heard himself telling Jack.

"When you're ready I'll be here."

"All right."

"I have to do something crazy now."

"Huh?"

Jack's face became red, blotchy.

"The company sent you around to check on me," he said vehemently. "They want to prove that I'm not crazy so they can stop my disability payments and then fire me!"

"Hey come on, Jack. You know better than that."

Jack looked ready to strike. "Get the fuck out of here before I punch you in the fucking mouth!"

Ron stood up and backed away quickly. Oh God, he *is* going to hit me. Someone please stop him. Ron looked at the bartender but the bartender was leaning toward him from behind the bar just like Jack, with a fierce wild look in his eyes . . . his face red and blotchy. Ron turned to Minnesota Mining who suddenly stood up and grinned a crazy, hillbilly grin at him, his cock-biting teeth protruding from his mouth like some old WW II caricature of Hirohito. He too was closing in, his face turning red.

There was no one else in the bar. He was about to be devoured by madmen.

"You're crazy," he said to Jack.

Jack stopped. He laughed. A hearty, happy, sane laugh, like some swashbuckling pirate in the movies. Minnesota Mining sat down and the bartender was back to wiping the bar.

"Give my regards to the boys," Jack said, waving and saluting as Ron continued to back out of the bar.

As Ron reached the exit he bumped the door jamb comically and the bartender smirked knowingly at Minnesota Mining, enjoying Ron's undoing at the periphery of their little world.

As Ron opened the door he wondered if there would be land or sea outside and was honestly relieved to set his shaky legs on solid asphalt.

CHAPTER 16

He went right back to the home office. He couldn't, wouldn't live this way. If word was really out and around and was going to stop his career, he wanted to know it. Action is the thing, procrastination the enemy. He'd been successful through action. By their fruits ye shall know them. Action is character, character is action. Fruits . . . Ha, I'm a fruit . . . All the old things are coming back to me today, he thought. Jack . . . Jack Gray, he's something new . . . new and marvelously powerful . . . scary but soaring . . . soaringly insane . . .

He caught McCloud in the hall, heading back to his office from lunch. "Hey," McCloud said, "how're you . . ." McCloud put his arm around Ron's shoulder. "Roaming the halls of the puzzle palace, are you? Come on in and have a little visit."

They seated themselves comfortably in McCloud's office. McCloud unbuttoned his jacket and gazed out at a splendid view of the city. "You know," he said philosophically, "I was reading an article the other day by some psychologist who talked about fear as a prime mover in American business."

"Oh?"

"Yes . . . talked about someone, for instance, who sells like hell, makes a lot of money, then gets frightened, terrified that he can't keep it up—so he becomes a sales manager—inspiring other fellas to do the thing that just scared the hell out of him . . ." McCloud chuckled. Ron chuckled with him. "And of course onward and upward, but it's not ambition, according to this psychologist, it's fear of not being able to keep it up . . . Ha, sounds goddamn sexual, doesn't it?"

McCloud looked at Ron and smiled. Ron smiled back but he could feel sweat in his armpits.

"You believe much of that?" McCloud asked.

"Sounds like a crock of shit to me, Tom."

McCloud laughed. "Me too. Hell, I wasn't afraid to stay out there in the field. I was making great money. You know I haven't made the money here in the home office that I was making out there as a general manager?"

"I can imagine. You were number one for a good many years."

"I came into the home office for what I now perceive as a solid reason. You know what that was?"

"What?"

"I was crazy."

Ron genuinely laughed.

"No, I'm serious. I was crazy. I had a great life out there. Money, stability—had it knocked, made in the shade—but I thought that I'd get bored doing the same thing year after year. And you know what? I do the same thing year after year in *here*. While I'm not bored, I'm vexed. I'd rather be bored than vexed, wouldn't you?"

Ron shrugged.

"I thought this'd be a challenge. Why, the only challenge I encountered here was how to keep my sanity. Like locking yourself in a nuthouse for a long period of time and seeing how you'd come out. Now Ron, I don't know if I've met the challenge— there are no statistics, like sales statistics, that can guide me. If you repeat any of this I'll certainly deny it. Sometimes I hear myself saying things that I'd lock myself up for. I say them at meetings or in conferences, expecting everyone to leap up and clap some irons on me and put me away. Anyway, I don't know if I've met the challenge or not . . ."

McCloud stood by the window, reflecting on the gorgeous skyline. Ron joined him—two American business philosophers gazing out at New York. "I can imagine that the perspective can be awfully difficult to come by up here," Ron said.

"You know, Ron, I long for the days when I was out in the field. I had a hell of a good time as an agent, and then a manager . . . a hell of a good time . . ."

"I know . . . it's great out there . . . the money, the independence . . . the satisfaction . . . I know . . ."

They paused. McCloud broke the spell by sitting down at his desk and Ron casually put himself in the chair near the desk. "Now, I've got to pick someone to come in and I sort of hate to do it," McCloud said, alluding to some papers on his desk.

"Yes. I can imagine."

"That's why I'm glad you dropped by," McCloud said. "You know the managers as well as anyone. Your recommendations would be very valuable to me."

It could be the recommendation tactic. He'd used it himself. If you recommend really good appropriate people you don't want the job. If you recommend people not exactly right, you do.

"I'll give it some thought. I'll put some names down if you like . . ."

"That's wonderful, Ron, that would help me a lot. We need more interaction like that between the field and the home office. I mean, you fellas know what's happening out there."

"All right."

McCloud stood up and stepped from behind his desk, signaling the end of the visit. Ron followed him to the door. "Get back to me on that as quickly as you can, would you?"

"Sure," Ron said. As they reached the door McCloud's hand just gripped his arm and squeezed it by way of goodbye, forestalling a handshake.

If a hand could cry, Ron's would.

And he was out in the street again. He went over every detail of his interview with McCloud, weaving every kind of interpretation available . . . McCloud did not want to put his skin and my skin together. Did the bastard think I'd give him the finger in the palm? Offer to suck his cock or something. Suck one cock . . . the old joke ran through his mind. A tourist on the banks of the Seine saw a Frenchman on a bench, crying. He asked the man what the matter was, and the man said, "Alors, . . . woe is me . . . do you see zat bridge over ze Seine? I built it. But am I known as Pierre ze great Bridge Builder? No. My art stands in ze Louvre, but am I known as Pierre ze Artist, ze Sculptor? No. Ahhh, but suck one cock . . ."

One cock . . . no, many cocks, but be suspected *one time* . . .

He found himself at the Nautilus again. Jack was still there. Minnesota Mining was gone. There were only a few more men at tables now.

Ron sat next to Jack. Ron's shot glass from before was still there, brimful and untouched. Jack said, without even looking at Ron, "First, I can't tell you what to do. Flipping out is like selling, everyone must develop his own style. Don't ask me what I did. It would do you no good. No imitation would be strong enough, and it would only get you fired. Do your own thing, like the fucking hippies used to say, but like selling there are basic principles that must be followed. I'll tell you what they are. First, let's drink up."

Jack took his shot glass and poured the contents on the bar. Ron did the same. He didn't look to see who noticed. The bartender wiped the bar and served up new drinks. All done routinely. Ron felt a certain measure of freedom from his little crazy act.

Jack continued, turning a bit more toward Ron. "First"—Ron had discovered that there were never any seconds with Jack— "you must know that your cause is just. You must operate from a solid ethical base. Any grudge, any rancor you harbor for those sanctimonious bastards up there is just. They are guilty of everything. Allow no qualifications to undercut you. Who the hell are they not to let you into their home office because you like what you do? Everybody does something, for Christ's sake. That doesn't mean that you should be denied what you have rightfully earned, does it?"

"No!" Ron burst out.

Jack smiled at the spontaneity. He was full face to Ron now and Ron felt a zesty comradeship forming.

"First, know what your real goals are. Know how you want to live. What you want to do."

His little apartment in the Village flashed through his head— a time when David was taking a shower and he was reading a book. Simple. Domestic. Peaceful.

"I felt the indignities of unjust imprisonment as deeply as if I had been chained to the hold of a slave ship, but I wasn't sure what to do."

The indignities of an unjust imprisonment. A general manager —selling and pushing all his life until sixty-five. He was thirty-seven now—twenty-eight more years!

"I wasted too much time—almost two years. Of course, it wasn't entirely lost time because I indulged in some nice obnoxious behavior and took a lot of time off. But in retrospect they were wasted years. I should have done one atrocious thing—a big blast all at one time, and I'd have achieved my present happiness that much sooner."

An idea came to Ron, but frightened him so much that he didn't dare visualize it. Jack divined something.

"What you're thinking is not insane—it's *not doing it* that's insane. Your reservations about your proper course of action result from distorted and neurotic thinking. Do you know where the answer was for me, when I was at your stage? From the water. Everything comes from the water. The answer to everything in life is in the water. I spend all my time now on my boat. We all belong on, in and around water. That's why humanity is messed up—because we came out of it. The devil is the first piece of life that evolved us out. I come up on land once in a while to recruit new people because I'm a new species and I must propagate myself.

"I was fishing for flounder one day in the bay and I caught a poor blowfish which I would normally throw back. Ever see a blowfish? They're fat and wide and they get the name because they puff themselves up like they're blowing."

Jack illustrated with his cheeks. Ron laughed, feeling that he and Jack were in a world within a world now.

"I put the fish on the rail of the boat, waiting for it to flip itself back into the water, but it kept jerking itself back into the boat instead of the water where it belonged. You see, the blowfish was insane. Any time you act against your own nature you are insane. The blowfish had an incorrect perception of reality. At that moment I knew that I, like the blowfish, was insane. My trying to make it as a manager instead of flipping out and going on disability was insane—an incorrect perception, an action against my own nature. As I picked the blowfish up off the deck and put it back in the water I vowed to do the same thing for my very self."

"How did you fool the psychiatrists?"

"I didn't."

"They declared you disabled mentally."

"I didn't fool them. I am disabled."

"You're not. You're here. Free. Talking to me . . ."

"And getting seventy percent of my income as well . . . just as you can get seventy percent of yours."

Ron had made one hundred and ten thousand dollars last year.

"First, they don't keep you in an asylum. As long as you're harmless, they let you out. All you have to do is to do crazy things and you are crazy. Once I was hypnotized by a stage magician at a hotel. On the stage I knew what I was doing the whole time. I could have disobeyed and ruined his act if I had wanted to, but I didn't. What the hell, I was a nice guy so I went along. The next day I ran into him in the lobby and I told him so. He kind of sneered at me, and I wished that I *had* ruined his act. Then he told me that I couldn't have even if I wanted to—he had measures for people who tried to disobey commands. But then he told me that part of picking a good subject—one of the reasons he had chosen me—was that he could detect the 'good guy' syndrome, the ability to fool yourself with the rationalization that because of your good nature you will go along with the proceedings. The act of acting hypnotized is part of the hypnotic process. The act of fooling yourself in your own mind fools your mind. The rational, sane decision to flip out and play-act crazy, then in fact implementing it, is in fact *it.* Doing it does it. You never have to worry about authenticity. Just do it—start it in a big way—sting them—hurt them so they won't want you back—make them glad to pay you for the rest of your life to stay away. Take your theme—like Beethoven or Berlioz—and twist it, turn it, torture it, invert and distort it—go to fucking town with it—and you will have *done* it."

Jack's eyes glowed with religious fervor. He fixed them squarely on Ron and moved closer. "Now what were you thinking before?" he commanded.

"They're giving me an honor luncheon . . ." Ron said without hesitation.

"An honor luncheon . . ." Jack sneered rhythmically.

"I'm number one."

"Number one . . ."

"I'd like to get up there . . ." Ron stood up. Jack gazed up at him from his stool as if he were a mad audience waiting . . .

"Get up there . . ." Jack echoed.

"Get up there and when it comes time for my little bullshitting speech about the fucking honor and the opportunity . . ."

"The honor and the opportunity . . ."

"I'd like to get up there . . ." Ron's voice was rising in the bar and he didn't give a solitary shit.

"Get up there . . ." Jack's voice rose a third below like a runaway Beethoven crescendo.

"Look them all over . . ."

"Look them all over . . ."

"And in a big, gorgeous, thundering voice I'd tell them all to go fuck themselves."

Jack rose and clapped his hands wildly. They were making a hell of a noise. They were in a world within a world.

"Tell you all to go fuck yourselves!" Ron shouted. Then he snatched his shot glass off the bar and spilled it.

"That's *my* insanity!" Jack yelled, jumping back onto his stool and pointing. "Now what's yours?"

Ron flung his shot glass to the floor. It bounced zanily. Two men raised their heads and looked over. Ron glared pugnaciously at them, fiery-eyed. They minded their own business. He loved the power of that.

Jack was grinning with great satisfaction. He extended his hand. Ron's hand, at last, found a home. It felt great.

Without a glance backward he turned and with sure sea legs strutted out of the Nautilus bar into the street.

He went back to the home office. He was sure—but first he had to make dead sure. There would be only one way.

McCloud's hostile black secretary was away from her desk. Ron walked up to McCloud's door and knocked twice, then just opened it. McCloud, a bit startled, said, "Well, I didn't expect you back so soon."

Ron walked right up to the desk and said without preamble or courtesies, "I've been thinking about names and there's only one that comes to mind."

"Who?"

"Me."

McCloud reacted as if he'd been tagged with a quick jab. "You." Ron watched his eyes. McCloud turned away. He wouldn't have to say another word. The reaction and the avoidance said it all.

"I'd never even thought about you, Ron. You're doing so well. What do you need it for? We're really not thinking too strongly about our top field people anymore... they're doing too well where they are... I don't know... I'll sure think about it..."

Ron leaned across the desk. "Tom, besides all that, is there any other reason that I wouldn't get it?" Ron paused. "I've known you a lot of years. Now, you don't have to tell me what the reason is, but just tell me if there is a reason . . ."

"Ron, you've got to be crazy to think about coming in here. Think of the cut in pay . . ."

"Tom. Is there any other reason?"

McCloud stood up to his full military bearing. Ron could see that he was putting on the mantle of the code—certain things you just don't tell the other fellow. He knew what McCloud was going to say before he even said it. "No, no, fella . . . no other reason . . . I mean, I'll think about it . . . I promise you that."

Ron couldn't help snickering. The interview was over. He turned and marched out of the office. When the time came, he would enjoy telling that bastard to go fuck himself the most of all.

Ron drove his car around a very long time before he headed home. He didn't think about anything—just drove with a sense of not caring, floating from street to street. When he finally came home, Doris was watching Merv Griffin.

Ron walked to one side of the living room to an old heavy, hated, ornate lamp that came from Doris' family—Napoli, by way of the Bronx—and yanked out the cord. "Where's Valerie?" he asked. Doris had hardly looked up as he came in.

"By her girl friend's . . . I think she'll sleep over tonight."

Ron picked up the lamp and walked to the TV set and he hurled the lamp at Merv. The screen smashed with a very loud pop. Then he yanked the cord from its socket and picked up the set and threw it through the back yard window and watched it smash on the patio. Then, without even a glance at Doris—who was cringing in shocked disbelief in her chair, he walked up to the bedroom, closed the door, barricaded it with furniture and went to sleep in his big round bed.

CHAPTER 17

He stayed in the bedroom the next day. He was totally rational and totally furious.

He did damage. With a hacksaw he cut through the chain that supported a large overhead lamp and left it hanging on a thread of metal until it finally snapped and tumbled to the floor. He guillotined imitation Hummel figures on the knickknack shelf. He dismembered cutesy dolls and he worked on some Keene eyes in pictures of children that Doris loved, trying to make them more sardonic with Doris' mascara. It didn't work though—those eyes are indomitable.

"Doing it does it," he'd repeat. He hated this bedroom. Nothing in it seemed to belong to him. And being he was locked in here, he reasoned—see, I know I'm not locked in. I know that I can walk out of this room any time I want but I'm acting—yes, that's it, acting as if I am locked in. That is insane. Doing it does it.

From time to time he'd hear Doris wailing at him outside the door, making concerned-wife noises. She wanted him to eat, have a drink, talk. He wasn't hungry. For the first time in years he didn't want a drink. He'd go to the bathroom from time to time and splash some water on his face and swallow it. Above all he didn't want to talk.

Toward evening, Doris came to the door and said, "Ron, Valerie has to come back soon from her friend's. I told her to stay the whole day. We can't let her know what's happening. Can we talk?"

He was giving the white shag carpeting a haircut—a crewcut, imagining it to be a sheep and himself the shearer. He hadn't chosen this fucking carpeting—it was that idiot decorator he'd hired. Why the hell didn't he do all the decorating himself as he'd done with David in the apartment? Now the rug in the apartment, that dark, smart beige that he and David had chosen, with just a touch of Persian . . . that was classy.

The apartment.

"Ron," Doris said.

"The apartment," Ron mumbled to himself. "It's ridiculous. The plants haven't been watered . . . those beautiful plants that David and I picked out together."

He rose from the floor, moved the dresser away from the door, opened it and walked past a gasping Doris who fought back tears as she saw the casualties in their bedroom and mumbled, ". . . place hasn't been dusted in a long time . . . probably smells musty."

As he was going down the stairs toward the garage, Doris said, "Ron, where are you going?"

"The roaches have probably carried the place away by now.

Thank God David's so immaculate. I'm sure the place is clean."

He was in the garage getting into his Mercedes. Automatically Doris found a jacket that was the best coverup for the mismatch of slacks and an open-necked sport shirt that he'd worn through the day.

She opened the passenger door of the Mercedes as he started the car and put the jacket on the seat next to him. "Ron, are you all right to go out? Ron? I'll have to call someone if this keeps up . . . the doctor or someone. Can't we talk? Put this on, it's a little chilly."

He didn't want a doctor, not now anyway. After the luncheon next week he'd see a battery of them, but not now . . . They might force him to take a pill or an injection that would take this marvelous fury away from him. "We'll talk when I get back, okay?"

"When are you coming back? Where are you going?"

Ron pressed the button on the dashboard of his car to open the garage door.

"Why did you do all those things in the bedroom?"

He started to back out and Doris had to slam the car door and hurl herself back against the garage wall. You're crazy, she wanted to scream. He'd have loved it if she had.

He parked in a No Parking zone and ran up the one flight to the apartment. He opened the door quickly and turned on the light. It wasn't going to be so bad, he thought, a bit musty, yes, and very dusty . . . oh look at the frames of those pictures, and the dead plants.

I'm sorry, plants.

I sent my money to the landlord, but not a drop of water to you. I'll never neglect you again. Rug, shelves, little plants, everything in this apartment, I hereby vow and pledge to you that I will take care of you. Nurture you. You are my heart of hearts on this planet and I must always keep you clean and thriving.

He cleaned and dusted, opened a window and played a Berlioz record, *Romeo and Juliet.* Jack knows his music, he thought, no one can torture a theme like Berlioz.

When he went back outside he saw with some dissatisfaction that he hadn't gotten a parking ticket. He'd wanted one. He could almost feel the cardboard ripping in his hand as he'd snatch it from his windshield and tear it up, scattering it into the face of one of those officious little imitation cops who wrote them out . . .

He drove straight home, put the car in the garage and went into the living room. Doris was sitting in a daze on a chair. She looked as if a piece had been taken out of her because she had no TV set to watch. She'd propped boards from the garage against the hole in the window. She'd been sitting there for hours, unable to decide what to do. Should she call Carmine if he acted up again? Next time he might hit her. Who knows, with the way he was acting . . . but then she didn't want to start with Carmine—the whole family would know and some of the rougher ones might come around and just sit in the living room to put some fear into Ron. Ron would hate her for the rest of her life if that happened.

Ron sat on the couch and they looked at each other. Ron crossed his legs and cleared his throat. "Where's Valerie?"

"At my sister Theresa's."

"Is she coming back?"

"Not tonight."

"What about school?"

"Theresa will take her."

"I'll have to see her. I'll have to make her understand."

Doris thought she must have missed something.

"Do you wonder what's going on?"

She nodded her head.

"I would think so."

Then he sat there stonily. "Well?" he finally said. "Why don't you ask?"

She still couldn't say anything.

"I'm being nasty," he said reflectively. "That's stupid. None of this is your fault. You've been perfect all along, totally blameless.

As a matter of fact, the most important person—the person who must understand—is you . . . If you help, it'll go easier for all of us."

She found her voice. "Ron, what *is* it?"

"You've got to tell Valerie that it's only a game that her father's playing—not to get alarmed. If she believed that I was really sick it would frighten her. All right?"

"All right what?"

Ron got off the chair and crouched in front of Doris. "Will you tell Valerie that her father's playing a game? And that he's okay?" He took hold of her wrist and she immediately blurted, "Yes."

"All right, good. Now, you've got to tell the doctors that I've been in bad shape lately. Tell them about this . . ." he gestured toward the broken window and absent TV. "Tell them more, tell them about raving, ranting, screaming at the neighbors, yourself, just turning into a lunatic . . . that kind of thing."

"Doctors? What doctors? Ron, please tell me what you're talking about."

"Didn't I?"

"No."

"I thought I did. You see, if you tell them all this then I won't have to do anything at home. I can just do what I have to do at the luncheon and that'll be that. I mean, what I've done I'm sorry for, but there won't need to be anything else."

"Do what at the luncheon?"

"Didn't I tell you?"

"No."

"You're very forgetful."

He let go of her arm and sat on the floor, running his hand over the thick wool carpeting. She thought of the carpeting in their bedroom and said quickly, "Please tell me . . . I'll try to remember."

"Good," he said with a half-smile. "See, you can report this conversation, can't you? I'm talking like a crazy man, aren't I?"

She wished she could run—she could say nothing.

"Say something. I'm talking like a crazy man, aren't I?"

"No."

"I am. I am!" he shouted and he got on his knees and held her wrist, more tightly this time.

"Yes. Yes you are."

He let go and relaxed again. "This must be a strain on you. You're blameless."

"Ron, what are you going to do at the luncheon?"

"I'm going to flip out."

"Flip out? What is that supposed to mean?"

He stood up. "I'll show you. Make believe you're Larry Edelman. After all the speeches extolling my virtues, you, as master of ceremonies, are finally introducing me . . . Come on, you've been to enough of those things . . ." He pulled her to her feet. "Come on . . ." He pointed her toward the broken window as if it were the audience at the luncheon.

"What do you want me to say?"

"Introduce me . . . come on, say after me . . ." He imitated Larry, ". . . As Ron's Meridian father . . . go ahead . . ."

Her voice came out of dry sand. ". . . As Ron's Meridian father . . ."

"To introduce my Meridian son, winner of the President's Trophy, number-one manager in the entire country . . . Ron Starr. Come on Doris, like Merv . . ."

"To introduce my Meridian son, number one in the country, Ron Starr."

Ron clapped his hands, playing audience. "Then I'm going to face everybody, and silence will prevail. It'll be a long pause . . . I'm going to look around at all of them—Brock, fucking Brock, McCloud, Edelman, and I'm going to say, thank you, I would just like to tell you all, individually and collectively, to go fuck yourself."

Ron laughed. Doris wanted to scream.

"And then I'm going to start throwing things . . . salt shakers, pepper shakers, and glasses and chairs and tablecloths, and I'll stand on chairs and kick water pitchers until they hold me down, and they'll call a hospital and they'll take me away . . . I will go fucking berserk! Oh, Lenny would love it!"

He envisioned Lenny out there saluting what he was doing with the middle "up yours" finger to the brow.

"Ron, why are you going to do this?"

"To get disability." Ron guided Doris onto the couch and sat next to her. "I'll get seventy percent of my income for as long as I'm disabled We'll have no problems."

"That's wrong."

"Wrong? Do you know how much premium income my men will bring in this year? Over five million dollars! Do you know how much the men brought in by my men will bring in this year? Another three million. Can you imagine what it'll be next year and the year after as my men bring in men and they multiply and bring other men in? Wrong? Do you know what wrong is? Wrong is that I'm not going to get anyplace in this company. I'm going to go downhill—eventually they'll fire me and I'll be too old and bitter to get anything else. Now is the time to strike out!"

"Why can't you get anyplace in this company? What happened with the home office?"

"Just some petty politics. I'm out. And they'll be out to get me from here on in . . . even as a manager. The minute I stop recruiting, they'll be on my ass . . ."

She sensed that he was evading something. "Well, Ron," she said after thinking a moment, "if you want me to cooperate, you've got to tell me why."

"I told you."

"No, about the petty politics. You must tell me what happened." Doris sometimes became dumb stubborn—Italian stubborn, Ron called it. Her jaw would set and she'd squat like a mule shitting, and now she was doing it again.

"All right," he said, as levelly as he could, a man finally having to come out with the painful truth. "A vicious rumor is going around. Brock started it and now it's all over like wildfire. The night we last had that gathering, Brock saw me talking with a young guy in the Baseball Diner. This guy was someone I was working on . . . hoping to develop to become an agent one day . . . you know how I am . . ."

"Of course."

"Well we were talking very intensely, and Brock thought I was . . . one of those . . ."

"What?"

"Gay."

"Oh, no."

"He spread it around. I think one of the people in Watergate said that once the toothpaste is out of the tube you can't get it back in."

"So that's what it is." Doris came closer to Ron and squeezed his arm. "We'll fight it. They can't do that to you."

"You can't fight something like that, Doris. What do you do, go up to people and say, look I'm not queer?"

"All right, then we'll stick it out. Memories are short and you are still number one. You won't go downhill—not you. Soon they'll be begging you to come into the home office. You'll see."

"I don't care anymore. Even if they begged me now, I'd tell them to shove it up their asses."

"You're just bitter and angry . . . It'll all cool down . . . you'll see." Doris stroked his face gently. It soothed Ron and he leaned back and rested his head on the couch. "Have you eaten?" she asked.

"No," he said, and for the first time in days he felt hunger.

"Would you like me to fix you a nice Scotch?"

He did want a drink. He kicked his shoes off. Doris bent down and removed his socks. The cold air from the broken window made his feet feel good. He sighed.

"I'll get you one," she said. She went into the kitchen and he heard ice plopping from the ice-maker into the glass, crackling as the Scotch poured over it. He was getting free of the tension that had possessed him and he spread himself on the couch. As Doris

304

came back with the drink, he said, "It's true."

She didn't react as she bent down and put the drink toward him. "What's true?"

"I am one of those. I am gay."

"Drink your drink."

The glass was cold in his hand. He spilled some of the drink on the carpet and then lazily dropped his glass.

Doris didn't seem to notice. "How about a sandwich? I have some ham and I have some Swiss."

"No," he mumbled, but she went into the kitchen as if he'd said yes and fussed in the refrigerator.

"Doris, come in here."

She slowly put down the ham and came into the living room. Ron was lying on the couch. He lethargically signaled her to come to him.

"Don't you believe me?"

"Do you want me to believe you?"

"I don't know . . . I haven't thought about us. After this is over . . . I haven't thought about it . . . I'm tired."

"I'll put you to bed. A good night's sleep will be wonderful."

"I would sleep down here but someone broke the window and the breeze makes it cold," he said, his eyelids drooping. Doris was very strong for a small woman and she managed to lift her dozing husband off the couch and in fireman's style get him up the stairs into bed, where she undressed and covered him.

When that was completed she went downstairs and made herself some tea and thought about what the hell she was going to do tomorrow about this. Doris knew well enough that Ron was not going to calm down about this insane notion. She wished he had a temperature or that his appendix needed removing so that she could rush him to a hospital—something like that. What does someone do when her husband is like this? If I call a psychiatrist and have him come look at Ron, that would be playing right into this crazy game.

Carmine might hit him and Doris couldn't see what good that

would do either. She just sipped her tea and decided to wait and see what developed.

The next morning she woke up and saw a suitcase on the bed, and Ron was up and about in his sports jacket, throwing clothes into it. When he saw her looking he said in a good-natured, businesslike way, "I'm going to take a quick trip out to California. To see Lenny. Don't worry, I'll be back in time for the luncheon."

CHAPTER 18

He approached Lenny's beach house in the late afternoon. He was dressed all wrong for California—a New York sports jacket, long-sleeved shirt and tie. It was hot and he was sweaty and uncomfortable.

On the beach in front of Lenny's house, young men played volleyball, jumped around and ran in and out of the water. They all seemed beautiful. Everyone seemed beautiful in this little beach town. It was a gay colony—more open, more everything than he'd ever imagined. The cars that passed were not filled with tourists gawking at the freaky gays. Tourists would have been the gawked-at ones here—the freaks.

For years now, all the old warmth had gone out of the relationship between the two brothers. Lenny came East perhaps once every year and a half—mostly to visit his parents. He never stayed long at Ron's, and while he was there he mostly played with Valerie—who adored her flamboyant-looking uncle with the bullet-like shaved head and the olive complexion and erect stride, who tumbled and flipped her around, showed her tricks for flipping her playmates, and little gymnastic feats. Ron would talk at Lenny about his blossoming career, how much money he was making (offering continually to loan Lenny any amount he wanted for anything he had in mind) and showing Lenny each new expensive accoutrement around the house.

A bore, Lenny always said to himself. Thank God that girl-boy he married manages to make herself scarce when I come. Isn't it funny though that whenever I play with Valerie, Ron has to be there watching as if to make sure that I don't somehow infect her. I bet he doesn't even know why he watches us so carefully. I wonder if that idiot knows anything about himself anymore. God, the way he drinks and the way he looks—it's horrible. We can't talk anymore. He pretends that what he is never was and that I never knew. I wonder what he's doing now. It's probably sneaky and sleazy. Idiot. He's letting the parade pass him by. There are plenty of guys in his position coming out now and their companies aren't firing them as long as they bring in the business. Moron. We talk about reaching all the others in hiding, and I can't even reach my own brother.

Ron knocked on the screen door. The door opened and before him was one of the most beautiful naked young men he'd ever seen. He was totally blond, tall, pleasantly this side of muscle-bound; his arm and shoulder muscles looked softly powerful. Ron wanted immediately to be nestled in them. He was hung like a horse.

"Hello," the young man said, "who are you?"

"I'm Ron. I'm Lenny's brother. Is he home?"

"Oh, Lenny's brother. How nice. Here from the East?"

"Yes."

"Come." Ron followed the young man into the house. After a few attempts he stopped trying to keep his eyes from the young man's gorgeous dimpled behind.

Lenny, dressed in a simple white ki and plain black trunks, walked out of a room and greeted Ron casually, as if he were long-expected and part of a process that he knew was going to occur.

Ron wondered why he didn't seem at all surprised. Lenny hadn't known he was coming.

"Have you met Buster?" Lenny tousled Buster's blond hair. Buster laughed and shied away. "Doesn't he look like Buster Crabbe?"

Lenny, seeing the puzzled look on Ron's face said, "Don't you remember the old Flash Gordon serials? Haven't you seen them on reruns?"

Buster was about to open the patio and run out into the sand when Lenny said, "Put something on, for God's sake, before the wicked gendarmes appear. This isn't Black Beach, you know."

Ron watched as Buster slipped on skimpy dark trunks that set off his blond beauty. Lenny, observing Ron's interest said, "Gorgeous, no?"

Buster ran out into the sand and dashed straight for the ocean. Lenny led Ron outside and they started to walk on the sand. They walked silently for a while, Ron forcing himself not to look at all the wonderful boys on the beach, sweating and feeling the sand slipping into his shoes.

There was so much he wanted to tell his brother. There'd been years of not talking. He wanted to get advice, justification, encouragement, to apologize, get close to Lenny again . . . he needed Lenny so desperately now. But he couldn't get into it because he kept getting distracted by the amazing beauty on that little beach.

"Most of them are my students," Lenny explained. "I wish we'd had any of them along with us that night in Binghamton. Remember?"

"Yes."

"You did all right then."

"I lost it . . . I lost it . . ."

"No . . . no . . . you didn't . . . It just went to sleep along the way . . . it's waking up now . . ."

"I'm going to be coming out." He hadn't really made that decision until he heard it emerging now. It sounded so right.

"Good. What about Doris?"

"She'll be well taken care of. I'm not much fun for her."

"Valerie?"

Ron felt sick when Lenny said that.

"I don't know. What do you do about kids? Another woman she'd understand, eventually. What do you do about this?"

"She's very special, you know. She has a deep, instinctive feeling for the truth, but, I don't know . . . it'll be rough. Don't tell her now. When she's older and can understand more . . . There's more education going around."

"Are a lot of men like me doing it?"

"In droves. The climate is changing—everything is different. It's still rough, but it's happening. What about your job?"

"I'm going to play-act flipping out. I'll get seventy percent of my income, enough to take care of Doris and Valerie and still live the way I want to live."

"Watch out they just don't fire you. You mustn't let them know you're doing it because you're gay. They don't know now, do they?"

"No. Just rumors. Don't worry, I'll do it well. Very well."

"You seem to have it all together."

"Do I?" Ron turned to Lenny but he didn't need Lenny to answer that question now. He needed no advice or justifications, no need to apologize or anything else. They put their arms around each other's shoulders and walked feeling now as one, two brothers . . .

"Welcome aboard . . ." Lenny said.

After a while, Ron said, his voice choking with an onrush of tears. "I-I love you, Lenny, you know that, I love you a lot . . ."

"I love you too, kid . . ." Lenny said and gently kissed his brother's forehead.

Later on that evening there was a bonfire on the beach and many of them sat around and there was a litany of stories, stories told many times before by each of them to each other and to their psychiatrists, friends and lovers. They talked about how it had been . . . their discoveries about themselves and working through the awfulness of their anxieties, still present, but better for the most part than before.

Lenny was the high priest, presiding with a sure touch rich in strength and compassion, devoid of the arrogance Ron remembered. Ron listened and for the first time in his life felt that he had come home and was in a place that made him totally comfortable. He was like a soldier who'd been in a terrible war all by himself, battling without anyone by his side—no comradeship, no bitching together, no cursing the first sergeants with each other. Now he was in touch with other soldiers, and each of them had had feelings and experiences that were like his own. Each of them was part of him.

Lenny turned and asked him something about himself. Ron said, "I don't feel I have a right. I'm still in, hidden . . ."

Someone else said that he was too, and the rest agreed that it was hard . . . it was all right though . . . it takes a long time . . . it's tough . . . Go on, Ron . . .

"I have a wife and a kid . . ."

Many said they did too, and Ron went on. "I feel so at home here . . ."

They made sounds like a prayer group, a chorus of amens. Buster said, "You're beautiful, Ron."

"I don't feel beautiful with my little pot belly and New York clothes . . ." They laughed.

They told him that when he came out he'd get in shape. He'd want to. Competition was tough out here, too. Ron laughed. "It's the kind of competition I'd like to enter.

"Why is it so fucking hard? Why do we have all these problems just being ourselves? I mean, here I am at thirty-seven with a whole life built up around something that I'm not. I look around and I ask myself where and how did this all happen. I've never talked this way, never said any of these things, even to my brother. I've avoided him for ten years or more. I've been ashamed of him and myself . . . afraid . . . cowering like a dirty little boy . . . I've been drinking a ton of Scotch and it hasn't done a thing for me except make me plump. Why has all this happened?"

Someone said to see a shrink. Someone else said that shrinks wanted to convert you if they were straight and fuck you if they were gay.

"I'm going to see plenty of shrinks soon. I'm going to tell them all to go fuck themselves, and they're going to take me to a battery of shrinks . . ."

"Right on . . ." "Go to it . . ." "Fuck 'em . . ."

"I'm going to get up there and tell them to go fuck themselves . . . all the bigwigs of my other life . . . all the fucking insurance executives with their phony macho shit . . ."

Someone who worked for a bank chimed in . . . "They're the same fuckers."

"I'm going to rip them off and go out on disability and collect plenty from them and live free and out in the open like this goddamn beach."

They rejoiced. Didn't great savages of the past sit around fires and boast of old and new feats of bravery?

"You're beautiful, man, you're beautiful . . ." Buster said. He sat next to Ron and rubbed Ron's knee hard with his large hand.

"I'm going to hurt them like they hurt us. I'm going to come the fuck out and I'm going to be fucking free!" Ron shouted, and they were with him around the fire, excited by what Ron was saying, and hands were going on each other and they were getting closer to each other, and Lenny sat in the middle like a conductor in a mighty orchestra and his eyes smiled, and Buster whispered to Ron, "You're beautiful, man . . . you're beautiful . . ." Ron looked deeply into his beautiful Flash Gordon face and kissed him as hard as he could; he put himself between those gorgeous shoulders and felt them envelop him as they moved away from the fire . . . and they made love to each other and Ron was so dizzy that he couldn't believe all this was happening to him. If his life ended at this moment, he thought, he'd die a very happy man.

CHAPTER 19

Ron came home the night before his honor luncheon. Doris
was in the kitchen when he arrived. When she saw him she felt
encouraged. He'd never looked better. He had a touch of sun and
he seemed jaunty and energetic. Yet no usual perfunctory kiss on
the cheek as he came into the kitchen—he simply said, "Where's
Valerie?"

"She's staying at Theresa's for a while."

"Good."

"Want a drink?"

"No. No thanks."

"How was California?"

"Fine."

"Lenny?"

"Terrific. I'm going upstairs to change."

In the bedroom he pushed one button to open the bedroom closet, then another and a clothes rack holding about six robes emerged. He quickly tossed his suit on the floor, put on his plainest terrycloth robe and stretched out comfortably in a low-slung modern chair. The suit in the middle of the floor somehow reminded him of his father's crumpled tea bags on the kitchen table. When Doris came in she picked it up off the floor and carefully put it aside for cleaning.

"How do you feel?" she asked.

"I never felt better in my entire life."

"You look great. You got some sun."

"Yes."

"Did you eat?"

"On the plane."

"No drink?"

"No. I'm going to cut down." He patted his midriff.

"You should."

"Do you have my suit picked for tomorrow?"

"Yes. It's the navy blue with the thin stripes. I bought a tie and shirt that'll go perfectly."

"Let me see."

The shirt was a deep beige and the tie a black and brown silk. Doris knew what she was doing with clothes. She sat down on the bed.

"Do you want a bath? I can run the water," she asked.

"Not a bad idea."

She stood up to go to the bathroom.

"Doris," Ron said, his tone stopping her. "What's going on? Why are you this way?"

"I'm no different than I always am."

"That's what I mean."

"I'll run the water." Doris disappeared and Ron heard the

water rushing in the tub. He picked up the phone and dialed a number. Doris came back into the bedroom as he dialed, wringing her hands.

The phone rang three times and Larry Edelman answered. "Ron, how the hell are you?"

"I'm fine, Larry. Are we all set for tomorrow?"

"What do you mean all set?"

"Tomorrow. The luncheon."

"You're sick."

"Larry, I have never felt better in my life."

"Somebody's pulling my leg then. Doris called and told me you were really sick, bad flu, couldn't come to the phone even. She said you'd never be in shape for tomorrow. I was just going to call McCloud and postpone."

Doris started to run out of the bedroom. Ron said, "Hold it a minute, Larry." Carrying the phone, he ran after her and grabbed her in the hall as she was going for the extension phone in the study. "You're not going to stop me," he hissed at her. He shoved her into Valerie's bedroom and held the door shut. He picked up the phone again, slightly out of breath, and said, "No postponing, Larry. I'm fine. I just went on a trip and Doris was afraid that I wouldn't make it back in time."

Larry paused. Ron was afraid he'd hear his breathless sound. Doris was banging on the door and yelling something. Ron muffled the mouthpiece.

"Jesus . . ." Larry said. "Well, I'm glad I didn't start making phone calls. You're really all right?"

"Fine. I just got back."

"Okay. See you tomorrow. Glad it's on."

"Right. Bye." Ron hung up. He opened Valerie's door. Doris was back against the far wall, looking as if she expected Ron to hit her.

"Doris, you're acting insane." Ron said in a reasonable tone. "You're acting against your own best interest. You have what an old friend of mine would say was an incorrect perception of your own reality. Instead of trying to stop me, you should be helping me. Can't you see that?"

She shook her head. "No."

"Come on," he said, "let's talk about it . . . let's not stay in Valerie's room."

Doris walked past Ron into their bedroom. They sat on the bed. "I guess there's one important missing link that you don't perceive that's making you act this way. One thing that you refuse to believe that once you do believe will make you change . . ."

"Ron," Doris interrupted, putting both her hands on his arm, "don't talk the way you were talking before you went to California."

"About my being gay . . ."

"Stop it."

"That's the point."

She squeezed his arm very hard. "Ron, you're not that."

"Doris, I am."

"Ron, you're not. I should know."

"Doris, I am. I should know. I've hidden it . . . I've played tricks with myself . . ."

"Ron, do you know what you're saying? We're married, we have a daughter. Do you know that you've been a beautiful man to me—a woman. Do you know how from the very first I've loved you the way a woman loves a man . . . a real man."

"Doris, you have a soap opera reality. You know when I first saw you at the desk at Meridian Life I thought you were a boy. I said to myself, they're hiring cute boys for jobs that girls used to do. That was my split-second reaction the moment I saw you —then of course you stood up and I saw the skirt and I was disappointed. But something remained and it grew on me as each day went by. I didn't just become attracted to you—I identified with you. When the men, Gil Sloane and the rest, would flirt with you, be pigs, it was like they were doing it to me . . . It was strange, fascinating and delicious in its way. When Gil would look at you walking down the hall and make that kind of fist that men do when they want to fuck a woman . . . it was like he was doing it to *me*. And I loved it. I felt what he felt for you and I could feel like you . . . Doris, do you know there were times that I used to go into my office and lock the door . . . No, don't turn away, you've got to understand . . . I used to lock the door and make believe that I was you, that Gil was jamming me and it used to make me come like crazy . . . like crazy, Doris . . . What do you call that?"

"Ron, you have been a man from the very first. From the very first time you stood there in the doorway when I was going out with that boy Jimmy, and your look told me in no uncertain terms that you wanted me and that you were jealous of Jimmy . . ."

"Is that what you thought?"

"That's what I knew. I knew you loved me. I knew I loved you. I knew that I wanted you to be the first and only *man* I ever had. I could see it all in that moment, Ron. It was the most beautiful moment in my life."

"So that's what you knew."

"Yes." There were stars in her eyes as she recalled that moment.

"Do you want to know what was? What really was?"

Doris did not want to know. She tried to move off the bed. Ron held her arm.

"Jimmy was so pretty." She just turned her head. "I could imagine that I was you, fending him off in the car after work . . . Come on Dor, how about a little feel? . . . Come on, whaddya say, kid? . . ." Oh God, Ron sounded just like him and then she felt his hand roughly over her breast and for the very life of her it felt like Jimmy McDonald's rough hand. "I was you, Doris. When I gave you that deep, meaningful look at the door that evening I was imagining I was you—a shy little Bronx virgin, lying naked in bed with the sheet over me to cover my nakedness, sneaking glances at Jimmy as he got undressed . . ."

"No . . . you were *jealous* of Jimmy."

"Oh no, I was dizzy with fantasies of you and Jimmy in bed. I imagined his hot freckled hands all over you, over me. I can see the freckles now . . . like little fireflies on a hot summer night. I saw him coming in bed with me . . . Look Doris . . . look it's getting me so hot . . . I'm you and I'm seeing Jimmy all over me . . ."

She turned and moved the folds of his terrycloth robe. He was shiningly erect. "No matter what you say," she said, "you are a man and I am a woman."

He lay back on the bed, his eyes closed, gyrating slowly . . . "I see him coming into bed with me. His shorts coming off and his hot Irish freckled cock coming at me . . . into me . . ."

Doris bent over him. "Ron, no matter what you say you are a man and I'm a woman. No matter what you say or what you do you can't change that . . ."

"Come on Jimmy . . . come on . . . I'm ready for you . . . I'm ready for you . . ." Ron pushed Doris' head gently down toward his penis . . . When the act came to its fruition and she was forced to perform the ultimate indignity, she kept saying to herself that no matter what he says or what he does he is a *man* and I am a woman. And my name is Doris and his name is Ron.

Afterwards he was calm—sleepy. He peered deeply into her eyes and asked, "Doris, do you understand how I am now?"

She nodded and said, "Yes, Ron."

"Will you stand in my way?"

"No."

"Everything will be the way it should be."

"Yes."

"Don't try to call it off."

"No. It's too late for that. Don't worry."

He fell asleep.

She put on a robe and quietly went into the kitchen. She put some water on for tea before she picked up the phone and dialed upstate New York to speak to Louis and Blanche.

When Ron awoke it was morning and he immediately saw that Doris hadn't slept with him. Where was she? Was he tricked?

Could he move his feet? Were they tied? He moved them. Was the bedroom door locked? He jumped out of bed and tried it. It was open. The time? Had he been drugged, overslept? It was nine forty-five. Plenty of time. He calmed himself. She hadn't betrayed him. She was going to cooperate. Good. Where had she slept, though? Probably in the guest room. He put on his robe and went out into the hall and he peered into the living room. Doris was there, serving tea to Louis and Blanche.

They looked at him for a moment. Ron remembered the time he'd looked down from a landing and seen Lenny pinning them cringing against the wall with his pointing finger. Thereafter he'd done all the right things and Lenny everything wrong, but now between his parents and Lenny there existed that bond which arises between fierce enemies who live through a battle.

When they spoke of Lenny it was with muted admiration. They looked forward to his visits. They wrote him—jointly. Blanche sent him her poems and Louis asked about running a business out in California: taxes, overhead, net, gross. They hardly ever visited Ron, or he them. Ron made ten times the money Lenny did, but his father never wanted to hear the numbers. Blanche could hardly pain herself to visit. To her he was like a beautiful concept of a painting that hadn't turned out right, so she'd simply blotted it out. When she did come she'd look around the house and invariably say, "Still no piano?" and never look at Doris or hardly notice Valerie.

Well, it's very appropriate that they should be the first ones in this world, outside of his sweet loving fucking wife who called them in to try to stop him, to feel the sting of his little seventy-percent act.

Ron went down the stairs with the middle finger of his right hand stuck in the air. No one moved. He studied them as if they were waxworks. Mother's been depressed lately—weird. She's gotten really old, growing into herself, hunching, gnarling as if she were trying to become a wrinkled Spalding ball. Well mother, sorry, still no piano, but here's the number-three finger for you.

Up yours, darling! And *you,* my dear phony father. You look fine and dandy. Mother says you've got a bit of action upstate with one of the local business ladies, and that's okay by her. You pig. Well, I'm sorry father, I have no Protestant vice-presidencies for you. All I've got for you is my ever-loving fucking finger! A digital spire!

With a departing look of fury at Doris he bounded back up the stairs into the bathroom for his morning shower. The cold water tapped on him, waking every nerve for this, the most important day of his life. He rubbed the bar of soap hard against his flabby tummy, his ever-present symbol of personal decay—soon it would be gone, flatness in its place like a badge of honor.

He shaved. Should he deliberately cut his face shaving? Yes. Doing it does it! He gave himself a deep, hurtful nick on the right side of his jaw. He brought himself closer to the mirror as he watched the blood run out of him and he giggled—Oh God, something about this whole thing feels so fucking good. He hit the mirror with his fist. Should I break it? No—save that kind of thing for the big show . . . the really big show. He combed his disappearing hair. He'd been contemplating a toupee—none of that shit for him now. Maybe he'd shave his head like Lenny.

He put a dab of toilet paper on his nick and quickly put on the suit that Doris had laid out for him. It was a good suit, shirt and tie combination. He looked terrific. It reminded him of the time he saw Professor Lavalle for the last time.

There was a timid knock on the bedroom door. Ron strode to it and threw it open. His father was caught in the middle of another knock.

"Come on in," Ron said, stepping aside and waving Louis into the bedroom. "I haven't much time. I've got to be there shortly." He stuck his head out of the door and yelled commandingly, "Doris, are you dressed yet? Are you going, or what?"

Ron could hear the jump in her voice as she answered from the kitchen, "Yes, Ron."

Mother was still sitting in the living room with her back to him like a statue. He went back into the bedroom and told his father to have a seat. Ron sat facing Louis on the edge of one of the swayback chairs near the window. Louis sat opposite on the matching one.

"Son," Louis said. For Christ's sake, Ron thought, sound Jewish for a change. Where the hell did you get that midwestern twangy "son." "You're not really going to go ahead and do those things that Doris' been saying you're going to do, are you?"

"Dad," Ron began. God, he thought, I sound like a midwestern Wasp myself. "I know that you are an officer of the court and must uphold the law in every facet of your life because you belong to a very high profession. I know that if I told you that I was planning on acting in an illegal and unlawfully boisterous fashion, you'd have no choice but to clamp your officer-of-the-court clamps on me and detain me."

"What are you saying, son?"

"What do you think I'm saying, dad?"

"Are you going to do this thing, or are you just having a spat with the wife and trying to scare her?"

Ron laughed. He knew he was coming off weird. He indicated that his father should examine the bedroom with its cut-up shag carpeting and other little damages. Examine the evidence counselor. Louis did.

"You know, breaking a few things and cussing people out doesn't make you crazy, legally or medically. If you do this thing and it backfires, you've thrown away a career. Those psychiatrists have a way of picking out the fakers . . . Say, you nicked yourself pretty badly . . ."

Ron had removed the paper from his cut, put his finger on the warm blood and wiped it on his new beige shirt. Louis blinked and stared. Ron stared back. Louis said, "That's . . ." and then stopped himself. Ron allowed himself the luxury of a small smile. He'd made his point.

Louis slouched back into the swayback chair, his features, arms, legs seeming to cave inward like the chair. He didn't look at Ron now, he just stared out the window at the quiet street. "When Doris told me about what you were saying to her . . . about being like your brother, it all came back to me in a bad way. I don't know if it's true or not, I don't have to know—I don't want to know . . . I go to meetings here in the city sometimes. These organizations for people like your brother have meetings for the family. They're good. They help me understand that I've got nothing to be ashamed of—doesn't mean I was a mollycoddle—it could happen to any family, no way of knowing, no predicting. The important thing they impressed on me is that it doesn't mean that he's sick—your brother, I mean. He can lead a good, useful life. And he is. He's really terrific, isn't he?

"I was crazy years ago when I acted the way I did—pure loco. I don't know if this is the right time to be telling you all this, maybe part of what you're going through is because of me. My attitude. Your mother's . . . I don't know. If it is it's too late for me to change the past. . . . I don't know what I want to say to you, son. Whatever you are, you are. Don't hurt yourself because of it . . . If there are bad rumors going around, ride it out. If they're true—"

Ron leaned forward, "If they're true?"

Louis turned and looked directly at Ron. "If they're true . . ."

"Yes, dad, if they're true?"

"I don't know . . ."

"Come on, dad, if they're true?"

"If they're true . . ." Louis mumbled, "don't live a lie, son, don't live a lie . . ."

Then as if what came out of him could strike him dead he shot off the chair and headed for the door. Ron followed him. Louis turned, wishing he could repeal or modify or qualify what he'd said, but couldn't. He now believed it too much. He turned and went downstairs.

Ron sat down on the bed. "I give you the finger and you gave me the truth," he muttered to himself. When he looked back at the doorway Blanche's head was in it.

323

"Come in," he said, and his mother moved into his room. She moved swiftly these days, the way birds do when they dart from branch to branch. She sat on the bed next to him and took a piece of white scratch paper from her purse. "I wrote a poem just now," she said. "Want to hear it?"

"Mom," Ron said. "I'm going to write again. I'm going to be a playwright. I was good, mom. I'm going to write again." He walked to the door and yelled down at Doris in the kitchen. "Doris, I'm going to write again, Doris. Do you hear, I'm going to write again."

"All right," she yelled up immediately. "We'll get you a type-writer."

"And a piano. We're going to get a piano. I'm going to play again—give Valerie lessons too."

"That's a good idea," Doris agreed.

He closed the door and sat next to Blanche.

"Let me hear your poem, mother."

Blanche read:

> I shot two bullets at him,
> One killed him.
> The other was a dud.
> It killed itself.
> I killed the bullets.
> I killed the gun
> I killed I.

"That's very good, mother."

"I'm going to send this to your brother in California. He got one of my poems printed in one of those poetry magazines out there, you know." Then she asked, "You mean you're going to be in the theater again?"

"Yes."

"Ohhh." Blanche stood up and walked about. "Maybe you'll run into Marsha."

Marsha? And then he remembered. Marsha, his fictional romance of many years ago.

"I see her all the time on television, in commercials and in the movies . . ." Ron said.

Blanche was thrilled. "Ohhh . . . that's wonderful . . . That's when all your troubles began when you broke up with her . . . She'll be on her fourth divorce by now, you know how those actresses are. You'll have a wickedly good time. She must be in her mid-thirties by now . . . a good age for a woman. She'll steal you away from . . ."

Blanche nodded derogatorily in the downstairs direction. She sat on the floor at his feet. The blood from his nick dripped down more slowly now, congealing a bit. She patted the blood off his chin with her hand, and she got on her knees and kissed him softly on his lips and warmly on his cheek and she smiled directly at him. Ron hadn't been this way with his mother since he was a teenage boy and at once he took her in his arms and put his cheek to her face and cried, feeling as his mother enveloped him in her arms that he'd come home again, that he was safe, safe and . . .

"Free," she was saying. "You're going to be free now, aren't you?"

Ron saw that his mother could never face, as his father had, her son's sexuality. No, her complicity was too great. No family meetings for her. She'd shot the bullets after all, it was her gun. Blanche could see Ron's chains and not see his sexuality just as she could now see Lenny's lack of chains and not see his sexuality.

"Yes, mom . . . I'm going to be free."

"You'd better get out of here," Blanche said. "Your wife is making phone calls."

Ron bolted up. Doris' pseudo-Mafioso family would enjoy pinning him down and stomping him. He dashed down the stairs. Doris was on the phone in the kitchen as he whizzed past her. She wasn't dressed yet and it was eleven o'clock. She had never intended to go with him. She was going to try and stop him. He went for the garage but stopped himself . . . no . . . she probably had Carmine planted in his Mercedes ready to grapple with him. He went for the front door, half expecting it to be guarded by some overweight Italian relative, and was overjoyed to not see anyone. He hailed a taxi, wondering if it was a plant—the way one sees it in spy movies. He looked at the identification before he got in. Irving Finklestein, an old Jew. He checked it against the face that was turning toward him, stepped in, closed the door and said, "Home Office of Meridian Life Insurance Company, please."

He was exhilarated by his escape. The late morning was bright and spring-like—good omen for the start of a new life—but as he settled back in the seat he realized that he'd asked for the home office instead of the Hotel Lancelot, which was two blocks away from the home office, an old-lady type of hotel owned by the company and used for company functions and housing out-of-town guests. He leaned forward to correct the address but realized that he wanted to see, perhaps for the last time, his secret man, Vice-president Morgan Gerhard.

He wanted the approval, bon voyage, give 'em hell kid, I wish I could be there with you. I wish I could still do it myself. Fuck 'em baby . . . fuck 'em up the ass for all of us—individually and collectively. It was silly and stupid and just a bit sentimental, but there it was . . . he wanted it. How? He didn't know—somehow they'd communicate.

Irving Finklestein, a true and open Jew, let Ron Starr, the son of a half-hidden Jew, off at the base of the Protestant citadel of America known as the Meridian Life Insurance Company. Ron Starr, who was giving up his inherited dream of ascending the spire of this financial cathedral, looked up at its height and wanted to punch it somewhere in the middle and have it quiver and shake with his blow. He was reminded of Ahab who would strike the sun if it offended him. He was delighted to be thinking literately again—he hadn't since coming in the insurance business. Maybe he could and would be a writer again—you never lose that kind of talent . . .

He went inside.

In the cavernous lobby he lost heart. Masses of people coming at him, surrounding him, all seeming happy, right, and proper, laughing and moving as if put there by the hand of God. And he was going to curse and yell at them. In the elevator he felt weak and was suddenly sweating. There were eight other people there, none of whom he knew, but if he told them how much money he made and what his life was like and what he was about to do they'd think he was stupid, not crazy. And he was. What the hell is wrong with a hundred thousand a year, a wife you don't have to pay much attention to, and all the freedom in the world? If they gave it to him now. If McCloud got on the elevator to go to the luncheon and met Ron . . . shook his hand at last, pulled him off the elevator and leaned against the sepia marble wall and there and then offered him the vice-presidency—lower rung and all—what would he do? He had no idea . . .

He mechanically got off at the thirteenth floor and went to Gerhard's office. The moment he opened the door and saw the redness around Miss Kearny's nose and eyes he knew something was wrong. When she saw Ron she turned away. Ron came to the desk and asked, "Is he in?"

She put a little lacy handkerchief to her eyes. She'd been crying. Ron walked around the desk and crouched near her. "What's the matter?"

"Oh, Mr. Starr," she said, the tears flowing now and her face a blare of redness. "He's no longer with us . . . he's no longer with us . . ."

"No longer with us . . .?" Ron echoed stupidly.

"He's passed away." And with that she stood up and cried fully. Ron put his arm around her shoulder and comforted her.

"How?"

She wouldn't answer and he had to know *now*. More forcefully than he'd ever been in his life, he pulled her wrist away from her face and made her look right at him. "Miss Kearny, how did he die?"

"He took his own life," she said. "He sinned and he took his own life . . ." then she broke down completely. Poor thing, Ron thought, you probably feel there was something you could have done, some way you let him down . . . No Miss Kearny, it wasn't you—he killed himself probably a long time ago. Maybe he had a clear choice and he didn't take it, and that was his death, and after that he had a long last gasp.

And now, Miss Kearny, it's almost twelve and I have to leave. I have to go to my luncheon.

CHAPTER 20

An insurance-company honor luncheon is not the dull affair that it sounds like. To be sure it has its share of easily satirized hullaballoo but there is also a quotient of warmth, wit and charm. A great deal depends on the subject being honored. For instance, it is axiomatic that the higher the vice-president, the duller the affair, because no one can take a chance on offending, except those vice-presidents who are higher than the one being honored. The higher the vice-president, the fewer there are higher than he, and those usually have their brains addled by that time and are incapable of any real wit. The speeches take their tone from celebrity roasts on television—insults and barbs are signs of regard, with a half-affectionate disclaimer at the end, something like ". . . yet seriously Joe, I want to say that it's been etcetera etcetera," then on to say how much that person has meant in personal growth, leadership, whatever.

Ron's luncheon was going to be memorable. His agents were going to see to that. Between Ron and his men there existed a relationship combining all the dynamics of a family. He could be a cruel and loving father to them, a mother, brother and sister, one at a time or altogether or not at all. He was the one who had found them and originally inspired them. He dispensed rejection if they did poorly, loaned money when they needed it, and got drunk or furious with them. His absences from the office lately had hurt their feelings, and unconsciously they were trying to retrieve him. They were fiercely proud that through their efforts he was now the leading manager in the country. They resented his absence. Where had he been lately, why had he become so innaccessible, and when they did see him why did he appear so distant? A salesman doing badly could no longer expect an upbraiding, which was almost in the same category as not getting Ron's praise when he did well. There's nothing worse than neglect in selling.

Speeches had been carefully honed, a skit depicting Ron in a typical sales meeting had been rehearsed, and signs were all over the staid old luncheon room in unprecedented numbers. The signs bore Ron's sayings:

> TURN YOUR LEMONS INTO LEMONADE
> WHAT THE MIND CAN CONCEIVE IT CAN ACHIEVE
> THREE FEET FROM GOLD
> PLAN YOUR WORK AND WORK YOUR PLAN

There was a chronological succession of blown-up photos depicting the course of Ron's receding hairline and his blossoming paunch, with arrows labeling the recession as WISDOM and the increasingly larger tummy as GROWTH.

In short they wanted him back among them as he'd been before, part of them, of them and over them. He was their synthesis. Their banner.

The home office people in attendance, the highest ranking being Vice-president McCloud, looked forward to an afternoon of great fun. Field luncheons were much better than ones honoring home office people. These were the gladiators who were beholden to no one—they earned their keep by commissions so they didn't have to be polite.

Ron entered the large room just before the bar was going to close. He was shaking no one's hand. Faces were turned toward him, hands swinging into position, feet stepping toward him, throats being cleared. Ron sensed emotions being stifled, edited, filtered, diffused, rationalized; warmth being generated like toasters in a kitchen—electrically, mechanically. He was having none of that shit. He knew what they knew, and he was going to let them know on a very basic level that he knew it.

He snapped his fingers at Larry Edelman and dodged, like a halfback, zigzagging down a field, a formation of greeters about to tackle him. Larry, relieved to see Ron, almost ran to him. Ron drew him into a corner and the greeters veered off to the bar to fill up before it closed for the luncheon—their spirits merely dampened. They were salesmen, after all, used to rejection. The afternoon was young . . . he was probably just nervous.

"Where's Brock?" Ron asked.

"Where's Doris?"

"Entombed. Now where's fucking Brock?"

"He can't make it. Sick or something, but he sent a congratulatory telegram." Then I won't get a chance to split his face, Ron thought, I'll do it now . . . in my mind . . . I see his face there and I take a plate yes I can see one of those blue-bordered china plates cracking him on the forehead and the blood trickling down . . . just the way it's trickling from my nick. And the wide-eyed look, just the way he looked on that night with David. Now instead of the look saying—oh I didn't know you were homosex-

331

ual, it would be—oh I didn't know you were homicidal . . . Oh God, I'm just as glad he's not here . . . If I get violent and hurt people they'll lock me away for years . . . No, take it easy . . . Flip out but don't hurt anyone physically, you idiot . . . a padded cell and bars isn't what I want . . .

"Hey, Ron," Larry said, peering strangely at the top of Ron's chest. Ron thought, what's the matter, baby, is my bra strap showing? "Jesus you cut yourself badly . . . look at your shirt . . ."

"Larry, you're a pimp, do you know that?"

"We'd better get back now. They're closing up the bar and starting the luncheon. Have a drink?"

"You're an oblivious fuck."

Larry tried to take Ron by the elbow to escort him to the bar, but Ron wouldn't allow himself to be touched. He simply marched to the dais. Larry caught up with him and asked, "Will Doris be here soon?"

Ron ignored the question. He seated himself in the center of the dais table in back of his melon. Larry seated himself to Ron's right in back of his. Danny, who'd never achieved anything by waiting, was digging in, but McCloud, legs crossed, was waiting for Ron before starting his. Ron was not going to touch the food. When that became apparent everyone went at their melons.

Larry asked Ron, "Why am I a pimp?"

You are a pimp, Larry, because you found me in a little room years ago—depressed, discouraged, talking about driving my cab off into the water and killing myself—and you nodded your dumb fucking head and proceeded to try to sell me a policy, and when you couldn't do that, you sold *me* to the Meridian Life. Why didn't you encourage me? Why didn't you sympathize—you were supposed to be my friend. That's what I needed then—someone to tell me I had real talent. Someone to tell me to write thirty plays like Noel Coward until I made it. That's why you're a pimp, Larry, and maybe I am too because I might have done the same thing in your place. Meanwhile, pimp, I will not deign to answer you.

The meal proceeded. To Ron's mind they were all like little fishes in the bay, and above them was an enormous yacht, Jack's yacht. Jack and Lenny were sporting above them like dolphins—flying, zooming, whirling about. Then they joined each other like Siamese twins stuck on the prow of the ship, like Norse gods, cackling at the little fishes in the bay—what fools ye fishes be. Yes, Ron agreed, what fools indeed we fishes be.

Ron saw people turning toward the entrance. He heard oohs and ahhs, saw smiles, nudges. Someone had come in and had caused a stir.

I'm not going to look, Ron announced to LennyJack. It's crazy not to look, so I'm not going to look. Doing it does it, right Jack? Jack, on the bridge like a wise old captain with a pipe suddenly in his mouth, agreed sagaciously. But Lenny was flying madly around, perversely urging Ron to look—watching to see if he'd weaken at the sight of the late arrival. Lenny knew. Doris had come in with Valerie in tow.

Larry was delighted. This will break Ron's mood for sure. Valerie and Doris sat at the dais and as the meal proceeded Larry thought, if only they'd family it up a bit—they're sitting like mummies in a tomb . . .

Ron still wasn't looking. He was lost in a contest with his brother's image. Lenny would look temptingly to Ron's left and his eyes would open wide. I don't care—fuck you, I'm not going to turn my head, Ron would tell him.

The main course was finished. Larry signaled for the proceedings to begin. The skit was first, depicting Ron, the eternally peppy sales manager, trying to get a pessimistic agent out of a depression. The key audience for this kind of material is always the person being satirized; if he laughs and enjoys it, then everyone else can, too. The skit was well done, the barbs sharp and in good taste, but Ron viewed it zombie-like and there was scarcely a laugh from the floor. When the skit was ended, a failure, the men walked back to their table to faint applause, let down and discouraged. The audience was truly uneasy now, and frequent trips to the bar ensued.

Larry was getting more muddled by the minute. Would he be blamed for this fiasco? So far, McCloud, perched there at the end of the table, totally poker-faced, had not expressed a thing. He wished now that he had called it off when Doris called. She was right, Ron was sick, sick in the goddamn head . . . He made the rounds whispering to all the speakers, imploring them to cut their speeches very short or not go on at all . . . telling them that Ron may be ill . . . just got over a touch of flu and it still hasn't left him . . . you know how the flu . . . ?

But they were salesmen, used to resistance, and each felt that his display of affection, his joke or his recollection of past experiences with Ron would do the trick—make Ron laugh or smile. So they proceeded to the dais and talked, forsaking the usual handshakes, hugs and kisses on the cheek (manly of course) which were common at these affairs. But their verbal affection was like pigeon shit on a statue, it splattered but didn't penetrate. Ron was still locked in an eye battle with his brother.

Doris had been patiently waiting for Ron to acknowledge Valerie, who was sitting next to him. She was sure that if she could just get Ron and Valerie into eye contact, he would not be able to go on with whatever insanity he was planning. She sat through speech after speech, her frustration, fear, and anguish increasing as her husband simply sat stonily. Finally she whispered in her daughter's ear, "You didn't even say hello to your father. Say something to him."

Danny Carpagian was up telling his age-old car-wash story. Lenny became convulsed, hysterical with laughter, and Ron was on guard. Was it a trick to get him to look at who was seated next to him? No, Danny Carpagian's oil-barrel-like ass was floating beside the yacht above, and Lenny zoomed around it wanting to know if Ron ever really wanted to fuck this—was this ever fuckable bending over cars? No, you idiot, Ron let him know. Now if it was Gil Sloane . . . where is Gil? There? Ohh, he's gorgeous.

Jack roared as Lenny zoomed to pick Gil up from his table and fly away with him—the crazy fish bandit kidnapping the sweet little prince . . .

Valerie was pretending not to hear her mother. Doris was about to press further, but now McCloud was getting up to speak and she didn't want to cause any fuss then.

McCloud talked about the multiplying effect of one good man. He had figures to show the business brought in not only by Ron's men but by the men brought in by Ron's men. "A journey of a thousand miles starts with one step and then another and then another. We count in this business by ones, one sale, one man— one at a time. The day that Larry Edelman asked one man to come up to Meridian he started a dynasty that I'm sure no one foresaw. One, gentlemen, just one."

Yes, Ron thought, and just one "fuck you" starts me on a new journey!

McCloud was finished and Larry stood. It was time to introduce the honored guest. Mysteriously, McCloud sat in Larry's seat, next to Ron. Larry was nervous as hell, his mouth dry and his heart beating hard.

Doris took hold of Valerie's hand and placed it on Ron's arm and said to Valerie, "Say hello to your father."

Ron jerked as if branded by a steaming iron and turned on Valerie and Doris with a look of withering malice.

Larry started to speak. "There are no words that I can really come up with to introduce this guy . . ."

LennyJack, together again, leaned far over the deck and with four all-seeing eyes took in the proceedings.

McCloud crossed his legs.

Everyone in the room was completely quiet, all eyes were on the honored guest. It was almost time for his speech.

Ron's glare burned into Doris' soul, feeling like it could knock her off the dais onto the floor. This was mad—crazy blazing insanity—and she wasn't going to stay there and subject her daughter to it. She had lost. He *was* crazy. Really crazy. This was no act.

Larry saw Doris leaving the dais with Valerie in tow, heading for the entrance just as he was saying, "One of the proudest accomplishments in my life has been bringing him into the life-insurance business." I hope McCloud figures that the kid is sick and that they're going to the john or something, Larry thought. I'm going to get blamed for this whole stinking show somehow . . .

The men saw Doris leave with the child. That look he gave her. They saw it and it made them uneasy. What was the matter with Ron?

McCloud crossed his legs the other way. He seemed to be counting the bulbs on the chandelier.

Ron felt force emanating from somewhere in his middle and now he could feel a great motor of destructive, deadly energy ready to be released at last. LennyJack was going totally insane inside of him.

Larry was saying, "Now, I'd like the leading general manager of the Meridian Life Insurance Company to get up here and say a few words . . . let's hear it now for Ron Starr."

Larry led the applause and everyone in the room stood up and clapped their hands with abandon. Each clap beckoned Ron to come back to them, each loud noise, hurtfully done by some, showed Ron that they loved him and wanted him back as one of them.

And as Ron was about to stand up and go to the podium, McCloud leaned over to him, put his hand near his mouth to muffle what he was going to say and whispered to Ron, "Are you still crazy enough to want the home office?"

And without a moment's hesitation Ron replied, "Yes." And McCloud said, "You got it." McCloud then stuck his hand out and Ron's hand went right into it, right up to the crook between the thumb and forefinger.

"Welcome aboard," McCloud said, smiling. Ron smiled back.

He stood and stepped to the podium.

Ron opened his mouth to speak but at first nothing would come out. LennyJack screeched—Tell them, tell them to go fuck themselves. Tell them. Tell them.

Ron found his voice. "Vice-president McCloud, friends, I would like to tell you all individually and collectively . . ."

Lenny was screaming "individually and collectively to go fuck yourselves!" Jack was laughing and rolling on the deck of his yacht.

". . . that you have made me the happiest man in the world today."

I am. I am! I'm fucking bubbling inside like a huge fucking atomic fountain!

Lenny snap-kicked at him viciously but it didn't hurt.

I'm free of you now! Ron leaped out of the sea and hissed at his brother like a crazy sea monster. Stay out there in California and suck your California cocks! I'll get mine here—my way! No coming out. No pink trumpets blaring for me.

Jack was rolling on the deck like an idiot. He's flipped out. He's flipped out! Welcome aboard blowfish, he laughed.

No. You flipped out, not me. Ron shot his sea-monster tongue at him and whipped him. I've got the Meridian by the balls. I get it all. I play the game and I win. I don't have to play crazy. I've won.

LennyJack teamed up to tell Ron something but the sea monster knew it before they could say it.

Vice-president Morgan Gerhard?!

A schmuck. He just didn't know how to do it right.

Lenny punched, hit, kicked furiously, but it was fading, it was fading . . .

"Men, I'd like to tell you that my being number-one manager is really your award. I conceived this for myself but *you* achieved it for me."

They bolted up and gave Ron a standing ovation. They almost danced. McCloud had been the first on his feet. Larry wanted to hug the world.

337

LennyJack was fading . . .

Ron looked toward the entrance and saw Doris standing there with Valerie still in tow. She must have come back when she heard the applause. She was crying. Valerie was annoyed, bored, but so beautiful and lovely. At least she won't have to go through an ordeal and Doris . . . she's strong, much stronger than I thought . . . The way she fought for me, stood up to me and tried to keep it all together . . . quite a woman there . . . "You know," he told the audience, "you don't do it alone . . . you just don't . . .

They all turned and saw her at the entrance.

"I want my family up here with me."

Grown men started to cry. It was the greatest luncheon any of them had ever attended. Doris almost ran up to the dais with Valerie. Oh God, Valerie thought, feeling sorry for herself. Do I have to go up there again?

As the *Meridian Monthly*'s photographer was flashing pictures of Ron with his arm around Doris and Valerie with McCloud handing Ron his President's Trophy as leading manager Lenny wished Ron a fond adieu.

Goodbye little brother. I hope they catch you sucking cocks in the executive washroom and that they thereafter hang you by your cowardly balls from the fucking spire of Meridian Life Insurance Company's home office.

Someone came up to shake Ron's hand, and as the handshake locked in place and Ron felt the strong warmth LennyJack went away completely and Ron, purged, took a deep, free breath. He kissed Doris, hugged Valerie, and stuck his chest out proudly. Vice-president Ron Starr and family.

Great.